FATED TO THE FERAL WOLF

The Hunted Omegas

APRIL L. MOON

THIGPEN-
GANDY
PUBLISHING

What Came Before

This is book two in an interconnected series. It's highly recommended that you read book one before this book. If you choose to forge ahead, there will be spoilers.

Designations in this world begin with alpha, as in most wolf packs. But they proceed all the way down the pecking order from alpha, beta, gamma, to the lowest of lows, the psi wolf.

Well, *almost*.

One designation is more hated than all others: the omega. Deceptively last on the hierarchy, omegas were rare and blessed throughout history with extra gifts from the Moon Goddess herself. They lived and used those gifts for their packs quietly for many, many centuries. Until Narcissa.

Narcissa was given the power of war and used it to turn the most powerful European packs against other magical races. The war that ensued was catastrophic, resulting in the near extinction of multiple magical races. They rose up together to overturn the wolves. A new Interspecies Governing Council was created, and the Omega Defense League was formed to prevent another like Narcissa from rising. From then on, omegas have been hunted to extinction, for the safety of all other species. Every brand-new wolf-shifter baby must be tested by the Omega Defense League, and any omega daughters are killed by their third day of life.

Fated to the Wolf Prince

Brielle and Kane have mated under the full moon, cementing their bond ahead of the fight to find Kane's parents' killers. An Athabascan shaman is waiting for our heroes, to celebrate their new bond, but also to examine Brielle's magic for the taint Kane found while she was shifted.

The rest of the Blackwater and Johnson City packs are celebrating their high alpha's bonding with a good old-fashioned afterparty. Leigh and Gael have left the dance floor to engage in... other activities, when a feral wolf arrows straight for Shay, our quiet best friend.

The dance floor empties, enforcers arrive, and a single shot is fired.

Present day ...

ONE

Shay

Being shot was agony. White-hot and furious, the bullet tore through my abdomen, leaving a trail of flames in its wake. The crowd of enforcers, the music, the lights, the screams —it all began to blur as my body processed what was happening to me in the only way it could: shock. I felt the impact, though, when my shoulder plowed into the floor.

Another time, I would have rolled, caught myself— anything to lessen the impact. But not this time. This time, I hit and bounced, my only saving grace the fact that it was my shoulder and not my face that took the brunt of my fall.

All my air was gone, the wind knocked straight out of me as I stared up at the ceiling, gaping like a fish as the fluorescent lights blurred into a too-bright mass overhead.

Something warm and wet touched my face, and a sharp whine pierced my ears, cutting through a layer of the shock.

He's important. My wolf was insistent, shoving at me to shift, get back to my feet. But I couldn't. Why couldn't I let her out? She'd protect me. She was the *only* one who could protect me, she insisted.

She shoved and snarled in my mind, growing more frantic

by the second, but cold dread filled me as my abdomen began to go numb far too quickly. Shifters healed fast, but not that fast, and it hurt like a bitch. Which meant...

Wolfsbane.

They must have used a dipped bullet, but why would they do that?

I sucked in a desperate lungful of air as realization hit me. The feral wolf. The enforcers used a dipped bullet because that was one of the only ways to fell a feral wolf.

But if it had hit him... he wouldn't have gotten back up.

"Stop, don't shoot him," I rasped out as pain racked me again, this time farther from the bullet. *The poison is spreading too fast.*

Holy fuck, my stomach was cramping, and it was excruciating. But I had to focus. I couldn't let them kill him. He might have been feral, but he was my mate.

Goddess, it didn't feel real. Was it real? Was he really mine?

"Get off her!"

"We have to shoot!"

"You can't, you idiots! It's Dirge!" Reed's voice was a half snarl, tearing through the others arguing over what to do and silencing them with alpha dominance. As third in command, he was stronger than everyone except Kane and Gael, and neither of them was here.

The warm, wet thing prodded me again, and I forced my eyes to focus. It was a nose. Above it sat two glowing red eyes, the hard, soulless pits the stuff of human nightmares.

Little did the humans know, those lycanthropy legends started just like this, with a feral shifter who'd lost control to the dark side of his beast.

We all had one, but the human side outweighed it, for most of us. But not this guy. He was massive, black, and dripping saliva as he stood over me, paws planted on either side of my body as if shielding me from further harm.

But the distressing numbness was a danger of its own, and if I didn't get him off me—and stop him snarling at the enforcers—I would have much bigger problems.

I held his nightmare stare as I spoke next, slowly and clearly. "They won't hurt me. I need their help—" My words choked off with a violent cough, the involuntary clench of muscles making me hiss through my teeth.

"Please." I reached up a tentative hand, trying again. He didn't flinch back, didn't snap as my fingers met his cheek. The thick fur was surprisingly soft under my fingertips, and since he was letting me, I tangled my fingers into the silken strands. He whuffed, nothing more than a gentle burst of air, and tipped his head to the side, leaning into my hand. He liked it, my touch.

At any other time, wonder would have filled me. But right now, I was too scattered—too hurt—to really dissect the improbability of the situation.

"Dirge, it's me."

A dizzying glance up and over my shoulder showed that Reed had coerced everyone else to step back, giving us a few feet of space. He was the only one still close enough to be in danger or be perceived as a threat.

"I'm your brother. You know I won't hurt you. But Shay's in trouble, and she needs medical attention. That bullet was coated in a lethal dose of wolfsbane, and if we don't get her to John Henry quickly, she is going to lose access to her wolf."

The glowing red eyes left mine, a vicious growl tearing from his throat, and saliva dripping down over my chest as he homed in on his brother.

Shit, shit, shit.

TWO

Dirge

T hreat.

He was too close, the male whose scent triggered memories of my past. Memories of before I was a being made up of living, breathing pain. I shook them off, forcing myself to step between him and my wounded mate.

The blood oozing from her smelled *wrong*. Tainted. The man had said that, though. His words meant something, but I wasn't sure enough of the man was left to remember what wolfsbane was or why it mattered.

All I knew was that the blood didn't smell clean; it smelled like three-day-old-carcass rot that turned even my stomach. But it shouldn't, since she was alive and the wound was fresh.

I couldn't focus on that. He wanted to take her away from me and give her to some other male. I didn't know who John Henry was, but if he laid a finger on my mate, I'd rip it off and swallow it whole.

Mine!

"Dirge? Is that your name?" My mate's quavering question stopped me in my tracks, and I turned back to where she still lay on the cold, hard floor. Her sweet scent was fruity and floral, and if she weren't wounded, I'd be trying to get it all over me.

Dirge.

Was I Dirge?

Confusion stopped me from moving toward her or toward the familiar-smelling man. His eyes held pain, but was that because he loved my mate? My mate who was hurt?

He couldn't have her. Another snarl parted my lips, flashing my fangs at the man who wanted my other half. *Never.*

Something tugged at my mind, the sensation unfamiliar and, at this point, unwanted.

The man. He lived deep inside, stuffed so far down, he couldn't ever come out again. I was wolf now, and nothing more.

The man was nearly dead. But that was okay, because I didn't need him to protect her, my female. If she would just shift, she would get better.

I turned my back on the man, ignoring his pleas, and nosed my female.

Shift.

I tried to force the suggestion into her mind, use the pack link, but nothing happened. Our connection was too new. But she knew, surely? That when you hurt, you took fur?

Shift!

I tried again, forcing all my will and intention into the communication.

Her body shuddered, and a bit of foam formed at the corner of her lips. Her lips, which were turning blue.

The man inside beat against my defenses, screamed into my mind. I shook again, trying to shed the uncomfortable sensation, but he wouldn't stop. Pounding and pounding against my defenses until a fissure appeared.

It's wolfsbane! Stand back! Let Reed help her, or she'll lose her wolf forever!

5

The man's demand had me stumbling to the side. He was so weak, so far back in my mind, that I hadn't heard him speak in many seasons. But was he right? Could my mate lose her wolf?

I threw back my head and howled at the pain of that thought. If she had no wolf, how could we be mated?

"Now! The tranquilizers!" the memory man shouted, as a split second later, stinging pinpricks hit me from all sides. I snarled and scratched, bit and yanked, trying to get the annoying projectiles off me, but it was no use.

Everywhere I'd been hit, cold seemed to flood my body. I blinked over at my female, her form growing hazy before my eyes.

Once, twice, as I swayed on my feet.

Don't crush her, the man in my head said, wresting control for a second and forcing me to the side.

He was right this time. Because seconds later, I collapsed.

THREE

Shay

"**D**irge? Is that your name?" I asked, trying to distract him with something, anything. Even something as mundane as his name. I didn't want to keep thinking of him as feral, even if it was technically true. Feral meant I was doomed, though. If he couldn't reason, if he couldn't let Reed and John Henry help me...

No, I couldn't think about that. About losing my wolf forever.

She whined, the sound high and mournful inside my skull.

Dirge stared intently at me, as if trying to communicate something, though all I saw was the red of his eyes flicker, a glowing hazel flashing at me before cementing back as red.

Was the man still fighting for control? I smiled at the thought, even as something wet touched my cheek. He suddenly howled, staggering to the side.

I heard Reed shout something, but it was distant, like he was down a long, cold tunnel.

Cold, yes. My eyelids were so heavy. I fought to keep them open as the lights danced over my head. And then Dirge was gone, replaced by the worried pack healer, John Henry.

7

"Shay? Stay with me. I've brought the antidote and a pain drug. Shay?"

Why was he shaking me? Didn't he know my stomach hurt?

A grip like a steel band held my arm, then a sharp pinch at the crook of my arm preceded blissful darkness.

BEEP... *Beep... Beep...*

What was that Goddess-cursed noise? I tried to scrub my eyes, but my arm was *so* heavy, it barely budged off the mattress.

Wait.

I wasn't on a mattress before.

The memories came rushing back, and my eyelids flew open.

"Dirge?" His name came out a hoarse whisper, and I cleared my desert-dry throat and tried again. "Dirge!"

"Shh, it's okay. Hold on, let me get you some water," Leigh said, her relief evident when she appeared over me, the blonde curtain of her hair filtering the overhead lights for a moment before she disappeared again.

She popped back into my line of sight with a Styrofoam cup complete with bendy straw. "Take it slow, okay? You've been out... two days? Maybe three. I'm not sure. Time's a bit squashed together at the moment." She shook her head, then carefully lowered the straw to my lips.

I drank the water down greedily, trying to process what she'd just told me. Two or three days? That wasn't good. As soon as I released the straw and took a steadying breath, I asked again. "Where's Dirge? Is he okay?"

"Uh, yeah. About that. The feral wolf—uh, Dirge—had to be sedated to treat you. The last I heard, they were taking him to a feral cell." She winced at the admission, watching for my reaction.

"A feral cell! Leigh! You have to get me up. I have to see him." I shoved at the heavy pile of blankets weighing me down, letting out a frustrated grunt when my shaking hands barely moved them. I tried again, and again, until Leigh swooped down and captured my hands in hers.

"Shay, you can't get out of bed yet." Her stern tone just pissed me off. She didn't understand. I knew in my bones that a cell would make him worse. To go from living wild to locked up, barely able to move, would be awful for any wolf. But a feral one who'd just found his fated mate? He'd be breaking himself trying to get free.

I knew, because it was exactly what I'd be doing. Snatching my hands away from Leigh, I went back to dislodging the blankets. When I succeeded, she just sighed, then helped me swing my legs around.

"Hang on, let me get your clothes."

I looked down at that and frowned at the realization that I was wearing a hospital gown and could feel the cool air from a nearby open window on my very bare backside now that I was upright. Though I supposed my other clothes were ruined, between the bullet hole and the blood.

Shifters had to learn early not to get too attached to our wardrobes. Sigh.

Leigh helped me into soft leggings and an oversized tee, the outfit finished off with my favorite pair of jingly sneakers. I was still a little bit sore around the bullet entry and exit points, but the more I moved, the more I came back to myself, and nervous energy thrummed through my veins like electricity or the staccato beats of techno-music.

I had to see him, make sure he was okay. Then it was the small matter of getting him out of the freaking *cell* they'd thrown him into. Uncharacteristic fury rose in me at the

9

thought. I shook my head, trying to shake the rage physically loose.

Getting hotheaded about things wouldn't help me spring him from wolf jail.

Leigh had her arm wrapped around my shoulders, carefully guiding me toward the door, when it flew open, nearly cracking us both on the nose in the process.

"Where is she? I'm going to skin whoever didn't tell me about this alive!" Brielle's furious tirade ground to a halt as soon as she saw me up and on my feet. "Shay! Oh, I'm so glad you're okay! You're not supposed to be up yet, though." She shot Leigh a pointed look for helping me break the rules as she stepped forward to wrap me in a hug. Bri hesitated at the last second. "Is there any way I can hug you without hurting your side?"

I shrugged my left shoulder, careful not to zhuzh the right side, which still ached from the bullet. She moved more slowly, carefully wrapping her arms around my shoulders and giving me a steady but gentle squeeze.

"Now, why are you out of bed? John Henry told me he was recommending two more days of rest. Since he *finally* got around to telling us this happened!" She shot an angry look over her shoulder, where both Kane and a browbeat John Henry stood in the doorway, watching our reunion.

"She's not supposed to be out of bed," the pack healer grumbled. "And you weren't supposed to be disturbed until seventy-two hours after your mating ceremony. Early interruptions usually end in bloodshed, and we took a vote. It was unanimous that any interruption before you two left the cabin on your own would be seen as a challenge for mating rights."

"I have to go get Dirge. They put him in a feral cell," I insisted, ignoring the hovering males. My hands shook as the awful thought came back to the forefront. I had to get him out of there. Confinement was no place for a wolf.

"A cell? Wait, you want to spring him *before* he's turned back?" Bri shot a concerned look at Kane, who stayed silent except for one lifted eyebrow, which was very loudly conveying his disapproval of my plans. "He can't stay in there. Please," I added, not caring if I sounded pathetic.

"You may see him, but he may not leave the cell until we know he's not a danger to any member of the pack, and that includes you."

Kane's words hit me like a ton of bricks. They were laced with an undercurrent of Alpha command, and it felt like someone rubbed their hand the wrong way up my wolf's back. Although... Where was my wolf?

I reached for her but found only silence. I tried again, shutting my eyes and digging deep, but again, there was no familiar tingle of the change starting, no pleasure-pain of her bursting free to go for a run. There was just... emptiness.

Dread climbed up my throat, its sickly fingers holding me frozen in a choke hold.

"M... My wolf," I stuttered, letting my hand float to my neck, as if I could wipe away the dread.

"I know, you think he may be your mate. That is *wild*. I mean, what are the odds?" Leigh cast a glance at Brielle for backup before continuing. "However, if it's not safe for him to be out—"

"No, *my* wolf," I said again, clutching the front of the oversized black tee. There was no fire, no magical light in my chest. Just darkness where my wolf should be.

Leigh sucked in a shocked breath, while Brielle launched into doctor mode. "How high was the dosage of wolfsbane?" She launched the question at John Henry like a torpedo.

"Seven point five ccs," he answered without missing a beat.

"And how long after exposure was the antidote administered?"

"Eight minutes."

"Eight minutes?"

"Give or take about ninety seconds."

"That's not a lethal dosage, but it's close." Bri frowned, her fingers drumming anxiously on her jeans-clad thigh. "You probably just need some time. You went through a major injury, even without the added complication of the wolfsbane. Your small intestine was clipped, and apparently, the bullet missed your ovary by less than half an inch."

I knew I should be grateful that the bullet hadn't mangled my ovary or poisoned me with fecal matter from an intestinal wound. But all that felt insignificant in comparison to being unable to contact my wolf. Without her, I was alone.

Weak.

Vulnerable.

And with a brand-new feral mate, that was the last thing I could afford to be.

FOUR

Dirge

I barreled into the silver-lined cell door, ignoring the burn and my own need to cower from the poisonous substance as I flung my entire body into the effort yet again. My mate needed me. She was wounded, grievously, and I was locked away inside this cell like an enemy of the pack.

How long had we been apart? I couldn't say, since I'd been sedated, and the cold lights overhead were sterile LEDs. A fact I knew with my human half, now come back to the fore. A small part of me thought I should shift back. They'd surely let me out then.

But I wouldn't. *Couldn't.*

So I launched myself at the door again, setting it rattling on its hinges. The smell of singed fur had burned my nose in the beginning, but now I was so used to it that my nose had gone numb.

The blood, though, from the pads of my paws where they came in contact with the silver still smelled somehow cloying. Probably because it wasn't constant. My fur insulated me more, and scratching at the door had yielded nothing, so I wasn't doing it as often.

I paced an anxious circle around the Goddess-damned cell, snarling low in my throat as I went.

Every few hours, the man's voice came over a speaker inside the cell—not just any man, I corrected myself. My brother.

Reed.

It was the same message every time.

"Dirge? I know you're in there. Please shift back so we can let you out. Don't do this to yourself."

Some part of me hurt to hear the pain in his words, over and over. His voice was wrung out with exhaustion, but that was a lower priority than her.

She was my everything. My light, my other half.

Even if I couldn't dare let the man out, I could still protect her, live at her side in wolf form. It was a half life, less than was meant to be. But it was all I was allowed by fate.

The thought sent rage boiling over inside me once again, so I flung myself at the door one more time. Sharp claws of pain lanced through my shoulder on impact. I bounced back, not landing on my feet this time, but rolling instead to my other side.

I shook myself, then climbed tiredly back to my feet. I ignored the crackle of the impending message, since I already knew what he would say. But it wasn't Reed's voice that froze me in my tracks.

"Dirge?" My mate's voice cracked on the simple word, pain, fear, and exhaustion warring for top spot among her emotions. I could sense each one, even with the wall between us. "Please, don't keep hurting yourself. I'm trying to get you out, but they say it's against Blackwater Pack law to release you in wolf form. The high alpha has forbidden it." Anger leaked into her tone at the last, and the speaker crackled again as her voice cut off.

I threw back my head and howled, sorry at even this small new separation spearing me. I needed her, needed to be at her side.

14

If I couldn't shift back, was there anything else I could do to be released? If they kept me locked in this tiny, silver-lined room permanently, I'd lose what little grip I had left on the man.

The thought knocked me back on my haunches with a whine. No matter how long or how far I wandered, I hadn't truly lost him, like most feral wolves. I was protecting him from his awful fate, keeping him locked away. And he knew it, so he lay quiet inside.

Shifting back wasn't an option, but losing the man to insanity would hurt almost as much as losing my mate. So what could I do?

I whined again, frustration and fear pushing me to move, to act, to keep trying to escape. But that hadn't worked, and now I knew my precious mate was watching.

How could I get them to see I just wanted to protect her? That I needed to be by her side, even if I couldn't shift?

When it struck me, the simplicity of the solution was undeniable. The only question was whether they'd understand and let me out, or leave me to rot in this cage for the rest of my life.

FIVE

Shay

"What is he doing?" Leigh asked, leaning closer to the screen, clearly confused. We were in the monitoring room, staring at a panel of screens mounted on the wall in front of us. Twelve views were empty. Only the four angles looking into Dirge's occupied cell were active. The trash can overflowed with empty coffee cups, and even the piney scent of the wood-plank walls couldn't overpower the scent of stale java.

"I don't care, so long as he's stopped hurling himself at the wall. He hasn't stopped since the drugs wore off, and it's beyond awful to watch." Reed ran a hand over his exhausted features, letting his eyes briefly drop closed. He'd been sitting vigil for Dirge's entire stay in the feral cell, and it showed. His clothing was rumpled, his eyes were red, hair askew, and even in human skin, he reeked. But still, I admired his dedication to his brother.

My mate.

I spun back to the camera, temper semicontrolled for the moment, so long as I didn't look at Kane for more than a minute.

But a completely different wolf showed on the camera.

Where before a raging, snarling beast had been hurling himself repeatedly at the walls of his cage, now there sat a calm, collected wolf. He stared up at the camera, the only thing betraying his feral status the glowing red eyes. And the blood-smeared walls behind him, but I was trying hard not to think about that.

When I thought about how the blood got there, I wanted to challenge the high alpha—my best friend's fated mate—which was an epically bad idea.

"Has he been taking breaks like this?" I asked Reed, not taking my eyes off Dirge's wolf.

"No, he hasn't been still since the sedatives wore off two days ago. I'm not sure how he's still upright, let alone fighting so hard."

"Almost three full years of hard living have made him strong," Kane murmured from his position behind us. "He was already a fighter, and now he's been honed by nature into a killing machine."

My lip curled up into a snarl without my permission. "He's not *just* a killing machine. He was trying to protect me!" The words were guttural in my mouth, but still, my wolf lay dormant. The reminder of her absence sent a pang of sadness through me.

"Yes, so the witnesses all agree. But why?" The high alpha paced forward, letting his hands drop to the desk in front of the security monitors.

They didn't know. Somehow, in all the commotion, *nobody* knew.

Was I even sure myself?

Part of me screamed yes, but the other part—maybe the larger part—wasn't ready to say it. What if I was wrong? What if, somehow, him being feral triggered the mate bond inside me, but not in him? Had anyone ever found their mate while they were feral?

17

I didn't know. Dragging in a steadying breath as Kane straightened, I looked just below the high alpha's eyeline, not enough to outright challenge, but enough to push the limit and get his attention.

"He won't hurt me. I want you to let me in to talk to him, and check on him. He may need medical attention."

"No."

"But—"

"It is pack law. Enforcers are the only ones allowed in, and then just to deliver food and water, or sedatives if urgent medical attention becomes necessary. We can all see that he's fine... but probably bruised from his own efforts." There was exasperation in his tone, and to his credit, he spared a glance to his third, who sat wearily in the monitoring chair. Reed's sorrow perfumed the air with a thickly sour scent, but he didn't comment.

"I respectfully ask for you to allow an exception." The words were bitter on my tongue. I didn't dislike Kane; in fact, I was happy Brielle had found him. But the situation was pushing me to fight, to argue, to rage against anything between me and my mate... and right now, that was Kane.

He didn't answer immediately, sizing me up in that unnerving way that alpha wolves have, as if their power is *tasting* you on the air.

I lifted my chin and kept my shoulders square. I wasn't going to back down, no matter how badly my body ached or how exhaustion threatened to pull me under.

"Everyone but Shay, out," Kane said, eyes still leveled on me.

Leigh squeezed my arm as she made her way past, toward the door. Brielle stopped and whispered something in Kane's ear, a stern look on her face before she followed Leigh. It felt like lead, filling up my chest as I watched my two strongest supporters in the world walk out that door. But if he was sending them out, I had to believe it was for a reason, that there was *hope*.

"Alpha—" Reed protested, but Kane held up a hand. "You need rest, food, and a shower. You can come back as soon as those are seen to. You have my word as pack leader that your brother will not be unattended at any time."

Reed followed Leigh and Brielle out with a sigh and a last, tormented look over his shoulder at where his brother's wolf still sat, patiently waiting, on each of the monitors.

When the door clicked softly behind them, Kane pulled the chair out and gestured for me to sit. "You've been through an ordeal, and hurting yourself won't help him."

I sank into the chair with a mixture of relief and indignation. Kane was no dummy, even though I wanted to wring his neck right now.

Once I was settled, he propped his hip against the table and ran a hand through his hair. "Tell me."

It was a command, no doubt, despite the fact that he withheld his alpha command. Probably out of respect for my relationship with Brielle. Or just because he was actually a good guy beneath all the responsibility.

"He's... I think he's my mate." I dropped my gaze to the varnished floorboards, suddenly losing all my bluster.

"You think?" I could hear the amusement he tried to squash in his tone. "Why aren't you sure?"

"He's feral! Can he even acknowledge a mate bond? I don't know if this has ever happened before or how to go about dealing with any of this." I was surprised when tears prickled and gave in to the urge to pull my knees up to my chest to give me something to hide behind.

Kane let out a weary sigh. "I would have to have someone check the records, but to the best of my knowledge, there's nothing that precludes a mate bond from forming with a feral wolf. In fact, if anything, they're likely to hit harder, given he's being ruled by his primal instincts and not his human side."

I stilled in the chair, letting that sink in. I hadn't considered that the reason he'd reacted so strongly to me was because the wolf was in charge and didn't know how to handle the bond in a more civilized manner. Though it made a lot of sense, now that he'd pointed it out.

"But it progresses through physical intimacy..." I trailed off, realizing I wasn't telling him anything he hadn't just experienced himself. "How am I supposed to form a mate bond with someone who won't shift from the wolf?"

Kane pressed his lips together in a grim line. "You can't, not unless he'll shift. Feral wolves have been saved over the centuries. Not many, but it has happened." He spoke gently, like I was a scared fawn poised to dart away. That lead from my chest had sunk to my bones, making me feel heavy and sluggish.

The possibility that I'd found my fated mate at twenty-six only for him to be feral and leave me alone for the rest of my life was too cruel to consider. The centuries of loneliness ahead of me stretched in a seemingly endless, bleak expanse. No family of my own, no children.

It was the worst fate I could imagine after growing up in foster care. I'd already lived it. No roots, no loving home to come back to after the end of a long day of harassment and teasing at school. Just me against the world.

The darkness of an unbonded wolf slowly sinking in, driving me insane as the centuries wore on.

I had Brielle and Leigh now, of course. But Brielle was already mated, and in time, the pups would come. Leigh longed for a mate with a fervor that was undeniable, so I was sure she wasn't far behind. They'd go their own ways, build their own families, and then I'd just be another pack mate, the single one.

The third wheel forever.

It took all my willpower to shove those thoughts aside. Getting Dirge back wasn't hopeless. I had to cling to that and let the rest go, or else I'd drive myself insane.

"Can I see him?" I finally asked.

Kane was silent for a long time. "I should say no."

Pain lanced through me, and not from my slow-healing bullet wound. If Kane really wanted to keep me from Dirge, he was strong enough to do it. I'd be no better off than Dirge, flinging himself against an immovable wall.

Unless I wanted to use my relationship with Brielle against him, but that felt wrong.

I steeled myself for the argument, but he saw it a mile away and lifted a hand in warning.

"I *should* say no. But I think this is a special circumstance. You may see him, but you need a second, in case he doesn't respond in a way we expect. Dirge is an incredibly dominant, powerful wolf, and that was before he went feral and spent three years living in the wild. He was head enforcer for our pack before the change—top five in my father's pack before he left to come with us to Alaska—and he's more dominant than Reed."

"So..."

"So, I will be coming along. Are you ready?"

"Yes." The word was out before it processed in my brain, a pure reflex. I craved my mate on a cellular level, and anything that got me a step closer to him, I'd say yes.

"Okay, then. He likely will respond badly to me being close to you. I will precede you into the room, step to the side, and allow you entry. I'd recommend waiting until I'm in the corner before you step inside. Freshly mated but unbonded males are easily set off at the best of times, and this is not the best of times." He shot me a wry smile before striding out of the room.

I followed hot on his heels, despite knowing I was going to

have to wait to go in after him. Something inside me urged me to hurry, to close the distance between us.

"Remember what I said," Kane warned before punching a pin code into the digital lock on the thick steel door. I shifted my body subtly to the side to try to catch it, but only saw the last three digits. It unlocked with a heavy *clunk* of metal bars sliding back into place inside the door, and then he let himself inside.

The door closed behind him but didn't relock. My hand was trembling on the handle within a second, but I forced myself to wait. No snarls or sounds of fighting came from inside as I counted to ten as slowly as I could manage. As soon as my count was up, I pushed the door open.

The scent of filthy, unwashed wolf hit me like a brick wall, but I didn't care. Because for the first time ever without being surrounded by gun-wielding enforcers, I was standing face-to-face with my mate.

SIX

Dirge

Waiting was torture and against every demand raging inside me. But after a few minutes of calm, I heard footsteps in the hallway. Two sets, maybe three. The urge to fling myself back at the door—or better, position myself just inside it, so I could force my way out when it opened—was overwhelming, but I leaned on my humanity to keep my muscles locked in place. This room was monitored, and if I moved, they wouldn't come in.

That certainty was the only thing that saved me when the door opened, and a dominant alpha strode through, the scent of *her* wafting in with him.

I wanted to rip his throat out.

But this was probably a test, a fact I remembered well from my years as an enforcer. Unstable wolves were dangerous, and if I couldn't control myself, they wouldn't let me out. So, I clamped my jaws shut and kept staring at the door, ignoring him as he walked to the far corner of my cell. I recognized the scent of the alpha; the name Kane floated up through my memories like a leaf on a still pond.

He was a friend of my brother's, from back when he was

still a young sapling I could overpower with one hand tied behind my back. But now... a dominance like no other rode him. He'd matured, and his power had multiplied a hundred-fold since I'd last seen him.

But what did he have to do with my mate?

I didn't have a way to ask, but the thought left me quickly enough when the door swung inward a second time. This time, her scent was fresh and strong, a soothing balm to my over-wrought senses as she pushed through the door.

Her emotions were running high—nearly as high as mine—when she crossed the distance between us and sank to her haunches in front of me. A tiny part of me was pleased that even with me, she didn't settle to her knees. My mate was too smart and careful to limit her escape options like that. She stayed alert.

I drank in the sight of her the way a dying man swilled whiskey, as I hung on to my control for dear life. She was beautiful, of course. There was no universe in which she could be unbeautiful to me. I believed in the old ways, which said she held the other half of my soul and I hers. But I could see the ragged edges of her, the telltale signs of a woman pushed to the brink. There were dark smudges beneath her gray eyes; her riot of dark curls was uneven, pulled back into a haphazard knot at the nape of her neck. And she still favored her right side, where she'd been shot.

If it had been a normal bullet, she would have healed within hours, so long as nothing vital was hit. A day, if a major organ needed repairs. But several days later... That was the wolfsbane. And being in this silver-laden death trap wouldn't help her any.

When she finally spoke, even her voice was worn thin around the edges, and for the first time in a long time, the man and wolf agreed, she needed our protection, our care.

"Dirge? Is that your name?" she asked, and paused for an answer.

I ducked my nose down, then back up, the closest I could get to communication at the moment.

She sucked in a breath, her gaze darting across the room to Kane. A low growl rumbled out of my chest against my will. I did *not* want to share her attention with another male. Not ever, but especially not now, when our bond was so new, and I was a prisoner.

"It's okay, it's okay," she murmured, her hand rising toward me tentatively before she seemed to catch herself and stopped. "Can I touch you, Dirge?"

"No, Shay. Don't push the boundaries. We don't know how far gone he is, and he could hurt you accidentally. Explain to him what needs to happen, but keep your distance."

There it was, that growl again. It was louder this time because I was angry at the other alpha's interference. There was nothing I wanted more than for her to touch me, brush her hands over my fur.

"Right, sorry." She met my gaze again, a soft smile lifting one side of her mouth. "No touching yet."

I liked the sound of *yet*.

"Dirge, we need you to shift back. Pack law states that you can't come out of this cell until there's no chance that you'll hurt any member of the pack, and until the man is back in control, we can't guarantee that. I know it's hard, but I'm here, and I'll do anything I can to help you. Do you understand?"

I ducked my muzzle again, even as frustration grew within me like a poison tide.

Shifting back was not an option. *I can't.* I sent the mental words with every bit of oomph I possessed, but she just continued staring at me, her hopeful expression unchanged.

At some point, we'd develop a mental bond. But my memories of when and how the mate bond progressed were hazy,

25

clouded by so many years of distance. Maybe I needed to keep trying.

I cannot shift back. Ever.

Nothing.

"Are you trying to shift?" she asked hopefully, quickly looking across at Kane again.

I shook my head, and her smile fell. "Dirge, I really want to get you out of this cell. It's no place for a wolf to be. But they *will not* let you out until you're back in human form. Can you try? For me? I... I hope you've felt the connection between us." Her voice quavered, the uncertainty there an arrow straight to my heart. She was my huntress, and I her willing prey.

I took a cautious step forward and, when she didn't move, another. The third step put me in range to lean my head against her chest.

She gasped, but clung to my neck, steadying herself against the weight of my much larger wolf resting against her small, fragile human frame. Her fingers curled into my pelt, the sensation better than anything I'd felt in the whole of my long, lonely life.

It was so little, and yet everything at the same time.

"It's okay. We can try together. I'm having trouble reaching my wolf right now, since the wolfsbane. But I've been where you are before. Not for as long, of course, but I've lived as a wolf too. And the longer you're in fur, the harder it is to shift back. But I know you can do it."

She whispered softly against the top of my head, while her fingers stroked along the ruff of my neck. She didn't shy away from me now that we were touching, and for a little while, everything else melted away. The cell, the silver, the other alpha. There was nothing but my mate and her sweet embrace. I found myself wanting to give in, to give her everything she asked me for. A shift was nothing. A matter of moments, and then I could take her into my arms and kiss her so well, she'd never question if I felt our connection as mates again.

Except... I couldn't do that. Not now, not ever.

The truth yanked me from our happy bubble, sorrow slicing through the happiness with ease.

I might have forgotten the steps of a mate bond or what it was like to walk on two legs. But there was one thing burned into my memory like a brand, so strongly imprinted that I could never forget. The thing that meant I could never take human form again, no matter how sweetly she begged.

Because what I knew, down to the marrow of my bones, was that the day I shed my fur was the day my mate died in my arms.

SEVEN

Shay

"We should step outside." Kane's words broke my reverie, stilled my hands where they were sunk into Dirge's filthy, matted fur. I didn't even care. There was something soothing about touching him, even if he needed about ten baths and a major haircut.

"Not yet," I pleaded, squeezing Dirge's neck a little tighter.

"Just for a few moments. We will return." When I didn't move, he added a hint of alpha command. "Come."

My limbs moved without my permission, releasing Dirge as I rose to my feet like a puppet on strings.

I bit back my irritation. I was trying to moderate my emotions so that Dirge could better control his. He was attuned to me. I knew it instinctually, even though he couldn't say. When I'd gotten upset, he'd comforted me in the only way he could.

Following Kane out of the room on wooden legs was a low point, but I was proud that Dirge didn't move, didn't throw himself back at the door as it shut behind us.

As soon as the door lock ground back into place, the alpha command dropped from my limbs, and I spun to face Kane.

"Why would you do that? I was making progress!"

"I agree," he said, so calmly that it stopped my fury midwindup.

"Okay... so if you agree, then can he come out?"

Kane sighed. "It's not that simple. To knowingly break pack law about something as significant as this, I would need to bring it before my top five."

That was surprisingly fair. I wasn't a hundred percent sure how the Johnson City pack ran, but I vaguely remembered a similar process happening a time or two over the years when a rule was changed. "How soon can you talk to them? And can I wait with Dirge while you do?"

"I think you're correct that he won't hurt you. He seems to have uncanny understanding, for someone who's been feral as long as he has. I'd like you to be there for the beginning of the meeting so you can speak on your own behalf. But in this case... I think seeing that with their own eyes will help convince the five to side in your favor. So, yes. You can wait with him after you speak to them. I just wanted you to be aware of what was happening. You're very dear to my mate, and I don't take that bond lightly. But as Alpha, your protection has to be my top priority, even if you don't like it."

I wanted to bristle at the implication that he knew what was better for me than I did, but I had to grudgingly admit that he knew more about feral wolves. "Where are we meeting them?"

"I've sent for them through the pack bonds. They're already on the way."

We walked back into the monitoring room, where we could see Dirge patiently waiting in the middle of the room, staring up at the camera above the door. My heart ached at seeing him locked up, and determination built in my chest, brick by brick, to get him out of there. A wolf I didn't recognize was first through the door, but Gael was only moments behind him. My heart lifted when Brielle walked in, pressing a quick kiss to

Kane's lips before coming to stand beside me and hold my hands tightly in hers. The touch of my pack mate and best friend anchored me in a way that little else could. I only wished that Leigh could also be here, so our trio would be complete.

One friendly face was more than I expected, though, and I'd take it. I'd forgotten that as the Alpha's mate, Brielle automatically became one of the top five.

Reed walked in with a pensive expression, but with his dark hair still wet from a shower. It was one of the few times I'd seen him out of a suit, but he still wore a crisp button-up and smelled of freshly applied cologne. He sank gratefully into the lone chair, sparing a glance for me before watching his brother on the monitors while we waited for the last member of the Pack Blackwater's top five.

My heart sank a little when Julius, one of the pack's senior enforcers, walked through the door. He was a sharp man in every sense of the word, a fact the graying hairs at his temples didn't detract from, and I couldn't imagine him voting to break pack law, not even for a good reason. He was thickly muscled and weathered from too much time in the sun. My pulse pounded loudly in my ears as Julius let the door swing closed behind him without a word.

"Thank you all for coming so quickly. This is an important issue. Quick introductions before we begin—Everyone, this is Shay of the Johnson City pack. You likely recognize her as Brielle's second from the challenge for mating rights last week." A hint of gravel entered his tone when he mentioned the challenge, when he'd come so close to losing his own fated mate. Kane cleared his throat before continuing. "Shay, you already know Brielle, Gael, and Reed. This is Samuel," he paused, pointing to the first wolf through the door. He had swarthy coloring and keen intelligence in his eyes. "He is my fifth, and Julius is my fourth as well as the top enforcer for our pack, after Gael."

I nodded to the two of them, too tense to say anything. Silence had always been my go-to in times of trouble, and now was no different. Silence, or music. Composing had been my escape ever since I'd become obsessed with music in my teens. Music spoke when words failed me.

"As you all know, Dirge is back. Unfortunately, there has been no change to his feral status, and he remains in wolf form." Kane pointed to the monitors, and every head in the room swiveled to take in the image of the patiently sitting wolf.

"He doesn't look feral at the moment, apart from the eyes," Gael mused.

"I agree, and there are some extenuating circumstances we need to discuss. There has been a request to release him from his cell."

"Seriously?" Samuel's voice was incredulous. "There's a very clear law on this. No skin, no release. What's there to discuss?"

A sharp growl poured through the room at his callous disregard, and it wasn't until Brielle nudged my shoulder with hers that I realized it was *me* growling like an idiot. I reeled it in, but it took an enormous effort. Clearly, my control was lacking today.

But was it the wound, or the proximity to my unclaimed mate?

"He was getting to it, asshole," Reed snapped, his bloodshot eyes narrowing on the pack's fifth.

Well, at least I wasn't the only one.

"Okay, we're *all* touchy today." Samuel raised his hands in a calming gesture, shooting a confused, what-the-hell look at Reed.

"As I was saying, there has been a request for his early release," Kane said again, mild censure in his tone at the interruption. "We believe he's returned because his fated mate has been found, and what we first interpreted as the attack of a feral wolf was actually his attempt to protect his mate."

31

There was a heavy moment of silence, and then everyone was talking at once. Brielle hung on to my hand like it was going to float away, and her grip was the only thing keeping me still as the testosterone level in the room went through the roof.

"Can a feral wolf even recognize a mate bond?"

"That makes him *less* stable. There's no fucking way!"

"How do you know?" The last, calmer question from my best friend brought the angry exclamations to a sudden halt. Every head swiveled, none daring to talk over the high alpha's new mate.

Kane sent me a questioning look, but I could no more speak past the hedgehog lodged in my throat than I could sing opera.

"Several things. One, look at him. As soon as she spoke, he settled, even in his feral state. For another thing, her wolf is not feral and has also expressed the desire to claim."

"Even so," Samuel interjected, "he can't actually claim her unless he comes back to himself. As long as the wolf is in control, he's going to be dangerous. Not just because he's feral —he hasn't harmed any human or shifter during his years in the wild, which we all know. But a new mate bond that hasn't been solidified by the claiming? He's going to be unstable, aggressive, and on guard until they go through the claiming rites. If any male touches her—even by accident—he's going to try to tear their arm off."

I drew in a breath through my nose, the weight of those words sinking in. He wasn't wrong. New mate bonds were precious, but it was also a fraught time for any relationship. Until the bonding ceremony was completed, cementing the lifelong bond under the Moon Goddess, another wolf could challenge for mating rights, just as had happened with Brielle and Jasline.

Dirge's wolf waited calmly, his black fur matted and over-long, red eyes glowing menacingly even in the wan fluorescent lighting, and the knot in my throat finally eased as resolve settled into me. He might look terrifying, sure, but I knew in the core of my being that he wasn't here to hurt me, or anyone else in our pack. "That's not going to happen," I said.

The males all turned to look at me for the first time, and Brielle gave my fingers a little squeeze of support as I continued. "Kane and I walked into the room already and he didn't react. He's got control, even though he's not shifted back yet. And if someone will volunteer to go back in with me, I'll prove it."

Silence was the only answer for one heartbeat and then another.

"I'll go," Reed said, meeting my gaze with equal dread and determination. "He's my brother, and I want him released as much as you do. He may not be able to shift back without help, and time around his pack will strengthen those bonds again."

"It should be me," Kane said. Reed bristled under his alpha's assessment.

"He's my *brother*, Kane." Reed raked a hand through his hair, standing from the chair and stepping into the open space between all of us.

"I know. And that's why it needs to be me. You're too close to it."

Reed growled, the sound starting low, then building as his anger crested and his eyes began to glow ice blue.

"If the situation were reversed, would you want me to turn away your help? I'm strong enough to hold him, even if he snaps. I hold the power of the pack bonds now." Kane tapped his chest, the place where he must feel the immense tangle of power fed to him through all the packs who pledged loyalty to him.

The growling dropped lower in Reed's chest but didn't stop even as he nodded. Reed turned his back to us, letting his head hang loose on his shoulders as he white-knuckle gripped the back of the chair.

"Okay." The word was hoarse, a strain for the usually composed male.

Kane nodded, then turned to me. "Shall we?"

I looked at Brielle, checking to make sure she didn't object to me putting her mate in danger, but all I saw there was compassion.

"You got this." She gave me a quick hug, and then we were back in front of the heavy steel door. Nerves swarmed in my stomach, a sickly sensation I wanted to shake off like water after a swim.

"Whatever you have in mind, move slowly and keep your calm," Kane suggested as the keypad chirped and the lock slid open.

But I didn't focus on that. My hand was already on the handle, pulling the door wide so I could see Dirge.

My mate.

The thought still didn't feel real. Maybe it wouldn't until he was able to shift—to speak to me, to hold me. I craved his touch in a way that went deeper than anything I'd ever experienced, even as a child dreaming of the parents I'd never had.

I needed Dirge with an intensity that bordered on physical sickness. Moving far too quickly, I closed the distance between us, dropping to my knees heedless of the bullet wound in my stomach and the hard concrete floors. I buried my fingers in his fur, letting my forehead fall against his.

A low, contented rumble started in his chest, the sound and gentle vibrations almost like a cat's purr, soothing me. How long we stayed that way or when Kane followed me inside, I couldn't say.

It wasn't until he spoke that I remembered why we'd come back in. "Shay? We should get started."

We had a show to put on.

EIGHT

Dirge

S hay pulled back a few inches, and my heart sank. Was she here to tell me they still weren't letting me out? I braced myself for it, even as I hoped with all I had for something else, I wasn't sure when or how, but the wolf was slowly letting me back to the forefront.

Maybe it was her, my mate. The wolf loved the girl, but the bond couldn't be solidified while the wolf was in charge, and he knew it. Even feral, he knew.

And so it was that I was present, *lucid*, if not in the driver's seat, when she spoke next.

"They don't want to let you out because they're afraid you'll be a danger to the males of the pack while our bond isn't complete."

I bit back the growl that wanted to escape. The last thing she needed was me snarling at her for having the bad luck to be mated to me. I kept it in and kept my eyes locked on hers. She grounded me, when nothing else had for a long, long time.

"But I told them you weren't a danger. You were protecting me, and we could prove to them that you wouldn't hurt anyone. You won't, right, Dirge?"

She stroked my neck, the sensation making me want to curl up in her lap. But instead, I jerked my chin down in a nod. Shay cast a pointed glance toward the camera at my acquiescence, as if proving a point.

"Okay, I know you may not like this, but we're going to show them that you can tell the difference between harmful touch and friendly touch. Kane is going to touch me now, and you're not going to attack him. Because he's our friend, and he's helping us." She spoke with conviction, but the pleading in her gaze was unquestionable, even as my feet shifted anxiously on the cold, biting concrete.

Nothing about this was okay with my wolf. *Nothing.* We didn't share our mate with other males; it just wasn't done. The Goddess gave us many gifts, and chief among them was a protective streak a hundred miles wide. There was no bridge I wouldn't cross, no fire I wouldn't leap through, and no foe I wouldn't face to protect my mate. Yet here she was, asking me *not* to give in to that urge.

It was a tall order for a man in control, and I was not that. But she was asking, and I had to try. For her.

I forced my chin down again and focused on her eyes as she stood, releasing her grip on my pelt. The loss of her touch was a wound, but I locked my muscles in place. If she needed my control, I would give it to her.

One step back, another. The tentative threads that bound us stretched between us achingly, until she stopped a scant three feet away. Too close to the Goddess-cursed silver lining this wretched room.

"Kane." She directed the moment, chin held high and palm outstretched. Pride swelled inside me, even as I fought the urge to get between them. My mate was *strong*, even wounded, and she didn't hesitate or back away from the overpowering alpha who approached. To his credit, he moved slowly, keeping his eyes on neutral territory and his posture relaxed as he extended his own hand.

Watching them link hands felt like a spike being driven through my ribs. I whined. I couldn't help it. My muscles were locked tight, but the wolf didn't understand why our mate would do this, even though I knew why.

"You're doing great, Dirge. So, so well," she soothed, her gray eyes soft and a little damp as she held my gaze. "I don't think this is enough to convince the five, though. Did you know Kane has mated with my best friend? When you and I first met it was at the afterparty for their bonding ceremony. It was beautiful, and the flowers smelled lovely. So many lights, and all the pretty dresses."

Her voice was wistful, and I wanted to give her that beautiful ceremony more than anything. Every flower, every decoration, the best food, and any gown she wanted. Hell, I still had money sitting in accounts from before. She could have every last penny if it would make her smile again.

"Kane, congratulations on your bonding. I don't think I've told you that yet." She squeezed his fingers in hers, and I forced down a twitch. I hadn't forgotten that they were touching, per se, but her words had distracted me. Probably exactly as she intended, smart woman.

"Thank you, Shay. I appreciate you standing up for my mate."

"She's my sister," Shay said simply. "May I offer you a congratulatory hug?"

No.

No, no, no. No hugs. My paws shifted on the cement, my best self-control flagging at the prospect of what was about to happen.

"Of course. You're family now."

Family? My paws stilled again, and I realized what they were doing. Family was no threat, no harm to a wolf. To harm one's own flesh and blood was anathema; no wolf would dream of it.

And as my mate, *her* family became my own, immediately. Even though I hated the power rolling off the other man, even if I wanted to tear his skin off for daring to look at the beauty that was *mine*, everything inside me stilled.

Hurting her family hurt her. And no part of me would do that.

I watched as she hugged the alpha, Kane, who I'd watched grow up. The memories came rushing back of the dark-headed boy who laughed too loudly for the responsibilities he would one day bear. The memories shocked me with their clarity. Nothing had been clear except pain for so long.

Until Shay.

The two of them pulled apart, and Shay leapt at me with excitement. "You did it! You did it, Dirge!" She wrapped me in a hug so tight, she nearly choked me. But rather than dislodge her, I pushed her forward, letting her back meet the concrete as I laved sandpaper kisses over her cheeks and forehead.

"Eww, Dirge!" She laughed, the first time I'd heard the sound, and I stopped licking just to listen, to appreciate the unbridled joy of it.

Something fundamental inside me shifted.

NINE

Shay

It was even harder leaving Dirge in the cell the second time, but I did it with renewed determination.

"If I hadn't seen it with my own eyes, I'd have called you a liar," Julius said as we walked through the door into the monitoring room.

"Can we let him out?" I didn't wait for a lengthy discussion or for people to start second-guessing what they'd seen. I needed him out. I needed him with me.

"We will vote on it," Kane said, laying a gentle hand on my shoulder before crossing to Brielle's waiting arms. She stared up at him with adoration.

"Have I told you lately that I don't like it when you put yourself in danger? That was terrifying to watch."

"I know, baby, but I could cow his wolf if I had to. This is part of being Alpha." He stroked her cheek reverently, the tender sight making my stomach tighten with jealousy. I was so proud of my friend for overcoming the odds and claiming her mate. But I wanted that for myself too, so badly it hurt.

Brielle leaned into his touch, even as the two of them turned together to face the rest of the group.

"All in favor of allowing a trial release period?" Kane posed the question with no further fanfare.

Reed and Brielle lifted their hands immediately, and I did too, though I likely didn't get a vote. Technically, I wasn't even *part* of Pack Blackwater, but I didn't care. The rest of the hands were slower to go up, but in the end, every one went up, except Julius's.

"I'm not saying no, but he needs a guard at all times until he's no longer feral and they're bonded."

"I will personally take responsibility for him." Gael stepped forward, shocking me in the process. I didn't know him well—only observing the crazy, angry chemistry between him and Leigh—but the grateful look Reed sent him told me everything I needed to know. He was no hopeless romantic, but he'd do anything for his pack.

Julius nodded, then lifted two fingers to signal his consent.

I headed straight for the hall, not waiting for anyone to change their minds.

Kane called after me, "Five, eight, two—"

"Six, eight, nine, I know!" I called back over my shoulder, already punching in the code.

They didn't need to know that Dirge was getting out tonight, whether they voted for it or not.

AN HOUR LATER, I was back in bed, Dirge lying plastered to my uninjured side and growling lightly at John Henry, who wanted to check my wound since I'd escaped my room earlier.

"I feel okay, just tired," I reassured the displeased healer.

"I understand, but your body can't process wolfsbane, and you're not healing at normal speed. Things like pulled stitches matter when you're healing at human rates."

I lifted the bottom of my shirt and frowned down at the

bright red bloom of blood on my bandage. I hadn't even noticed, but it probably needed changing. I cast a glance at Dirge, whose hackles were raised as he tried to engage the man in a staring contest. John Henry was carefully keeping his eyes averted, and the whole thing would've been comical if I didn't need his help.

"Can Brielle check it?" Leigh asked from her post in the corner chair. "She was grabbing our lunch, but she's trained, and maybe Fido will be a little less touchy about a female doc." Her pose was casual but alert, one arm slung around her knee, the other foot bouncing on the ground with boredom. She didn't fully trust Dirge yet, and I couldn't blame her, really.

The glowing red eyes were unnerving.

"Don't call him Fido, Leigh." I stroked down his back again, ignoring the filth in favor of connection. But we'd have to get him cleaned up somehow, and soon.

"We can wait for Brielle, yes. But if he doesn't allow *her* to help..." John Henry pressed his lips into a grim line.

He didn't have to finish the sentence; I already knew. They'd take him back to the cell. My grip on his fur tightened reflexively.

"Don't stress, Shay. It's all going to work out, because *Dirge*" —she said his name with a heavy dose of censure—"wants you to be healthy, and he won't stop the doctors from helping you. Will he?" She squinted over at him, making eye contact and not shying away when he returned it. Even from her seated position, her wolf rose to the surface, eyes glowing a stunning gold as her wolf pressed forward.

To my surprise, though, he didn't growl at her or take offense. It was like he knew that she was family.

"I'll wait in the hall until Brielle returns." John Henry ducked his head politely and then stepped out of the room. As soon as it clicked shut, Dirge visibly relaxed, letting his tongue loll out and wagging his tail.

41

"You're a real piece of work, dude," Leigh muttered, but the corner of her lips twisted up. "There might be something wrong with us, Shay. Why do we like assholes?"

"We? Do tell. I haven't heard anything since Gael carried you off the dance floor." I waggled my eyebrows at her in a move I'd seen her do hundreds of times over the years when she was ribbing me or Brielle about our nonexistent love lives.

Payback's a bitch.

My loud, brash friend blushed. *Blushed.* "There's nothing to tell," she said, trying and failing for a casual tone.

"The heat between you two is enough to melt the ice caps. You would really deny me details when I'm laid up in bed, wounded?" I dramatically slouched into the bed, doing my best to look pitiful.

"Stop it. Don't make me feel worse! It's bad enough I was busy— Ahh, shit. Fine!" She dropped her head in her hands for a second, then smoothed her fingers over her long, blonde ponytail. "We hooked up, okay? But he's an arrogant ass, I got him out of my system, and I'm *never* going there again. Hell, I'm never speaking to him again. I'm through."

I watched all this with barely suppressed laughter. It was so rare to see Leigh ruffled, I hated that Bri wasn't here to see it.

"So, was he that good, or that bad? I know it's one or the other."

She sighed, a wistful admission. "He was great, okay? The best I've ever been with, if I'm honest. But I'm not going to tell him that, because his ego does *not* need to get any bigger. He's already impossible."

"Fair enough—you know I'm no snitch."

She smiled at me then, the tension easing out of her shoulders and melting away. "You? Never." There was a comfortable pause. "It's still early for lunch, and Bri was going to get something special. Why don't you try to rest."

As soon as she suggested it, I yawned, a wave of exhaustion

I'd been studiously ignoring washing over me and making my eyelids heavy. I still had questions about what had happened between her and Gael, but they could wait for another time.

Leigh smiled, pulling her phone out of her pocket and waving it at me. "I've got a book to read, so don't worry about me."

I quirked an eyebrow at her as I scooched down the bed, rearranging my pillows. "Is it at least something good? Or is it another one of those boring, dry—"

"Hey! Kinesiology and physiology books are informative, not boring."

I yawned again, not buying a word of it, when, to my surprise, a soft rumbling came from Dirge, where he lay pressed against my side. He was still facing the door, on alert even as he soothed me. He was a good wolf and, I hoped, a good man underneath.

"But if you must know," Leigh continued, "I'm reading the new Lindsay Buroker. She's the only one who gets the dragons right. Pompous asses, every one of them."

"Good," I murmured, sleep pulling me under with a smile on my lips and my hand wrapped in Dirge's coat. Even as I thought that Leigh was full of bullshit. She'd never met a *dragon*.

TEN

Dirge

The room fell quiet, nothing but the soft sounds of Shay's deep, even breaths to keep us company, and the occasional tap from Leigh—the mouthy blonde female who was as close as my mate's shadow—doing something on her phone.

When Shay released a relaxed sigh and rolled onto her stomach—fully asleep now—Leigh dropped the phone along with the air of disinterest she'd been wearing.

Her eyes snapped up, the regular blue fading away behind the bright, golden glow of her wolf pressing forward. It wasn't lack of control, though; far from it. It was *intentional*, a display of force.

I met her gaze, never one to back down from a predator.

"Listen up, Fluffy," she said in a low, threatening tone. "I'm tolerating you because Shay thinks you're her mate. But I want to get one thing very, very clear."

She paused, waiting to make sure I comprehended her, so I dipped my muzzle down to nod without breaking eye contact.

"If you hurt her, I will slit your throat and bury you out back before she knows you're gone. And I won't feel a single second's guilt, you can believe that. This girl right here?" She pointed at

44

Shay's sleeping form. "She's not my friend. She's not my pack mate. She is my *sister*. And I won't let anybody hurt her *ever again*. And until you've got full control of yourself? I don't trust a hair on your stinking, shaggy head."

I whuffed, a wolfish laugh I couldn't restrain even in this form. But inside, a happy warmth filled me. She could threaten me until she was blue in the face, because I would never hurt Shay. But it made me happy to know that my she-wolf had such fierce, loyal friends on her side. I would keep an eye on this one too. She was unmated and surrounded by aggressive males. But if she was my mate's sister, she was mine to protect as well.

I would do that for Shay. I laid my head oh, so carefully over her arm, where I could still keep an eye on the door, but not wake her. Just feel her closeness. Revel in her soft, sweet floral smell and the warmth of her skin.

So long... I'd waited *so long* for her, I didn't want to miss a second.

Leigh was still staring me down when the door cracked quietly open again, and our attention snapped to the intruder.

"Well, you two are tense. Everything okay in here?" Brielle whispered as she stepped quietly through, waving the male healer in behind her. I sat up, my hackles rising as he followed her.

"Easy, Dirge," the alpha's mate crooned, as if I were a cuddly puppy and not a three-hundred-pound feral killer.

Oddly, though... the hair on the back of my ruff lowered of its own accord, and my eyes drifted away from the male and back to the woman. She had shining, dark curls and a pleasant scent, even if it couldn't hold a candle to my Shay's. It hung heavily in the air around her, over the strong scent of food she carried in a stack of small boxes.

Brielle's scent wasn't attractive. It was... calming. Like a pool of still water surrounded by sweet grasses. The kind my wolf would love to sleep beside.

45

I shook my head, confused about why I'd risen in the first place, until the healer moved at her elbow. My eyes snapped to his, but he quickly and respectfully ducked his head, averting his gaze.

"John Henry isn't going to approach Shay, so you can stay calm for me. Right?" She smiled easily at me before passing the food to Leigh, who set all but one box on the small table next to Shay's bed.

Ducking my muzzle in acknowledgment, I still didn't look away from the other male.

"Excellent. I'm here to check her bandage and discuss anything else we may be able to give her to support a more normal healing pace. Wolfsbane is some nasty stuff, and it's unfortunate she was dosed with it at all, but especially such a strong dose." Brielle gave me a gentle smile before stepping closer, unafraid. "I'll need access to her bandage." She pointed to the side of the bed, the order clear.

I huffed but obeyed, shifting so I was out of the way a few inches from Shay's back.

"Thank you, Dirge. I'll try not to wake her, but the bandage change might do it anyway." Her soft murmur was soothing as she worked, all while I monitored the healer at his position just inside the door. I saw the vivid red blood on the bandage as she removed it, causing Shay to whimper and shift in her sleep. I pressed a bit closer to her back, unable to stop myself from offering whatever comfort I could. It was pure reflex, and I couldn't have done anything else when my mate was hurting.

"Shh, shh." Brielle made little soothing nonsense sounds as she worked, and Shay calmed under her touch much as I had under her voice, not waking even as Brielle applied a thick, stinking unguent and another padded bandage. It was uncanny, and if it weren't so damn soothing, I might have found it peculiar.

When she finished, she carefully settled Shay's blankets

back over her and removed the gloves I hadn't noticed her putting on to begin with.

"Okay, she's settled for now. The only question I have is how can we help her heal faster? Do you think a turmeric tincture might help? Or I could prepare it in a tea," Brielle said, looking to the male healer for confirmation.

"That could work. We could also get some sage candles in here, so long as we get her into a room that's not hooked to the oxygen." He jutted his chin toward the wall, where a little tap extended out for oxygen tubing to be connected.

"Oh, yes. Sage for sure. Anything to clear that nastiness out of her system. We can transfer her to a lower-level room."

"I'll speak to Emory about it, then." His hand was on the doorknob, and then he was in the hallway without a glance back.

I relaxed as the door clicked shut, inching over so more of my body pressed against Shay's where she lay quietly.

"Okay, then. I'll get out of your hair until I've got some tea leaves ready. Leigh, do you want to trade off with me for the night? I don't want her to be alone, and you need to rest too."

"Nope," she answered, popping the p. "Rover and I have come to an understanding, right, poochie?" She blew me a sarcastic kiss, daring me to argue. In this form, I'd just bite her.

I rumbled my annoyance at her teasing, but nodded instead of using my fangs. She might have been a mouthy bitch, but she was a likable bitch. And under my protection, even if she didn't know it.

Brielle rolled her eyes at the two of us. "I'll be back in an hour or so, after I get the tea leaves prepared. Call me if she wakes up sooner, though. I'd like to talk to her and make sure she doesn't need anything extra for the pain."

"Deal," Leigh answered, shoving in a mouthful of noodles and giving the Alpha's mate a thumbs-up.

Brielle chuckled as she left, shutting the door softly on her soothing scent. The absence of it made a part of me deep down feel bereft, and I didn't like it. But as I settled in next to my mate, her soothing floral scent settled me once more. It had just a hint of sharp, tart fruit to it that made my mouth water. *The man would know,* I thought as my eyelids drifted shut.

SOMETIME IN THE middle of the night, the sickroom door slammed open. I was on my feet, standing over Shay in a heartbeat. The big, dominant male in the doorway radiated fury, and I snarled, baring my fangs at his audacity, coming in here and waking my sick mate.

She shifted beneath me, startled awake and grabbing her side with a gasp. But it was Leigh who spoke first.

"Hey, asshole, we were *sleeping* in here. Do you mind?"

"You're supposed to be in your room sleeping. But when my patrol checks, you're not in your bed. Instead, I find you in here with a *feral alpha* who could rip you limb from limb! Get up, now. We're going."

I growled again, the sound low and deadly in my throat. I didn't like how he spoke to her, not one little bit. If he moved a muscle into this room, I would tear him a new asshole. I'd already sized him up, and he was plenty dominant, but I could take him.

"One, you don't get to tell me what to do. Two, it's not my fault Reed didn't tell you I came in while he was watching the door. Three, the only one getting ripped apart is going to be you if you don't cool your jets. He's protective of Shay if there are other males in the room, and you coming in all alpha-hole isn't helping." She thrust a hand in my direction for emphasis, not moving from her spot curled up in the chair by Shay's bedside.

"This is not negotiable. If you won't walk out of here, I'll carry you out."

"Try me, Gael. I'm not leaving her bedside." Leigh stood then, both hands on hips and chin lifted in defiance. I could smell the anger rolling off her, her arms shaking a little with the repressed urge to shift.

"Guys, I'm okay. Can we all just settle down? Dirge is still working on his control," Shay said. She'd managed to sit up in the bed, moving her legs from underneath mine at what must have been great personal expense. "Since you're guarding him, Leigh's fine, right?"

"And he can practice his control again once I get Leigh out of danger and back where she's supposed to be."

"Oh my *Goddess*, do you even hear yourself? I'm not a toddler! Get out of here. You stood up for him and now you're going to act like he's some slavering monster unsafe to be in the same room with me?" Leigh's eyes began to glow gold as her wolf pressed the issue.

Gael lunged toward her, and I leapt for his throat.

ELEVEN

Shay

"Dirge, no!" I watched in horror as Dirge flew through the air, deadly sharp canines flashing under the fluorescent lights as he arrowed toward Gael's shoulder.

Thank the Goddess, Gael dodged back and raised an arm to block. Not enough for Dirge to miss, but enough for the deadly bite to sink into his biceps instead of his jugular.

"Shit! Shit, shit, shit! Fluffy, down! He's a dick, but you can't kill him!" Leigh ran forward—faster than me, in my wounded state—and, to my utter shock, wrapped her arms around Dirge's neck and pulled.

Dirge released Gael with a throaty snarl, blood and saliva dripping down his chin as he stared up at Gael.

Gael's face was painted with shock as he looked down at the gaping wounds in his arm. His black T-shirt was shredded, not having stood a chance against shifter fangs.

Not knowing what else to do, I pulled the red emergency call rope hanging next to my bed, and alarms sounded as lights flashed in the hallway.

The sound pulled Gael back into the present, because between one moment and the next, he'd shifted, clothes exploding into useless shreds as a massive tan-and-gray wolf appeared where the man had just stood. He snarled and paced toward Dirge, his maw open, saliva dripping from his dagger-sharp canines.

"Stop, please, both of you! Stop!" I swung my legs off the bed, cursing my wobbly knees as I tried to close the distance and put myself between them.

Dirge barked, short and sharp, warning me back as he shook off Leigh's grip. She swung toward me, swearing again as she saw me standing, then dodged the two alpha wolves. As soon as she was at my side, she bear-hugged me so I didn't fall, then proceeded to yell at the two wolves.

"We're both fine! You two are fighting for nothing! Would you knock it off before you *both* get thrown in a cell?"

Dirge didn't attack again. To my surprise he simply backed up, putting himself between us and Gael. Who was guarding who here?

"What's the meaning of this!" Kane's dominance barreled into the room ahead of him like a freight train, and I winced as it hit me. He usually kept it pulled in, at least around his own pack mates, so we weren't getting slammed with it constantly. But right now, he had it on full display, nearly leveling us all to the linoleum with the force of it.

I couldn't speak, couldn't do anything but cling to Leigh and try to stay on my feet.

Luckily, Leigh was stronger than I was at the moment, because the two wolves weren't going to answer him. "Gael stormed in here and spooked Dirge. It was *not* Dirge's fault. We were all asleep when Gael slammed the door open, and Dirge didn't attack until Gael lunged for me."

"He lunged for you, or Shay?" Kane asked, pulling back on the power just a little, allowing me to take a deeper breath.

She didn't have a chance to answer before Brielle elbowed her way past Kane into the overcrowded sickroom, her own fury palpable despite the crushing alpha dominance already stuffed into the small room. "Holy hell on a double helix! You boneheads have her out of bed way too early. You should *both* be ashamed of yourselves," she snapped, and moved to skirt them, but Kane threw up an arm to block her from the shifted males.

"Shift back *now*," she ordered from behind his arm. To my utter shock, Gael yelped once, and then he was a naked, angry man again. Dirge howled, the sound pained, but retained his fur even as he sank to the ground on his side, twisting and panting with the effort not to shift.

"Leigh, let me go. I have to help him, please," I said, my hands shaking. I didn't care, though. I couldn't see him in pain. I had to go to him.

"We'll do it together. Come on." She bore most of my weight as we crossed the small space, and she carefully lowered me to the linoleum next to my shaking mate.

I lifted his head into my lap, gingerly stroking his fur as Kane dressed Gael down not two feet from where we sat. Brielle was at my side in a blink, focused not on Dirge but on my bullet wound.

"Gah, the stitches are out again. You're bleeding, and I'm going to have to get you back on the bed and close this back up," she murmured, clearly upset as she pushed back to her feet and rounded on Gael. But Leigh was already there, a furious blonde tornado.

"I don't care what you thought—we spent one night together. *One.* And whatever your pea-sized caveman brain might think, we are not together. We are not a couple. You're not my mate, and you don't get to say *shit* about where I am or what I do. Are we clear? I'm not part of your pack. I'm not your girlfriend. Hell, we aren't even friends. Capiche?" She jabbed a finger into his naked, naked chest, and layered one last insult on the pile. "Now get the fuck out of my sight before I shift and finish what he started."

"Fine. You want it that way, princess? You got it." Gael's tone was so cold, it scared me as he turned on his heel and marched out of the room, all military precision and no feeling. Kane exchanged a few whispered words with Brielle before following him and shutting the door behind them.

I sagged against the bed as the alpha dominance left the room, replaced instead by a soothing surge of energy I couldn't place.

"Okay, now. Everyone's okay, and Kane will see to Gael. Dirge, I need you to hop up for me. Can you do that?" Brielle used her doctor voice, no-nonsense but kind. "Shay shouldn't be out of bed yet, and Leigh and I need to get her settled again so I can fix her stitches and put a new bandage on."

He stilled under my touch, then heaved himself upright with effort. Relief washed through me, but it was replaced by wonder when he turned toward me, and I saw his eyes.

His gorgeous, green eyes.

The feral red was gone.

TWELVE

Dirge

I was hesitant to sleep again after my mate's wound was stitched back up. Adrenaline ran through my veins at top speed, whispering that danger was near, even as the long hours of the night stretched on. Her pack mates—her family, I corrected myself with a glance at the blonde and brunette heads tilted together in sleep in their chairs—stayed with us, meaning I had not just my precious mate to protect, but them as well.

What was precious to her was precious to me. And after seeing them interact today, I had no doubt that they were precious to Shay. So I kept watch, doing the only mate thing that was left to me in wolf form: protecting her.

Brielle groaned softly in her sleep, clutching her stomach and curling tighter into Leigh's side. That concerned me, but she settled after a few moments. Still, I stayed vigilant.

So it was in the very early morning, when the sun's rays had only begun to crest the horizon, I was awake and felt a strange power flood the room.

It was unlike anything I'd ever sensed before, and the flash that accompanied it had me on my feet, a low growl in my throat.

"Dirge? What's wrong?" Shay's sleepy voice was soft and rough, her hands in my fur gentle, soothing. "I don't sense anyone nearby who shouldn't be. Can we rest a little longer?" She dropped her forehead to my shoulder, stroking my ruff lightly as she waited for me to decide.

I had no way to tell her what I'd felt or to find out if the magical surge had invaded the whole area or just this room. I hoped for the former, but feared the latter. Still, though, as we sat and quietly watched the sunrise together, there was no sign of anything amiss, and gradually, the tension eased from me.

"I wish you could talk to me," Shay murmured, twisting a lock of my fur around her fingertip. "There's so much I want to know about you, but I can't, like this. Like, why did your eyes go back to normal? Can the man hear me, or are you all wolf now? Are you trying to shift back? Do you need something from me to do it?" Frustration leaked into her tone, and I whined as I leaned my head against her chest.

I couldn't answer her. And while it was a sorry situation for her mate to be confined to a wolf's body, that was the only way it could be between us.

And so I swallowed down the pain of not being able to give my mate exactly what she wanted and let a low, soothing rumble vibrate from my chest. She sighed when she felt it, hugging me a little too tightly to her chest for comfort, and fell back asleep.

I relished every second.

"GOOD MORNING!" Brielle's singsong voice elicited grumbles from the other two women in the room. "Oh, come on. It's after nine. Even I'm awake and caffeinated! Plenty of time for us to be up and check that wound again. May I?" She directed the question to me, where I still lay clutched in Shay's now-loose grip. I gently nosed her hand, and she released me so I could sit up and allow the exam.

"Excellent," Brielle said with a smile, her efficient hands already shifting the blankets and Shay's shirt so she could access the bandage. "Okay, good news—there's no fresh blood here, which means your stitches did their job overnight. Now let's just peel this off and see— Holy hell in a handbasket!"

I stiffened, nosing her hand aside to see what had alarmed her about my mate's condition.

But what I saw was nothing. Smooth, brown skin stretched over a taut stomach. The stitches were gone; the wound was gone. Shay's scent was stronger there, brightly floral with tart fruit, as if it was concentrated on the area where she'd healed miraculously overnight. I snuck in a lick, but she batted me away with a laugh.

"Don't try anything, playboy. Now is not the time to get frisky." My mate tried to sound stern, but the warmth in her touch as she pulled me back toward her shoulder and away from her bare stomach was undeniable. It stoked a warm coal of feeling in my chest. I couldn't place it in this form, but it fueled me nonetheless.

"I've never seen anything like this—especially not with wolfsbane," Brielle whispered, eyes round with shock as she looked from Shay to Leigh and back to the nonexistent wound. "Wolves heal quickly, but the *stitches* are gone. Where did they go? I need to palpate your abdomen. Tell me if anything hurts."

Shay nodded, and Brielle began a gentle series of pokes and prods to the area, even asking Shay to roll over so she could check her back.

But to my utter relief, there was no wound, no pain, and

nothing of evident concern. Not even a scar, which was common with wolfsbane injuries.

"I need to speak with John Henry. This is unprecedented as far as I know, but he's older and might have seen... whatever this is."

"Am I cleared, though? Do I need to stay here if I'm better?"

Brielle hesitated, which gave Leigh an opening.

"Aw, come on. Don't be the doctor right now. If she feels fine, let her sleep in her own bed."

Brielle nodded her acquiescence. "If *anything* hurts or feels weird, call me immediately. I'll swing by after I talk to John Henry and let you know if he has any idea how this happened. But for now... enjoy your miraculous recovery." She shrugged, then paused. "Also, after a lot of hemming and hawing last night, it's been agreed by the top five that Gael *guarding* you didn't work out the best, given... your roommate and the tension. So, on a strictly *trial* basis, you're guard-free."

I sat in shock as I watched her hurry from the room, an anxious tinge to her usually peaceful scent.

But I didn't have much time to focus on that because my mate was stretching before jumping out of bed with long-pent-up enthusiasm. "I get to go back to my room and get out of this fishbowl of a sick ward!" She turned a blazing smile on me, then Leigh.

"You're welcome, milady." Leigh bowed extravagantly. "But if you're bringing the mutt to *our* room, I must insist that he be bathed. Thoroughly."

Both women swiveled toward me, eyes lingering on various parts of my matted coat. I lowered my ears and rumbled displeasure as what she'd said sank in. A bath? *No way.*

There was soap in my eye, my ears were wet, and I had imagined things going *far* differently if ever my mate stroked my hindquarters. Instead, I was sneezing because the fake-oatmeal-scented wash she was using was terrible, and there were bubbles everywhere. *Everywhere.*

"Oh, come on, now. Is it really that bad? You're getting a rubdown. Surely that part feels good, at least." Shay emphasized her point by really digging her fingers in and then using her nails to lightly scratch behind my elbows.

I huffed in answer. That part did feel good, I guess.

"Time to rinse, anyway." She hummed a quiet tune as she sprayed me with the detachable showerhead, and I bore it with all the dignity I could muster. Before she got the towel, I shook the water from my coat to her squeals.

Now, *that* was fun.

After she dried me to her satisfaction, she cleaned the bathroom and then showered herself. But not until after shooing me out the door, because "gentlemen don't peek"—a fact I found amusing. I was no gentleman when it came to her. Though, my wolf form was less concerned about her nudity than her happiness. I kept vigil outside the door until she was finished and settled onto her bed, looking exhausted.

"You should have let me help, woman. You're too stubborn for your own good," Leigh said, flipping through a magazine on her own matching bed. She appeared bored, but I didn't miss the worried looks she kept tossing Shay's way.

"I'm fine now, just a little overheated." She fanned her face.

"Hey, be a good puppy and go bump the switch for the fan with your nose," Leigh called to me, gesturing toward the far wall, where a row of switches was indeed lined up next to the door.

I growled lightly at the *puppy* remark, but crossed the room and nudged each switch until a fan began to spin lazily overhead.

"You know, having a service dog might be useful after all." Leigh shot me a shit-eating grin, and I grumbled again before climbing on the foot of Shay's bed to keep her company.

"Leigh, quit," Shay admonished, patting the spot by her side for me to come closer. As soon as I did, she kissed me on the top of my nose. "He's not a dog. He's... mine." The words were a soft caress, the claim she staked on me, however tenuous, a balm to my weary soul.

I'd spent hundreds of years alone. With my parents, yes, and then eventually Reed when he was born. But there was a hole in a wolf's soul, one that couldn't be filled by any but his mate. The looming darkness of despair that I had no mate and was destined to be alone forever was the reason I'd done the impossible and sought an audience with the Fetya.

The thought of the challenge of finding them and then the horrible future they'd imparted with no small measure of glee soured my stomach. I wouldn't let it poison what I could have with Shay, though. I wasn't alone anymore. I wasn't a man who could hold her, sure. But I had her in my life. More than I ever dared hope after the awful news they'd given me.

It turned out that even the Fetya hadn't foreseen this possibility. Or if they did, they hadn't shared it. Only that the first time I held my mate in my arms would be the day she died. Not in so many words; that wasn't the way of the fates. They cackled and gestured, the shortest of the three slapping me on the forehead to instill a vision.

And oh, a terrible vision it was. A stunning beauty. Tight black curls flying in the wind, beautiful tawny skin in the pale morning light. She was everything. And then I saw myself rushing to hold her, and the explosion of light bursting out of her as soon as we touched.

The vision darkened after that, and I was left more bereft

than I'd entered. Because what torture was it to know that I had such a beautiful, perfect mate and that I'd find her, only for her to die in my arms?

So I shifted, and I ran. That vision couldn't come to be if I never took skin again. Which was why I hadn't.

And I won't.

THIRTEEN

Shay

"I t's me. Can I come in?" Brielle called through the closed door.

"Always!" Leigh called back, answering for both of us as she so often did. Dirge didn't budge at my side as she entered, unconcerned by either of my besties' presences anymore, something I hadn't put together until just now.

"Okay, so, John Henry agrees that your overnight healing is completely unprecedented in the presence of wolfsbane. So... I've got nothing. Except news. That I have." She pressed her lips together for a moment, a streak of sadness stealing over her features before she quickly schooled them back into a smile that didn't reach her eyes. "Our flight for the north, to the Athabascan pack lands, leaves tomorrow. Given everything going on here... I'd like to offer you and Leigh the option to stay here. I want you by my side, of course. But it feels selfish to drag you along when you have your own things going on." She tucked a loose lock of hair behind her ear, ducking her head to look at her shoes instead of either of us. "I would understand if this is where you two say you're done. It's probably safer if you both take some time."

"Hell no." Both heads snapped toward me and my uncharacteristic outburst, but I didn't care. "If you think we're abandoning you now when you're newly mated, in a new pack, and with no idea what's going on with your magic, you've got another thing coming. We are getting on that plane with you."

Leigh gave me an air high five, grinning like a loon. "Everything she just said," she added.

"But..." Brielle's feeble protest died on her lips, tears rolling over her cheeks. "It's not safe. The Omega Defense League is going to keep investigating. We don't have any information about who killed Kane's parents, or why, or if they're after *us* now that he's high alpha. The wolf's out of the bag that I'm a weak link, and after how many people saw me try and fail to shift... If they weren't after him before, they might decide to come after him now." She threw up both hands in a helpless gesture and then angrily dashed away a tear. "It's bad enough I painted a target on my mate. But I can't do that to the two of you. And dragging you along is doing that. Being selfish. So, please. Stay here, or go home. But don't put yourself in the line of fire for me."

Leigh shoved to her feet so fast, she blurred a little. Her eyes glowed the gold of her wolf—that was happening a lot more since my accident—and she closed the distance between her bed and Brielle in half a second.

"Do you think our friendship is worth so little to me that I would leave you to deal with all this alone? I thought we knew each other better than that, and if you suggest that I stay behind—that *we* stay behind—one more time, I'm going to be insulted. For real, not kidding. You two and your knuckleheaded males are all I have in this world." Leigh bit her bottom lip for a second. "We are coming with you. Don't suggest otherwise again."

Brielle nodded, too choked up to say anything else as she fell into Leigh's waiting arms. I climbed off the bed and finished the group hug, the shifter need for physical touch driving me. I was surprised when Dirge nosed his way in, licking me on the arm once before leaning into the huddle, providing his own support.

I know the man is in there. But why won't he come out? The thought was going to plague me until I had a human mate standing in front of me.

"I'm okay, I'm sorry, I— I'm fine." Brielle waved us off after a few minutes, swiping hastily at her eyes to hide the evidence of her momentary breakdown.

"Of course you are, you lucky bitch. You have us." Leigh winked and blew her a flamboyant kiss, making us all laugh. The tension evaporated like magic as we all settled around the room. Brielle took a cushy armchair between our two beds on the opposite wall.

"So." I hesitated to bring up an unpleasant topic, but we needed to discuss it. "The killers. There's no news? No sign of what happened?"

Brielle shook her head, shoulders dropping in sadness. "No. The only thing we know is that there were no physical wounds, but the test for known poisons in his blood was negative. It doesn't mean it wasn't poison, only that it could have been an unknown substance. And if it's not a known poison, it's harder to pin on any one group or person. Apparently, killers have favorite methods they tend to go back to, and this is brand-freaking-new."

I scratched behind Dirge's ears as I thought.

"So, we have to go back to opportunity, then, and motive. There were members of almost every pack in the modern world on-site. Opportunities abounded. Motive, well, there's power, obvs," Leigh mulled aloud. "But I think that actually narrows it down. There aren't that many packs strong enough to think they could *keep* the throne after pulling something like that. They'd have to be strong enough to take on not just Pack Blackwater, but Kosta's home pack, the Caelestis. And be able to get past Kosta's personal guard. Have you seen that Sergei guy? I wouldn't want to tangle with him unless it was in the sheets." She made a claw motion with her fingers and shook her shoulders suggestively.

"Didn't you get enough alpha asshole energy with Gael?" I asked, rolling my eyes at her over-the-top self.

"Wait, *what*? Back up, rewind, and tell me everything." Brielle leaned forward, eyes glued to Leigh, who was now blushing furiously.

"Okay, so, this is *way* low priority given the topic we were just discussing"—she shot me a narrow-eyed glare—"but Gael and I may have spent the night together after your bonding ceremony."

"Shut the fuck up!" Brielle blurted, then slapped a hand over her mouth. "Pardon my French. But seriously, you guys slept together? I thought you hated each other. You're always fighting."

Leigh shrugged one shoulder. "I got it out of my system, and that's it. I blame all the pheromones you and Kane were throwing. We were under a spell." She wiggled her fingers mysteriously in the air. "But back to the point. Killers. Motive. Bad stuff."

"I'm sorry, I need more than three seconds to process the fact that you hooked up with Kane's broody, grumpy—"

"Hot as heck," I supplied, to which Dirge growled and shot me a look over his shoulder.

"Oh-ho! Fuzzy-wuzzy is jealous!" Leigh cackled.

Dirge's only response was a haughty huff low in his throat.

"He has no reason to be jealous," I countered, then met his eyes with a grin. "He just needs to shift into a man again so we can all talk about how hot *he* is."

"Maybe he's got a bad butt, so he's too embarrassed. Is that the problem, Fido?"

"You've already used that one," I said drily.

"I know. I need to look up some new ones. Who's a poochy with a bad butt?" she crooned.

After that, serious discussions devolved into long-overdue best-friend chatter, a *Leader of the Pack* hairbrush singing montage, and three pints of ice cream, which extended late into the night. Even after Kane found us and took up a position at Brielle's side, content to let us enjoy a rare moment of peace.

FOURTEEN

Shay

The next morning found us hastily shoving clothes and toiletries into our smallest suitcases for the road. I peered at my favorite black sneakers with dismay, unwilling to pack them when the silver buckles were coated in blood from my injury, the stale copper tang making my stomach churn.

Leigh walked by and plucked them out of my hands. "I'll get someone to clean them for you while we're gone. You know Grace can find someone who won't mind lending a hand, given everything that went down. Just pack your blue ones." She pointed to my second-favorite pair, tucked in a corner of the room and forgotten.

With a nod, I tossed them into the bag. Leigh always seemed to know when I was hung up on something. She was going to make an excellent mother one day. The thought gave me pause, and I looked at her a little more closely with my hand still on the suitcase zipper.

She was bustling around the room, tossing things helter-skelter into her own yawning suitcase. But things started to coalesce into a pattern as I thought over the last few days.

She was on edge, her wolf close to the surface. She was

overprotective of both me and Brielle, which wasn't unusual in small doses, but this was a *whole 'nother level* of protectiveness. She'd been fighting with Gael like shifters and vamps, yet she'd spent a hot night with the man instead of lighting his shorts on fire. But with no heat, it couldn't be. Shifter pregnancies were rare under the absolute best of circumstances, but a random one-night hookup leading to a pup would be almost unheard of.

Although, just before the wedding, she'd been burning up hot. Could she be pregnant? Without a mate bond?

Surely I was reading too much into it. I shook my head, clearing the ludicrous thought and zipping up the bag.

Leigh tossed a sparkly minidress and a pair of ridiculously high black heels on top of her mountain of clothing before sitting on the case to zip it.

"I don't think you're going to need those, Leigh. They said it's really rural where we're heading. The pack lives close to the land, and the shaman especially spends most of his time in isolation, communing with nature. That's why they told us to wear hiking boots." I pointed to my leather-clad foot, but she ignored me, the sounds of a zipper wrenching under her super-natural strength preceding her crow of triumph.

"Got it! Let's go. Come on, Cujo." She clucked her tongue to Dirge, who gave me the most long-suffering look I'd ever seen on a wolf's face.

"I know, she's impossible. But I love her, sorry." I scratched him under the chin before hauling my suitcase off the bed. At least it was light, though I had plenty of energy since my wound had healed. I clammed up as we walked through the halls, wolves from Pack Blackwater milling in and out of the dorms, some cleaning, others moving furniture in the wake of the mass exodus of all the other packs.

I still wasn't comfortable around strangers—particularly men—and might not ever be. Maybe the silver lining of meeting my mate while he was stuck in fur was that I wasn't self-conscious talking to him.

To my surprise, when we walked out of the dorm, there was a six-seater UTV waiting, with a rack on the back for our luggage.

"Aren't we going to an airstrip?" I murmured to Leigh, confused.

"Yeah, on the pack grounds. Small plane, hence the luggage limits." She huffed as she hefted her suitcase and flipped it onto the rack. I picked mine up and placed it next to hers, looking at Dirge, then the utility vehicle, and back again. I hadn't thought the logistics of all this through.

"Can you run alongside, or do you want to try to get into a seat?" I asked, as if he could answer me. Though in his own way, he did. When I pointed to a seat, he sat next to it, waiting for me to get in. Once I was in, he continued waiting, standing at attention as pack members passed by, talking and laughing.

Okay, run alongside it was.

THE AIRSTRIP WAS small but tidy. To my surprise, it was paved, with equally spaced lights tracing either side of it for safe night landings and a fairly large hangar off to the side at one end for storing the pack's small planes. One was already waiting on the tarmac for our trip. Or so Reed told us when we arrived, and he offered us champagne while we waited for Kane and Brielle. Leigh declined for us both.

Sometimes, I forgot that Reed was richer than Solomon and owned dozens of fancy restaurants, but when he was casually drinking fancy French champagne before 10:00 a.m. and wearing an expensive suit while the rest of us wore sweats and tees, I remembered.

"Hey, brother," he said to Dirge. He was clearly aiming for

casual but missed the mark. His jaw ticked with tension in the silence that followed his greeting. When he sighed in defeat, I decided to speak up despite my anxiety. Reed had gotten a little closer to "safe" in my circle, even if he wasn't all the way there yet.

"He can't talk back to you, but it doesn't mean he can't communicate at all. If you ask simple questions, he can nod yes and shake his head no."

"Right. You're right, he did that in the cell on the video." Reed rubbed his jaw, even though there was no trace of stubble to be found there.

"Are you looking forward to the flight?" he tried again, then laughed. "This is stupid."

But I was watching Dirge, who dipped his muzzle once to answer. "See? He said yes." I scratched him behind the ear, and he leaned tightly into my leg. It wasn't perfect, but it was something. We were making progress, little by little.

"Yeah, I guess he did." Reed tipped up his champagne glass and drained it, leaving Dirge and me while he went to pour another, all the way to the rim.

It was my turn to sigh at that.

The sounds of another UTV approaching brought us all to the door of the hangar, where Brielle, Kane, and Gael were getting their luggage unloaded.

"Morning," Kane called, lifting a hand in greeting. A man in a pilot's uniform appeared from somewhere, coming to shake Kane's hand and brief him on the flight plan. After a quick exchange of hugs with Bri, we were ready to board.

"Does he have to come on *every* trip?" Leigh muttered as we climbed the short staircase that led into the aircraft, staring death daggers at Gael, who was studiously ignoring us, his back turned and his arms crossed a few feet away.

"I imagine he's here to support and protect Kane, much like we are Bri," I answered quietly.

"I know, I know," she groused, sliding into a plush leather seat at the back. The plane was the smallest I'd ever been in, just single seats on either side of a small middle aisle. It appeared that we were maxing it out, with only one empty seat after everyone was accounted for. Dirge had followed me up the stairs, but there was no good place for a three-hundred-pound wolf except the aisle, so that was where he sat, right between me and Leigh. Bri settled on the row in front of us so she'd have a seat for Kane.

"Can you tell us anything about the man we're going to meet? He's Athabascan, correct?" I asked, nerves over visiting an unfamiliar culture hitting me. I didn't always do well in my own culture. The last thing I wanted to do was flub up in front of people we needed help from or offend someone with my silence.

"Yes, Kane filled me in over breakfast."

"Breakfast. We definitely should have had some, Shay," Leigh grumbled, closing her eyes and leaning against the small window next to her seat.

Bri ignored her in favor of answering my question. "He's a shaman from a long line of healers. He's nearly thirteen hundred years old and struggles with mobility at this point, which is why he didn't attend the great pack gathering himself. That, and they didn't have many singles. But his name is Inuksuk, and the invitation we've received is very rare. Their pack is small, about forty members, and keeps out of wider shifter politics. Everyone speaks English, but their traditional language is Dena'ina, and Kane taught me a few phrases. *Yaghali du* is the traditional greeting. And in response, you say, *aa'yaghali*."

"Aa-ya-gha-li," I tried, without any of the smoothness Brielle had picked up in a morning.

She grinned at my attempt. "Aa'yaghali."

"Aa'yaghali?" I tried again.

"Much better! We may not be perfect, but it's always good to try."

I nodded, casting a nervous look at Dirge. Maybe I should try again to shift and just offend no one as a wolf.

But that would be cowardly. So, I spent the preflight repeating the word in my head over and over again, with hopes of cementing it in my brain correctly.

Leigh kept her eyes stubbornly closed as the men climbed aboard, and I had to try hard not to chuckle at Gael's pointed efforts to ignore us. He sat in the front row and stared straight ahead, speaking to no one but Reed and Kane. They were a hell of a pair.

Kane made his way down the aisle to drop a kiss on Brielle's waiting lips before settling into the seat in front of Leigh. He nodded to me and, to my surprise, Dirge as well. Leigh, he just grinned at before turning back around.

The plane started rolling a few moments after the door was shut, and I cast a worried glance at Leigh. Her face went pale— she *really* hated flying—but she stayed quiet and kept her eyes screwed shut.

Just in case she needed it, I ruffled through the seat back pocket and found an airsickness bag. Somehow, I suspected my poor attempts at speaking Dena'ina wouldn't make up for arriving covered in puke.

OUR FLIGHT TOUCHED down less than an hour later and was thankfully sickness-free. As soon as the door opened, though, Leigh was on her feet, stepping around Dirge and bolting for the front. She nearly bowled Gael over, who'd clearly had the same idea of bolting first. They both froze, awkwardly avoiding eye contact, until Leigh dodged him and hurried down the stairs without a word.

The sound of retching hit us thirty seconds later, and I winced.

So much for arriving puke-free.

"Oh no, let me go see if I can do anything for her." Brielle hurried forward, past the still-hesitating Gael, and out of the plane.

Kane turned to me. "Does she always get airsick?"

"When she's not drunk, yes."

He grunted in response. "I'm sure Brielle has a tea or something that can help for the flight back." He paused. "How are you and your new mate doing?"

There was real concern in his question, and I was as surprised as I was touched. But I didn't really know what to say.

"We're okay, I guess. He still hasn't shifted, so it's hard to get to know him. He won't leave my side, though. I hope that doesn't cause a problem when we meet Inuksuk and his pack."

Kane didn't look as worried as I felt. "I'm sure he'll behave himself. He's done fine so far, and as long as everyone remains respectful"—at that, he cast a pointed look toward Gael—"I don't see why there would be a problem."

I nodded, but the knot of nerves in my belly didn't ease. It probably wouldn't until we'd met the shaman and heard what he had to say. I really hoped he could help Bri. She hated her weaknesses, and while we loved her anyway, I knew how it felt to be the one who was always *other*, who didn't fit. If she was able to change that, well, I wanted it for her.

Resolved, I stood.

"Ready to go?" I asked Dirge, who jumped to his feet, tail wagging. "Well, at least one of us is excited. Stay with me, okay?"

FIFTEEN

Dirge

I could smell the nervousness and tension in my mate's usually lovely floral scent. Now that I had been smelling it longer—or perhaps, now that the man was steadily rising back to the surface—I was certain it was freesia. And pomegranate, maybe. Delectable, except for the hint of uncharacteristic sourness.

I kept close to her side as we stepped off the aircraft—a whole new and not entirely pleasant experience in wolf form when I couldn't chug water to relieve the pressure on my ears— but she didn't have to ask. I wasn't leaving her side ever again, unless she sent me away.

She might, if she couldn't adjust to me staying in wolf form. I was still excitedly awaiting the first time *she* shifted, so that our wolves could meet. We'd be on equal footing for the first time. But those thoughts were distractions from the task at hand, and as we walked down a small footpath leading away from the grassy airstrip, a plethora of unfamiliar scents hit my nose. Unfamiliar, but not unpleasant.

There were dozens of new shifter scents, yes, but also the smells of cooking meat, soft hides, and, if I wasn't mistaken, an extensive garden nearby. And perhaps the sharp tang of a tannery, which made me wrinkle my nose. *That* I could do without, but the rest of it was invigorating.

The path was soft underfoot, shade-loving mosses with gentle ferns lining the sides. On any other day, I'd run through them, soaking my fur and enjoying the coolness of an Alaskan summer. But we were on a mission, and Shay's fingertips were tangled in the fur on my ruff. Keeping me close. I relished that little bit of contact. The man chafed at the fact that if we shifted, we would have had much, *much* more contact by now. But that wasn't possible. So I pushed it aside, despite the intense pangs of longing coming from the man.

The Athabascan pack's meeting grounds were small but inviting. A series of tidy modern buildings laid around an open shared central space governed by a large quaking aspen. The tree was lush and shady, with that garden plot I smelled situated at one end of the grounds. It overflowed with life, and the itch to run through it nearly won out over common sense.

But I had a purpose. And so it was that I stood proudly beside my beautiful mate as she waited to make her halting introductions to the pack's representatives who came to greet us.

"Yaghali du, friends of healer Inuksuk. We offer our condolences on the death of your father, but are pleased to host you and congratulate you on your recent bonding." A middle-aged woman with golden-bronze skin and dark, shiny hair greeted our party with a smile. "I am Ilana, daughter of Inuksuk, and this is Iaoin, my twin brother. Tonight, we hold a feast in your honor."

"Aa'yaghali, Ilana. Thank you for your generosity." Kane stepped forward, offering his hand to shake first to Ilana, then to Iaoin. "We are grateful to be among friends at this tumultuous time."

The two made their way through our group, repeating a

shorter version of the greeting and shaking everyone's hands. Iaoin came to Shay first, and I immediately bristled at the dominance he freely exuded, with no attempt to rein it in.

A cocky grin lit the male's face as he appraised Shay, giving her a subtle once-over that pulled a growl from my throat. Shay frowned down at me, ignoring his appraisal.

"Yaghali du. Are you Shailene?" He said her name like a lover's caress—one that sent a molten barb through my chest because I hadn't even known her full name—and I hated every second of it. She was my mate. I should know her better than this pup with more power than sense.

She looked startled that he knew her name, but recovered quickly, shoving her thick curls back over her shoulder before offering her hand for a shake.

"Aa'yaghali, Iaoin. Everyone calls me Shay."

"Shay," he murmured, accepting her hand, but instead of releasing it, he leaned low over it and sniffed. One long, deep inhale, his eyes closed in bliss. When he opened them, they glowed turquoise with his wolf.

I shoved forward, putting myself between Shay and Iaoin, forcibly pushing her back with my body.

"Dirge! Stop! You're being rude," she scolded me, tugging on my ruff to try to get me to relent.

But his eyes glowed brighter as they met mine. *A challenge.* Let him try. Shay was mine.

"You claim this female, in wolf form?"

I growled, the sound a promise now, not a warning.

"And yet, she is unbonded." He cast an entirely too wolfish smile at Shay before once again fixing his stare on me.

"It's complicated. We—"

"Everything okay over here?" Leigh sidled up next to me, not blocking my view, but edging her hip in front of mine to at least slow me down.

"Everything's fine. I don't know what's gotten into Dirge

when he's been doing so well. All we did was shake hands."
Shay sounded irritated, but I didn't spare a glance backward.
Iaoin still held my gaze, the challenge growing by the second.
Our power filled the air, the thick dominance a physical
presence.

"Oh, I think I do," Leigh said, but then called out in a breezy
tone. "Kane? I could use a little help over here."

But Kane was engaged with Ilana, and two other members
of the Athabascan pack who had wandered up to pay homage
to the high alpha. Gael, however, was in front of Leigh in a
heartbeat.

"What's wrong?" His voice was all gravel, a barely concealed
threat that his heavily muscled physique left no doubts he
could make good on.

"Just a friendly chat, but your friend here seems to have
taken offense. Why is he shifted? It's considered quite rude for a
diplomatic envoy." Iaoin answered Gael, but never broke eye
contact with me. I put subtle pressure on Leigh's hip, slowly
edging her further behind Gael and out of my way.

But the stubborn bitch wouldn't go, angrily shoving at the
male's shoulder instead to try to get him clear.

"Please, we have no intention of rudeness," Leigh said as
soon as she edged past Gael, which earned her a stony glare
from him. "Dirge here is more comfortable in fur, and their
mate bond is very new, which has them both... edgy. If we could
just give them a little space—"

Iaoin threw back his head and laughed, the first time he'd
broken eye contact besides flirting with Shay. "New, and he
won't shed his fur?" There was heavy censure in the male's
tone. "I challenge for mating rights."

Kane and Ilana both stopped, stunned for a moment at our
sides, having disentangled themselves from the others to see
what was happening.

"Iaoin, *no!*" Ilana gasped and tugged on her brother's arm, but he wouldn't budge. "We cannot dishonor Father with this bullheadedness. My sincerest apologies. He will rescind the challenge immediately."

"I mean no dishonor, but I will not desist. Her scent... It calls to me. They have not consummated the bond. Do you bear mating marks?" He directed the highly impertinent question to Shay, and I charged.

SIXTEEN

Shay

"**G**oddess's tits!" Leigh swore as Gael dragged her back from the charging wolf.

I stood frozen in horror as Dirge leapt for the unshifted Iaoin's throat. Time seemed to slow, every ripple of his fur in the wind clear and outlining the deadly muscle underneath. Something inside me snapped.

My own wolf ripped free of my body in one hot wave, taking control as she had so many times before. When I needed her most, she never, ever failed me. She was already in motion before my conscious mind had caught up to the need. My relief at her reappearance was strong, but I didn't have time to dwell on it.

The impact of my shoulder slamming into Dirge's left me breathless, but did as intended, knocking Dirge's deadly flight off course. We both landed roughly off to the side, and somewhere in the dim distance, I heard gasps and shouts, but none of those mattered. Because for the first time, I was standing nose to nose with my mate, in the same form.

His eyes glowed a startling green, more vivid in this form. We stared each other down and paced in a circle. Was he going to leap? Attack, unable to stop now that he'd been triggered by Iaoin? I stopped pacing, lowering my front end, ready to spring if he made the wrong move.

But he did the only thing I wasn't ready for. He threw his head back and yipped, a joyful, celebratory sound. When he pounced, it was playfully, tail wagging like a pup instead of a full-grown man. Wolf. *Whatever.*

My wolf took over then, dancing with his and exchanging yips and playful swipes. A rush of warmth suffused me as I connected with him on a new level. I froze midcircle when I realized we had an audience, the human side embarrassed at such an unfettered moment being witnessed by strangers. As I cast a look over my shoulder at the gathered crowd, though, Dirge didn't stop. He took full advantage and pounced, knocking me onto my side and then following as I rolled over onto my back.

It was the most vulnerable position for a wolf, and mine didn't like it one bit. But then he was there, over us, eyes glowing a merry green. I held his gaze, staring deeply as we shared the moment. He broke eye contact after a moment to lean down for a better angle to lick my muzzle. First one tentative swipe, then another, and another.

It took me longer than it should have to realize what was happening. He was grooming me. Emotion swelled in my chest, even in this form, at the primal rush of connection that flowed between us then. He might not have been able to speak to me, not in human form, but the intent here was crystal clear.

He cared for me. Wanted to *take care* of me.

And my human heart broke just a little bit, even as the wolf reveled in the attention from her mate.

I COULDN'T SAY how long we stayed in fur, as time passing rarely bothers wolves. All I knew was that the crowd wandered off, night fell, and the only human who stayed with us was Leigh. Well, not the only one. Gael hovered fifty yards back at the corner of the building, keeping an eye on all three of us.

That male was confusing most of the time and then painfully clear at others. Their plight was far from my mind, though, by the time the urge to shift back finally came over me. Hunger gnawed rabidly on my belly, but I didn't want to risk hunting on lands where we were guests. So, with regret, I shifted back.

The cold night air hit me at once, sending goose bumps flying over my skin as a violent shiver racked my naked body. Dirge whined, pressing himself against my now-human legs.

While we were no longer in the same form, I could still feel his sorrow at the loss of familiarity plain as day. It was anchored in my chest like one of my own ribs.

"Here, I thought you might need these," Leigh murmured, offering me a pair of thick, lined leggings and a hoodie to pull on. I accepted them gratefully and dressed, the familiar scent of my bestie's clothes settling around me like a cloud.

"Better?" she asked at my contented sigh, and I nodded.

"Thank you." I paused, the ramifications of my afternoon-turned-evening interlude hitting me afresh. "Is Brielle mad? We messed everything up." My voice was small, faint in a way it usually wasn't with my best friends.

Shame pulled at me, the dereliction of my duty to someone who'd been nothing but loyal to me like a crushing weight over the fragile high of shifting with my mate. Everything with Dirge felt fragile. We had no mating signs, not truly, and if he couldn't shift, we might never.

The sorrow of that realization gutted me worse than any bullet, and I sank to my haunches, right there in the middle of the village.

Violent sobs racked me, and Dirge tried to push in, lick my face, but I shoved him away. He wasn't what I needed, *couldn't be* what I needed. Leigh's arms came around me in a tight hug, and she rocked me right there in the grass, on the cold ground under the waning moon.

Only after the tears stopped did Leigh's words come. "She's not angry at you, Shay. She's thrilled. Thrilled, do you hear me?" Leigh shook me lightly, making sure I didn't miss her meaning. "No one begrudges you this time with your mate. I mean, Iaoin was disgruntled, but Ilana tore him a new one for trying to lay claim to you when we're on a diplomatic mission. I like her." She said the last bit with an impish twist to her lips.

But I found no joy in it. "We're supposed to be at the feast. It's bad enough that I'm not there, but I took you from her too. She needs your support right now—*our* support—as much as I do. It's just... our lives were so simple before. How did they get so messed up so fast?" I scrubbed at my scratchy eyes, trying to erase the evidence of my breakdown.

She shrugged, unperturbed. "Shit happens when it's supposed to. Maybe lover wolf is important to all this. Maybe he has a piece of the puzzle we need to fix Bri."

"I hadn't even considered that," I murmured, sparing a glance for Dirge, who lay not ten feet away, a mournful expression clear on his wolf features as he watched someone else comfort me. But I hardened my heart and looked away. "We should go now. The feast is probably going to go on all night."

My stomach chose that moment to rumble, and Leigh laughed, throwing her head back, face tilted to the moon, soaking up the rays.

"I'm sure it is," she said once she could breathe again. "But what about Fluff Butt? Isn't he going to take issue with being around Iaoin?"

I thought about it, really thought about it. I didn't know

how or why, but I knew in my soul that he'd been pulled free of his feral state. He *could* shift back.

He was choosing not to.

And I wasn't sure I could forgive him for that. I needed some space to process.

"I think it's time we're honest about where this is going." I swallowed hard, speaking difficult even as I felt the rightness of what I had to say. "The feast is for human participants. If he's unwilling to shift, he should wait in our rooms."

Leigh's jaw dropped as she glanced from me to Dirge, then back again. "I don't know if you've noticed this, but, uh, he's unwilling to leave your side. And anyone who tries to separate you two is in danger of meeting the business end of those canines. Droolius Caesar is *determined*."

"Are you ready to shift?" I met his gaze, lifting my chin in challenge when I delivered the question.

He dropped his eyes, and my broken heart turned to shards. Tiny fragments that could blow away with the faintest wind.

"Then I don't need you by my side this evening," I said, the words leaving me hollowed out.

He threw back his head and howled, the mournful sound raising the hairs on my arms and the back of my neck.

Gael appeared from his position by the nearest building. "I can see him to a room." The offer was a pleasant surprise, and I nodded, even as Leigh tensed at my side. I gripped her fingers tighter.

"Thank you, Gael. You can take him to whichever room I'm assigned to."

He nodded and turned, not wasting any time, but Dirge hesitated. I wouldn't meet his eyes this time, keeping mine firmly fixed on the inoffensive blades of grass that were tinged silver by the moon.

"Come on, then," Gael murmured to the wolf. "She's not

going to change her mind." Then, more quietly, he added, "Neither of them is."

I could tell he didn't mean for us to hear that last part, uttered under his breath. But we did, and Leigh leaned against me as if I were a raft, and she was adrift at sea.

The two of us were quite a pair as we watched the men we shouldn't love walk away into the night.

SEVENTEEN

Dirge

My mate rejected me. She finally shifted. We shared that time together. At last, we were equals.

And her response was to reject me.

I'd always known I was unworthy. But her confirmation of it cut deeper than any blade.

I sat in her room and howled until my throat was raw. And then I howled some more, my pleas to the Moon Goddess falling on deaf ears.

Mercy wasn't mine to have.

Not now, not ever.

And so I howled, and nursed a broken heart.

EIGHTEEN

Shay

Brielle jumped to her feet and hugged us when we arrived at the feast, and I knew then I'd made the right decision. Her face was flushed in the firelight, eyes glowing with her wolf. It was a rare sight, and I started to believe what they said about Inuksuk's people. They were closer to nature, to the powers that drove our shifter sides. My eyes skimmed the gathered crowd, and relief washed over me at not seeing Iaoin among those seated at the long, wooden tables. We feasted under the moon, on more dishes than I could count. Some familiar, some not. *All* delicious.

Ilana came to our table and personally apologized to me for her brother's actions. Apparently, they rarely saw female shifters outside their own pack, and Iaoin had been unable to attend the great pack gathering due to his training to take over Inuksuk's duties.

"He's getting older, feeling territorial, and a bit put out that he missed the opportunity to meet his mate. If you ask me, he's grasping at the wind, and father should send him to the city for a while. His mate is out there somewhere, but it's clearly not you," she said with an eye roll.

"Clearly not," I agreed, for lack of anything else to say to the fountain of information. I was often uncomfortable in conversation with new people and tongue-tied. Thankfully, Ilana held the conversation quite well on her own.

"I don't mean it offensively, of course, but you've already got a fated mate. Stealing you wouldn't fill the hole in his chest. Our males all face the same fate, though. Venture out into the wider world on hope, or stay here and grow old, never finding a she-wolf to bond with. It's a lonely life that stretches before him, but duty ties him here more than most. My father grows frail with the years, and he's insistent that I not be the one to carry on the family tradition." She frowned then, looking toward the endless, dark wood.

"That must be painful for you. To be passed over."

Her head snapped around to where I sat, the stiffness in her shoulders making me antsy. Had I overstepped? I cast around for Leigh or Brielle, but they'd been pulled into a deep conversation with an older couple, each dandling a giggling young pup on their knees.

"Most people don't see it that way," she finally admitted, finally letting her shoulders droop. "It's always been a male healer. A male tribal leader. A male *Alpha*. But Iaoin and I are twins. He's technically the same age that I am, save for a few minutes my junior. And yet, he's still green. I'm capable. I'm steady. I'm not hungering for a mate, despite my nearly five hundred years on this earth." She clenched her fist and dropped it angrily to the table. A sharp *crack* of wood splintering came from the table in response. She immediately flattened her palm over it, looking sheepish for the slip-up.

"My apologies. This is not your burden to bear. You are here for your friend's healing, not to hear my woes." She ducked her head and made to leave. I don't know why I did it, but I reached out, putting my hand over hers. It was a hundred percent out of my comfort zone, and I immediately second-guessed the physical touch with such a new—and important—acquaintance.

"It's okay. Sometimes you need to share a burden rather than hold it alone." I offered a small smile, which she returned, and then withdrew my hand.

"Thank you. Wine?" She waved at someone walking around with a pitcher, and her pack mate hurried over.

I blinked in surprise at the swift change of topic, and she laughed, the sound genuine despite the heavy conversation we'd just been having. "I know it's nearly impossible to get drunk, but my father has a special herbal blend he adds to the wine. Increases the potency at least tenfold."

I swallowed hard, then quickly checked to make sure Leigh wasn't drinking it—she could get herself drunk *without* a legendary shaman's assistance, thank you very much. To my surprise, though, her lovely crystal goblet held water and nothing else.

Maybe she didn't want to encourage a round two with Gael. *Wise.*

I, however, had a semiferal, fully confusing fated mate who was waiting in my room, still howling. I could hear him from here, though I tried my hardest to ignore the plaintive notes.

I held out my goblet for the herb wine.

SOME... *many hours later*

I stumbled into my room, ignoring the first rays of sun already peeking around the blackout blinds, and arrowing straight toward the double bed pushed against the wall. The blankets looked handmade, and I was determined *not* to vomit on them. That wine wouldn't make a great addition to the decor if it came back up.

Why did it want so badly to come back up?

Oh, yeah. We'd drunk a lot. Two whole pitchers between us. All specially blended. It was delicious. I burped and winced. It was less delicious this time around. Blech.

I fell face-first onto the bed, kicking off my second-favorite sneakers and falling straight into deep, blissful sleep.

NINETEEN

Dirge

I waited up for Shay. How could I not? She might not ever choose to love me; she might choose to hate me. But I knew to the depths of my soul that she was the only one for me. And no matter if she chose to end this fledging relationship between us, I would always protect her. From afar if need be. Her silent, distant shadow, keeping the dangers away.

It would be half a life, but if it saved hers, I'd consider it well spent.

So when my very inebriated mate stumbled into the room and didn't even bother to shut the door behind her, I stayed still until the snoring began, and then quietly nosed it shut. I couldn't lock it in wolf form, but I could lie in front of it until she woke and took care of it herself.

I couldn't say when I dozed off; the nights were long when you spent them telling the Moon Goddess your woes.

And when I slipped into the dream, it was smooth as an early morning stream, unbroken by ripples. I only noticed because for the first time in a long time, I was a man. Panic nearly sent me right back *out* of the dream, until I turned around and saw my sleeping wolf guarding the door so his mate could rest. His mate who was still lying conked out on the bed.

Except... she was *also* standing by the window, humming a tuneless song as she opened the blinds a crack to let in the golden morning glow.

It highlighted every angle and plane of her face, gilding her beauty and making me catch my breath. It was Shay, and not.

We were dreaming, both of us, and had somehow come to this shared awareness.

She froze, the tune dying on her parted lips as she stared at me, drinking me in.

"Who are you, and why are you in my room?" she asked, sounding more surprised than angry.

Dream logic. It had to be. It was a weird dream, being outside my body, but... with the power of this pack, who knew what was influencing us? Did it matter?

"You don't know?" I asked, cocking my head to the side and willing my eyes to light up with the wolf. Although, would that work with him sleeping? Who knew?

"I—" She stared at me, considering. "I dreamed you up, didn't I? You're who he would be if he could be a man again," she said with sadness, the smile slipping from her stunning face. I had to put it back there. It was like the sun falling from the sky at noon, so utterly wrong, I couldn't stand it.

I wanted her to always be smiling so I could bask in the rays of her warmth.

"Hey, don't look so glum. If this is a dream, and we're here together, we may as well enjoy it, right?"

She snorted, one perfectly shaped eyebrow rising up her forehead. "What exactly are you suggesting?"

I took one step closer, then another. She didn't back away, didn't run. Her pupils blew wide with arousal as it clicked what I was suggesting. She was blissfully unafraid in this dreamscape, and I took full advantage. I closed in on her personal space, taking in a deep lungful of her scent. Even in my dreams, it was potent. More so as a man, where I could identify the subtle scent of freesia, the sharp tang of tender-sweet pomegranate highlighting the flowers so tantalizingly as her arousal bloomed around us. It was completely and utterly *Shay*, and I wanted to drink in every drop straight from the source.

I lowered my nose to the base of her neck, letting it trace the tender skin there. Although I knew this was a dream, she felt solid in my hands, her warmth branding my bare chest and my thighs through the thin pants I wore. When I inhaled, she shivered, her hands coming up to land on my shoulders. For a moment I thought she'd push me away, demand that I keep my space. But she clung to me, her breasts pressing against my chest, nothing but a wisp of thin fabric between us.

My blood heated at the small encouragement, and then my lips were on her neck. The first taste of her branded my soul. If she'd had me before, she owned me now. Every inch of my being was in her delicate palms. She could crush me without a thought.

But she wouldn't.

Her surprised gasp when my lips made contact drove me to explore. I kissed up the column of her neck, leaving a trail of wet kisses across her jaw, until I was teasing the corner of her full, wide mouth. She had lips a man dreamed of seeing wrapped around his cock, but right this minute, all I could think of was tasting them. Devouring them.

I nipped her lightly, and her lips parted for me. Only an idiot would waste an invitation like that. Threading my fingers into her sleep-mussed curls, I tilted her head to the side and melded our lips together in a kiss.

But *kiss* was too small a word to contain what passed between us. There was fire and light, victory and exultation, surrender and ecstasy in such a small space of time, I might have missed it. But time slowed, and the whole earth narrowed to just the two of us, then and there. I pressed her back against the cool window, letting my hands roam down her sides as she melted beneath the onslaught.

I didn't consciously strip her out of her pajamas, but once my fingertips brushed her bare stomach with that intent, her simple tank top disappeared.

Damn, I love dreams.

She moaned as I spanned my hands across her narrow waist, then trailed the touch around to her back. Shay was strong, but small compared to my considerable bulk. I could easily tuck her beneath my chin if I wanted to. But I had something better in mind at the moment.

Reaching down, I hitched my hands beneath her ass and lifted her, spreading her thighs so I could step between them. She hissed between her teeth when her bare back made contact with the cold glass, but I was happy to warm her up.

My dick tried to punch a hole through my cotton pants as her molten core settled against me, and I couldn't contain a hoarse groan at the sensation. Good Goddess—if I didn't get a grip, I'd come in my pants like a teenager.

That wasn't about to happen. So, I focused on her, trying to block the overwhelming onslaught of being this close to my mate for the first time. The urge to bury my dick inside her and sink my aching canines into her neck was hardest to suppress, but I managed by taking the hard bead of one of her nipples into my mouth and sucking hard.

Should I be gentler? I didn't know. I hadn't been with a woman in decades, at least. Even if I had, none of them mattered. That was before. Before her. She was all that existed as I tasted, teased, and nipped until she cried out and dug her fingers into the back of my neck, pulling me to her other breast. I gave that one the same treatment, keeping her anchored to me with the weight of my hips against hers.

"Dirge, I— Oh." She breathed out little nonsense words as I

drove her higher. When nothing was left but cries of need, I lifted her again, looping her thighs over my shoulders and shredding the impeding fabric of her thin sleep shorts to bare her gleaming, wet pussy to my gaze before sliding up to bracket her rib cage and hold her steady against the window.

"Shay." I whispered the word against her heated flesh, so honored in this moment that she was here with me. I didn't deserve her. I never could, but I was grateful she deigned to let me touch her anyway.

She gripped my shoulders tightly with both hands. "I'm going to fall, Dirge. Put me down," she ordered, voice shaking with need and curiosity as much as fear. I looked up at her then, from under half-shuttered eyelids.

"Give me two minutes, and if you still want me to put you down, I will." I dove in before she had a chance to argue further, her keening cry as my tongue speared her core drowning out any objections she may have had left.

Her orgasm had her soaking my chin in less than ninety seconds. But I didn't stop, ruthlessly circling her needy little clit with my tongue as she arched against the pressure.

"Dirge! Dirge, put me down. Please, I need you. I need you right now." She tugged a fistful of my hair, the sharp sting only driving me to lick her again, from the bottom of her slit all the way to that crown jewel of pleasure. She moaned then, long and low, but didn't release her grip on me. "Put me on the bed. *Now.*"

She growled then, the low sound driving me to obey my female. I carried her across the room still on my shoulders, face buried in her stomach until I reached the mattress. I settled her with extra care on her back, letting my fingers trail up to toy with her reddened nipples again, but she was done with fore-play. Leaning up on one elbow, she dragged my lips down to hers in a claiming kiss.

Heat bloomed inside me at the possessiveness of it. I

wanted it, every bit she had to offer. There was heat across my chest too, but I paid it no mind. She consumed my every thought.

She used my hair to anchor me so she could pull back, panting. "Inside me, right now. I need you. Hard."

My dick pulsed with unfettered need at the command. I was as dominant as a wolf could be, but I loved that command on her lips in a way that I'd never loved anything before. I straightened just enough to peel down my pants, kicking them away as she drank me in with dark, hungry eyes. The soft gray of them shone in the darkness as I climbed back onto the bed, hovering over her on my hands and knees.

She bent her knees to cradle me with her hips, greedy hands on my hips pulling me down, down, down until the head of my cock bumped up against her.

She whimpered, and I was lost. One stroke, to the hilt. She enveloped me with heat and desire, and the sound I made when she squeezed me was not human.

"Please, please," she whispered, hoarse with need. "More," she urged, and then I was moving, plunging inside her heat, lost to my mate in the most primal way possible. She cried out as need spiked in my blood. My canines lengthened, the wolf still present even in this dream state, urging me to mark her. Mate with her.

"Shay." My words were guttural, almost unrecognizable.

"Yes." Just one word. So simple, yet it held the weight of the whole world. I reached down to stroke her clit for a half second before I struck, fangs sinking deep into her throat as ecstasy and connection surged through me. She screamed and arched underneath me, her nails scoring my back deep enough to draw blood of her own as I plunged into her once more, twice, and then roared my own release into the night.

Something deeper pulsed in the air between us as I collapsed over her, letting my lips find her neck, my tongue trace the wound there to seal it. She whimpered at the tenderness, but pulled me closer. "I'm too heavy. I'll crush you," I murmured, trying to pull to the side.

But my stubborn mate wrapped her legs around me, defiantly holding me in place. "Stay with me. Just stay with me."

And so we lay there, wrapped in each other's arms, just breathing in the early morning glow and the unexpected gifts we'd found together.

TWENTY

Shay

When my eyes cracked open the next morning, a warm, languid feeling suffused my limbs. That had been a *hell* of a dream. Was it possible to orgasm in your sleep? The sticky residue between my thighs said yes, yes, it was.

The question had a blush burning in my cheeks as I quickly scanned the room, only to spot wolf-Dirge—not to be confused with hot-as-sin dream-Dirge—sleeping peacefully in front of my door.

Who knew that the instant I tried to consciously distance myself from my mate, my subconscious would nip that idea in the bud? Well, more than that. Drive me to dream of the mating bite.

I'd never been one for vivid dreams, beyond the occasional flashback-style nightmare. But that... it had been so vivid. Granted, I felt a little sheepish considering I had no idea what Dirge actually looked like. I could just have had insanely intense dream sex with somebody's mailman, for all I knew.

That thought had me biting my bottom lip and making a mental note to ask Reed if he could show me a picture of his brother.

Another guilt-laden peek at Dirge, and I mentally amended, *Today. I'll ask for a picture today.*

If my brain was going to provide crazy-good dream sex, it should at least be with the right man.

I shook my head and then went about the business of getting ready after a quick scratch behind Dirge's ears. I had a hard time looking him in the eye after the night I had, but otherwise, things between us slipped back into the same routine we'd had before I asked Gael to escort him to my room last night.

He followed me out when it was time for breakfast, and I didn't argue. If last night had shown me anything, it was that while it might be painful to hold on to a mate who wasn't actively choosing me... I still wasn't ready to let him go.

Clearly.

Knocking on Leigh's door only got me a grouchy "Go away until lunch." So I moved on down to Brielle and Kane's. I wouldn't have known it was theirs—they'd left the gathering last night hours before I had—except Reed was stationed outside it.

He seemed fresh as could be, no sign of overimbibing the spiced wine, like my idiot self had.

"Good morning, Shay, Dirge." He nodded to me, and then his brother. The look of sadness never quite left his eyes these days, and I couldn't blame him. But maybe sharing old, happier memories with me would cheer him up? "Come to see Brielle?"

Remembering could make him worse, but I had to hope not.

"Good morning." I was getting better at talking around the most trusted men of Kane's pack, but the words were still quieter than I would have liked. I cleared my throat and tried again. "I am, but I also have a question for you. If you don't mind," I added, still feeling preemptive guilt about dredging up memories that might be painful for him.

"Of course, anything." His voice dropped low, his eyes holding mine with a worried question. When I didn't immediately respond, he took a step forward. "Is everything okay?"

"Oh, yes. Sorry." My cheeks burned. Asking a simple question shouldn't be this hard. Probably *wasn't* this hard for most people.

Granted, most people hadn't been through what I had as a child. I shut those memories down hard and fast, not letting the fear-tinged visions of men who beat you for speaking, or rusty shipping-container walls close in around me right here in broad daylight, thousands of miles away from where it had all happened.

With a quick shake of my head, I forced a smile. "I was just wondering if you had any pictures. Of Dirge, from before?" Reed's blank stare prompted me to continue. "When he was a man. I was just wondering what he looked like and realized you knew." More blankness. "I mean, if it's too painful, I—"

"No! No, of course not. Yes, I have pictures of the two of us. Hold on." He fished a sleek black cell phone from his pocket. After a pause where it scanned his face, he thumbed through the device and spun it around. "I can't believe I didn't think to show you sooner. Honestly, I—"

He continued talking, but the words faded into background noise. I was too wrapped up in the stunning hazel eyes staring out at me from a deeply tanned face. Long, straight, black hair framed chiseled cheekbones over a devilish smile. A five-o' clock shadow ran along his cut-glass jaw. The fierce *beauty* in and of itself would have stunned me plenty.

But nothing could compare to the shock of recognition.

The face beaming from the photo next to young Reed was the man from my dreams. I'd had *real* dream sex with my mate. And I had no idea how.

I thought I might be sick.

"You look like you've seen a ghost. You okay?" Reed settled a hand on my shoulder, and I shuddered beneath the unwelcome touch.

Dirge stepped forward, nosing his brother back and whining up at me.

I forced myself to meet Dirge's eyes for the first time since the night before. "It was you. Do you, I mean, *did* you also, uh —" My cheeks burned as I quickly glanced up at Reed and changed my mind about airing our activities in front of Dirge's brother.

A single dip of his muzzle.

Beethoven's shiny white composer ass, I swore mentally.

I had dream sex with Dirge. He nudged my hand, then snuck a lick in before I could snatch it away.

"Don't get fresh with me right now, dude. I am *processing!*"

"Uh, Shay, you feeling okay?" Bri's question startled me from the utterly ridiculous one-sided argument with Dirge.

"I'm not sure," I murmured, heat still suffusing my cheeks. I might not want to tell Reed, but bestie time was way overdue. "Can we talk?"

"Absolutely. Let me grab my sweater." She ducked back inside the room for a second, then appeared with a true, granny-gray cardigan slung over her shoulders. My bestie prior-itized comfort over style.

"Don't give me that look. It has great pockets." She empha-sized the point by looping her arm through mine then jamming both her hands into them. "Reed, we'll be on the porch. I already told Kane—he's still showering."

"I'll give you some space. We *both* will." Reed shot a pointed glare at Dirge, who huffed but walked by his brother's side instead of mine.

I breathed a little easier as we stepped out the front door of the small bunkhouse we'd been put up in and settled onto a creaky porch swing. I loved everything about it, from the weathered wood to the little bounce from the springs as we started to swing.

Brielle let the silence stretch comfortably between us, unhurried. She was never one to rush me, no matter how badly I struggled with words.

But frankly, there was no way to tiptoe around what I needed to say.

"I had hot sex in my dreams last night with a stranger, but Reed just showed me a picture of his brother and *it was Dirge*. How did I imagine sex with the real him if I've never seen him out of wolf form?"

There was only silence in response, so I braved a glance at Brielle. Her face was stunned, mouth agape as she stared at me.

"I'm sorry, I... You had sex with a man. In your dreams. But it was Dirge?" She paused for my confirmatory nod. "The real him," she muttered under her breath. "Wait, did you drink the special wine last night?"

"What do you mean, *special* wine? The herb stuff?" She nodded apprehensively. "Yeah, Ilana said it increased our chances of getting drunk. Why?"

"You weren't there at the beginning of the feast. The first pour came with a warning that it can increase your chance of dream walking."

"What the hell is that?" I blurted. I had no calm left in me this morning.

"Well, I'm no expert, but my understanding was that if you stayed awake, you'd hallucinate, and if you fell asleep... you'd enter the dream world. Leave your body behind, and..." She lifted her fingers in a floating gesture.

It wasn't much, but any level of explanation made me feel better. I wasn't crazy. I hadn't somehow developed weird prescience. I'd just... drunk hallucinogenic wine and met my mate for the first time. Instead of *talking to him*, I'd banged his brains out because I thought it was just a dream.

Oh my Goddess. He'd *bitten me.*

My hand flew up to my neck, and relief that there was no scar under my fingertips nearly knocked me from the swing. So, there were still physical limits.

"So... I drank the wine. But Dirge didn't, so how does that work?"

She shrugged one shoulder. "How does any of it? Sometimes, it just does."

Then realization hit, determination and excitement both filling me. "Bri, do you think our hosts would be willing to share another pitcher of that wine tonight? I need to have a conversation with someone, and apparently, the only way to do it is to get piss drunk."

Both of us looked up to where Reed and his brother stood at the far end of the porch, facing away from us to give our conversation privacy.

Brielle turned a wicked grin on me. "Goddess, yes."

TWENTY-ONE

Shay

I lana was more than happy to procure me another pitcher of spiced wine, with a stern warning that it would be the last. Apparently, overuse could get you stuck in a dream state, and their pack only imbibed it twice per year as a rule. Unfortunately, I couldn't do anything with it until nightfall. I had no desire to sit around and hallucinate while Brielle finally met Inuksuk, even though I was dying to have a real conversation with Dirge for the first time. So I carefully tucked the ceramic pitcher away in my room and headed out to join our party for the big meeting.

Ilana and Iaoin were subdued as they led us down a twisting path into the forest, deeper than any of us had ventured since we'd arrived. Kane held Brielle's hand as we walked down the path, the sight sending a pang of longing ricocheting through my chest. Leigh and I trailed just behind, while the men in our little party followed more slowly still.

We walked for nearly half an hour in the dappled sunlight before a small fire ring came into view. It sat in a tiny niche tucked into the forest, hardly a clearing. Behind it was a more rustic cabin, hand-sawed logs stacked up to form the walls, a moss-covered roof blending into the deep greenery like it had always been there. Meant to be. The front door sat propped open, colorful rugs on the floor welcoming us inside.

We waited at the bottom of the steps while Iaoin entered first, a quick, patterned rap on the door the only warning before he charged inside.

"Father, we've brought the guests. Do you want all six— well, seven, I guess—of them inside? Or do you want to come out to the fire?"

An ancient voice, reedy and thin, barely reached even my excellent wolf-assisted ears. "Take me to them, please."

"As you say," Iaoin said, respect evident in his tone as he addressed his elderly father. All traces of the cocky hothead who'd challenged for mating rites three seconds after meeting me were long gone, in his place a tender son who helped his elderly father down the steps with his cane.

We parted, letting them have a clear path to the giant half-log benches that circled the smoldering fire ring. The thin trail of smoke coming from the pit was almost blue in the light. The dual scents of sage and ash were oddly calming as we settled onto the other benches, forming a semicircle around the elder. Dirge settled himself in front of me, lying down where his side pressed against my shins.

"Yaghali du, Pack Blackwater." He bobbed his chin, the barest motion of acknowledgment. He was unimpressed by Kane's status as high alpha, and I liked that about him.

"Aa'yaghali, Inuksuk," we all said with eerie oneness, and he smiled, the motion turning his wrinkles into deeper creases on his cheeks.

"Very good. If you don't mind, I would like to get right to the meat of the issue. I'm old and impatient as my time on this plane wears thin. Tell me." He propped both hands on top of his intricately carved cane, scanning our group as if guessing which of us would tell him what was going on. His eyes settled heavily on Brielle, and I had to work to unclench my fists as the nerves overtook me.

"I have trouble shifting, Inuksuk. I can occasionally, under the moon. But it's very draining, and I always collapse within a few moments of taking my wolf form." Embarrassment had her ducking her head at the admission.

Inuksuk nodded, shifting his gaze to Kane, who continued. "The first time I shifted with my mate, I sensed a sickness, a witch taint to her wolf. There was a green ooze coming from her sides, draining down into the earth." He hesitated, and at once I realized that he wasn't sure if he should share his suspicions about Brielle's omega status.

Could they help her if he left any details out? And if we trusted this pack with the illness, couldn't we trust them with the rest?

"She's special, sir," he finally said. "And incredibly important to me, as well as my pack. But most of all... we suspect that she may be an omega."

Brielle's hand looped around his biceps, gripping him for dear life as we waited to see what the shaman would say.

TWENTY-TWO

Dirge

If I weren't lying down, I might have fallen down. The girl was an omega? Reed's pack had been *harboring* her from the ODL?

I was floored, though clearly, nothing terrible had happened to anyone close to her thus far. She seemed sweet and intelligent, not the type to go on a worldwide rampage of destruction and genocide. Brielle had only ever been kind to my mate and, by extension, me.

The Omega Defense League wouldn't care, though. They'd kill her without hesitation if what they suspected was true. Suddenly, the secrecy and urgency of all this made much more sense. I'd assumed this special audience was merely because she was the high alpha's mate, but it was so much worse than all that.

"Hmm," was all the elder said, staring through wizened eyes at the young shifter. "I need to see your wolf." He waved a hand to the edge of the forest, a small opening between our seats and the dense woods.

"Sir... Inuksuk. Respectfully, I don't think I can shift again so soon. I faced a challenge for mating rights to Kane and had to shift not long ago. If I try to shift now, nothing will happen."

The old man pursed his lips, squinting at her as if she were pulling his leg, even as Brielle lifted helpless hands.

Leaning heavily on the cane, and with both his children steadying one elbow from their seats at his sides, he rose on shaking legs.

A change came over his face. The silver glow of wolf eyes, yes, but it was more than that. His words were guttural, his face seemed to shimmer, and dominance buffeted us like a tidal wave, flowing from the deceptively frail man.

"*Shift!*" The command hit us all square in the chest, and I was grateful to already be in fur, immune to the order. The rest of my pack, however...

Yelps and yowls tore out all around the clearing as wolves were pulled out against our will, Kane the only one who managed to grit his teeth and resist, his eyes glowing green with indignation at the order.

But it served its purpose. For there in the middle of the circle of benches was a small, mostly white wolf with dark-tipped fur. She had sorrowful eyes and swayed on her paws. I didn't see anything wrong with her—certainly nothing so foul as a magical ooze—but it was still clear she was unwell. Her entire body shook with the strain of holding this form that was as natural as breathing for most. Shay's honey-brown wolf bolted past me to her side and leaned against her friend, bolstering her under the shaman's scrutiny. Leigh's tawny wolf was only a moment behind, hemming Brielle in from the other side like a sandwich.

Everyone seemed to hold their breath as Inuksuk stared, his eyes raking over the fragile little wolf in a way that even I wanted to stop. But eventually, he said, "Enough," and waved a trembling hand to release the pull on our wolves.

106

I shook like I was trying to shed water off my coat, the feeling an unpleasant one. But Brielle collapsed, a nude human appearing where her wolf had been. Averting my eyes, I waited until Shay returned to my side, wrapping her fingertips into my fur to anchor herself after slipping on a pair of borrowed sweats and tank top.

"Your wolf is indeed sick, but I can't say with certainty if you are as you suspect." There was kindness in his eyes as he examined Brielle. "But it is not an illness, not in so many words. Your sense of witch magic was correct. This was no accident of fate, but a multigenerational curse."

Fuck.

Kane looked grim as he spoke. "Can you tell the nature of the curse or who put it there?"

Inuksuk lifted one shoulder absently, looking lost in thought. "The curse is old, older than her. Someone in her family likely suffered from it before?" he asked Brielle for confirmation, and she nodded.

"My mother, sir. She died in my teens. We thought it was cancer."

He nodded solemnly. "It could seem so, I imagine. We are beings of immense power, but even we can withstand only so much loss. Even as some wounds are too great for our wolves to heal, so too are some curses too heavy for the spirit to bear. You are not in imminent danger of death"—everyone let out a sigh of relief—"but this situation cannot go unresolved indefinitely. You must find the witch who did this to your family line and get them to remove it. As for the other... I know of one who may have the answers you seek."

The other? Ah. Her omega status.

"Jada of the Kodiak bear sleuth. She is the only one alive who can say."

A bear sleuth? Interesting. I'd heard of the Kodiak shifters, but they were even more reclusive than this pack. They lived in total seclusion on an island, surrounded by *actual* Kodiak bears. The only way to get there was by seaplane, and to go without an express invitation was certain death. Even a small wolf pack at full strength would be hard-pressed to take down a single angry Kodiak, let alone an entire sleuth.

And with our females to protect, well, it would be insane to try it.

"I will let her know that you're coming." His eyes lifted then to the sky, and I could sense that his attention was elsewhere.

"We should go," Ilana whispered, sparing a reverent glance toward her father, whose hands were now lifted as he stared into the clouds. One by one, we followed her down the path, each wrestling with this new information in our own minds.

AFTER THE SHAKY Brielle was taken to her shared room with Kane and our hostess excused herself to handle pack business, the rest of us had nothing to do for the rest of the evening.

Shay looked down at me, a crease between her eyebrows. "Would you like to go for a run? Sometimes, when things get too heavy, I need to run them out of my system." The sadness around her was palpable, her sweet scent soured by a tinge of decaying rose. Sickly, and it made me want to sneeze in this form.

I dropped down on my front paws, wagging my tail in the universal sign for *let's go*. She laughed before turning her back and quickly shucking the borrowed clothing. In seconds, her beautiful brown wolf appeared, pouncing on me. We rolled head over tail for a few feet, yipping and barking before taking off into the woods.

She led the way, and I followed, nipping playfully at her heels as she dodged between the trees. Every now and then, she'd cut a tight turn and send a clod of dirt flying into my mouth.

But my wolf didn't mind. All he felt was free, and happy to be with her. By the time we finished running, all the worry was gone, and only contentment remained in its place.

TWENTY-THREE

Shay

A run was exactly what I needed to clear my head, and doing it with Dirge was somehow better than running alone. In the past, I'd always enjoyed being alone. It never bothered me because people—outside a very select few—were dangerous.

But being with Dirge filled a hole I hadn't known I carried inside, lent me an air of safety even as we tore through unfamiliar surroundings. When my sides heaved with effort and the sun sank below the horizon, we turned back for the guesthouse where we were staying.

I shifted back to let us into our room and dropped my abandoned shoes inside the door. Dirge waited while I showered, humming to myself as I scrubbed out the shampoo and then slathered on the conditioner. Thoughts whirled through my mind like little tornadoes, each new line of thought demolishing something in its wake. The news about Brielle was heavy, and I knew tomorrow, when she was feeling better, we'd need a plan. But despite that, all I could think about was the pitcher of spiced wine waiting next to my bed and what I wanted to say to Dirge tonight.

What I wanted to ask him.

How I'd feel if I didn't like the answers he had for me. It was enough to make me shiver under the warm deluge of water, so I quickly rinsed and got out.

I felt uncharacteristic nerves as I slipped on a black sleep set, the soft material making me tremble as it caressed my skin. I couldn't help thinking about the set dream-Dirge had destroyed last night as I fingered the hem and turned out the bathroom light. I checked the stainless-steel water bowl I'd set out for him in the bathroom and then walked into the bedroom.

It was silly to be nervous now, when I'd been naked and writhing under the man last night, but I was anyway. So I did what I always did when my mind was racing: I pulled a little speaker from my bag and set it on the bedside table. Once my phone was connected, I flipped to one of my favorite pieces. As the plaintive piano notes of *Gymnopedie No. 1* slowly filled the empty air around us, I fluffed up some pillows and leaned back on the bed. Deciding to just go for it, I poured the spiced wine into a regular glass cup from the bathroom and took a deep swallow before patting the bed next to me for Dirge to jump up.

He did smoothly, barely making a ripple in my wine as he settled next to me, laying his head gently across my stomach.

I listened to the familiar piano in contented silence, sipping the wine and playing with the soft, shorter fur on top of his head. Somewhere around the third full glass, my tongue began to loosen, and I found myself talking to him as I stroked.

"I was a foster kid. I know that's weird for a shifter. Usually, your pack takes care of you, even if your parents die. It happens, right? But I never knew my parents. I don't know if they're dead, or if they abandoned me, or hell, I could be a half-breed, even. An accidental kid left behind after a one-night stand." I snorted, the absurdity of not knowing where I'd come from striking me as funny in my half-drunk state. I poured another refill. Best to get fully drunk, the way this was going.

A drop sloshed over the edge of the cup, trailing like blood down my hand. But before I could wipe it away, Dirge's tongue swept out and licked it away, the warm sandpapery feeling making me giggle.

"Don't feel sorry for me, though. Not for that. If you want to feel sorry for *something*, I would be sorry about the human trafficking. Well, no. Actually, I don't want to talk about that. Those guys..." I tipped the cup up, draining half of it in a single chug.

"Did you know I learned to play piano in the public school's band class? Once I'd found the pack, I had to catch up on school. I was behind on so many things, but the music just made sense right from the start. I play three instruments proficiently and half a dozen more passably. One day, when my career takes off, I'm going to have the fanciest music studio you've ever seen. All that state-of-the-art stuff I drool over in the catalogs." I swirled the cup of wine, staring down at the bits of green I could see floating in it. It sounded gross on the surface, but I didn't mind it. It was earthy and rich, and paired well with the natural sweetness of the wine. "DJing has always been a temporary plan, but it pays the bills until I can sell some of my compositions."

Unsurprisingly, Dirge didn't answer as he watched me drink. It still felt nice to talk to him, though.

"I am going to have a headache tomorrow, I have no doubt. But I'd like this conversation to be less one-sided, so, bottom's up."

After I drained the *fourth* cup of spiced wine, I set the cup down, hoping that was enough. Drowsiness was trying to drag me under, even as I fought to keep my eyes open.

"They got what was coming to them," I confessed to the top of Dirge's head as I curled around him, slipping into the soft embrace of sleep.

I COULDN'T SAY how much time passed before my eyes popped open. I was sitting on the edge of my bed, wearing the same black pajama set I'd gone to sleep in, but a quick glance back showed my body still curled around a wolf. But I couldn't think too hard about the weirdness of that, because a grinning human-Dirge was sweeping me off the edge of the bed and straight into his arms.

"Hello, beautiful," he said, his cocky grin giving way to a soul-searing kiss. I resisted the urge to wrap myself around him and get a repeat dose of last night's orgasmic bliss, but only barely. Shoving at his shoulders, I created some space between us.

"Hold on, lover boy. We need to talk."

He smiled again, only half his mouth curving up in a devilish invitation. God, I wanted to taste those lips every day until I died. He was pure sin walking, and even as I knew better, my blood thrummed with heat. One look! I was pathetically easy if that was all it took.

But damn, it was a good look.

"Why don't we talk *after*. Wouldn't want to waste a good dream, after all." He tried to kiss me again, but I swatted him on the shoulder. He just laughed and dropped his lips to my shoulder, trying to tease the strap of my tank top to the side without me noticing.

"I'm serious. And this isn't a dream, not really."

That froze him in his tracks. He lifted his head, eyes glowing slightly with the influence of his wolf. "What do you mean?"

"I mean the Athabascan pack has a special herb blend that makes you dream walk. This is... really us. Mostly." I waved toward our bodies still on the bed, and his expression grew solemn. "I want to know why you won't shift back."

He jerked like I'd slapped him. "But I bit you last night. If this isn't a dream..." He tipped my head gently to the side, baring the side of my neck where he'd sunk his teeth into my skin the night before. "Shit! You're marked. You're still marked." He let go of me, backing up a step with a tortured expression and raking both hands through his long black hair.

"Don't be silly. I checked when I woke up, and..." My fingers felt the evidence on my neck, tidily healed scar tissue in the shape of his bite. My flesh felt real and solid, despite the fact that I was outside my corporeal body. "What the hell?" I whispered, looking up at him in shock.

"I'm so sorry. I can't believe I— No, no. I thought it was a dream. Shay, you have to believe me. I'd never mark you without your consent if I knew—" He backed up until he hit the wall, his eyes closing in abject horror.

"Shh." I stepped into his personal space, grabbing his arms and pulling them down to my waist before he could do something truly regrettable, like rip out all that gorgeous hair. Pulling it was my self-appointed job as of yesterday.

The memory of what we'd been doing when I pulled that hair sent a bolt of liquid heat straight to my core. Damn, I was horny. But I needed to focus.

"It's okay. Neither one of us knew what was happening, and like I said, there's no real mark on me. Whatever this is..." I risked letting go of one arm so I could wave at my neck, "it's not the real deal. If I'm honest, I'm not really sure how this works, but if it lets us talk, I'm willing to try it."

He gazed sorrowfully down at me, not convinced that I wasn't upset. "It is the gravest of sins to hurt your mate. And taking that choice from you..." He shook his head, refusing to meet my eyes. "It is an injury beyond any I could ever forgive myself for."

"Okay, would you lay off?" Anger was starting to burn off the haze of lust surrounding me. "I get it. You got caught up in

114

the moment. Whatever. Neither one of us knew this was more than a hot sex dream. I'm not mad about an accidental mark, even if it's... never mind. I'm a lot more concerned about the choice where you're refusing to shift when we're *not* asleep. Can we talk about that?"

I don't know if I was channeling Leigh or what, but I'd never been so sassy in all my life. Especially not with a man. I resisted the urge to slap a hand over my mouth, though. It needed to be said, and I didn't want to waste whatever time we had on him kicking himself over an accident.

His eyes sprang open, a different kind of fear filling them as he gazed down at me.

"I can't shift back, not now, not ever." He was adamant, resolve straightening his shoulders as he pushed off the wall and let me go as he began to pace in agitation.

"Ever?" The beginnings of anger ratcheted up to eleven as his words sank in. "So I'm just supposed to live essentially alone for the rest of my life? Dirge, I'm only twenty-six. I need more than a dream to hold on to for the next nine hundred years."

"I would understand." He swallowed hard, his jaw tensing before he ground out, "I would understand if you needed to take a lover."

My jaw dropped.

"You fucking bastard!" I leapt at him, my wolf enraged at the suggestion. I could barely hang on to my shift, and if we weren't in some drug-induced dream state, I'm pretty sure she'd have torn his throat out for the suggestion.

I tackled him, both of us falling to the plush, patterned rug at the foot of the bed. He didn't resist, and I landed on top of his chest, straddling his rib cage as I struggled to keep my wolf from shredding out of me.

"How could you even say that to me? You are my mate, and if you think I care so little about the mate bond that I'd take another partner while you're right here, well, you don't *deserve* to be at my side anymore. You can get the hell out and not come back." Granted, I was pinning his shoulders to the rug with claw-tipped fingers, so leaving was a little difficult.

"Shay. Shailene," he crooned, his hands gentle as they caressed my sides, sending tingles of anticipation and need through me.

I growled, baring my teeth as I refused to let up.

"It would destroy me, watching you with another. But if protection is all that I can offer you, I don't expect you to remain chaste."

"I don't want excuses or pretty condolences, damn you! I want an answer. Why? Tell me why." I held his gaze then, challenging him, hell—*dominating* him in this pose.

He sighed, the sound weary as his hands continued their slow work of stroking, soothing.

"I am old, Shay. Old enough that the darkness was starting to get to me. Drag at me. So, I went hunting for a mate. For nearly a hundred years, I traveled. Looking for dense populations of shifters, hoping to happen across my female. But I never did. My mother's second pregnancy brought me home, as childbirth takes more wolves than any war has in living memory."

My anger started to wane as his fingertips massaged the sensitive skin beneath my breasts, and as I was consumed by this piece of his history. I hadn't known he and Reed had a younger sibling.

"For a while, my family anchored me. The joy of a new pup is not small, and for years, I was content again. The darkness held at bay. But as Benedict hit his teenage years... that surge of alpha pheromones triggered my own, and it grew harder and harder to contain the need inside me."

My grip on his shoulders loosened, my claws retracting as the need to comfort Dirge took over. "I'm sorry, that must have been incredibly difficult."

116

"It was. And in my desperation, I sought the lore. Who could help me find my mate? Unfortunately, or fortunately, depending on your perspective, I found an answer."

A chill went down my spine, and now I was clutching his shoulders for a different reason: fear.

"What did you do, Dirge?"

Sorrow painted his handsome face as he continued the tale. "I sought the Fates."

"Wait, like the Greek myth ones? They're real?"

He bobbled his head from side to side. "Yes and no. They've always existed, but the name and lore surrounding them have changed many times. The Fetya, as they're called in shifter lore, can only be reached by great personal sacrifice and from certain points on the globe. With nothing to stop me, I sought the nearest mountain. The journey was long. I took no food or water, weakening myself sufficiently to meet the requirements of personal sacrifice. By the time I had reached the top—in human form—I was on the edge of death, even for a shifter."

I worried my bottom lip between my teeth, not at all feeling warm and fuzzy about where this was going, even though he was here, solid, and very alive beneath me. Had these Fetya cursed him? Could I force them to take it back? I would climb a mountain if it meant getting him back for real.

"By the time they appeared, I wasn't sure if it was hallucination or reality. But I asked them to show me my mate. And they did."

This time, a wide smile showed me his straight, white teeth. He trailed a fingertip up between my breasts to touch my lower lip with his thumb. I shuddered, ridiculously aroused as I waited on tenterhooks for the conclusion of this story.

"You were radiant, the most stunning creature I'd ever seen. But the Fetya do not simply give visions. They give prophecies. And the vision they showed me was a nightmare." Grief made him avert his gaze, grip me more tightly to his chest.

117

I melted down his chest, the urge to comfort him with my body overwhelming. "It's okay, Dirge. You can tell me. I'm here," I whispered into his neck, curling my body over his as if I could protect him from the past with sheer stubbornness.

He dragged in a deep, shuddering breath as our legs intertwined. Even in his grief, his arousal was hot and hard against my thigh.

"They didn't just show me you. They showed me you on the day you die."

I froze. The day I died? They knew?

More importantly, did I want to know? I held my breath and my questions, silently urging him to continue.

"We were in a field, somewhere I'd never seen. And you were radiant, smiling. The mere sight of you took the breath from my lungs. But then everything changed. The vision grew hazy. The sky darkened, and you were falling. I shifted out of wolf form to catch you, and..."

I stroked his cheek, silently supportive.

"That's when they told me. The first day I hold you in my arms. The first day I leave my wolf behind in your presence, that is the day you are taken from this world. I saw it happen, Shay. As soon as my hands touched your skin, light burst out of you. You were consumed, taken. And all I held was your broken, lifeless body."

My hands stilled, a secondary horror washing over me. Not only was I going to die, but *he* would be left alone. If we were unable to complete our bond, he wouldn't be taken with me. With the darkness already dragging at him, with no mate...

He would be feral.

Forever.

TWENTY-FOUR

Shay
_____

We lay there quietly in each other's arms, soaking in the comfort of a mate, of another's presence. I had so many questions and so little time he could actually answer them.

"What if it's not what you thought? Maybe... maybe it's not the first time, maybe it's five hundred years from now." I pushed up off his chest, looking down at him hopefully. "We could have a hundred lifetimes together before that happens."

He shook his head, adamant. "They were very clear, Shay. The first time. The first time I touch you, it's your death knell."

Frustration rose inside me, bound by iron chains of help-lessness. We were cursed.

"No, sweet Shay, not you. You could never be cursed."

I hadn't meant to say that out loud, but he was brushing my hair back and looking at me with all the devotion I never knew I could have. Tears pricked the corners of my eyes, desperate to fall.

It was torture. Pure torture to be this close to the one my soul was meant to love, only to be cruelly told that this was all we could have.

"You are light in the darkness, sweet honey in a barren land. You are *everything*. I only wish I could give you the full life you deserve. See this belly swell with my pup," he said, trailing his hands over my abdomen.

Flutters filled me at the contact, even though the picture he painted was apparently never going to happen. I wanted to live in a world where it could.

Not because I wanted babies. I actually might *not* want babies. Ever. But I wanted a life with my mate. I wanted to love and be loved, to be held in his arms as the sun came up on a thousand mornings. To make love in the middle of the night while the rain fell outside.

And it wasn't fair, it wasn't even remotely fair that this was it. This was all we would get.

A tear fell, and then another. It didn't matter what he said, if this was the life I was doomed to, I must have been cursed.

I crashed my mouth against his then, the salt of my own tears mingling with the taste of his lips as they finally broke free. His hands tightened on my waist, pulling me harder against his thickly muscled chest. The action ground my clit against his washboard abs, sending sparks of pleasure through me.

A low moan escaped my throat as I pulled back from the kiss, arching against his hold. He began to rumble then. The sound was low, but the effect was instant. Vibrations rippled through his chest, sending me from the starting line to the edge in a matter of seconds.

"Shay—" My name was a harsh promise, a demand.

I rocked in his grasp, seeking pressure, friction—

He dragged me down until I was riding the ridge of his dick, and I cried out at the desperate need it ignited. He was hot and hard and every single thing I needed.

I flung my shirt off, not caring where it landed. He lifted his hips, shucking off his own thin black pants as I hastily leaned forward, letting him drag mine down right after them. There was no hesitation, no sweet nothings whispered, only hot need as he steered me back on top of him.

"Are you ready?" Dirge's question was guttural, and I answered him with all the pent-up wildness inside me by slamming myself down, taking him to the hilt in one motion.

The burn and stretch of him had me howling, head tossed back as he began to move. His knees were up, supporting my back, so his hands were free to wander. He cupped my breasts with unexpected tenderness, and some part of me rejected it. I didn't want tender. I wanted fury, passion.

I lifted up and slammed down again, ignoring the gentle rocking he was building. He grunted, but didn't pick up the pace. He was still rumbling, that low soothing sound tearing at my control. I ground down onto him, taking the friction I needed to climb the mountain of bliss.

He didn't stop me, his hold remaining gentle as he let me drive us forward at a breakneck speed. I kept working him, up and down, grinding with a twist of my hips at the end until the orgasm took me. His name was a gasp on my lips as stars burst behind my eyes.

"That's it, beauty. That's it, easy now," he whispered, holding my gaze as my body turned boneless atop him.

All the fight went out of me, and he could clearly sense it, because between one heartbeat and the next, I was cradled beneath him. I didn't know how he flipped us without slipping out of me, but he was still there, shallowly thrusting in and out.

The head of his cock rubbed that spot, the one I didn't know lit me up before Dirge. But now my eyes were wild, searching his face as if he knew why my body was a live wire under such a small touch. As if he could anchor me in the storm of pleasure.

I gripped his shoulders, fingertips digging in as he continued teasing, still not giving me his all.

"Dirge, it's, it's—"

"Let go. Just let it all go," he murmured. His smile returned, that cocky grin that I loved. I pulled him down with greedy hands, sucking and biting at his bottom lip as he continued his shallow thrusts.

The second orgasm took me by surprise, and I screamed against his lips as it shuddered through me.

He moaned, eyes closing as I squeezed him in my bliss. His pupils blown wide, he finally sank in deep, hands lifting my hips to hold me flush against him.

"I love you," he said, his eyes open now and glowing green as they bore into mine. "I know you don't know me well enough to say it back, and that's okay." His words faltered as his pace quickened, chasing his own release as he drove me higher so soon after the last wave of pleasure.

"I know it's too soon, and I know I can't be everything you need." His voice cracked, head bowing under the strain of speaking as he fought his own peak. "But I will give you every-thing I have. Whatever I am, no matter how broken, it's yours."

Tears spilled down my cheeks. All the emotions I tried to shove aside with rough sex poured through me like acid. I wasn't able to stop the tears, only let them fall as I rose to meet him, our bodies saying so clearly what words could never convey. Every hurt I tried to repress billowed through me, mixed with sweet care as a rough fuck turned into slow, tender caresses.

He reached between us, thumbing me just right and sending me over that cliff of pleasure one more time as he roared his own release to the heavens.

But even then, in that last moment of breathless, clinging bliss, I could feel him fading, slowly beginning to drain away from me.

"No, please, not yet, please!" I wasn't ready. I was breaking, shattering to bits. I wasn't ready.

I was sobbing then, clutching his biceps, trying to hold him to me just a little longer. I wasn't ready. *I'm not ready to lose him.*

"I'm so sorry, Shay, my beauty. I'm so sorry." He faded faster then, and that was when I felt it. I was fading too, being pulled out of the dream walk and into my body, still asleep on the bed. He lowered himself to kiss me one last time, but it was barely a whisper against my lips before we both winked out into noth-ingness.

TWENTY-FIVE

Shay

I was hollow inside. It felt like someone had taken a cold metal ice cream scoop and carved out all my guts. How was I still alive if I had no organs left? No beating heart, no muscles. I was nothing but a living bruise as I stared at the ceiling, the cold light of dawn leaving me frigid.

There was nothing but pain and sadness left where my heart used to be, even as something odd thrummed beneath the surface. Not even my favorite instrumental playlist, still running from the night before, could put a dent in my melancholy.

Dirge was still there, his wolf form burrowed into my side as if he too felt hollow without that contact. My fingers wove into his fur, and his eyes blinked open. Canine sorrow was clear in them, and I held on to him a little too tightly as the odd thrumming turned into a vicious burn.

A gasp froze in my throat, my eyes going wide with terror as the searing centered itself on my chest, over my heart, between my breasts.

"Ahh!" The cry finally escaped, and I arched into the bed, Dirge's howl twining with my pained scream in a morbid song.

"Shay? Shay!" Brielle was at the door, pounding against the wood.

"What's happening?" Reed's question was next.

"I don't know. Something's wrong. Get me in there. Now!" Brielle barked the order with alpha power, and then the splintering crack of wood followed by the *boom* of the door falling to the ground was all I could hear.

I clutched my chest, mouth stuck in a frozen *o* of pain as Reed lunged through the door, Kane and Gael coming more slowly behind, blocking my friends from any danger.

When it dawned on the men that it was just me and Dirge writhing in pain on the bed, they allowed my friends to pass.

"What is this? What's wrong with her?" Leigh's voice was desperate as she watched Brielle check my pulse, tug at my hands.

But the searing heat was starting to leave, numbness filling in behind it. My hands collapsed to my sides as I sucked in great, cooling lungfuls of air. What was wrong with me?

Brielle clawed the neck of my sleep tank down, her eyes going wide as she bit her bottom lip between her teeth and shot a worried look at Leigh.

"What is it, love?" Kane was at her side, a possessive arm around her waist now that she'd stopped checking me.

"I think... I think it's her mating marks. But..."

The words filtered through my numbness, something clicking inside me.

Mating marks.

Oh, Goddess.

I bolted upright and brushed past Leigh, tearing into the bathroom. The light blinked once and then stayed on, the heavy square mirror showing my disheveled hair and wild gray eyes. But I didn't care about any of that. I peeled off the shirt, not caring in the least about stripping down with people right outside.

My breath caught in my chest at the sight.

I'd seen my bare chest a thousand times. No surprises there since puberty, really. Until today. Painted over my skin were the most gorgeous marks, thick green swirling lines so smooth, no tattoo could hope to replicate them. They started at my left collar bone, swooping down over my left breast, teasing the edges of my areola and scrolling across to my sternum, but the magical ink began to fade there, as if it ran out of steam halfway with the pattern still unfinished.

My mate marks were beautiful, and I couldn't help but trace them with my fingertips, a sob breaking from my lips as I reached the midpoint over my sternum, where they petered out to bare skin. The truth was clear, written right on my skin.

The marks were incomplete, and they always would be. My mate wasn't human. And without him changing back, his marks couldn't take hold. The magic was unfinished, stretched painfully between us to the breaking point.

I could feel him, though, in my chest. Closing my eyes, I searched for that tenuous connection to Dirge. He was a warm ember, glowing and alive, that replaced the numbness I had woken with.

A whine came at the door, followed by the sharp scratch of wolf claws. Despite myself, I smiled a little at his insistence. I stepped behind the door to open it, letting him in without flashing my boobs to the three males hovering anxiously in my room. Not that they would likely care, but the first person to see my marks should definitely be Dirge.

He padded in on quiet paws, and I shut the door behind him.

A tortured whine slipped from his lips, and he rubbed hard against the front of my thighs before turning around to get a good look at me.

I sank down to sit on the bathroom floor so he could see

them at eye level. They were there for him, and he should have matching ones for me.

But I would never know, never get to see his marks or run my fingertips over them.

Rage and sorrow were a knot tangled up inside my chest. Dirge stared, taking in each graceful line. And then he threw back his head and howled, the sound sending goose bumps rippling over my skin. It was heavy-laden with emotion: sorrow and joy, pain and pleasure. It was all wrapped together like barbed wire.

What should only be joy was tainted, broken.

Tears streamed down my cheeks, and I didn't bother to wipe them away. As his howl faded off into nothing, a tentative knock came at the door.

"Shay? Do you want us to go? Or to come in, or..." Leigh trailed off, even my usually chatty friend lost for words in this shitty situation. Brielle had obviously filled her in.

I didn't know what I wanted, so I stayed silent. Though, that wasn't true. I *did* know what I wanted. Dirge, in human form. Completed mate marks. A small, beautiful bonding ceremony where we promised to love each other always under the Moon Goddess's approving glow.

But I couldn't have any of that, and sitting on the floor crying about it wouldn't fix it. Dirge nudged my hand with his nose, and I reflexively stroked the soft fur on his muzzle.

It was a small thing, but it was something. I wasn't alone, even though the pain in my chest said otherwise. My brain started spinning, possibilities and thoughts threatening to drown me in their deluge.

So, he saw a vision. Was that gospel? Could it be changed? Or maybe he'd misinterpreted it somehow.

Maybe yes, that would be how I'd die, and it would be while he was in human form, but not *the first time*. Or maybe I would have died anyway at that time, whether he shifted or not.

Shit. Why couldn't the future be changed? What would happen if he shifted and we were inside, not in some field like the Fetya foresaw? Would I still die?

I reached for my shirt, tugging it back on as possibilities and determination replaced the sorrow. We might have been dealt a tragic hand. Maybe we couldn't change it. But we sure as hell wouldn't if we didn't at least *try*.

I was on my feet again in an instant, Dirge my faithful shadow as I flung open the bathroom door a little too forcefully, slamming it into the wall by accident.

"Shay? Are you all right?" Brielle and Leigh were leaning against the wall, wearing matching expressions of worry. The men had left the room, giving us some privacy. But privacy wasn't going to fix this.

I opened the door to see all three of the men standing in the hall and had to fight back the ridiculous urge to laugh at how similar they looked to Leigh and Brielle.

"Come in, please." I waved them through the door, my throat tightening at the realization that I had a lot of talking to do, and the old familiar discomfort of speaking around men threatened to choke me.

But I couldn't let it. These were my pack, my people. And just as much as they were working to help Brielle, I knew they would help me—*us*—if I let them in.

So I had to let them in.

TWENTY-SIX

Dirge

I paced the long side of the room, unable to hold still after seeing my beautiful mate's new marks. She was stunning, and perfect, and it tore a hole right out of my chest that the marks were unfinished. I didn't know it was possible for them to form at all with me still shifted. Had our nighttime meetings done something more permanent than we'd realized? It was a worry I had no one to bounce off.

So I continued wearing an unsettled track into the floor-boards as Shay filled in the rest of the pack's inner circle on our situation. She faltered at times, but her shoulders were straight as she outlined our midnight meetings—leaving out the private bits, of course—and what I'd shared about the vision from the Fetya.

Reed's face paled and he sank into an empty chair as she finished the tale. When his eyes met mine, it was with intense sorrow.

"Brother," he whispered, reaching out a hand toward me. I quickly butted it with the top of my head in acknowledgment, but couldn't stop the urge to pace. It itched, telling everyone.

But not as much as the realization as I listened that my mate thought they could *fix it*. Change our cursed destiny.

I knew, deep down in the marrow of my bones, that this was not going to happen. Nothing we did, nothing we tried would change it. And if she didn't honor that, the Fetya could take her from me even sooner.

I could absolutely not live with that.

"M'kay, so..." Leigh was the first one to wade in after Shay finished speaking. "There's nothing actually *preventing* his shift right now? He's fully aware and the man is in control but... Darth Furder's afraid of the vision?"

I lifted my lip in a halfhearted snarl at her insult. Leigh just grinned, enjoying herself, the incorrigible little shit.

"Well, if you were in a field and now we're not, just shift now. You can't complete the vision if you don't play by its rules, right?" She slapped her hands on her thighs as if the matter was settled.

It was absolutely not settled.

"It's not so simple, I'm afraid." Kane's expression was grave as he spoke. "The lore of the Fetya is shrouded in many mysteries, but one thread of truth runs through them all. What they foresee is as much price as it is a promise. They *will* extract the truth of the vision, whether it is now or at the foretold time in the future."

Ice water flooded my veins, even though I already knew the accuracy of his words.

"He's right," Reed said. "If they foretold Dirge's first shift leading to Shay's death, then his shift will in some way bring it about, sooner or later."

"Okay, sooner or later. Fine. But what if they could have years together before then? Why have nothing if you could have something!" Leigh stood from the edge of the bed, raking frustrated fingers through her long blonde hair. "Even if they

130

got a week. Wouldn't you rather have a week with your mate than *nothing*?"

"No! It's reckless, and it could end with both of them dead sooner. Do you care so little for your friend that you would throw away what could be *centuries* of life for a few days of pleasure?" Gael held his position leaning against the wall, but the grating derision in his tone was enough to slough off a layer of skin.

All of them and their bickering were driving me nuts. I didn't care what they decided; I wasn't shifting. It was too risky, and none but Kane had the power to force the issue. I paused, casting a glance at him and then at the little she-wolf at his side. Brielle was a wildcard, but somehow, I didn't think she would press beyond what Shay and I wanted, even if she could.

Leigh spun toward Gael, fury tingeing her cheeks red. "You don't know that—you're just guessing. So, get off your fucking high horse. Wolves age so slowly that it could be tomorrow or five hundred years and he wouldn't have been able to tell in that vision. But you also don't know that they'd only have moments. She could get those five hundred years *with him* before the price comes due. And yeah, if I was blessed enough to find my mate, and I had the choice between any amount of time with him and none? I'd choose him. *Every fucking time.*"

You could have heard a flea jump, the room was so quiet.

"Guys, I think we all need to take a step back, here." Brielle's voice was calm but firm, and Leigh immediately spun away, giving Gael her back. He took a step after her, his rage at the obvious diss tingeing the air with an acrid sulfur scent that burned away his usual wolfy pine. I stepped between them, lifting my lips in a snarl.

Leigh was Shay's family, which meant she was mine too, and for some reason, this male couldn't seem to stop pissing her off.

I didn't like it, and I wasn't sure I liked *him*. Inner circle or no, if he didn't stop hurting the females under my protection, I'd tear his throat out and piss on his corpse. That I could still do in wolf form, and at this rate, I'd enjoy it.

"Back off, Dirge. This doesn't concern you," Gael said hotly, meeting my gaze in a challenge.

I growled, but then dainty hands grabbed me by the ruff and pulled me back. Shay. "Stop it. Both of you," she said, casting a disapproving look at Gael too, though she quickly ducked her head away from the other male.

That just made me want to leap at him more. But I didn't. Her hands were tangled in my ruff, anchoring herself as much as me. So, I leaned into her thigh, soaking up the contact.

Reed stood from his chair, casting the two of us a glance I couldn't decipher in this form. His scent was bitter, though, like coffee left too long to burn. "I don't think this is a decision they can take lightly, and regardless, it's not something we can decide for them. As much as I hate to say it, for now, he needs to stay in wolf form. We need to do more research on the Fetya before we can say with any certainty what might happen. And, unfortunately, the discussion is going to have to wait. Our plane is ready to take us back to the pack grounds so we can wait for word from the Kodiak sleuth."

"It's okay, we'll figure this out. I promise." Brielle crossed to loop her arm through Shay's, grabbing Leigh with the other. "Maybe this Jada will know how to help you too. If she's old enough to recognize omega magic, surely she's seen a Fetya vision before, right?" Her chipper smile and soothing presence had the intended effect, the tension in the room ratcheting down several notches as the men filed out. I stayed back, watching them go—keeping a particular eye on Gael, though he didn't spare the women another glance.

"Come on, we'll help you pack up your stuff, then let's get

out of here. The Athabascan pack have been lovely hosts, but I need some space," Leigh said as she headed into the bathroom.

Seconds later, the sounds of her roughly shoving toiletries into a bag reached us, and Brielle chuckled. "Those two are like oil and water, aren't they?" she whispered to Shay.

"More like gasoline and firecrackers," Shay muttered as she hurried to pack.

TWENTY-SEVEN

Shay

The trip back to Pack Blackwater grounds was uneventful, and I let out a sigh of relief when my feet touched familiar territory once more. But we weren't even to the UTVs we'd left parked beside the hanger when a runner burst out of the woods.

I tensed as he approached, only relaxing when I realized it was Julius, the top enforcer. After Gael? I thought that was right. A lot had happened in the past month, but in-depth conversations about Pack Blackwater's structure weren't on the list, and we'd only been briefly introduced.

Dirge tensed at my side, then took a tentative step forward.

Did he know Julius? I watched Dirge closely, but Julius had eyes only for Kane.

"High Alpha, an urgent missive came in less than ten minutes ago. A..." He checked the paper in his hands, "Jada, reported to be a Kodiak bear shifter, if you can believe that, is requesting an immediate audience."

Kane lifted one eyebrow in surprise as he held his hand out for the letter. Julius passed it to him before finally surveying the rest of our group.

"You lot look like you just came from a fucking funeral. Haven't we had enough of that?" He shook his head, eyes finally landing on Dirge. "Holy shit. That you, man? You back?" Julius dropped to his haunches, getting on eye level with Dirge. "Red's all gone, at least." He reached up slowly and then rubbed Dirge behind the ears.

"He can understand you," I said, cursing the waver in my voice, how weak I sounded. Would I ever get used to speaking up around men? If Dirge couldn't speak for himself, I would have no choice.

"Yeah, excellent. If you shift back, we could use another good enforcer. Technically, all the spots are full, but with all this shit going on, we could use another trustworthy man."

Dirge snorted, but didn't answer otherwise.

"Julius," Kane said, and Julius stood, leaving Dirge at my side.

"Yes, Alpha?"

"Who delivered this? We were expecting a significant wait, given how reclusive the Kodiaks are."

Julius shrugged. "Nobody saw, Alpha. One of the patrol shift found it stuck to your office door between one round and the next. He brought it to me, and I opened it, given the strangeness of the situation and your absence."

"I'm glad you did. This says they want us to come as soon as we can, as early as today. I don't know how Inuksuk contacted them, but apparently, he conveyed the urgency of the situation." He swept us all with his gaze, settling on Bri. "What do you think, my love? Do you need a few days, or—"

"Hell no. Let's go find out what they know. We're already packed, right?" She smiled, but it was forced, not reaching her eyes.

"We are. We'll need to top up on fuel, but we could be flying again in half an hour."

135

Leigh stifled a groan as Gael jogged over to the pilot, letting him know of the change of plans. "So much for space."

I looked down at Dirge. "You better go hunt before we leave. Stay close?" I asked, and he nodded, darting off into the woods.

"ALPHA, WE'VE GOT AN ISSUE."

Never reassuring when the pilot says that. I reached down and tightened my seat belt, nerves ratcheting up ten degrees. I spared a glance at Leigh, her face pressed against the small window. She was queasy and pale, but so far had managed not to puke.

Kane removed his seat belt, then made his way carefully up the small aisle to where the pilot sat. "What is it?"

"The weather is rapidly deteriorating. I can request permission to set us down at the nearest airstrip, and we can wait for it to blow over. Or we can fly through it. We're going to fly slower, though, and burn through more fuel than I'd like."

"How much more?" Kane asked.

"We'll be below ten percent reserve. Closer to five."

Kane grimaced, looking back at all of us. "Whose territory are we over if we set down? I'll need to contact their alpha and let them know why we're in the area, which I'd rather not do."

The copilot answered. "We're over Lake Clark National Park. The current Alpha is Caesar, of Pack Effelin."

"Pack Effelin? What's their affiliation?" Kane asked Gael.

Gael thought for a moment, and the plane began to shudder as raindrops splattered against the windshield. I was stiff as a board in my seat, back pressed into the soft leather like that would be enough to cushion a fall from this height. "Neutral, as far as we know. They shouldn't mind a visit, given the circumstances. They're mostly fishermen by trade and stay out of most interpack drama."

Kane nodded. "Take us in if the air traffic controller allows. We'll phone the Alpha as soon as we're wheels down and ask for shelter and pay for a fresh tank of fuel."

The plane took another terrifying dip before the pilot got it back under control.

"Yes, Alpha," the pilot said in a strained tone, then raised his voice so we could all hear. "Please fasten your seat belts, if you haven't already. It's going to be rocky for a bit."

Kane took his seat once more as the shuddering intensified. I drummed on the armrest of my seat, nervous energy making me want to shift, even though Dirge was already taking up two rows' worth of the aisle. He whined low in his throat, then licked my fingers. He didn't like it when I got anxious, could probably smell it on me.

"I'm fine," I whispered. A second glance at Leigh, though, showed that she wasn't. She sat with her hand over her mouth, looking horribly nauseated. I passed her an extra sick bag.

"I'm so sorry," she said quickly before gagging, the airsickness finally getting to her. She retched off and on through the storm until the pilot finally took us back down, all of us bumping and jolting hard in our seat belts when the wheels finally touched. As soon as we landed, I jumped up and guided her out of the seat.

"Come on, you'll feel better once we're on the ground with some fresh air." I wrapped my arm around her shoulders, turning sideways so she could lean on me as we walked down the aisle. Dirge dogged our steps, nose bumping occasionally against the back of my leg.

"Thanks, Shay, you're a lifesaver," she murmured, voice rough from the strain. She was clammy under my fingertips by the time we made it down the stairs. The rain pounded down now, soaking us to the skin as soon as we were on the ground, but Leigh didn't care. She turned her face up to it, letting it wash away the ick. The smell of wet earth was soothing and the grassy ground beneath my feet comforting to my wolf.

Dirge braved the rain right along with us, pressed against the front of our legs in a protective stance. I noticed that he seemed to have adopted Leigh too, and it just made me love him all the more for caring about my bestie.

"Come on, there's a shelter right over there," Brielle shouted over the rain, pointing as she joined us. There was no fancy hangar at this airstrip, but what amounted to a little bus-stop shelter. It was better than nothing, though, and we half jogged through the grass to get under it.

"This sucks. Can I just say that this really sucks?" Leigh sounded exhausted as she let herself drop to the bench, leaning against my side for support.

"You can, and I'm so sorry. It wouldn't be so bad if we could take the pack's bigger jet, but on these little planes, you feel every bump." Brielle was all mother hen, feeling her forehead and then taking Leigh's pulse at her wrist. "Hmm, your heart rate is a bit elevated. We need to get some fluids in you, and let me have those, there's a trash can." She fished the sick bags out of Leigh's sweaty grip and disposed of them without even a nose wrinkle.

Doctors. Nothing fazed them.

Before we could go hunting for drinks, though, the men appeared. To my surprise, Gael was at the front of the line. He stepped toward Leigh, but Dirge put himself between them, growling low in his throat.

"Easy. I've just got a soda for her." Gael held up the green can. "Ice-cold ginger ale. I grabbed a few from the hangar fridge before we left."

"Oh, good idea." Brielle plucked the drink from his fingers and popped the tab before passing it to Leigh. Drink up, and then we'll chase it with some water when you're less queasy."

Gael nodded as Leigh took a sip, then stepped back out into

the rain, leaving the shelter for us. He didn't complain as the rain drenched him, and once again, I wondered what was going on between the two of them. But I didn't have long to think about it because Kane walked up, phone pressed to his ear.

"Yes, myself plus my delegation of six pack members, and two air personnel. Nine total. Thank you. We're waiting at the airstrip." He hung up, finally looking at the paltry shelter. "They have a driver on the way to retrieve us and take us to pack lodging. The Alpha wants to speak with me, but they have enough beds for the night, and hot showers."

"Thank you, Kane." Brielle stood and pressed a kiss to his lips, hands going around his neck as he pulled her closer. I looked away, giving them a moment of privacy even as the sight of what I couldn't have made my chest ache.

"I hear a vehicle." Gael's tone was sharp, alert—and everyone tensed as a small passenger van bump-bumped out of the forest, headlights blurred by the downpour.

"We trust these people, right?" I asked, the chill and nerves both combining to raise gooseflesh along my arms. The previous high alpha had been assassinated mere weeks ago, and now Kane was the new one, standing six feet from me. If someone came after him next, we were all in danger.

"We have no reason not to, but stay alert. We take no risks and we stay together." Kane's tone was calm but hard, brooking no arguments.

The van pulled right in front of the little shelter, a harried-looking middle-aged man with a receding hairline cranking down the window a few inches. "Heya, folks. Climb on in and we'll get you dry as quick as we can." He plastered on a smile to match his too-chipper tone, but ducked back from the window as rain splattered up.

We all piled in, the pilot and copilot last after securing the plane right on the airstrip. The ride was bumpy and dark, and

Leigh was groaning quietly from her position on Brielle's shoulder between sips of ginger ale.

Dirge and I took up an entire row of seats ourselves because the side aisle of the van wasn't large enough to hold him.

"Nothing like the smell of wet fur, eh?" The driver chuckled, looking at us in the rearview mirror far longer than was comfortable. "Your man there doesn't shift, even with a frog strangler like this?"

I shook my head, uncomfortable and unwilling to try to explain to this complete stranger our complex situation. Though... I'd have to get used to it. A nonshifting mate wasn't a complication that was going away any time soon.

I bit my bottom lip and dropped my gaze, hoping he'd likewise drop the issue.

"Well then, my name's Mick, and I'm one of Pack Effelin's support staff. I understand you're expected by Caesar, Alpha?"

"*High Alpha* Kane will be making brief introductions with Alpha Caesar," Reed corrected, an unusual imperiousness lacing his tone as he addressed the male. "But we have been through quite a lot this evening, and we appreciate your pack's understanding in granting us some privacy and rest."

"Okie dokie, understood." Mick's smile turned forced, but he lapsed into blessed silence for the rest of the ride.

We pulled up in front of a small but well-maintained log cabin, a light on in the front window, with a woman visible running around frantically inside.

"Uh..." Leigh lifted her head, squinting.

"Oh, don't worry. That's just Marge. She's another of our support staff, and she's getting things prepared for you. Head on in, she won't bite." Mick began to whistle as we climbed out of the passenger van.

"So..." I looked anxiously from the van to the house, the stranger inside still darting back and forth.

Gael stepped forward, brushing past us and tromping up

the front steps. He rapped once on the door, hard, and then pushed it open. The woman inside let out a loud yelp, and then a quieter exchange took place just out of earshot.

"Gael will clear the cabin, and then the rest of you will wait here while Kane and I go speak with Alpha Caesar," Reed said.

Brielle spoke up, a worried edge to her tone. "Shouldn't Gael go with you too? We've never met this Alpha before, and we don't know how safe it is. The two of you are strong, but three would be stronger."

Reed smiled gently. "Kane will be fine, I promise. The most common method of taking out a powerful alpha is by using his mate. You are what needs protecting." Reed graciously extended his gaze to all us females as he said that.

"I'm a strong fighter, Reed. And we have Dirge. If you need Gael, nobody will get past us," I argued.

Reed just shook his head. "High Alpha's orders, I'm afraid. But don't worry. I don't sense anyone with a tenth of Kane's power anywhere within a half mile. He could probably flatten every alpha in this pack with his pinky finger." He shot me a wink as Gael walked back to our group.

"It's clear. Everyone inside."

Brielle shared a quick goodbye kiss with Kane, and then the van pulled away.

"THIS IS A BEAUTIFUL CABIN. Thank you so much for your help, Marge." Brielle played diplomat while I hauled Leigh to the kitchen, and poured her a glass of water. She was still green around the gills, but she'd kept the entire can of soda down so far.

Baby steps.

"You don't have to coddle me, Shay, I'm fine." Leigh took the water with a sullen expression, but drank it down greedily nonetheless.

"I don't have to, but if I don't, who will you let do it? Certainly not the brooding alpha-hole who just walked off." I leveled a *try me* look at her, but she ignored it.

Leigh was top-level delusional when it suited her.

"I don't know who you're talking about, but Gael certainly wants nothing else to do with me."

"Right, right. So we're going full ignorance campaign? Got it. I'll tell Bri."

Leigh snorted, hiding her grin behind the rim of the water glass and taking another sip.

"There's nothing ignorant about acknowledging a one-night stand for what it was."

"So, the ginger ale? That was nothing?" I leaned back against the counter, crossing my arms over my chest.

"A concerned pack mate. He probably was worried I'd vomit on *him* at the rate I was going."

"Right. I don't have the most sexual experience of the three of us, as you well know—" Dirge growled at my side, but I nudged him with my knee to get him to shut up. "But even I know that one-night stands don't bring you things when you're sick, hover, and worry about your safety."

"Okay, now *you're* going full ignorance. The man despises me! Okay? Des-pi-ses. We shared a hot night between the sheets, and then the next morning, I—" She stopped midstream and slammed the water glass down so hard on the counter, I worried it would crack. "One can of soda doesn't equal caring. Just... never mind. I need a shower and a bed. Stat."

I watched in shock as Leigh stormed out of the kitchen, just as Brielle was coming in.

"Umm, everything okay in here?" Brielle asked, concern

tilting her eyebrows down, making the little frown line appear between them.

"I have no idea. She's really sensitive about the Gael topic."

Bri popped her hip out and leaned against the island, mirroring my pose. "He's standing guard on the porch. You never did fill me in on the details, but should we follow her first?"

I sighed and mindlessly tangled my fingertips in Dirge's fur. He'd become my touchstone so quickly, it was scary.

But also right.

"I don't really *know* the details. They spent the night together after your bonding ceremony. She was dancing with another pack mate, he got jealous, a fight turned into making out, and then they left. I woke up with her at my bedside after the whole..." I waved at my side, where the bullet wound had been. "She won't talk about it, claims it was a one-time thing, and that he was good. That's all she was willing to say. But I get the feeling *something* happened, good or bad, between them. I just can't put my finger on it."

I worried my bottom lip between my teeth, debating whether or not to take this moment alone to tell her the *rest* of my suspicions.

Brielle crossed her arms over her chest. "Out with it, Shay." She used her best doctor voice on me, and then, more softly, "This might be our only chance to talk for a while."

I blew out a hesitant breath.

"She can't be pregnant, right? From a fling with someone who's not her mate?"

Brielle's eyebrows nearly flew off her face, they jumped up so quickly.

"I'm sorry, why would we think that, exactly?"

I shrugged, already regretting mentioning it. "I don't know, just little things. She had a fever the night of your bonding ceremony. By the time I came to, she seemed perfectly fine. But if you'd seen her on that dance floor... she wasn't herself. And then she went off and had a one-night stand with Gael, who she usually can't stand. Not like her at all. She's a serial monogamist, and you know as well as I do that even *briefly* messing with two guys on the dance floor is weird for her."

Brielle sighed and rubbed her forehead a few times before shrugging.

"I mean, anything is *possible*. But based on my studies, it's far more likely that she went through a false heat. You can think of it almost like a practice heat. All the emotional"—she used her hands to make a roller-coaster motion—"with none of the results. True heats don't start until you're closer to a hundred, a hundred fifty if you haven't found your fated mate. We're a long-lived species, and while we reach maturity relatively quickly like humans, we lack the rush to procreate before our fertility dries up."

Relief washed over me. "Okay, that makes a lot of sense. I won't bring it up to her again, since it's upsetting. And, honestly, for the best. Whatever is between them, if she doesn't want it to continue, I don't want it for her."

Brielle smiled at that, then cast a worried glance over my shoulder toward the front door. "How long do we say it takes for him to appease Alpha Caesar's feelings before I worry they've been kidnapped or drugged?"

I chuckled, then crossed the space between us to give her a quick hug. "Longer than the fifteen minutes it's been. Kane's a big deal now, so he's going to have to have long, boring political conversations. Kiss babies, shake hands. That sort of thing."

She laughed, some of the tension leaving her. "That's true, very true." But she stared down at her shoes, not looking back at me.

"Is that all that's worrying you? You're not having more symptoms, are you?"

Her head whipped up. "No, no! Please don't worry about

that. I've been much better since Kane and I completed our bonding and the, umm, physical relationship also seems to keep the worst of it at bay."

Now it was my turn to be surprised. Mate bonds were a powerful thing—the *most* powerful thing in the shifter world, really—but his touch curing a witch's curse, even temporarily, was next level. "That's kind of cool. But... if it's not that...?"

She sighed. "I keep racking my brain for why my family would have a witch curse. It would explain why no medical treatments—or the endless tests I've been running for years—ever turned up results. It's just that nobody before my mom ever died young or of a sickness. And thinking back, my parents were so accepting of it all. Now that I feel the terror of it hanging over my own shoulder, knowing if I don't fix it, I will for sure die and take Kane with me... It doesn't make sense. None of it makes sense. And I wish I could go back and shake them, make them try harder to stop it, but they're not here, and, and—"

"You didn't know then what you know now?" I offered, feeling her frustration.

"Yeah, exactly. It's too little, too late."

"It's not too late for you, though. That's the most important thing. If your parents were resigned, well, that is weird. But it's possible they thought it was truly just a freak illness." I shrugged, unable to think of any other reason they wouldn't have hunted up an answer. "Besides, witches aren't so common that they would have suspected a curse."

Brielle's head snapped up, her eyes widening. "Holy shit."

"What is it?" I stood straighter, my wolf pushing close to the surface at her sudden shift in mood. She considered Bri under our protection and had since the first time she admitted to me that she couldn't hold a shift herself.

"My mom's best friend was a witch. I don't really know what kind or if she was in a coven... Honestly, I hadn't thought of her in forever. Karissma lived far away, but she was shipping my mom potions, trying to prolong her life there at the end."

"You think her friend cursed her?" Horror filled me at the thought.

"No, of course not. Karissma was a real hard-ass, but she loved my mom. Mom used to say she was the closest she had to a sister, and I grew up calling her Aunt Kari. But, if Karissma was treating her, maybe she knew what kind of curse it was, and how it got there."

"That would be huge, Bri. Where does she live?"

"Well, she was always moving, when I was a kid. She'd blow into town a time or two every year, but then she was off again. We lost touch after my parents died. I pushed her away the first time she tried to visit after that."

"Do you still have her number? I know it's been a long time."

"It's been more than nine years," Brielle corrected with a remorseful grimace.

"I don't think it would matter if it were a hundred years. You were grieving, and she was close to your mom. I bet she'd be thrilled to get a call from you. Even if she's not, if she has information..."

"You're right," she said with a tight smile. After a deep breath, she pulled her cell phone from her pocket and flipped through the contacts. "I still have her number, but I've got no service out here. When we get back to the pack grounds, though, I can make the call. I can't imagine reception's any better on the island we're heading to."

"Probably not." I shot her a grin. Even if she was hesitant, I was happy to have any possible lead, no matter how small a chance it might be. It felt like we were making progress. Well, somewhat.

Kane hadn't shared any updates with us about the investigation into his parents' killer, but we'd been a little busy. One look at my friend's exhausted pose and I decided to wait to bring that up until after we met the Kodiak shifters. Progress on her health was enough for one day.

"Come on, you. Let's go find our rooms and check on Leigh. I should probably apologize for bringing up Gael again anyway. Then we can hit the showers."

"Good idea." There was a pause. "But I won't sleep until Kane's back."

"The good news is you don't have to. We'll keep you company."

My sweet, brilliant friend had tears in her eyes when she said, "Thank you, Shay. This is all just so much. I mean, I'm mated, which was the last thing I expected out of this, and my magic is on the fritz, and Kane's parents, and I just... I don't know what I'd do without you and Leigh to keep me steady."

I smiled and wordlessly wrapped an arm around her waist and dragged her toward the stairs. The sooner I got her showered and in pajamas, the better. I had a not-so-sneaking suspicion that she'd be out the moment she crawled under the covers, whether Kane was back or not.

TWENTY-EIGHT

Dirge

L eigh waved off my mate's apology when we arrived at the rooms, her hair wrapped in a towel as she brushed her teeth while blasting "Disturbed" from her phone. Shay pushed Brielle toward the shower and then sank onto the end of the bed, curling into a ball where she could still reach to distractedly rub my ears. I leaned into the touch, craving it down to the center of my being.

Memories of our last time together blurred into a haze behind my eyes when I closed them, so I didn't. It was bittersweet, having a taste of the connection we couldn't ever have again. She looked into my eyes as she stroked, and I could practically see the thoughts buzzing behind her serious gray eyes, even as sleep started to weigh her down.

My thoughts were scattered too, after all that had happened in the last few days.

An incomplete mate bond wasn't the least of the complications. The music and the connection with my mate put me into a physical lull, the tension I always carried leaching out of me in the calm. Within a few moments, she was sound asleep. But as my mind continued to wander, I sensed something outside the cabin.

I stood slowly, carefully pulling out from under Shay's limp fingertips so as not to wake her. Padding to the window, I gazed out at the dark forest, where rain still came down in torrents.

There was absolutely no sign of trouble, and whatever I'd sensed had already faded. I was tempted to go out there and see if I could track it down, but Shay was asleep, and I wouldn't wake her to open the door for a passing suspicion.

I paced into the bathroom next, where Leigh was now dancing in her nightgown as she brushed out damp blonde hair. I whuffed, the quietest noise I could make to get her attention.

"What's up, Hairy?" she asked, not pausing her brush-strokes.

I whuffed again and jerked my muzzle toward the door.

"You thirsty? You can come in. Your water's right there." She pointed to the steel bowl Shay now carried for me. "I don't have any meat to give you at the moment, but—"

I shook my head, and she frowned.

"It's really inconvenient that you can't talk to us. Seriously." She dropped the brush on the counter and faced me fully. "It's not food, it's not water... Is Shay okay?" She stepped past me into the room, where she could see my mate sleeping soundly. She walked over and flipped the end of the comforter over her, then turned on a lamp so she could switch off the overhead light.

"Okay, she's good, Sir Barks A Lot." She patted me on the head and went to step by, but I stopped her. "Seriously, I don't know what else you need."

I walked to the door and stuck my nose to the crack, whuffing again.

"Uh, I'm already in my pjs, dude. Besides, I think we should all stay together. The guys aren't back, and we're in unfamiliar territory." She crossed her arms over her chest and stood her ground.

I whined, scratching the door this time.

"Fine. *Fine*. But you better piss quick and get back inside so I can hide before the guys get back. I don't need any more Gael time tonight, so if you're not back in three minutes, you can wait on the porch. You copy?"

I nodded quickly as she yanked open the door and followed me down the stairs on bare feet.

We crossed the living area toward the front door, but it opened before we reached it.

"Shit on a stick," Leigh muttered under her breath and spun on her heel.

She didn't make it two steps before Gael was in the doorway, shaking raindrops off his hair.

"Leigh? Everything okay?" His tone was terse, but I could see the concern in his tense pose, the sweep of his gaze over her retreating form.

"Fine." She waved over her shoulder, then reluctantly turned. "He needed to use the little wolf's room."

"The... oh. I can let him out."

"Thanks. Just knock, I guess, when he comes back in. We're all bunking together."

Gael nodded, then watched her every step until her legs finally disappeared from sight at the top of the stairs. He sighed, shoulders slumping as he turned to me. "Sorry. Come on."

He pulled open the front door, then followed me onto the porch. I didn't actually have to pee, so I stood at the edge and sniffed, checking for signs of the strange magic I'd sensed. There was no trace, and in this downpour, all physical signs would be washed away.

But my mate was safe and sound, and I didn't mind the

steady patter of rain on the porch roof, so I sat there and watched, waiting in case it came back.

Gael stood next to me, fingers laced behind his back in a rigid stance as he too stared out at the rain.

I was surprised several minutes later when he spoke, breaking the easy silence between us.

"I really messed it up with her. I don't... I'm not good with words." There was a lengthy pause. "But I want you to know that I don't want to hurt her. She's just this itch under my skin that I can't get rid of, even now that she hates me." He rocked back on heels as I looked up in surprise at the admission.

I whuffed an approving sound.

"We don't need to be enemies is all I'm saying. You're Reed's brother; you're not feral now. Hell, I don't think you need me to guard you anymore either. We don't need division in the pack, with killers out there probably gunning for Kane since his dad's gone."

At that, I nodded, in complete agreement. Packs were always strongest when all members worked together. Tiny rifts left unmended turned into chasms over time that you couldn't later cross.

I wished I could tell him that as long as he treated Leigh well, we'd be square. But he'd have to accept my nod and fill in the details on his own.

He froze and looked off toward the right.

"They're on the way back. Kane just told me through the pack bond."

Ahh.

We waited together, and for the first time, I found I didn't mind Gael's company all that much.

TWENTY-NINE

Shay

After a night of tossing and turning in an unfamiliar bed with scratchy blankets, I woke up with a deep-seated sense of unease wrapped around my chest like a vise grip. To ward it off, I curled around Dirge like he was my own personal body pillow.

Which, to be fair, he kind of was now.

But other body pillows didn't lick you in the face before your eyes were fully open.

"Eww! Dirge, that's gross."

"Ha! Get her again, Fluffmeister!" Leigh crowed happily from her position on the bottom bunk across from mine.

"You suck too," I groused as I shoved Dirge's nose away from me and pointed at her accusingly. "Can't a girl have five minutes to think before she jumps out of bed? That's not too much to ask, is it?"

"It is today, because I want out of this place. I'm ready to get to this island, meet some hot poly bears," she punctuated that statement with a salacious hip wiggle, "and then get back to the pack grounds. Frankly, I want Bri-Belle better and to move on with our lives."

I wasn't even going to ask what qualified as a *hot poly bear*. Nope, not happening, skipping over that like it never happened.

Hell, maybe I would get lucky and this would turn out to be just a sleep-fueled hallucination.

Although, wait.

"You want to stay in Alaska? Not Texas?" I sat up slowly, pondering the question and ignoring the strange feeling of foreboding in my chest. Did I want to go back to Texas? I hadn't even considered it in the whirlwind that was the gathering, Bri's bonding ceremony, and then getting shot.

Hell, when had my life gotten so crazy? I hadn't even composed a new piece since... well, since Texas.

"Heck no. I mean, Gael sometimes makes me pine for the days of PT at the little gym with no psychotic jealous wolf exes, but no. I couldn't leave Bri to turn into a wolf-cicle without us in the frozen tundra alone."

"True, and Kane can't leave his pack." Bri had married the Alpha of a different pack, which by default meant she was now a member of Pack Blackwater. But Leigh and I still belonged to the Johnson City pack, and it would be paperwork and a headache to officially move to Alaska. "I guess we're not going back to Texas, then."

The thought was strange, but deep down, I agreed with Leigh. Bri was family. While, yes, we were part of the Johnson City pack, they weren't my family. Three single females, we hadn't really fit in with the rest. All of us had no biological family left, so we'd become that for each other, and as such, we stuck out like sore thumbs.

Bri popped out of the bathroom, looking half-asleep. I needed a few minutes to think when I first woke up, but she took *not a morning person* to a whole different level. "What are you two talking about?" She rubbed her eyes, then wandered back toward the bed. Leigh grabbed her by the shoulders and gently turned her toward our luggage, piled in the corner.

"Get dressed."

"Right, right," she murmured, but still shot us an *answer the question* wave over her shoulder.

"Well, when this is all settled, we're still going to need to go back to Texas and pack. Also, I'm pretty sure there are transfer forms."

Brielle shimmied into a pair of jeans with a confused expression. "Transfer forms for what now?"

"Switching to Pack Blackwater."

She blinked slowly as she buttoned the pants, while I headed to the bathroom to get myself ready. Dirge rolled around on the empty bed, tongue lolling with glee at having the space to himself.

"Rub it in, why don't you?" I muttered.

I heard Bri gasp from the other room as I went through my quick morning routine. As soon as I opened the door to come out, she was there to squeeze me in the world's tightest hug.

"You're joining my pack. Oh my Goddess, I love you guys so much, you know that?"

She continued gushing and swiping at would-be tears while we finished dressing, but that was our Bri. She never expected kindness, even though she knew we were together for life. She wasn't getting rid of us, just because she married the most powerful male in the shifter world. Far from it.

BREAKFAST WAS a quick affair of granola bars and water bottles in the van back to the airstrip, but it sat like a rock in my gut. Brielle got a single bar of service, and sent off a text to her Aunt Kari's number, since we didn't know how long we'd be on

Ushagat Island. Hopefully, by the time we got back, she'd have responded.

Leigh had politely abstained from the paltry food options, citing airsickness and taking a motion sickness tablet Brielle gave her instead.

I pretended not to notice when Gael handed her a lemon-lime soda as soon as we got off the van. Whatever there was between those two, I hoped her false heat passed quickly and my bestie got back to her usual self soon.

The pilots had preflight checks to do, so I stood near the edge of the woods so Dirge could run before the flight. He wouldn't go far, even though we were well protected by the other males in the pack and in the middle of nowhere.

Leigh jogged over, grinning despite the early hour. "This airstrip is perfect for a run. Wanna go?"

I looked around, assessing the terrain. She was right; it was basically a flat field, with little dots of wildflowers clustered here and there making it idyllic. But I didn't share Leigh's obsession with fitness, so I declined with a shake of my head.

"Fine, but you're missing out. Runner's high, man. There's nothing like it."

"I'll stick to pack runs on the full moon, thanks." Shifters had such high metabolisms that we didn't really need to run or exercise to stay fit. She just liked it. Back in Texas, she'd worked as a personal trainer, and all her human clients had wondered at the fact that she had such strength "for a woman." Even that was less than half power, so she didn't give herself away as *other*.

Brielle wandered over a few minutes later, a cup of pale, steaming coffee in hand that she was sipping slowly. I could smell the hazelnut creamer from here. "Did Leigh try to get you to run too?"

"Yep." I rocked back on my heels, hands under my arms for warmth. If we were going to be moving here, I'd have to get used to the constant chill, even in warmer months.

"She's something else." She shook her head and took another sip.

We stood there in contented silence for a while, until a strange ripple of magic in the air brushed over my skin, instantly sending the hairs on my arms standing on end.

"Did you feel that?" I turned a worried gaze on Bri, but she shook her head.

"Feel what?"

"Strange magic. We should call—" I spun on my heel, but before I could wave the guys over, I saw him.

An unfamiliar man armed to the teeth bolted out of the woods, arrowing straight toward Brielle. He was unnaturally fast, even for a shifter. I didn't think, I didn't hesitate as he pulled a forearm-length dagger from the scabbard on his side.

"Brielle!" I screamed as I lunged, shoving her aside.

I saw it all peripherally, out of the corner of my eye. The men surging forward. Dirge's form swerving out of the woods, teeth bared in a horrible snarl.

But none of them made it; none of them intercepted. And as the attacker swung, a hot stab of pain tearing through my chest, everything narrowed down to that moment. Shock and searing agony, white-hot and drowning in its intensity. I looked up, meeting the man's crystalline gaze for a split second before he fell away, Dirge's teeth tearing out his throat.

But I couldn't turn my head, couldn't turn my gaze as my body grew cold.

Brielle was there, then, trying to stanch the flow of blood. My unflappable doctor bestie... She was crying.

Saying something I couldn't hear through the ringing in my ears.

Her hands scrabbled at me for a second before a man was there, dragging her away. Shock poured through me, pricking the bubble of pain I was in.

He was the man from my dream.

Dirge had finally shifted.

THIRTY

Dirge

I felt the explosion of power first. It was that same fleeting signature I'd felt the night before, but a hundred times stronger. I was already turning, my claws cutting through the soft loam of the forest floor to get back to my mate's side when I heard her scream.

I pushed myself harder, my wolf straining at his limits as I broke through the tree line. There she was, but I was too late.

Sorrow bombarded me as the scene clicked in my head. The airfield was a meadow, untamed and lovely from this angle. The sky overhead, which had been sunny when I'd left for a quick hunt, was overcast, heavy black clouds threatening to deposit their load over the airfield any second.

But all that was secondary. Shay, my beautiful Shay, had put herself between an assassin and her best friend. I watched as the wickedly curved dagger entered her flesh to the hilt, right over her heart.

I didn't stop to mourn, though. Lament what I knew marrow-deep was happening.

No, there was no hesitation as I leapt, taking out the throat of the fucker who would dare harm her. I ripped and tore, the spray of blood from his carotid bathing me in hot spurts as I clawed until I hit spine. When he was dead and glassy-eyed seconds later, I turned to her.

Brielle was there on the ground, trying to stop the bleeding, but it was too late. Shay's whole body was pale, shaking from shock and the overwhelming damage.

Between one heartbeat and the next, I was human. I didn't know how. The change slipped over me as easy as breathing, despite the years of struggle since I'd last worn my own skin. And then I was there, kneeling at her side, lifting her off the cold, damp grass.

"Shay, oh my Shay. I'm so sorry, my love. I'm here. I'm with you."

I cupped her face, her gray eyes fixed on mine as I held her, shuddering in my arms.

"I'm so sorry. I love you, I love you," I whispered as I stroked her soft cheek. I was unable to tear myself away and couldn't hear anyone else around me as the life faded from her eyes. Mere seconds later, she went limp, lips parted as if to say my name, though I knew she would never speak it, never again.

Something inside me broke, cracking right in two as her heart stopped.

I threw my head back and screamed my anguish at the thunderclouds. It was raw, and painful, and questioning. Why, when she was the most beautiful soul in this whole cursed world, *why* would they take her from me so soon? It wasn't enough. It would never be enough. Red haze prickled at the edges of my vision.

The wolf was half-rabid with pain and horror, fighting against my control. If I gave in, I would be feral once more. But this time, I had nothing left to live for. If I gave in, I would murder every single person in the clearing, and there would be no one who could stop me.

I couldn't give in, so I held him back with all the vicious

sorrow pounding through my veins. I had to give my mate the burial she deserved. I had to hold on for a little longer, long enough to give her a warrior's funeral—an honor she deserved, to the bitter end, as she protected those she loved—and then bare my neck for Kane to take me out before I could hurt anyone else. The pain in my chest was so horrible, my wolf would burn the world to ash and never stanch it, even as he reveled in the flames.

It was the only way.

It was exactly as the Fetya had foretold, except—

Pure-white light blasted out of Shay, brighter than the sun and as violent as any explosion. I screwed my eyes tightly shut, but held on for dear life as her body jerked against my chest.

This time, I heard the screams, but there was nothing I could do. The threads of time seemed to warp, as if someone was snatching the weft in a way it was never meant to go. Whether a minute passed or twelve hours, I could never say. All I knew was that when the feeling passed and I cracked my eyes open again, the light was slowly fading, sinking into her skin.

THIRTY-ONE

Shay

M y entire body felt like it was floating. There was nothing at all except a tantalizing scent. Cedarwood, with hints of bergamot and something distinctly male and delicious. I wanted to roll around in it, wrap myself up in it like my own personal cocoon on this sea of... Hold up.

I couldn't float. We were in a field. That was illogical.

Wait.

We were in a field, waiting on... our plane. Preflight checks? Yes. So why was I floating? And who was I sniffing?

I opened my eyes, and a concerned, handsome face stared down at me. One I'd seen before in a *very* hot dream.

And just like that, everything clicked.

The attacker, Brielle, me getting stabbed, Dirge shifting— I gasped and clutched at my chest, but there was no pain, no wound that I could feel, just a torn shirt sticky with half-dry blood. How long had I been out? I really had to stop getting mortally wounded. It sucked.

"Not long, my love."

"I— But the wound is gone. How has it not been long?" I mumbled the first idiot thing that came out of my mouth before clamping my lips shut. I was clearly not fully back with it yet and lay dazed in his arms as I searched his eyes.

Goddess, he was beautiful. He'd probably hate that description—shifter males didn't like anything that poked at their masculinity, as far as I could tell—but it was the truth. His hair was tousled, dark chestnut and straight, almost to his chin. He had olive skin and the most piercing hazel eyes I'd ever seen. And now that I was seeing them in the daylight, I knew without a doubt that the dream had been a mere shadow of the man.

He was stunning and powerful and *wholly* overwhelming.

"I don't know. It's a miracle."

"Umm..." I tried to bring myself back around to the present, but when he was staring at me so intently, it was hard to focus on anything except my very needy pussy. She wanted him, pronto.

Chill out, Shay. It's not a good look to be drooling over him while you're covered in blood.

"A miracle? More like some badass magic. Holy shit, Shay. You got stabbed. It was bad. Blood everywhere, instant shock, you were pale and fading, and you *fucking died on us*—we were all gutted, by the way—then BAM! Bright lights and holy shit, you're awake again." Leigh's eyes were wide, hair wild as if she'd run her hands through it a hundred times in the minutes I'd been out.

Minutes? It just didn't make sense.

"Leigh, if I died, I wouldn't be talking to you right now."

I scanned the group, waiting for confirmation, but Dirge was still holding me—in his lap, I realized belatedly. When I moved to sit next to him, he held me tighter around the waist, as if I were going to disappear into a wisp of smoke if he let me go.

I mean, I guess if he thought I just died, I couldn't blame him. But that clearly wasn't the case. Hello, I'm still here.

But when my gaze landed on Brielle, and I saw her shell-shocked expression, I started to believe it a little bit more.

"Is everyone okay?" I asked, fingers twining into Dirge's chin-length hair. Even if I did feel awkward sitting on his lap with all our pack mates around, touching him soothed me on a primal level. Anchored me.

Aroused me very inappropriately for the number of our friends staring at us.

"Everyone but the assassin, thanks to you," he said, nodding toward the corpse a few feet away.

I looked only long enough to see that there was, in fact, a dead body not ten feet from where we sat in the grass, before quickly jerking my gaze away from the grisly sight.

"Assassin?" My brain processed slowly, as if I were coming back to the present in a big bubble of molasses or honey.

"Assassin," Gael agreed, from his position kneeling next to the body. He seemed the least rattled of us all, focused on the task at hand and not on whatever had revived me.

Holy hell, had I really *died*? It didn't seem possible. I felt fine. Better than fine, actually. Energetic. Ready to take out a dozen assassins.

"He's carrying a sword, the knife he used on Shay."

Dirge growled beneath me at that reminder, so I brought my other hand up to rest on his bare chest, trying to calm him as Gael continued.

"A pouch full of all kinds of vials, possibly poison? To be determined. He's also got a pistol, both wolfsbane and devil's trap bullets, and a sat phone."

I blinked at the laundry list.

"Is he a shifter?" Kane asked from where he was crouched next to Brielle, hand on her shoulder. She had both arms wrapped around her knees, and she couldn't seem to stop staring at me.

"It's harder to tell postmortem once the essence fades, obviously, but I don't think so. He's got pointed ears and magic I've never felt before. The ears narrow it down to elf, goblin—mixed, given he's not green—fae, or... I'm not sure. Pixie, maybe? He doesn't smell like any of those."

"Drakenia guild." Dirge spoke, still holding me tightly yet cautiously, like I was a precious china doll he was scared to break. "Rare to see them this far from Europe, but clearly, the payout was big, since he's here."

I blinked at that. I'd never heard of the Drakenia guild, and I had no idea what kind of payout he was talking about.

"But why would a Drakenia killer be here in Alaska? Do you think they were after Kane, trying to wipe out Alpha Kosta's entire line?"

"He was running straight toward Bri," I said.

"And you paid for my life with yours," she whispered, tears flowing freely down her cheeks. "If it weren't for you, Kane and I would *both* be dead."

Oh yeah. They'd bonded, which meant when she died, he would too. Shit. My best friend was going to have an even larger target on her back now that they were bonded. It was way easier to take out the high alpha's weaker mate than the most powerful male shifter in the entire world. But knowing that intellectually and watching it happen was very different.

"But I'm okay, Bri. And so are you." I brushed off her tearful appreciation, which wasn't usual for me, but the discomfort I had was growing by the minute, as everyone stared at me as if I were some sort of miracle. I was no miracle, just the same messed-up, shy female they knew and loved despite my idiosyncrasies. And I wanted to keep it that way.

I looked up at Dirge, a silent cry for help in my eyes.

Goddess's hem, he was human. Full, rock-hard abs, stunning eyes, chin-length hair, *human*. Real, solid, and not a dream.

I mean, he might have been a wet dream, but he was not a figment of my imagination.

"You shifted," I whispered, not wanting to have the conversation publicly, but nobody was moving, and I had to say it.

"I did," he murmured against my hair, tucking me closer and holding me right under his chin. He stroked my back soothingly, as if I were a spooked fawn about to bolt.

Which was fairly accurate, so, wise on his part.

"But the vision—"

"The vision came true before my eyes, Shay. You, collapsing under the clouds, life force draining away in my arms. Down to the light, every detail was as I saw three years ago."

"Except I'm alive."

"Except that," he said with a nod.

"So that's it? We're free?"

He tensed beneath me and didn't answer. But I didn't have the chance to push further, because the pilots came jogging over.

"Alpha Kane, sir, I'm sorry to interrupt, but we've got a small window in which to get off the ground with this weather. I recommend we load everyone up—including, err, the body—and get back to Pack Blackwater territory to sort this out."

"So not the Kodiak? But they're waiting for us," I murmured.

Dirge shook his head against my hair. "No, it's not safe. You need to be surrounded by pack until we figure this out."

I shoved back from his chest so I could see him better. "We don't have that luxury, Dirge. We need to figure out what's going on with Bri, and heck, I'd like to know what's going on with me too. If Jada can tell us, we still need to go."

Brielle pushed to her feet on shaking legs, but her gaze was firm when she leveled it on me. "No. I've put you in enough danger. You two are going home. Kane can take me to see Jada once you're settled safely back on pack grounds."

Anger burned through me, pushing away the last of the groggy confusion. I moved to stand, and this time, Dirge let me. He was on his feet a half second later, hand on my waist as he stood at my back. He was solid and comforting, and I resisted the urge to lean back into him. I had to stand on my own two feet right now.

"No. You don't get to just shut us out, not now, not ever. We are your pack, your *family*, and you're not going through this alone. Leigh and I knew this would be dangerous," I said, surprising myself with my own vehemence. But damn it, she wasn't allowed to martyr herself. I'd been scared and alone, and I would wrap myself around her like a rabid spider monkey before I'd let her go off into danger alone.

"You *died*, Shay. Dead. No pulse, I checked. You didn't sign up to die for me! And you shouldn't have to!" She was yelling, backing away as if she was about to bolt for the plane, as if that would stop us. But Leigh, with her infinite near-mind-reading senses, was there first.

Leigh wrapped her in a hug, taking the spot Kane had vacated to speak with the pilot and deal with the assassin's body. "It's okay, Bri. She's not dead. Goddess knows how *any* of this works right now, but she's alive."

I crossed the distance, adding myself to the hug ball. Brielle sniffled into our shoulders, shaking with sobs. When she finally spoke again, her voice was small, terrified.

"I couldn't save her, though, Leigh. I couldn't save her. Her blood is on *my* hands."

The words made me suddenly aware of my own bloody, sticky clothes. But I'd already hugged her, so I just stayed where I was.

"Her blood is not on your hands. It's on that asshole assassin over there." Leigh jerked her thumb toward the corpse, which was being carried to the plane like a sack of potatoes. "Whoever sent him? Also responsible. You? Not responsible.

You're the victim here. Do you hear me? Doctors—even omega ones—can't save everybody. And trying to will drive you crazy."

Brielle bit her bottom lip and looked over at me, the unspoken question hanging between us.

"I agree. This was not on you," I said, holding her gaze the entire time.

She shuddered again, the two of us hemming her in until Kane returned to gently pry her from our grip.

"You should listen to your friends, baby. You're in a position of power now. People always try to tear down those they see as above them. All you can do is lead well and surround yourself with good people." He quickly smiled at the two of us. "And you've already done that."

She nodded, going gratefully back into his arms.

That familiar pang started to hit me, but then I remembered. And when I turned, Dirge was there, eyes glued to me as if I were about to disappear. There was still a small distance between us—it was odd, knowing him as a wolf, but now having him standing before me all manly and muscled— distractingly so—and I was suddenly shy.

He stepped forward, hands clasped behind his back politely as he stopped in front of me. "May I escort you back to the plane? The assassin has been loaded, and Reed bagged up the knife for lab analysis as soon as we can secure a courier."

I nodded and took his proffered hand. When our fingers laced together, something inside me settled ever so slightly into place.

THIRTY-TWO

Shay

After locating a courier, the world's fastest shower, a plane ride, and Dirge inhaling about a dozen sandwiches later —he'd really missed human food while he was living as a wolf for three years—we landed on Ushagat Island.

It was lovely and serene, the wind whipping off the Alaskan Gulf bringing the taste of salt to my lips and the smell of grass to my nose as we stepped off the plane onto the undeveloped grassy knoll. The whitecaps on the sea couldn't distract from the three imposing figures waiting for us.

They were the largest males I'd ever seen, broad through the shoulders and thickly muscled. Even their necks were as big around as one of my thighs. They each wore their hair buzzed on the sides with a bit of length on top and had deep, terra-cotta-toned skin.

The one in the middle stepped forward, extending a hand to Kane first with a wide smile. No one would have been remiss to call it slightly predatory, but it seemed like the man just couldn't help it.

"Welcome to Ushagat Island. I am Finn, and these are my sleuth mates, Hudson and Dax." He gestured as he spoke, and the correct male nodded and stepped forward as they were named. Once the first round of handshakes was finished with Kane, they moved down the line.

Our travels and meetings with various leaders were starting to take on a familiar pattern, and I found myself bored but simultaneously acutely aware of Dirge's presence at my shoulder as we waited to greet the three emissaries.

Heat radiated off him, even in this cool weather. He wore a shirt of Gael's, plain black and stretched tight over the lean muscles of his chest. Reed had offered, but Dirge had shrugged off his more formal button-ups in favor of enforcer gear.

I could still see the shape of those muscles, both from my dream and from waking up in his arms a few hours ago. But somehow, it didn't feel real yet. I'd just started to accept what life would be like going forward with a shifted mate, and it was like whiplash now that everything had turned on its head in a moment.

It was good, though. Overwhelming too. I let the side of my hand brush his, the barest touch, just to feel that energy flow between us. He smiled and cut a quick glance my way as he felt the slight touch.

But it was the return trace of his fingertips over the inside of my wrist that sent my heart hammering, my pulse racing in sheer, burning *want*. Which was utterly ridiculous. Wrists weren't sexy, and we'd had sex twice already. Dream sex, at least. So why did I feel like we were back to the beginning, like hormone-fueled teenagers in the early days of lust and exploration?

Mate bonds were wild. I suddenly had all-new empathy for what Brielle had gone through, not to mention all the stress of pack dynamics on top of these insane emotions. I cast her a quick glance, but she was smiling kindly and shaking the massive bear shifter's hand as if this was what she did all day, every day.

Finn—no, Hudson—stepped up to shake my hand then, and I welcomed the distraction from my own untethered thoughts.

"Hello," I murmured, extending my hand with a polite smile. I ignored the small growl from Dirge as Hudson returned the gesture with a nod.

"Lovely to meet you...?" He trailed off as our hands touched, but it was me who startled as a near-electric shock passed between us, and his eyes started to glow ominously.

Bears and wolves had some similarities, of course, but the sight of amber ursine eyes peering down into my soul made me want to hide behind Dirge like a big fat chicken. He was *other*, and my wolf's hackles were up at his unwelcome attention.

Dirge must have felt the same because, with supernatural speed, he flew between us, knocking Hudson's hand from mine.

In my shock, I hadn't even realized he was still holding it until the contact was severed, and it felt like the tight band around my chest released.

"You," Hudson spoke, his tone guttural and deep with the influence of his bear as he looked eerily past Dirge to me. "You're unbonded."

"Umm," I stammered, confused and concerned that he could even tell. Was he going to make an issue of it like Iaoin had? That hadn't ended well.

I mean, nobody died, but that was a pretty low bar.

"She has mate marks," Dirge said with a warning growl, eyes locked on Hudson.

"Everything okay, brother?" Finn stepped up to Hudson's side as I shrank back.

Hudson shook his head as if confused while his eyes faded back to human with painstaking slowness.

"I'm sorry, that was strange..." His brows were drawn down as if he didn't know what had just passed between us.

What the hell was happening? I had lived my adult life in

170

blissful invisibility from pretty much all males that I didn't come on to first. I only lost my virginity because I was lonely at a full-moon ceremony and approached one of the less dominant, lonely pack members first. We'd dated for a bit after that, but there was no spark when the sun was shining, and we'd broken it off within a few months.

Now three very dominant shifter males had locked onto me within a matter of weeks, and I was freaking out.

As if he could sense it, Dirge turned his back on the other shifters—a bold move, which my wolf rumbled her approval of —and put his hands on my upper arms.

"It's going to be fine, muzică mea." His tone was soothing, and I found myself swaying toward him. My hands landed on his chest, and the world seemed to stop shifting under me. I was okay; he was okay. Hudson had turned to confer with his pack mates, and I pointedly ignored the hand gestures toward me.

After a moment of calming down with Dirge, I nodded, and he slipped an arm around my shoulders. We turned to face the group together. Leigh shot me a supportive thumbs-up, which I returned. We were just going to pretend my hands weren't shaking and my wolf wasn't pushing me to shift.

The three bears broke up their discussion, turning toward us with apologetic smiles and raised hands.

"I apologize, Shay. My bear is usually under much better control than that. The rest of us will refrain from touching you, if that doesn't offend?" Hudson said with a genial smile.

"No, that's fine, thanks." I let out a relieved sigh. Touching people was dangerous at the moment. Though talking was a bit easier with Dirge at my side.

"We appreciate your understanding," Reed said with a Hollywood-worthy smile. He slipped into pack politician mode with ease, smiling widely and taking over the conversation.

I was going to have to send the man a fruit basket for that.

He clapped Hudson on the shoulder as they led us away from the plane toward a path cut through a rocky outcropping that loomed high overhead. When Hudson threw back his head and loosed a roar-like laugh, I finally breathed normally.

Dirge was a staunch, comforting presence at my side as we followed the narrow, pebble-strewn path.

THIRTY-THREE

Dirge

The Kodiak encampment was sparse to the untrained eye, but the bare cave opening they led us to opened to a world of hidden wonder. Skylights dotted the ground with natural light as we walked deeper into the cave, the narrow mouth of the tunnel quickly opening into a wide, spacious cavern. The ceiling and walls were crusted with sparkling gems, as if we'd walked directly into a geode. Oversized furniture that looked hand hewn was dotted around the space, and more bear shifters milled about, talking and laughing.

They fell quiet as they noticed us, though, joviality turning to curious whispers.

"We'll wait here for Jada," Finn said, turning that sharp smile on us again.

Bears were strange, and my wolf's hackles were half-raised at the light in his eyes as he appraised our group.

Unlike wolves, who found fated mates blessed by the Moon Goddess, bears mated in groups. One female to every three males. The thought of it made me want to tear someone's arm off—which I would if they touched Shay again—but it was the way of things for their species.

If I was reading the situation correctly, Finn, Hudson, and Dax were an unmated sleuth still on the hunt for their female.

When Finn's gaze settled on Shay for a little too long, I lifted my lip and snarled, letting the wolf's eyes glow through mine. He was still close to the surface, and after so long in fur, I'd have no trouble calling him forward if we needed to remind a bear—or three—that wolves did *not* share.

He felt my wolf and moved on, keeping his hands carefully behind his back, clasped and out of danger. Dax, though, had a wildness to him that I recognized, and while he wasn't looking at Shay, he was edging closer and closer to where she stood.

As if he was going to just accidentally-on-purpose bump into her.

What had Hudson told them, when they were in that circle? My wolf went from half-alert to fully on edge as the bear took yet another step toward my mate.

"Shay," I murmured, getting her attention.

She turned to me at once, tidily moving out of the bear's path. "Isn't it the most beautiful thing you've ever seen?" she asked, eyes glowing with excitement as she pointed to the crystalline ceiling.

I had to chuckle at that.

"Not by half, muzică mea."

"Oh, I—" She seemed disappointed, but I stopped her with a finger to her lips.

"A pretty rock pales in comparison to the true beauty standing right in front of me."

Her eyes went wide as understanding hit her, and a blush stained her cheeks. The scent of her heated arousal took her sweet scent and turned it utterly irresistible. My wolf rumbled in my chest, voicing his own approval of our perfect one. I couldn't resist the urge to stroke my thumb over her bottom lip, her lips parting under the tiniest caress.

I was so wrapped up in our little bubble of discovery that it confused me when she lurched forward, squeaking in surprise as she fell against me.

But the confusion evaporated as I looked up and saw Dax at her back, hands on her hips and nose buried in her hair as he reveled in the scent of her arousal.

I saw red.

The snarl that ripped out of me at the insult to my mate was inhuman.

"Oh, shit on a stick." Leigh swore like a sailor as I pushed Shay toward her, barely controlling my wolf, who was clawing to burst from my skin.

The bear didn't register the threat immediately, his odd, ursine eyes still locked on my mate, mouth slightly open as desire poured off him in a cloud, the obvious competition making my wolf even more rabid to tear into him.

His hands had shifted to claws, though, and when I barreled into his shoulder at full speed, he swiped at me with those two-inch long daggers. His body shuddered as he toppled to the ground beneath me, but I didn't relent.

I had the upper hand, and while I lost some advantage to his sheer bulk, when my fist connected with his jaw, he felt it.

I only got in three strikes before my pack mates dragged me off the downed bear, who was now bleeding from his lip as well as a cut on his eyebrow. My knuckles throbbed and had split in several places, but it was a good burn as I shook them out, ready for round two.

"He put his hands on her. *Scented her.*" My voice was not my own, the deep, angry wolf inside demanding that we tear his head off for the affront.

"We saw, Dirge. It's going to be okay."

"He has to pay," I snapped, finally realizing that it was my brother standing in front of me.

"He does, I agree. But right now, your mate is scared and she needs you." I reeled back as if he'd punched me in the gut, scanning for Shay as if my life depended on the sight of her.

The world narrowed to nothing when our eyes locked, and the scent of her terror registered in my nose. I broke Reed's grip and ran to her, but she flinched back from me when I moved to wrap her in my arms.

It was a blow like none I'd ever experienced. *She was afraid of me.*

"Easy, killer. She's spooked. Somebody just manhandled her without her consent. It's not you."

Leigh's words sank in, and fury bathed me again. The desire to turn to that bear and finish what I'd started nearly pulled me under. The shaking of an impending shift started in my hands, then my arms, as I willed my wolf to stay put.

"Ah-ah, that's the wrong direction. Calm, please," Leigh said sternly, and it clicked that Shay hadn't said a word. Her expression was drawn, her face pale. She was shaking as her friend hugged her, and her wolf's golden gaze held mine, clearly on the edge of her control.

"Muzică mea, please, tell me what to do," I begged. I hated seeing her like this. The urge to turn back and keep pummeling the bear was overwhelming, but I knew that wouldn't actually help Shay, and she would always be my top priority.

She shook her head, a tear sliding down her cheek.

"I'm here, I'm here if you'll still have me. I'm so sorry."

A single, shaking hand extended toward me, and I took it gratefully, chafing it between mine to warm her.

Many voices twined behind us, rising to a chaotic din, but I ignored them. In this, I trusted my pack. I could turn my back and focus on my mate and let the diplomats do what they had to.

Besides, Kane should have enough juice to handle the bears if it really came to that.

But it didn't.

"What is the meaning of this?" The feminine voice was low but filled with pure steel. It brought everyone else to instant silence, the weight of power subduing the gathered bears as if they were kittens, not apex predators.

"It was our fault, Jada. We have failed you and submit ourselves to your hand for punishment." Finn's chagrined voice spoke into the silence, and I turned halfway so I could see both them and Shay as the thuds of knees hitting rock echoed through the chamber. Finn and Hudson held Dax between them, his shoulders bowed as if with great effort to stay down before the leader of the Kodiaks.

"Explain yourselves." Her eyes were cold, with no hint of softness in them for the errant males. I placed myself in front of Shay when I realized three *more* giant bears loomed behind Jada.

They were older, with none of the youthful vigor the three cubs who'd been sent to greet us had, and I relaxed a fraction when I realized that they were her sleuth—her three mates. They stood guard much as I did and had no interest in harming Shay.

"It's strange, Jada. I just shook her hand, and it was like she zapped me," Hudson said, sounding apologetic.

I stiffened, shocked at the assertion. She'd zapped him? How the heck had that happened, and what did it mean?

"I mentioned it to my sleuth mates, and they agreed that we should all shake her hand, to see if she responded to all of us."

Fury built in my chest, scalding me like acid. These fools thought that my mate was theirs. What else could be the purpose of all of them touching her? Now I wanted to rip *all* their heads off, not just the handsy one's.

"These are our honored guests, come to seek my counsel." Jada's voice rang with indignation, and Hudson ducked his head. "And I sincerely hope that the rest of this explanation involves you being respectful and speaking with the girl about your suspicions rather than doing something asinine."

"It's my fault, Jada." Dax's voice was heavy with his bear when he met her eyes, and I noted with concern that fur had sprouted along both his forearms, thick and golden brown as the bear fought to break free. "I was just going to stand next to her, try to catch her scent without risking the touch. You know I have poor control."

The woman nodded, eyes narrowing.

"But when I got a whiff, I couldn't stop. She smells like heaven, like home. I— I touched her. Grabbed her. If there is any shame brought to my sleuth, and to you, I bear the burden of it." His head dropped, hanging off his shoulders with the weight of it.

Meanwhile, my wolf was clawing at me even harder. She smelled like heaven? I'd give him a piece of hell for daring to take liberties with my female. Shay was *not* his. Gael sidled up to my side.

"Easy, friend. They are not going to take her from you. Jada is reputed to be a fair, wise leader, and she will deal with him appropriately. You got your licks in. Now it's time to let it go."

My head swiveled toward him as my lip lifted, the snarl right there on the edge, fangs fully descended in my mouth.

He held up both hands in a placating gesture. "You've come so far in a short amount of time. I'd hate to see you slip back because of this."

The words struck me like a battering ram. Was I slipping backward? My vision was still red tinged, my wolf on a hair trigger.

Shit, shit, shit.

I couldn't let myself go feral again, not now, not ever. The mocking voice in the back of my head taunted me, eager to watch me fall.

You're a feral wolf. Finding your mate isn't going to change that.

Once a loose cannon, always a loose cannon.

You skirted the Fetya's prophecy. Going feral again and killing her yourself would be a solid punishment for that.

Oh, Goddess save me from my own critical thoughts. But once I'd thought them, they wouldn't let me go. We *had* skirted the Fetya's vision. Shay, my beautiful Shay, was alive and whole. Smiling at me and looking up at me like I hung the stars to shine on her.

She was supposed to be dead, and they would exact that price. But would it be me who killed her, with my own lack of control? Or would they strike in some other, unexpected way?

I didn't know, and the fear that took hold of me then was worse than anything I'd ever felt, except the pain of her lying limp and bloody in my arms.

I never wanted to live through that again.

"Is she not mated to the one who guards her? It's extremely unusual for a wolf to mate with a bear sleuth. It's not in their nature to live as we do." She gestured lightly to the three men bracketing her, then to the clustered youths kneeling before her.

"We don't know, Jada." The last one spoke up. Finn, the leader of our star-crossed welcoming party. "We've never felt anything like it. I have not touched her, and even so, I feel the pull."

The woman's brows drew down as she peered past me to where Shay now stood more solidly, still hanging on to Leigh.

Jada paced forward, her complement of mates flowing behind her like water. Before I could move to intercept, Gael grabbed me by the biceps.

"Hold tight. She's not going to hurt Shailene, and she might know what's going on."

I nearly broke a tooth, I ground my jaw so hard. But I held on, letting the touch of a pack mate steady me. It was foreign after so long being on my own, but we were wolves, and some things ran deeper than others. The need for comforting touch was the deepest of them all.

I watched in tortured silence as Jada approached Shay, whose coloring was thankfully starting to return to normal. She nervously tucked a wild, curly strand of hair behind her ear as the bear leader stopped in front of her. Jada sized her up silently for a moment, before extending her hand.

Brielle stepped forward, shaking her head. "Shay, you don't have to do this. You've been through a lot today, and this can wait for another time. Or never." Her words were firm, and that still-water scent I'd come to associate with her was charged, as if a lightning bolt had struck the pond and ozone hung heavy in the cave.

"It's okay," my brave mate whispered. Shay slowly raised her hand to Jada's, even as she leaned back, away from the contact.

When their palms met, nothing happened that I could tell. But Jada's eyes widened, and she held on tightly with both hands for a moment before pulling away.

"Those imbeciles mistook a fae's warning as mating energy. Goddess have mercy on me." She shook her head and rounded on the young males, but my brain was stuck like a truck in a mud pit.

Fae warning? What the fuck was she on about?

Jada dressed down the males for a solid two minutes before sending them out of the cave with an escort and a promise of punishment after our delegation had left their island. Once they were gone, the tension around us eased. The rest of the bears in the cave all went back to their happy chatter since the show was apparently over.

One of Jada's mates spoke next. "If you will please follow us, we've prepared a small reception for you in our private quarters." He nodded politely and held up a hand the size of a dinner plate to indicate the direction.

I wanted to take Shay's hand or wrap my arm around her

again, but I hesitated, the surety that my touch was unwelcome stopping me. As long as I lived, I'd never forget the way she looked when she jerked back from me as if I was going to hit her.

So I stayed at Gael's side and followed the bears, leaving Shay in her friends' care.

THIRTY-FOUR

Shay

Jada's private quarters were surprisingly luxurious. Though that probably shouldn't have been completely unexpected. Not everyone lived close to the land, like Inuksuk and his people, and many shifters were very wealthy. Compound interest did wonders when you lived for centuries on end. Plus, Reed wasn't even that old, and he was already rich as fuck.

The receiving room was full of ornate furniture with scrollwork details on the back, plush rugs underfoot, and heavy gold sconces on the walls. It reeked of Old World wealth, sitting right on the verge of overpowering the natural beauty of the rock the room seemed to be carved from.

But as I settled into an extremely comfortable settee, I found myself grateful for it. I did at least resist the urge to pull up my feet and curl into a protective ball, but only just barely.

I felt like one giant, exposed nerve, walking around frayed and vulnerable. The last thing I wanted to do was be polite and social when I really needed quiet and solitude after getting manhandled.

So many memories were fighting to drown me, tugging at

my clothes and pulling me under the surface until my wolf came out and saved me.

Because that was what she did. She guarded me as closely as my friends and wasn't afraid to take control if I froze up.

She'd done it before.

A server pressed a cup of steaming coffee into my hand, and I accepted it. The first sip had me closing my eyes, willing the world to fade back just a little bit so I could grit my way through this. It's funny how something as small as a cup of coffee can ground you with its familiarity in times of stress. But after a few sips, I felt marginally better.

Jada settled on the couch across from us that was oversized and large enough to hold her entire sleuth comfortably, though only one of them sat.

To my chagrin, I realized Dirge was hovering a few feet away as well. I was a woman divided; part of me wanted to drag him close, bury my face in his neck, and let him shield me from everything. The other part—the scared little girl who'd been hurt by bad men—she wanted to be alone. Safe. Untouched.

I didn't know which part was bigger, even though I was certain Dirge would never harm me. At least not on purpose. When the server had finished his rounds and bowed to Jada, he backed out of the room and one of her mates shut the door behind him.

Once we were alone, she didn't waste any time.

"So, is your fae wolf the one who's brought you here, High Alpha? I may have misunderstood, but when Inuksuk contacted me I thought he said it was your own mate who had power troubles." She let her gaze linger on Brielle, then flicked it back over to me in question.

There was curiosity there, but all I felt was confusion. She'd said that before, when I shook her hand, and I had no fucking clue what she was talking about.

"I'm not fae," I blurted. I immediately regretted it, as every

183

eye turned in my direction. I was getting really friggin' sick of feeling like a bug under a microscope today.

Belatedly, I realized it might be construed as rude to argue with this leader we'd come to beg a favor from. But... she had to be mistaken. I was a garden-variety wolf shifter, with nothing but a terrible childhood and excellent friends to distinguish me from any other.

She arched one eyebrow, as imperious as any queen while she sipped her coffee and stared at me. Stared *into* me, more like.

"You *are* fae, in part. Greater fae, not a lesser. But it is curious that you don't know it. The relation would have to be close, for you to be as strong as you are. A parent, grandparent at the absolute least."

I was stunned into silence. She thought I had a fae parent?

It wasn't really possible for me to argue the point since I didn't *know* my parents, but if I wasn't a wolf shifter—*fully* a wolf shifter, I corrected as my brain tried to process what she was saying—wouldn't someone have noticed before now?

Unease filled me at the idea of not being who or what I thought I was. Wouldn't I have known?

"How is that possible?" Bri asked from her position seated next to Kane.

Jada shrugged, while one of her men chuckled. "The usual way, I suppose. Fae wander into this world eager to mingle with all the different species. They are a sexually curious race. Wolves are often highly physical. It's not the worst match I've ever heard of."

I really didn't want to think about my existence being started by a randy fae and a lonely wolf's one-night stand. If that was true, why didn't I know at least my wolf parent?

No, there had to be more to the story, surely. I stayed silent, not eager to hash out my childhood trauma for this stranger's perusal. Besides, we were here for Brielle, not me. Although...

"If I were part fae, would that explain why everyone thought I died and then I came back? Or why a wolfsbane bullet wound would heal too quickly?" I forced the words out through gritted teeth.

Out of the corner of my eye, I saw Dirge tense, focus fastened onto me, instead of Jada. I couldn't return his gaze, though. Not yet.

Guilt gnawed at me because I knew it had to be hurting him, this distance. I hadn't meant to flinch when he tried to touch me. I truly hadn't. But sometimes instinct just took over. And if anyone could understand that, surely it was him?

I made myself a promise to tell him that as soon as we had some privacy for a real conversation. It would suck, but... he was my mate. He deserved the truth.

She pursed her lips and squinted at me, then turned to whisper something in one of her mate's ears. He whispered something in return, and anxiety began to crawl up my throat like a spider. I could feel the flush spreading through me under their scrutiny.

She contemplated long enough that I was on the verge of self-combustion by the time she finally spoke again.

"Not much is known about fae-wolf hybrids, frankly. But yes, I think it's possible. But more than that, it's possible you may be immortal, as are the fae. A strong enough sire or dam, the right circumstances... that mortal wound may have triggered your fae side to finally express itself after a lifetime of latency."

My brain was running slower than nineties dial-up. It was all static and off-pitch screeches up there.

Immortal?

Surely not. Wolves were long-lived, yes. But did I want to stay the same while everyone I knew got old and died? We'd just seen Inuksuk in his frail later years, so the image of the future was very fresh. Hell, one of my besties could die in childbirth. It happened more often than anyone would like to think about.

Did I want to stand by and watch that, unable to grow or change myself?

And my mate... was a wolf. A wolf who would also grow old one day. How could I be immortal if I was spirit-bound to a mortal being?

I couldn't even begin to comprehend that possibility. So, I did what every sane, twenty-something woman did in untenable situations. I packed that shit in a mental box, duct-taped it shut, and stuck it on a shelf for another, less insane time.

I was going to live close to a thousand years anyway; I'd deal with year one thousand and one when I got there, if I got there. Besides, there was so much unknown. She could be wrong.

Right?

I finally broke down and let my eyes flick to where Dirge stood, still as a statue, but gazing at me with shock and awe. *Shit.*

How would he feel about being mated to some sort of fae hybrid? I didn't know who my parents were; that hadn't changed. But when they were both wolf shifters, it wasn't really news. This... Would it change how he felt about me?

The carpet was suddenly very interesting as Kane cleared his throat from his position behind Bri's seat on the couch.

"Thank you for that insight, Jada. We appreciate your wealth of knowledge on so many topics."

Jada inclined her head magnanimously, a small smile teasing her lips. "But that's not why you called me, so let's get down to business."

Kane smiled in response. "My mate has a concerning curse that is affecting her health, but also some... different abilities. Did Inuksuk tell you—"

Jada lifted one hand, stopping him in his tracks. "Boy, I'm

not getting any younger. You think your mate is an omega, and you want me to verify."

Kane looked like he was about to choke on something at her bluntness. "That... would be excellent."

Jada nodded gravely, attention now pinned to Brielle. "I can do that. Do you know why?"

"From what we understand, you've met one in the past."

The idea of her being old enough to have *met* an omega and still being alive? Wild. Wolves lived on average a thousand years. Some, like Inuksuk, made it over twelve hundred. But the Omega War happened... in the sixteen hundreds, and even before the wars they were incredibly rare. It was possible for a wolf to live their entire life and never meet one.

"That's correct. What you don't know is that she was my brother's mate. She was killed in the purge after the Omega War, taking their entire sleuth with her."

The room fell silent as that sank in.

Holy hell.

The sorrow in her eyes was fresh, though the war was centuries past.

"I want to be very clear with you what you risk if you pursue this path. There is much sorrow and much pain. Strife will dog your every step if it's true and it becomes known."

Brielle let out a shaky breath, but she was steady when she answered, and I'd never been prouder of my friend.

"If it's true, I'd rather be armed with knowledge than caught by surprise." Brielle's back was straight, her jaw tight with determination.

"Very well, then. I will help you. Do you wish to know your gifts as well?"

"I... Is that an option? To find out?"

Jada nodded.

Brielle looked up at Kane, and I could tell they were

speaking through the mate bond as the silence stretched a moment.

Brielle took his hand before turning back to Jada. "Yes, if it's possible, we'd like to know."

"Very well. There's a purification ritual, and then you'll be presented before the Moon Goddess for her to reveal your gifts. Anyone who wishes to attend must complete the purification." She leveled us all with a stern look. "It's not for the faint of heart, so consider wisely if your presence is necessary. In the meantime, you'll be shown to your temporary quarters."

With a wave of her hand, we were dismissed.

THIRTY-FIVE

Dirge

We were led to a private corridor with two doors on either side of the hallway and one at the end. As soon as our bear guide left us with the sheet of purification instructions, we all stood awkwardly in the corridor until people started heading into the five available rooms.

It was clear that they intended each couple to room together, but I wasn't sure that was a good idea, given how things had gone with the bear sleuth. Shay probably still wanted her space, and I didn't want to push. This day had been a complete clusterfuck, not to mention a roller coaster of emotion. She died in my arms, I was human again, we flew straight to a new pack—sorry, *sleuth*—of shifters who then reacted to my mate...

It was a lot, even if we weren't in the middle of the mate bond taking hold. Which we were.

Goddess, I didn't even know if her mate marks finished filling in. I didn't appear to have mine, but it wasn't the sort of thing you asked in a hallway, even one with glittery walls.

Damn, I wasn't sure I *should* ask. Especially not given the nagging fear that the Fetya's price was still unpaid, without considering the new complication that my half-fae mate *couldn't* die. So how would they be paid?

I shook my head, trying to shake off the unknown. I couldn't do anything about those things right now; all I could do was speak with my mate and prepare for the purification rituals.

Shay stood with Leigh, both of their heads bent over the purification instructions Jada had provided for us.

"Shay, can we talk for a moment?" I stayed a few feet away so as not to spook her.

Her head flew up in surprise anyway. She swallowed hard, but nodded, handing the paper to Leigh before stepping halfway toward me.

The distance stung—my wolf was pacing unhappily in my mind, demanding we close that distance and make her see that she should stay close by our side. We would protect her, not hurt her. But I ignored it and forced a smile I didn't really feel.

"It seems like they gave us enough rooms for the couples to pair up, but if you'd feel more comfortable rooming with Leigh, I'd understand. Or I can room with one of the guys, if you two would both like your space." I worked to keep the smile steady, ignoring my wolf's angry protests.

"Oh, I—" She quickly took stock of the number of doors, and I could practically see her doing the mental math. She shook her head. "I would like to room together, unless you don't want to? We should talk before we dive into all this." Shay hesitated. "About earlier."

Ahh.

"Yes, I'd love to room together. If you're ready..." I glanced over at Leigh, who was waiting to see how it all shook out.

Shay spun back to her friend with an apologetic expression.

"Go, make kissy-kissy with Fluffy. I'm going to lie in the middle of the bed like a starfish and stare at the ceiling for the next forty-five minutes before we have to start this." She shook the paper and turned to leave, but I called after her.

"I'm human now. Don't you think you should call me Dirge?"

"Nah, you'll forever be my pet, wolf-man." She flipped me the bird over her shoulder, then shut the bedroom door.

I just laughed.

"Sorry about her," Shay murmured, a pink flush staining her cheeks. "She grows on you, I promise."

I had an *intense* urge to throw my arm around her shoulder as we walked to the only remaining empty bedroom, but I held back. "Don't apologize. I like her fine. Not as much as you, obviously, but it's hard not to like someone who's so devoted to your other half." I winked at her as I held the door open.

She ducked her head as she slid in past me, and the need to touch her, run my fingertips along her cheekbones, and see how far down that blush extended rode me hard, but I just took a deep breath in through my nose as I shut the door and steeled myself.

I could not get handsy after this morning. Could not, *would not.*

When I turned back toward her, she was walking around the room, running her fingertips over everything. Ours were smaller, less opulent quarters than Jada's sleuth's had been, but they were still the nicest we'd been in so far on this journey, and not just because I was actually human to enjoy them.

Our room was equipped with its own private hot spring, with steps into the steaming water carved right out of the sparkling stone, worn smooth. A single, king-sized bed loomed against one wall, carved out of beautiful, dark wood and spread with sumptuous, white blankets. And of course, the walls were rough-cut gemstone, casting a pinkish-purple hue over everything where the light reflected off them.

Mostly, though, it was Shay who took my breath away. She was quiet as she perused the room, the buckles on her shoes making soft music as she walked. But even in silence, she was

191

music personified. Every motion a graceful note that added to the symphony. The air around her bloomed with her scent, soft and inviting. Her profile was stunning, from her perfectly straight nose and soft cheeks, down to lips kissable enough to make a man do stupid things.

She was perfection, in every sense of the word.

When she spoke, it caught me off guard because I'd been so wrapped up in studying her.

"I'm sorry about earlier."

I rocked back on my heels in surprise. "You have nothing to apologize for, muzică mea. Absolutely nothing. You don't owe me your body, and I hope you know that. Mates or no, you owe me nothing."

She shook her head. "No, that's not—" She broke off with a sigh, then sank to sitting on the end of the bed. "I'm not good with words."

A chuckle escaped before I could stop it as I crossed the room to sit at her side. "I've been stuck in wolf form for years. I guarantee you're better than I am."

She snorted, but her gaze flitted quickly up to meet mine, then skittered away. She was still nervous, and I hated that. I wanted her to trust me enough to be comfortable, as she had been before. Though, it hadn't escaped my attention that she was nervous around men and often silent in mixed company.

"Do I make you nervous now that I'm a man again?" I asked the question, even though I suspected I already knew the answer.

She ducked her head, and my suspicions were confirmed. But I still wanted to hear it from her lips, to understand her. I craved knowing her, every little facet that made her who she was. I would never get tired of listening, of learning my mate. But I had to be patient.

Luckily, we had a lifetime.

"A little," she finally admitted.

I thought for a while before slowly extending my hand, palm up. She stared at it for only a second before carefully placing her hand over mine and lacing our fingers together.

"I would never, ever hurt you, Shay. And just because we've experienced some things, doesn't mean I expect—"

"Please, no. Don't... don't backtrack or apologize. I'm not afraid of you, not really. My wolf knows you won't hurt us. It was just instinct, if that makes sense?"

I froze, not wanting to move or breathe or do anything that would stop her from talking to me, even though my wolf was howling about the fact that her past had been terrible enough to give her *instincts* to flinch away from us.

When I realized she was waiting for an answer, I nodded.

"Dax grabbing me like that..." She shuddered, then forced herself to continue. "Him grabbing me brought back some bad memories. And in that headspace, I wasn't here, safe with my mate. I was... there, then. A little girl whose wolf had to save her from the bad men."

She shook her head. "I don't want to talk about that, really. I just... I just wanted you to know that I don't think you'll hurt me, and I'm sorry. Sorry for letting the past get in the way of the present. And I hope you can understand that it might happen again."

Shay bit her lip when she finally looked up and held eye contact with me.

I moved slowly as I reached up and freed her bottom lip from her teeth, and she didn't pull away. Her skin was smooth and soft beneath my thumb, and I had to resist the urge to shudder at the heat that ignited inside me at the small touch.

Resisting my mate was going to be sweet, sweet torture.

"You never have to apologize to me. All I see is a strong, gorgeous woman sitting in front of me. And if you'll let me in, we can conquer those bad memories together. On your terms."

She gasped as my thumb traced the shape of her mouth, tongue darting out to tease the tip.

I growled low in my throat then. I couldn't help it. She was playing with fire, and I was desperately holding on to my control, trying to ignore the halfie already pressing against the zipper of my borrowed jeans.

"I would like that. A lot," she added on a whisper. We leaned in, each of us subconsciously closing the distance as electricity seemed to crackle in the air around us.

But the air had nothing on Shay. When our lips met, it was like the world tilted on its axis. Everything that mattered in the world faded in comparison to the woman in front of me, whose lips tasted like the sweetest pomegranate and who smelled like home. Her small hands landed on my chest, fingers twisting into the front of my shirt as I buried my fingers in her curls, anchoring myself so I couldn't lose her.

Our heads tilted in perfect synchronicity, and when her lips parted, I plunged in, sweeping through her mouth, tasting, teasing. She matched me stroke for stroke, still holding me tightly as I devoured her.

When an insistent knock at the door interrupted us, I groaned, but didn't let her go. We pulled apart just enough to let our foreheads touch, our heavy breaths mingling as I took a second to compose myself before calling out.

"Yes?"

"If you don't start showering now, you won't be ready for the ritual start time. If you two are coming, that is?"

There was a question as well as a suggestion in Reed's voice, and Shay blushed again, ducking out from under my touch.

"I'll go hop in first," she murmured, darting for the bathroom door.

I walked to the door of the room and pulled it open so I could see my brother face-to-face. "We're coming."

Reed nodded, but took a step back, waving his hand in front

of his face. "The pheromones in that room are enough to knock me on my ass."

"Say that to Shay and *I* will knock you on your ass. She's shy."

Reed grinned. "I know, and I wouldn't dream of embarrassing her. Your wolf picked a good one."

I nodded, gravely this time. My wolf had picked the best one, and I needed to keep my head on straight and *protect her* instead of getting caught up in the physical. We still needed to talk about the news regarding her parentage, if for no reason other than to tell her it didn't change a thing for me. But we had time. Time to talk and figure out what to do about the Fetya's curse.

"What is it? What's wrong?" Reed asked, concern immediately replacing the good-natured teasing from a moment before. "Is she still upset about Dax? I've been assured by Jada's people that they were removed from the island and won't be a problem again."

"That's good," I said as the shower flicked on. "But everything's fine."

"Why do I not believe you?" Reed asked as I shut the door and turned the lock.

He'd better believe it, because I was going to make it okay, whatever it took.

THIRTY-SIX

Shay

Dirge and I showered separately, and I dressed in the unbleached linen clothing Jada's people had laid out on top of the dresser for the ritual while he was in the bathroom. It was softer than it appeared at first, simple linen that did nothing against the Alaskan cold. Or to hide my pebbled nipples. I was debating whether to cross my arms over my chest to hide them when he walked out in a towel, steam caressing his bare chest and immediately erasing all other thoughts from my mind.

A few drops of water escaped his damp hair and skated down his broad, flat pectoral muscles, over his abs, and finally across that mind-meltingly-hot V of muscle that disappeared into his towel. I traced its path with my eyes, swallowing hard when I noticed the bulge hiding behind that one little towel. In my mind, I was already ripping it off him even as he cleared his throat.

"As much as I like where your head is at, I'm pretty sure that if we get all up in each other's business, we have to start the purification instructions over again." He grinned salaciously as he rubbed a hand over his damp hair. "But I'm game if you are."

"No, no. We need to be there for Bri. Absolutely." I bit my lip as he reached for the towel, and forced myself to spin and look the other way. Otherwise, I couldn't be responsible for making it to the purification ritual on time, and I wanted to be by Brielle's side as she found out what her omega gifts were under the moon tonight.

After that?

All bets were off. Just knowing he was naked on the other side of the room had me soaking my panties, and I had a feeling the longer we spent together—in that big, fluffy, king-sized bed, no less—the hotter things would get.

I kept myself busy examining the wall in front of me as the sounds of the towel dropping and a hairbrush pulling through his wet hair tormented me. But it wasn't until my eyes landed on the wall mirror, and his bare ass in it, that my jaw dropped.

Goddess, I was lucky. It was insanely unfair that he'd lived as a wolf for years and yet had a perfect, unbroken tan over a thickly muscled back and perfect, bitable ass. And dream us really hadn't even scratched the surface yet.

My temperature ratcheted up what felt like another hundred degrees as I quickly glanced away, not feeling right ogling him without his knowledge.

Granted, based on that cocky grin he'd given me, I didn't think he would mind. But if I kept staring, I was going to want to start touching.

Later, you thirsty bitch. I scolded myself and tried to think unsexy thoughts.

By the time he was done getting dressed, I was mostly back under control. But the knowing look—and the very obvious sniff of my neck before we walked out the door—told me he knew exactly how aroused he had me, without even lifting a finger.

Damn him.

PURIFICATION CEREMONIES SOUNDED bad and a little bit cult-esque, but in actuality, it was almost like a free trip to a spa. We'd been sent to a natural hot spring sauna to steam, covered in mud, scraped clean of mud, and plunged into a deep, icy stream—that part was more suck than spa—before being put back into our linen clothing.

Now we'd all been sent out of the cave and into the forest, where we were deposited under a large spruce tree to meditate until the moon was at its zenith.

I didn't put much stock in meditation, frankly, but it gave me time to mentally work on a new composition, which I hadn't had the time for since... well, since Texas. The notes started slow and languid, soft and supple, before building into a heart-racing crescendo and crashing again.

The moon climbed across the sky as I played it over and over inside my head, tweaking it with each pass, adding more depth and heat. But it wasn't until the bear attendant came for us—in full shift, no less, so he towered over even the tallest of us—that I realized it was the feeling of falling in love with Dirge that I was composing. Every up and down, every sweet sigh and heart-pounding touch, represented by notes floating in my mind.

I wasn't sure I wanted to share it with anybody but him.

We followed the lumbering golden-brown bear through the forest to the edge of a stream. The water was a silver ribbon undulating in the moonlight as it flowed steadily through the banks.

Jada stood at the edge, her bare feet in the stream and her own pure-white linen dress draped over her imposing frame. Her hair was tucked underneath some kind of ceremonial scarf, thick smudges of something green painted over the bridge of her nose and down the center of her lips. Her mates were all shifted, and nerves shimmered in my belly. If they made us all shift, Bri would faint. Would the ceremony still work?

I cast a nervous glance her way, and she looked apprehensive as well. Kane hovered at her shoulder, ever protective even though he was careful not to touch her and risk breaking the cleansing rules.

We stopped a few feet from the bear priestess, and her voice rang out through the clearing as her eyes fixed on Brielle. "Step forth!"

Bri hesitated only for a moment, pulling in a deep, steadying breath before holding her head high and walking into the stream at Jada's side.

Jada began to sway on her feet, circling around Brielle as she danced to a slow, undulating rhythm none of us could hear. As we watched, the moonlight seemed to intensify, and I started to itch. So entranced was I that I almost didn't notice as the shift washed over me.

But sure enough, within moments, I was watching it all through my keener wolf's eyes, and I could feel Dirge's presence at my side. He leaned his shoulder into mine, the wolf wholly unconcerned by human ideals of purity. Contact was pure, was love. And I really felt it as we stood there shoulder to shoulder, supporting our pack, our family.

More surprising than that, though, was that once I was in wolf form, I could hear the softest strains of music. Was it the wind? Was it something else? I didn't know, but it was beautiful. The notes were high and clear and pure, and I was overcome with the urge to howl, to join in the music.

So I did, lending my own voice to the beauty of it. One by one, the rest of our pack joined the song as Jada's movements grew faster and the moonlight seemed to intensify, a strong beam of light making Brielle's dark hair shine like she was

Moon Goddess touched. The light expanded, bathing her in silver light.

It felt like the world froze, like I felt the pulse of nature, and then the light shot out, swallowing us all.

The light left me blinking as it faded, and when my vision cleared, I was shocked to see Brielle standing in wolf form, drenched as if she'd been dunked in the stream. But more surprising than that were the sparkling silver sigils carved into the stream bank.

They weren't in any language I knew, but Jada stood over them, studying them intently.

We all stared in silence, as if the fate of the world hinged on whatever Jada would say next.

After a long time studying the sigils, she bowed her head. "Goddess, as you have writ, so let it be."

With a mighty clap, the sigils went up in a burst of dazzling light, and then all fell still.

Brielle's wolf began to shake, but before I could run forward to bolster her, the change took over. To my surprise, she stayed on her feet for once, swaying drunkenly in the ankle-deep water. Kane was already back in human form, passing her a fresh set of clothing—warmer than the linens provided by the Kodiaks—as we all shifted back to skin.

There was a pile of sweats behind a nearby tree, and as soon as I pulled on my own, I rushed to Brielle's side. Her hand was cold and clammy as it gripped mine while we waited for Jada to share with us what she'd learned.

When Dirge reached for my other hand, it startled me—but as soon as we exchanged a smile, warmth flooded me.

This wasn't his fight. He barely knew Bri, and yet here he was at my side, strong and steady. Because she mattered to me. He was a good man, and he was mine. I squeezed his fingertips, and he returned the motion, even the small touch igniting a fire of arousal in my belly.

There were no barriers left between us now, and a massive bed in a private room waiting for us when this was done. All I wanted was to get tangled up with him in it and see how much we'd missed in that dream. I had a feeling the real thing was going to be a thousand times better.

Jada cleared her throat as the last of her mates joined us, now in human form. "The Goddess has spoken, and quite plainly at that." She gave us a smile that was probably meant to be reassuring, but looked much more concerned than joyful. "You are, in fact, an omega. You have been gifted with great blessings of fertility."

"I— What?" Brielle spluttered. "As in I'm going to have a lot of babies? That doesn't—"

Jada waved her off, and she quickly fell silent. "Omega gifts don't impact the wielder so directly. They *can*, but you'll find over the years that you have a measure of control once you learn to use it. The omegas were always meant to bless the packs they were part of, which means that you will bring fertility to those around you. If my senses don't fail me, you've already been at work, whether you realize it or not." Jada arched an eyebrow as she scanned the rest of our group.

"So, lots of people are going to get pregnant in Pack Blackwater? That's it?" Brielle's brows drew down in confusion.

"Not quite. The fertility gift has been held by omegas in the past, and it's more subtle. You have the power to help wolves get pregnant—a boon in times such as these—but much more importantly, some would say, your presence guarantees maternal safety. You possess the power to fix almost any pregnancy issue, so the wolves in your pack will suffer few to no losses of mothers or babies in your presence. Have you helped any mothers in labor before in your capacity as pack healer?"

"Yes, actually." I could practically see Brielle's mind spinning a mile a minute.

"And how did it go?"

"She was in distress, but when I got there, my wolf took over. We were able to repair a tear in her uterus, and it made no sense at the time, but..."

Jada nodded. "That is your gift. If word gets out, you will be sought by every pack, for you hold the key to the salvation of their precious mates. You hold the strength of wolves in the future, the power to bring your kind back from the brink of extinction. But take care, because many will find you a threat."

Holy shit. Bri had always been good with the pregnant mothers in our home pack, but what she'd done with Gracelyn was next level. If she had the power to fix *anything*, she wouldn't just be sought... packs would fight *wars* over that kind of power.

"Thank you, Jada," she whispered, looking up at Kane. His eyes were troubled, and hers seemed to hold the weight of the world.

Jada nodded. "There is more." When her gaze landed on me, the hair on the back of my neck and down my arms stood on end. "When the Goddess's light shines, it reveals much. You have a soul bond, but all is not well. It's fractured, left incomplete."

Dread filled me as I thought of the painful, unfinished mate marks on my chest.

"It is incredibly dangerous to have a fractured bond. I would advise you to complete your bond as quickly as possible before more damage can be done."

"What kind of damage?" Dirge asked, stepping forward as if he would shake the details out of her. I put my hand on his shoulder, anchoring him to my side. Her mates were keeping a close watch on him, and I was still unnerved by their ursine eyes.

She shrugged, and he tensed under my touch.

"It's so rare, not much is known about a fractured bond. It

takes extreme duress to create one, and it's very painful if not corrected."

"Thank you for telling us," I murmured, even as Dirge turned toward me, a frown marring his handsome face.

She nodded, then sighed. "I must rest now, but you may stay as long as you need." She gave us all a parting wave, and then her mates led her away into the darkness.

THIRTY-SEVEN

Dirge

"Dirge!" Reed caught my arm before we walked back into the cave. Shay paused, standing between her two friends, clearly holding back a question.

"I'll be there shortly," I told her with a soft smile. She nodded, and then headed inside. Gael and Kane would watch over them.

"I just wanted to talk to you for a minute, see how you're doing. Today... was a lot."

I laughed, dragging my hands through my hair as I tried to decide what to tell him. He was my brother, my twin. But I'd stepped out of time when I went feral. He hadn't. It was hard to peel away that distance in our relationship and open up to him.

"It was a lot. I'm a little worried, if I'm honest."

Reed's brows drew down. "About the half-fae thing? That's a wild card, for sure, but with more power, she'll be safer—"

I waved a hand, cutting him off. "No, that part doesn't bother me. Hell, anything that makes her stronger is something I'm glad of. It's the Fetya."

Reed laughed incredulously. "You're kidding, right? Dude, the prophecy was fulfilled exactly as you saw." He grabbed my shoulder and squeezed reassuringly. "She died in your arms. She's back, probably immortal. What could possibly be worrying you now?"

"Exactly that. The Fetya might feel cheated of their price because she can't die."

He grew still, studying my face. "Did the vision just cut off after the light?"

I nodded. There was more, though, I realized as I finally let myself delve into the depths of my worry. What if they took it out on someone else now that Shay was unavailable? "Brielle has untrained powers of fertility. What if Shay and I bonded, she got pregnant, and then the Fetya took our child as payment?" The words were acid on my tongue, and Reed blanched at the possibility.

"Surely you don't think... That's a big if, brother. Have you told Shay?"

"No. How can I? It's bad enough she almost died because of my stupidity. If I had just been patient, the gathering would have happened, and I'd have met her the same way Kane did Brielle. But the darkness was already creeping in, and... I didn't wait. And now I've not only put her through physical pain, but what do you think will happen when she hears that we're still at risk? What then?"

Reed shook his head with that same stubborn expression he always got as a toddler when I'd take something dangerous away from him. "No, Dirge. You're speculating. The vision ended. The Fetya didn't predict what would happen after she died. And even if there is still a price to be paid—you can't keep that from your mate."

"I can bear that burden. She doesn't need it. She's been through enough."

He snorted. "You know, I always thought you were the smart one, but I guess I was wrong."

I cuffed him on the back of the head, and he shoved my hand off good-naturedly.

"No, I'm serious. You're dumber than I thought. Really, brother. How do you think it's going to go when she realizes you're keeping something from her? Or worse, she *doesn't* realize and eventually goes into heat? You're going to not serve your mate? Let her turn to another?"

I snarled, the vision he painted making me see red. "She will *never* have another."

"Uh-huh. Well, if you expect her to ride out a heat *solo*, you sure as fuck better fess up that you're scared to get her pregnant. Shit, she might not even need a heat, between being half-fae and Brielle's fertility mojo. We have no frame of reference for how either of those things would impact her or any other she-wolf in our pack. The records were pretty much all destroyed after the Omega War. You going to just never have sex again? Even after the bear priestess just told you that your bond is fractured, and you could both be hurt by not completing it? How does that work out?"

The red haze over my vision made me want to shift and tear my brother a new one, but instead, I turned and punched the trunk of the nearest tree. Somewhere after the fourth punch, Reed dropped a hand on my shoulder and spun me away from the splintered bark.

"Knock it off, and stop being an asshat. The solution is simple. Talk to her. Tell her what you're worried about. You're not stuck in wolf form anymore. You can *talk to her*."

It couldn't be that simple. All telling her would do was scare her. Upset her. Make her pull away from me again, and I couldn't bear that.

But was he right? Was I asking for trouble if I didn't tell her?

I was damned if I did, damned if I didn't.

The question was, did I trust her not to run if I shared the awful reality with her?

THIRTY-EIGHT

Shay

The three of us walked quietly back to the hallway where our rooms were. I didn't know what I was feeling about any of what Jada had shared, so I could only imagine what Brielle was thinking. She'd lived her whole life thinking she was psi, and here we found out she was actually omega. If Kane couldn't somehow get the law changed, she would be hunted to the end of her days.

It was heavy and terrifying in and of itself. But now she had fertility powers she had no idea how to use, and no living omega to speak to about it.

We stopped in the hallway, but none of us let go.

"You two okay?" Leigh asked, worried gaze flicking between Brielle and me.

I shrugged one shoulder, unsure how to respond. I was confused, concerned, and about a million other things I couldn't quite put my finger on. It wasn't a good answer, so I kept it to myself.

"I'm better than expected," Bri said with a forced smile. "At least now we *know*. What the heck to do with this information... no idea. But we know, and that's something."

"Knowledge is power," Leigh murmured, giving Bri's arm a supportive squeeze.

"Exactly. And believe it or not, I got a message back from Aunt Kari earlier. She said she'd love to meet and asked when we'd be back in Johnson City."

"That's good news," I said, finally summoning a smile. "She's got to know something about... all this, right? At least the curse part."

"I hope so." Bri blew out an unsteady breath. Gael and Kane finished their conversation off to the side, and Gael took a position at the mouth of the hallway, ready to stand guard for the rest of the night. I pretended I didn't see Leigh checking out his butt, even though she *absolutely* did.

"We should all get some sleep, my love." Kane spoke quietly as he walked up to Brielle's side.

Leigh yawned, then nodded. "I agree. I'm beat. See you babes on the flip side."

AT FIRST, I curled up in the giant king-sized bed as I waited for Dirge to come to our room. But then the nerves got to me, and I moved to sit on the edge. Being nervous was first-rate stupidity, but telling myself that didn't tamp down the wild beaver that had taken up residence in my stomach. There weren't any trees in there, so he was just gnawing on me instead.

So much had happened, and we'd had no time alone. Other than earlier, when we'd almost fallen into this very bed. But now there was the fact that I was at least some part fae, possibly immortal, and oh yeah, we had somehow created a fractured soul bond.

Nothing at all to derail a couple. Ugh.

Was he going to be weirded out that I might be immortal? That still worried me. He hadn't seemed bothered when he'd been taking all the air out of my lungs with that *kiss*. My panties got soaked just remembering how his lips felt on mine.

The nerves had me wanting to stand up and pace, but I didn't want him to *know* I was nervous. If confidence was sexy, then jaw-clenching, leg-shaking anxiety had to be a whole 'nother level of *un*-sexy.

There was a soft knock at the door, and then he was there, letting himself into the room and stopping my mental gymnastics with his dominating presence. He was drop-dead gorgeous, and my pulse picked up as we locked eyes. I had to resist the urge to squirm, the heat building in my belly as he crossed the room.

"Hi," I murmured.

"Hello, beautiful," he said. The cocky half grin I'd already come to love was there, but there was a sadness in his eyes that didn't mesh with the heat I was feeling.

"Everything okay?" I asked, even though I was suddenly scared the answer was no.

"Not exactly," he murmured, stopping in front of me. He raked his hand through his hair, and I gasped when I caught sight of his hand.

"For Goddess's sake, what happened? Did you and Reed get into a fight? Oh, shit. Did Finn's sleuth come back?" I stood and carefully grabbed his wrist, pulling his hand closer so I could see his bloodied, busted-up knuckles.

"No, nothing like that. Just... got a little angry and decided to box with a tree."

"Umm." I stared at him, confused. What the hell had happened in the last twenty minutes that had him beating the fuck out of a tree? "Should I ask what you were angry about?"

His sigh was weary, and his shoulders were tense under my fingertips after I dropped his hand.

"You can tell me anything," I whispered, searching his face as if the answers were written in the sculpted shape of his eyebrows or the hard line of his jaw. The jaw I wanted to kiss every inch of.

Clearly not the time, Shay, I scolded myself as he slipped his arms around my back and buried his nose in my hair.

He drew in a few deep breaths, dragging my scent into his lungs as if it was what kept him upright.

"I don't think we can take the bond any further, but I don't know how to do that without hurting you."

Shock and anger whipped through me like a tornado. Whoosh, there went a flying cow, because it was soft concern to unbridled fury in a second flat.

I jerked back like he'd slapped me. "What do you mean, we shouldn't take the bond further? Why would you say that?"

Chagrin was on his face, but a solemn resolve too. And it *really* pissed me off.

"It's for your own good, Shay. I—"

"Oh, *fuck* no. Did you really just say that to me? What are you, my father?" I yanked my hand out of his grip and began to pace. "You had better explain yourself right now. Because what I'm hearing is some misguided patriarchal shit, which boils down to you rejecting our mate bond, and I am seriously going to lose it if after everything we've been through, you're going to reject our mate bond *for my own good.*"

"I am *not* rejecting our bond. I just don't know what else to do." The sorrow in his tone stopped me midstride, and I turned to face him. To study him, really. What had changed?

"You'd better start from the beginning," I hissed through clenched teeth. I was still hot under the collar—no, scratch that. My *wolf* was pissed off. She was strong, and she didn't take kindly to him backing out of the bond. He was ours, damn it.

As soon as I realized it was her riding me so hard, it got a little easier to separate her fury from my own emotions. Confusion, mostly, but there was fear too.

"I've been thinking about the vision."

"The Fetya's vision?" Okay, that was not at all what I was expecting.

"Yes, that one. They showed me you dying, but you're still alive. Your fae background meant that you couldn't die, not really. And as beyond fucking grateful as I am, I'm scared that they might feel cheated that they didn't get their price."

I ran my hand over the back of my neck, confused but trying to process what he was saying. "I thought me dying *was* the price."

"So did I, but you came back. What if they demand something else in exchange for your life?"

"Like what?" I asked, disbelief and the first trickle of fear starting to win over the fury as my wolf settled. Dirge wasn't abandoning us; he was concerned for us. We could work through this, right? "Do you think they'll take your life if I'm immortal?"

He shook his head. "They had the chance to take me, and they didn't. But Brielle has fertility powers now. What if... what if you get pregnant, and they take our child?"

Shock didn't feel how I thought it would. I'd experienced it a time or two, like when that assassin had stabbed me. That had felt cold, as if I'd been dunked in a bucket of ice water.

This shock felt numb, as if all the blood had drained out of me between one heartbeat and the next. My fingertips started to tingle, and I forced myself to breathe again. But then my brain caught up, and objections to what he said were popping up left and right like those annoying New Year's poppers.

"You can't know that. It's not set in stone that they would take another life. Your vision only saw me dying, and I did. We have no reason to believe they'd take my immortality out on our unborn children."

"No, it's not. But it's a possibility. And I promise you, I couldn't live with myself. I couldn't bear it if I caused you that pain." His shoulders slumped under the awful weight of it, and my heart broke at the sight of him. The fury was gone as quickly as it had sprung up, leaving nothing but determination in its wake. He didn't get to make this choice for me.

I could make my own choices, and I was choosing him.

"No, *no*. Stop it." I closed the distance with a speed I didn't know I possessed, wrapping him in my arms. "This is not your fault. Surely you know that?"

"It is a hundred percent my fault. How could you love me if I cost us our children, our future?" His words were a hoarse whisper, but I felt them like a dagger to my soul. He meant every word, and the pain in that question almost drove me to my knees.

"I could love you because you're my other half, Dirge. My soul mate. The one the Goddess made for me. Because you're brave and strong and loving. Because in your arms, I feel safety that I've *never* felt anywhere else. That's how."

"But what if—"

"No." I put maybe a little too much force behind the word. "No, we're not going to even consider that possibility."

"Muzică mea, we have to." Even as he said it, he gripped me tighter, like he was scared I was going to run away any second.

"No, we don't. We can't live our lives in fear like that, okay? We just... no. If these Fetya are so all-powerful, all-knowing, wouldn't they have *known* I was half-fae? That the assassin would stab me and my other side would kick in?"

"I-I hadn't considered that." He frowned down at me, brows drawn tight and low.

"Well, do. Because I'm not willing to live apart from my mate for a maybe."

He studied me carefully, fingertips tracing the line of my jaw before trailing down to my throat. He gripped the back of my neck, pulling me closer.

One second, we were balanced on the knife's edge of deep emotional pain; the next, his lips were on mine, devouring, wiping away everything but him in this moment. I opened up for him, and he backed me toward the bed as our tongues tangled. His hands were everywhere, one branded on my hip, the other anchoring me at the back of my neck, then roving to the hem of my sleep shirt.

His scent was heavy in my nose, spurring on my lust as I could smell the arousal spike his cedarwood with a layer of musk. My wolf growled her approval at what she sensed, loving that we'd brought our mate back around.

He pressed me back into the soft duvet with a look in his eyes I'd never seen before, passion and primal need, all rolled into one.

"Take this off," he demanded, tugging at my shirt as he sank to his knees, already peeling off the thin pajama shorts I'd slipped on while I waited for him.

I didn't hesitate, flinging the shirt across the room in my haste to strip. He was already shirtless, so I held onto his shoulders for dear life as his lips fastened onto my inner thigh.

A hiss escaped between my teeth as he roved higher, not hesitating to swirl his tongue around my core, driving me wild within seconds. I bucked up against him, wanting more, wanting all of him, but he pinned my hips with one hand, the other on my inner thigh keeping me spread for him.

He licked and sucked, straight past teasing into *everywhere, all at once* and not stopping until I screamed out my release, arching off the bed. It hit me out of the blue. One second, I was climbing toward that peak, the next, I was falling, stars bursting in my vision as he worked my clit with the flat of his tongue.

He rumbled low in his chest, a satisfied sound, and as I came back to myself from the orgasm, I thought it was enough to shake the whole bed. But when he froze between my spread thighs, I realized something else was shaking us—not just the bed, but the whole *room* was rattling.

"What the hell?" he murmured, extending a hand to pull me up.

My bones were still liquid, but I accepted the hand up as a pounding knock came on the door. I melted against his chest, my breath still coming in too-rapid pants, my knees useless jelly.

"We're under attack! We need to get to the airstrip right now!" Gael yelled over the din of rattling fixtures as an explosion sounded nearby.

"Holy shit, holy shit," I said under my breath as I frantically patted around for clothes. I snatched on a pair of jeans and a T-shirt that were lying on the bed as Dirge pulled on a pair of black boots and a black T-shirt. There wasn't time for more, though my soaking, needy pussy did *not* enjoy denim so soon after Dirge had just rocked my world.

The thought faded as we ran out into the hallway, the rest of our pack pouring out in stages of half sleep, half confusion.

"What's going on?" Dirge asked at Gael's grim demeanor.

"ODL. They must have sensed Brielle's omega during the ceremony, because they sent a lot more than just three representatives this time." The cave floor rattled under our feet, and dread filled me like lead. *Shit*. This was not good.

"Oh my Goddess, this is terrible. They're attacking the Kodiaks because of me?" Brielle brought a hand to her mouth to cover a half sob.

Kane wrapped his arm around her. "We've got to get out of here. The Kodiaks are strong, yes, but the ODL can't find us here, or they'll suspect us after the issue at the gathering. We need to buy some more time to figure this out."

A bear shifter lumbered into the hall, letting out a vicious roar before shifting with painful speed back into a naked, thickly muscled man.

He was graying at the temples, and his eyes were full of

death. One of Jada's mates. "We're keeping them at bay, but you need to go. To the airstrip, and straight to the skies."

"Thank you. We're in your debt," Kane said solemnly, and the shifter nodded once before sprouting fur along his arms and running down the hallway half-shifted. Another deafening roar echoed through the hallways a moment later, evidence he'd completed his shift and was heading back into the fray.

We bolted down the hallway as chunks of crystal began to fall from the ceiling, and the only thing that kept me together was the strength of Dirge's hand, tightly gripped in mine.

THIRTY-NINE

Dirge

We made quick work getting to the mouth of the cave, despite the pandemonium. Bears were everywhere, towering over us as they raced out into the night to defend their ancestral home. Children cried and women sobbed as the cave itself shuddered every time an explosive detonated. More than once, we had to dodge chunks of falling crystal, and we weren't successful all those times. Reed was bleeding, Brielle had a scrape down her entire forearm, and everyone's eyes glowed with the force of our wolves.

Gael held up a hand, stopping us at the cave mouth. After a quick look and another tooth-rattling explosion, he waved us forward and darted into the night.

I called on my wolf, leaning on his superior night vision as we sprinted over the rocky ground. We made it back to the path through the rocky outcropping without incident, most of the fighting happening on the other side of the caves. Apparently, the ODL had used their fae connections to appear inside the forest, giving themselves the element of surprise.

Though why they were starting with bombs instead of

inspections, I didn't know. We were forced to slow as we weaved through the narrow walls of stone, but I never let go of Shay. Keeping her safe was my number one priority, even if it meant wiping the ODL off the face of the earth.

Frankly, if this was how they reacted, maybe it was time to wipe the sons of bitches out for good. The night grew marginally quieter the farther we got from the caves, but steady explosions still caused the ground to tremble under my boots.

Perhaps that was how Gael missed it, the pebble plinking down from above. It was understandable, really, though the ODL soldier that followed it was harder to miss.

"Gael, watch your back!" I shouted even as I threw myself in front of Shay, halting the pack mates running behind us.

The vampire ODL soldier flashed his fangs with a hiss, then dove at Gael while he was still midturn. Wolfsbane was the only truly deadly substance to shifters—at least that we knew about—but vampire venom? It burned like a bitch and would put you on your back for a solid week while your wolf worked it out of your system. We didn't have a week.

My own fangs descended as I moved to intercept, fingertips shifting to claws without conscious thought. I swiped at the vamp's neck, aiming for a kill shot. Gael spun in time to get his arm up and block the attack, but only just. He ducked under the vampire's lunge, clothes exploding off him as he took fur.

I missed the vampire by less than an inch—they were fast motherfuckers—as he leapt into the air, high overhead and out of reach even from my over-six-foot frame. But what went up must come down, and he angled for me, jaws extended as he fell.

Braced for the impact, I caught him around the waist as he tried to topple me. He managed a vise grip around my head, but I'd planned for that. Letting his momentum carry us, I flung us to the solid rock underfoot, letting my superior weight drive the air out of his lungs. He didn't have to breathe, but the sudden lack of sensory input was still enough to distract almost anyone. He was no different. He froze as he gasped, dragging in a lungful of air on instinct as I pinned him. Before he could try to buck me off, Gael was there, wolf jaws clamped around the vampire's throat.

It took a few rips, but he succeeded in severing the vampire's neck, sending the bloodless head flying over the rocky wall and out of sight.

Gael's wolf spat and grunted as he tried to get the taste of vampire out of his mouth. The blood wasn't harmful, but it was nasty, especially to the wolf's heightened senses.

"Let's move!" I barked the order with alpha command as I spun, finding a pale-faced Shay standing not five feet back, clutching Leigh for all she was worth, the rest of the pack at their backs. Leigh looked nauseated, but the command had already kicked into effect, spurring her forward as she averted her gaze from the headless body. It would turn to ash when the sun rose, incinerating the black-and-silver uniform right along with the headless corpse.

I softened my expression as I approached. "We've got to keep moving. The bears are strong, but there aren't that many of them. We need to get off this rock before they realize we were here."

Shay nodded, resolve straightening her shoulders. I'd never been prouder of her than I was in that moment. She was quiet, my mate, but she was all steel under her soft curves. She clasped my hand again, and we ran hell-for-leather toward the airstrip. Gael stayed in wolf form, darting ahead on swift paws to scout for more ODL soldiers, but no more boogeymen appeared. The pilot was grim faced, but already strapped into his seat as we dove through the door, copilot at the ready to seal the hatch behind us.

No sooner had the light flashed green and the cabin was

sealed than he had the throttle down, and we were moving down the runway.

I ushered Shay to a seat with my hand on her lower back, even the simple contact lowering my heart rate. We'd made it, and as the plane lifted from the runway with a familiar lurch, I breathed a sigh of relief. She was safe. We were all safe.

"WHERE ARE WE GOING?" Brielle asked once the plane had leveled off to cruising altitude.

"Away from there, mostly," Gael said, sarcasm heavy as he tiredly pulled on a pair of gray sweats kept stashed in the plane. Shifters tended to have stashes of clothes everywhere. It was well past midnight, closer to dawn than dusk, but still it felt like the day that just wouldn't end.

"We should stay on the move for a while, until we figure out a course of action," Kane said, stroking his mate's dark hair.

Brielle nodded, guilt painting her expression as she turned to gaze at her two best friends. "Are you sure you two don't want to go back? It's me they're after—we've got that confirmed now."

"I'd love it if we could stop flying," Leigh said, already looking pale and queasy, "but how many times are we going to have to tell you that you're stuck with us?"

"At least one more," Brielle said with a watery smile.

Shay was quiet at my side, half-burrowed into my shoulder as her friends bantered quietly. When she spoke up, all eyes turned to her, and I could feel her flinch into my chest as if she could disappear there.

"Any word back from your Aunt Kari on when she can meet?"

Brielle dug her phone from her pocket—luckily, she'd grabbed it on the way out of the caves, because we'd been forced to leave our luggage behind. "No signal yet. But that's a good point. Should we head to Texas? That's where she asked to meet me—"

"Is it safe to sit in one place? They sensed your powers," Gael interrupted, arms crossed over his chest and wearing a disgruntled expression. "We got lucky this time, but we don't know how long the bears will keep them occupied, or if they'll figure out we were the ones who triggered their wards. We should find a safe house, somewhere remote where we can see them coming. Then we can wait it out and see if they're able to track *you* or if it was just the ceremony."

"They've never been able to track her before, so I think it's a fairly safe assumption that the presence of the Goddess's magic was the key difference," Reed said.

"You want to park ourselves in Johnson City like sitting ducks on a *fairly safe*? Bad idea."

Reed scowled at Gael's haughty tone. "Just because you're head enforcer doesn't make the decision yours. It's up to Kane."

"The Alpha—"

"Can speak for himself," Kane interrupted the brewing argument. "Right now, we need rest and a moment to get our bearings. We're not making any decisions yet. The plane is fully fueled, and we're all going to try to get some sleep. They can't attack us in the air."

I nodded, appreciating his level head. Shay sighed against my arm, clearly relieved at the diffusion of the testosterone spike. It seemed like she was uncomfortable any time alpha energy ramped up, which was something I should ask her about when we had some time alone.

Like when we'd had that very delicious interlude that had been so rudely interrupted. Best not to think about that, though, or I'd have an awkward boner for the whole damn flight.

But when Shay sighed again, I settled my arm over her so

she could get comfortable against my chest. And somehow, with her safe and snug against me, the rest of the world and all its problems faded away. I soaked in her scent, reveling in her perfect softness and warmth, and let my eyes drift shut.

We'd figure out the rest in a few hours.

FORTY

Shay

The solid jolt of the plane's wheels touching down woke me sometime around midday. My neck was a little stiff, but I'd slept surprisingly well, cuddled up to Dirge's side. Though when I looked up at his face, I was fairly certain he hadn't slept all that much.

"Everything okay?" I whispered the question, not wanting to disturb anyone else. The plane was quiet, nothing but the steady hum of its propellers and the rush of wind outside as we rolled to a stop to break the steady white noise.

"Yes, everything's fine. We're just stopping for fuel, as far as I know." He stroked my back, smiling softly down at me.

It hit me in that moment, that steady reassurance, his solid calm, the tender touch, and how long I'd been thirsting for the *security* that I felt. It wasn't the least bit logical; we were on the run, in the ODL's sights, while there was so much still unknown about our future.

They could catch up to us tomorrow, or in five years. But somehow, I felt safe. Grounded.

Loved.

That internal whisper knocked the breath right out of my

lungs. Was this what it was like for all fated mates? I didn't think so. Because something about Dirge called to me, healed me, on a level nothing and no one else ever had. I didn't need children if I got to keep him. And I would make him understand that in time. We just needed to figure out a solid plan for now until we figured out the mess with the Fetya.

His thumb stroked lazily over my cheek, but still left a trail of fire in its wake. I felt it everywhere, straight down to my bones. He lit me up with even that small contact, and I was pretty damn sure I'd never get enough. Even if I lived forever.

"Penny for your thoughts?" He asked the question a low rumble in his chest meant only for my ears.

Sometimes I hated how bad I was with words. I wished I could tell him everything, how it felt to be in his arms, safe for the first time in my life. How he made me feel like a new person, a better person. How exciting it was to know we had our whole lives ahead of us, to learn and explore each other. It was poetry, and I was no poet.

Those were words I didn't possess. The reason I composed music.

"I think I love you," I whispered. But when I tried to duck my face against his chest, hide away from the aftermath of my confession, he caught my chin with his fingertips. Dirge's touch was gentle even as his grin was wild, half-cocked up on one side, his eyes were crinkled at the corners with joy.

"You think so, huh?" His voice grew husky, the evidence of his arousal making my own blood sing with answering need.

I nodded, suddenly speechless for a different reason.

He kissed me like someone was going to snatch me away from him, hands tangled in my curls so he could angle me to better plunder my lips. After a few moments, I pulled back, but I didn't let go. If he kept kissing me like he was a drowning man and I was his last hope for salvation, I'd be a puddle of need with no way to do a thing about it. There was no way we were joining the mile-high club two feet from our pack mates.

The plane had stopped, and people were stirring, so it was *no time* to be getting hot and bothered.

Unfortunately, that ship had sailed. The molten heat at my core demanded I find a quiet spot and do something about it.

Kane stood at the front of the plane. "We're just making a quick stop here for fuel. If you'd like to get out and stretch, use the restroom, or get a drink, there's an open hangar right over there."

He pointed out the window to where a bay door stood open on a very large hangar.

It must have been evidence of how small—or maybe just how broke—the Johnson City pack was, but I had no idea so many wolf packs were out there with private jets and hangars that rivaled small airports.

"Where are we?" Leigh asked groggily.

"Colorado. We have no personal ties here, so it should be relatively safe and give us a chance to touch base with Julius back home, see what the news is on the ODL attack at Ushagat Island."

"Great," she murmured, pushing to her feet and heading for the door before anyone else had moved. Leigh *really* hated small planes. I wouldn't be surprised if she was out there kissing the tarmac. Not that I could blame her; if I puked my guts up every time, I'd be making out with the lawn too.

"Shall we? I would love to stretch my legs, maybe take a quick walk in the woods?" Dirge whispered against the rim of my ear, the heat of his breath making me shudder with need pulsing just below the surface. I nodded frantically, my pulse pounding a rhythmic tattoo at my temples as I shoved aside the ridiculous image of Leigh, a blade of grass stuck in her teeth.

Dirge led me off the plane—where Leigh was nowhere to be found, probably already in the hangar—to the breathtaking sight of the Colorado Rockies. The white-capped peaks were stunning, majestic in the distance, even if not quite as large as what we saw heading into Alaska a month ago. Had it only been a month? It felt longer. A large lake next to the runway reflected the peaks. There was no wind, and the surface was crystalline blue glass.

It was pretty enough to be a postcard or a painting, and the fresh, clean air—slightly warmer than Alaska had been too—was a welcome change after we were breathing stale plane air all morning.

Dirge and I both quickly used the restroom, and when I came out, he was holding out an icy bottled water for me. The water was so cold, it hurt my teeth, but I drank it gratefully.

"Go for a walk with me?" The half lift of his handsome lips had me wanting to throw myself at him, but I hesitated.

"Are we clear to go wandering off?"

"Already let Kane know. He's getting a debrief from Julius right now, but things are quiet. We've got some time."

"Okay. But I had an idea first."

He cocked an eyebrow in question, but followed me silently as I crossed the hangar to where Brielle sat quietly on a couch, sipping her own water.

"Hey, Bri. I have a question. I know it's still new, but do you think you could try out those fertility powers and see if you could maybe... block a pregnancy?"

Brielle's eyes went wide. "Well, I've never done it before, but she did say that most omega powers took practice to learn... So, I could try? Do you feel a heat coming on or something?"

"No, nothing like that." I smiled. "Just more uncertainty with the information about me being half-fae if I'll even go into heat or require one to conceive. And this is too new, and we're not close to ready for a baby with all we've got going on."

She nodded. "I get it. If you're willing to wait until we're back in Johnson City, I could see about an implant or IUD for

225

you, but frankly, those are spotty at best with our magic, and that's not accounting for your fae half. Hmm." She tapped her chin idly. "Worst that can happen is I can't figure it out."

Brielle leaned forward and placed her hand on my forearm, then closed her eyes. After a moment, she popped them back open. "You too, buddy." She waved for Dirge to proffer up an arm. He did, and as soon as her eyes fell closed, he shot me a wide-eyed look.

At first, nothing happened. We stood quietly while she hummed under her breath. But then heat blossomed, radiating through my abdomen. It didn't hurt, but it did start to itch after a few minutes, and I had to resist the urge to scratch. And then, as quickly as it started, it stopped.

She blinked up at us slowly, swaying a little from her seat on the couch. "That was interesting."

"Do you think it worked?" Dirge asked, and I noticed him subtly adjusting the waistband of his pants. I wondered if he'd gotten itchy too.

"I am 99.9% certain that you two will not be having babies any time soon. We can recheck in a few months, but... My wolf seemed to know exactly what to do, just like with Gracelyn." She smiled tiredly, and Kane appeared at her side.

"What are you doing over here?" he asked, rubbing her shoulders lightly.

"Testing out what my wolf can do. I could use an energy recharge, though, if you're done arranging things." She wiggled her eyebrows at him suggestively.

"I think that's our cue to leave. Thank you, Bri." I leaned in for a quick hug, then let Dirge lead me out of the hangar.

There was a small trail cut into the deciduous forest bordering the lake, and Dirge arrowed toward it as if he'd been here a hundred times before.

He was over three hundred years old... Maybe he had?

I didn't ask, though, because I didn't want to break the spell being woven between us as we walked, fingers linked, through the lovely wood. Soft, still-damp leaves bent underfoot with hardly a crunch as we followed the winding path. I couldn't tell you whose pack lands these were or how far we walked. All I knew was that the sound of running water reached us eventually, and a rocky outcropping came into view between the trees.

The sound got louder and louder until we stopped at the edge of the rocks. Dirge squeezed my fingertips with excitement, looking back at me with a giddy grin.

"Trust me?" he asked.

"Umm, yes?" I said, confused. Trust him to—

He scooped me up in his arms so quickly that I couldn't dodge him. In three great strides, we were at the top of the rock, and I was still confused as I clung to his T-shirt.

"Hold your breath."

"What?"

He didn't answer, though. He just leapt.

Wind rushed past us, our surroundings went dark, and after a short screech, I remembered to clamp my mouth shut. Just in time, as water rushed over my head a heartbeat later. Dirge kept me crushed to his chest as we made entry, and it wasn't until I felt his strong kicks pushing us back to the surface of the water that I shoved free, kicking and stroking my own way to the top.

I broke the surface with a shocked gasp, dragging in air as he surfaced two feet away.

"Are you crazy!" I shouted and splashed him.

He ducked back from the spray and laughed, his grin showing off his straight, white teeth. "Not crazy, just a bit of an adrenaline junkie. Tell me you didn't feel like we were flying."

"Flying to our *deaths*, maybe!" I splashed him again, not really angry. But my pulse was pounding, my heart in my throat. The water was chilly, right on the edge of being uncomfortable.

In one strong stroke, he closed the distance between us, wrapping his arms around me as he kept himself afloat with his legs.

"I've been here a few times in the past, and one of the local pack showed me this spot. It's private, far from the main lands. Most people using the airstrip pass right on by without ever knowing it's here. A crime, if you ask me."

"It is beautiful," I murmured against the warmth of his neck. The heat radiating off him was enough to keep me cozy, despite the water temperature. The sound of running water had come from here, I realized, as I noticed the waterfall at one end of the grotto. The pool below us was deep, so deep the bottom wasn't visible in the limited light let in through the opening in the rocks above.

Dirge pushed us toward the falls, and I let him. Toward the rim of the pool, the water grew shallow, and before long, I felt the smooth black rock bump against the back of my legs.

We kept scooting back until we were horizontal, legs still in the water, but head and shoulders dry against the smooth river stone beneath us. The waterfall was close enough that we occasionally got splashed with a few droplets, a steady mist sparkling in the air like tiny diamonds.

Dirge hovered over me on his forearms so he was holding his own weight.

"You're the most beautiful woman I've ever seen." His words were low, his touch reverent as he ran his fingertips along my clavicle, along the collar of the soaking shirt plastered to my skin. "How did I get so lucky? Goddess knows I don't deserve you."

"Goddess knows we're meant to be and that you're perfect for me," I said, correcting him gently. He was never going to stop kicking himself for going to the Fetya if I didn't make him. One mistake, one that he saw as a weakness, and it was enough to condemn him as flawed to himself forever. But I didn't see it that way. "Three hundred years is a long, long time to be alone. I don't fault you for wondering, and I don't fault you for what happened with that assassin."

He opened his mouth to object, but I put my hand tenderly over it. I had to work to focus when he sucked my fingertip into his mouth, working the digit with his tongue.

"I'm serious, Dirge. You haven't known me very long yet, but I can guarantee that even if you hadn't been there, I'd have jumped in front of that knife. Whether we'd met or not been mates, I was destined to take that knife for Bri. I protect my family."

"So fierce, muzică mea." His fingertips wandered down my side, leaving goose bumps in their wake. He teased the bare strip of skin under the hem of my shirt, making me suck in a breath through my teeth. I was still aroused from before, the heat thrumming just beneath the surface. And now I was riding an adrenaline spike too. "That's part of what makes me love you so much."

His finger continued to play as I tried to make my tongue work again. "Only part?"

"Mm, yes. A large part, but there's so much more to you."

I kept my eyes on his, deep down still uncertain that he could see me that way. I was so broken. Surely he saw that? I was as flawed as they came.

"You're fierce, yes, but also sweet. Soft and caring with those you love. You see everything, even though you say so little. Intelligence that matches your beauty inside and out."

His hand swept up under the shirt, fingertips trailing along the underside of my breast. The interplay of hot and cold was driving me wild. I arched into his grip, and a smile spread slowly across his face.

"That's it, Shay. Tell me what you want."

"You. I just want you." I breathed the words, and I meant every one. I wanted him, all of him, with no holding back.

FORTY-ONE

Dirge

"**Y**ou. *I just want you.*" Her words hung between us like unlit tinder for one heartbeat, then another.

She kissed me then, soft and slow and deep. It felt like she wanted to drink me in, meld the two of us together until there was no telling where one of us ended and the other began. In that moment, I wanted it too.

It was a slippery slope, and while something inside still screamed that I should be holding myself back, how could I? I wanted her in a way that was unholy. I'd never done drugs before, never had much taste for alcohol or the oh-so-fleeting buzz it brought to a wolf. But was this what addiction felt like?

The hot burn of *need* in my veins? I didn't know, only that she was my oxygen and I was hers. In any way she would have me, I was hers.

I kissed her back with every ounce of passion I had in me, and when her hands moved to the hem of my shirt, I leaned up, letting her pull it off over my head. It landed with a wet plop behind us, and within seconds, hers followed. Her nipples were beaded up tightly, begging for my kiss.

I circled one areola with my tongue—not quite where she

wanted me if the arch of her back was any indication—then moved to the other. I teased her, back and forth, back and forth, until she wove her hands into my hair and pulled, driving me where she wanted me.

Her moans of pleasure as she anchored me to her breast had me harder than steel, itching to drive home into her warm grip.

I hadn't planned this, this slow frenzy of lovemaking. All I'd wanted was to show her the grotto, give her a good memory to hold in this uncertain time. Share something of my past with her.

But when she shoved me back and hooked her thumbs into the waistband of my sweats, I was lost to her thrall. Reason and worry were gone, and there was no one and nothing but Shay, muzică mea.

She gripped me tightly with her small hand, my head bowing under the strain of staying up and not crushing her. And that was before she started to stroke.

"You're going to embarrass me if you keep that up," I murmured, frozen to the spot as she worked my dick.

She hummed happily, not easing her pace as she grinned up at me.

Saucy little she-wolf.

If she wanted to play dirty, I could be dirty. I flipped her hand away from my shaft, then quickly shucked off her own sweatpants before switching our positions. When I was flat on my back and she was sitting with her burning core plastered to my abs, I urged her up my torso.

"What? I—"

"Ride my face."

Her eyes went wide, casting around the grotto as if someone was going to burst out of the stone and stop us.

"I've never, umm." She blushed prettily, and pride filled me. She'd never?

Excellent. I'd be the first to blow her mind, and the last.

"I won't let you fall." I urged her, my hands steady on her waist as she slowly scooted up. She hovered above me with a look of heat mixed with uncertainty.

"Trust me?" I echoed the question.

"Always," she whispered.

"You're in control. Take what you need." I winked at her, then pulled her down, fastening my lips to her lower ones, laving her with my tongue.

She cried out and arched above me. The sight of her perfect, small breasts against the backdrop of the grotto burned itself into my memory. I never, ever wanted to forget this moment. Forget her.

I moved from her cunt to her clit, making slow circles at first, until she began to whimper. Following her cues, I amped up the tempo, chasing her over that edge.

Her scream of pleasure echoed off the stones that made up our private little haven as she soaked my chin with her slick arousal.

Shay's fingertips were on mine, then, insisting that I let her move.

I loosened my grip but didn't let go. She wobbled a bit before her strength came back, and she eased back down my chest. It was her turn to take me by surprise when she didn't pause, didn't catch her breath. She notched the tip of my cock at her opening and held my eyes as she sank down in one long, torturously slow movement.

All my breath went out of me in a rush as she took me to the hilt, our bodies grinding together as she chased that friction. Goddess, when she took charge... it was sexy as sin, and I loved every second of it.

I grabbed her hips when she tried to lift herself to plunge again, bucking up into her instead. She was heaven. Her walls gripped me like a vise, and I wanted to flip us over and pound

232

into her until we both crashed over that edge together. But I forced myself to hold back.

"Shay, what about the risks?" I hated the words. Loathed them. But they had to be said. We couldn't lose our heads here.

She dropped her hands to my chest, digging in with her nails just enough to get my attention. As if she didn't already have it.

"There is nothing standing between us anymore, Dirge. You are mine, and I am yours. I'm not in heat, Brielle did her omega magic... At some point, we're going to have to trust. I want this. I want *you*. And if you say no, if you stop this bond forming between us... that's your choice. But you need to understand that I don't want that. I want to face whatever comes *together*."

My chest seized at her words, that fierce look in her eyes that I loved so much. Was she right? Should I really let go?

She clenched around me, and my eyes fluttered shut with a groan. "You're killing me."

"No, I'm showing you what I want. What do you want, Dirge?"

What did I want? I wanted her. I wanted to chase this passion, live it every day for the rest of our lives. I wanted her, every day, forever.

I lifted her up and slammed her back down. Her head fell back, soft keening sounds falling out of her mouth as she rode my cock like my queen.

"That's it, Shay. That's it. You going to soak me? Come all over this dick?"

"Yes, yes." She took over the motions then, faster and faster, chasing her pleasure and bringing me right along with her. I rose and met her stroke for stroke, even as I tried not to blow. I wanted to match her, fall over that edge together.

The pleasure built to an unsustainable height, the pressure in my balls begging for release as she cried out once more, locking down around me as she came. I followed her over the edge, eyes locked and glowing with our wolves as we fell into the abyss of release.

SHAY LAY on my chest in the quiet aftermath, and I held her like she was the most precious woman in the world, because she was. There was nothing between us but the steady drumming of the waterfall and the mingling of our shared breaths.

When she gasped and her hand fluttered up to her chest, concern ripped through me like a lightning bolt.

"What is it?" I sat up, bringing her with me to rest on my lap, straddling me.

"I think—" She stared down at her chest, and I watched with awe as the beautiful green scrollwork of her marks spread, reaching almost all the way across to the other side.

"Oh, shit. It burns." She held my shoulders as the ink seemed to peter out, breathing hard before she let her forehead drop against mine. "Why does that hurt so bad?"

She whimpered, and the sound broke my heart.

"I'm so sorry. It's got to be the fractured bond. I'm here, for what it's worth," I murmured against her lips, stroking her sides gently. It wasn't much, but all I could do was hold her and soothe her.

Then the searing pain hit me square in the chest, and my own breath left me.

Fuck, fuck, fuck.

I grunted, and she pulled back, mouth dropping into an *o* of surprise as my own mate marks finally made their belated appearance.

"Just hang on," she said, grip on my shoulders steady as she watched.

It didn't take long. They were no bigger than the size of my palm when the mark stopped spreading, not even leaving one pectoral muscle. Nowhere near the broad span of her marks, and they were still incomplete.

Shit.

"I know it's not a good sign that they didn't finish, but that's got to be a step in the right direction, right?" she asked, worrying her bottom lip between her teeth.

I thumbed her lip, the sight of it popping free and glistening wet making me instantly hard again beneath her.

"I guess we'll just have to keep working at filling them in, won't we?" My suggestion was husky, strained with a renewed surge of need.

She giggled, a sound I hadn't heard from her before, and I immediately craved more. I wanted to hear every laugh, every facet of her. Each new thing was a piece of the beautiful puzzle that was my mate.

"If you want to call that work, I suppose," she finally said. "But we need to get back. This was only a pit stop."

I grimaced when I realized she was right. "But do we have to put those clothes back on? There's nothing worse than wet clothes."

She smacked me lightly on the shoulder, then stood, crossing to our very sad, very soggy clothes, which were also now full of grit from the stone.

Shay seemed truly chagrined when she felt them between her hands. "Walk of shame it is, then. Assuming you know how to climb out of here?" She glanced around the cave, concern turning her sweet scent slightly acrid.

I levered myself up off the floor with a chuckle. "There's a trail. Come on, gorgeous."

FORTY-TWO

Shay

W e survived the walk of shame, but only barely. Leigh whooping like a psycho and then doing an off-key rendition of *Tequila Makes Her Clothes Fall Off* was something I could have lived my entire life never experiencing.

But luckily, no one was mad about our brief escape. If anything, they were happy for us. Bri gave me a tight hug as soon as I pulled on a spare pair of sweats, grinning happily at me.

"How are you feeling?" she whispered, even though we huddled in an empty corner of a hangar.

"Pretty great," I admitted, a blush heating my cheeks as I stared down at the concrete below our feet.

"No more issues, no more pain?" She gestured to her own chest, mirroring where my mate marks lay.

"Well, actually, yes. So, my mate marks filled in a little more, but not completely. His started, but they're still small. The size of his fist, maybe? But I thought..." I paused, trying to figure out what to ask her. Then I decided, screw it, she was my best friend and a doctor, no less. "Did you and Kane have sex more than once before your marks filled in? I don't want to make assumptions, but—"

Bri chuckled, shaking her head before I even finished. "We'd barely done anything. A hot make-out session, really, and we had full marks."

My shoulders slumped, confusion and worry weighing me down.

"Hey, look. Our case was unusual. Our theory is that my wolf *needed* the bond because of the curse and pushed for it to complete early so we could lean on his wolf's power. My symptoms have gone way down since we completed our bond, and now I only really get hit with pain when we're either apart—hasn't happened much—or when I have to call on what I'm now realizing are my omega powers."

Interesting. And it actually made me feel a lot better that it wasn't crazy that we didn't just *instantly* bond like they did. Her omega designation really had changed everything, it seemed. Although that made me feel guilty for asking her to tap those powers for me.

"That makes a lot of sense, actually. Thank you for telling me. And are you okay, after helping us out before?"

She hugged me again. "You don't have to thank me, Shay. We're sisters. Nothing is off the table, so don't be afraid to ask. And I'm fine. Let's just say you two weren't the only ones who snuck away for a little connection time with their mate."

Grateful tears clogged my eyes, making her blurry.

"Hey, now, it's okay, honey." She hugged me tighter, and a soothing scent flooded me, billowing off her like perfume. Like fresh rain, or actually the waterfall. I gripped her back every bit as tightly, trying to shove down the unhelpful wave of emotion.

I was so not that girl, the one who cried. Not because there was anything wrong with it, more because... crying hadn't helped me survive. It made me feel weak, and I hated it.

Dirge's warm presence at my back a second later made me smile even as the tears escaped onto Bri's shoulder.

"What's wrong? Are you okay? Did the pain come back?" He rapid-fired the questions as he patted me down, as if there was a physical wound he could find and fix.

"No, I'm fine. Stop that." I batted his hands away as I turned. "Just... a lot of stuff to process right now."

His eyes were kind as he smiled down at me, but I only saw them for a second before he pulled me into his chest. "It's all going to be okay."

"Is it? What about the ODL?" I managed to peek away from his chest to include Bri in the question.

She shrugged one shoulder, trying to seem nonchalant even though I could feel her repressed worry. "So far, there's no news."

"Kane said there has been no word of the attack, no word of omega magic, nothing. Our working theory is that the ODL themselves are covering it up, because if word spreads that an omega slipped through the cracks..."

Shit. That would not go over well at all.

"So they're actually covering for us to cover themselves," I murmured.

"Pretty much."

"What do we do, then? Just go on hoping they don't sense Bri again?"

"What else *can* we do? If they do sense me, it's not going to matter where we are. We have to stay ready for an attack at any time, while hoping I don't accidentally trigger their senses again." The smile she plastered on was tight.

Kane walked over, interrupting our conversation. "The pilot says we're fueled and ready to go. We were able to procure some lunch from the local pack's chef. A bonding gift for the new high alpha and his mate."

"So that's how the other half lives, huh?" Dirge playfully slapped Kane on the shoulder, eliciting a groan.

"Don't get me started. I'm not used to this level of politics. People have always tried to ingratiate themselves before, but it was to get in my father's ear. Now, they want to talk to me, and it's not an improvement. Did you know they have a border dispute with a pack out of Wyoming? Yeah, I didn't either. They want me to mediate their negotiations. I told them I'd send Reed when things settled down. He's going to be the one who murders me," he added with a mutter.

"Not funny," Bri scolded. "No jokes about anyone else dying, please. It's too soon."

"I'm sorry. Sometimes gallows humor gets me through."

"Did somebody say *gallows*?" Leigh wandered up, a hefty sandwich in one hand, a bottle of lemon-lime soda in the other.

"It was nothing," Kane said, shooting a chastised glance at Brielle. She smiled up at him, never one to hold a grudge.

"Don't let her whip you this soon, man," Leigh said with a grin, then took a giant bite of her sandwich.

"Are you sure it's a good idea to eat that right before we fly again?" I asked, remembering her repeated retching through the morning's flight.

She shrugged. "I don't know, I'm just too ravenous not to eat. Bri gave me the good motion sickness meds, so we better all hope they hold." She took another bite, eyeing me as if I was going to steal her turkey sandwich.

"Let's move!" Gael barked from the airstrip.

Leigh handed me her soda, flipped him the bird over her shoulder, and then took an overly aggressive bite of her sandwich.

I was pretty sure she was imagining her wolf ripping a chunk out of Gael's hide.

"We're heading to Johnson City pack grounds. That way you three can gather more of your things, we can get the pack transfer paperwork finalized, and hopefully meet with Karissma," Kane told us as we headed for the plane.

"Great," Leigh muttered around a mouthful of sandwich. "Bureaucracy and long-lost relatives. What could possibly go wrong next?"

I really wished she'd stop asking questions we didn't want the answers to.

DESPITE OUR TENSION over the looming ODL threat, landing in Texas went off without a hitch. It had been four days since our escapade in Colorado, we were about done packing, and there was not a whisper of trouble in the wind. No sign of ODL retribution, or even the fact that they knew Brielle was the omega.

Meanwhile, the little plane—*of death*, Leigh added any time it was mentioned—had left, replaced by the full-sized Pack Blackwater jet, awaiting our convenience at the nearby private airport. The Johnson City pack didn't have an airstrip or a plane of their own.

My days were spent tying up loose ends together as a pack, but my nights were spent in my room with Dirge, making love and listening to classical composers until we drifted off in each other's arms. It was a little slice of paradise in the midst of turmoil, and each time we came together, a little more of our mate markings filled in. Mine had completed, finally, while Dirge's were slowly crossing the broad expanse of his chest.

To my surprise, where my marks went straight across, almost like the graceful curve of butterfly wings, Dirge's extended down, filling in over his left pectoral and skating down his abdomen. His eight-pack was starting to take on color, and I waited eagerly each night to see what would happen next, even though I hated that the markings hurt him.

I was pulling on my second-favorite blue sneakers when Dirge cleared his throat from the doorway. The scent of strong coffee and hazelnut creamer wafted my way, and I think I fell in love with him a tiny bit more. He was enjoying our foray into domesticity, and in between helping me haul boxes, he was studying my every move so he could learn how I liked things. He'd been working on my coffee order yesterday, and from the smell of it, he'd nailed it.

"Penny for your thoughts?" he asked, passing me the coffee once I straightened.

"Just reflecting, thinking about how different it is having you here with me than it was before."

"Good different, I hope."

I stood as I sipped the coffee, closing my eyes at the perfect blend of sweetness and depth. "*Very* good different."

He stepped up behind me and slipped his arms around my waist. "Well, I'll just have to keep working until I get to excellent, then." He rumbled low in his chest, a contented sound, as I leaned back into him. "What do you have left to pack?"

I sighed. "Me? Nothing. We all agreed to leave the furniture, and we took the last load of boxes last night after the pizza break. My instruments will be the last thing to load up on the day of. Alpha Todd's second has our transfer paperwork finalized. All three of us have to go sign at noon."

"Are you sad about the piano?" he asked.

I shrugged. "A little, but I got it secondhand, and it's over the weight limit for the pack jet with all our other stuff. I'll just have to buy one locally once we're settled down. At least I'll have my keyboard with us now."

He nodded gravely. "We'll get you a new one. A fancy one, on me, and you can pick out anything you want."

I arched an eyebrow. "I'm not spending your money. I have a little bit in savings, and the music store is buying this one back from me." He opened his mouth as if to argue, but I cut him off.

"In the meantime, I really need to go help Leigh. She doesn't have a mate, and she's got way more stuff than me. Maybe more than me and Bri put together."

He chuckled. "I can swing by this afternoon to lend a hand, but Kane's asked any of us who are free to visit his loaner office. Apparently, he's expecting forensic results on the knife and wants to debrief with his people working on Alpha Varga and things overseas."

"Do you want me to come?" I spun in his grip so I could look up at him, careful not to slosh a precious drip of my hazel-nutty perfection.

"Entirely up to you. If you want to help Leigh, I can fill you in after?"

"Deal," I said with a nod. Dirge smiled and pressed a kiss to my lips.

When we parted ways in the hall, I was humming the tune that had been playing on repeat in my brain since my night of meditation. Each time, a little more detail filled in, the song growing more complex. And now I finally had my instruments back to work on it.

FORTY-THREE

Dirge

K ane's loaner office was barely bigger than a broom closet, and with four of us squished in there—Brielle had also opted to help Leigh pack, rather than deal with politics and investigations—it was about one degree of separation from a sardine can.

Kane seemed a bit peeved as he dug through a pile of papers on his temporary desk, but I was enjoying our time in Texas. Not the heat; that could fuck right off. But getting a glimpse into Shay's normal life, learning about my girl? That was something I would happily spend all my time doing.

I was the last one in, so I shut the door carefully behind me, then stood in front of it. It was that or Gael's lap, and we weren't that close. Yet. He was growing on me, slowly, especially knowing that he cared about Leigh.

Reed sighed, smacked Kane's hand back, and efficiently flicked through the papers. He paused on one, then pulled it from the stack and handed it to Kane without a word.

"Thank you," he murmured, scanning the page with a furrowed brow. "What is Midazolam?" He questioned the four of us, but I had no idea. "The lab results on the knife are in with the DNA, but they also found a coating of Midazolam along the blade, mixed with Shay's blood, and a codeine pain reliever. Why the fuck would an assassin put a pain reliever on his blade before stabbing someone?"

"I'm more curious what the fuck kind of lab will only fax paper results these days?" I asked.

Gael sighed, scrubbing a tired hand over his face. "I think it's a sedative? We could look it up to be sure."

"A secure lab that uses government-level secure lines to send and receive transmissions," Reed said with a droll tone. "Email can be hacked." His thumbs were already flying over his cell phone, presumably looking up the two medications.

"If they have secure phone lines, they could use them to call us," Gael muttered.

"Do you really want some scientist to dial you up and rattle off that string of numbers?" Kane held up the page, the diagnostic results enough to make me go cross-eyed.

"Midazolam is a sedative—points to you, Gael—and a preliminary search says that it can have negative interactions when mixed with certain painkillers, such as codeine. The combination can repress breathing or stop it altogether in sufficient doses. This is obviously based on human anatomy, but Brielle would probably know a lot more about interactions with shifter biology."

Kane's mouth pressed into a grim line. "So, not poison. But a potentially deadly combination of ordinary medications."

"Sounds about right," Reed agreed, sliding his phone back into his pocket.

"Did they test your mother for normal drugs?" I asked, thinking of the mysterious deaths of Kane's parents. From what they'd filled me in on so far, his father's blood tests were completely clean, neither of them had any physical wounds, and poison was suspected, though none was detected. The only other option was some sort of magical attack, but even those were hard to execute without a trace or signs of struggle.

"I think... I don't know. Frankly, that period leading up to their funerals was hazy, a blur of grief and worry. I know there were no actual poisons, though." Kane cast a quick glance at his top two, who both nodded agreement with his statement. "I'll ask Brielle tonight what she thinks of the effect that combination could have on wolves."

"Perhaps they should run both of their labs again, check for a combination similar to this." I pointed at the paper. "The Drakenia assassins use a lot of tricks that average killers don't. They're the best of the best when it comes to hunting magical beings, an elite force you can only hire with a private bank deposit that is more than what most people's homes cost. With that price tag comes efficiency, a guarantee of discretion, and fancy tracking magic that could locate us in the middle of nowhere on an unscheduled stop."

Kane nodded solemnly. "We can send the lab in Romania the details and ask for another round of tests. But right now, it's time to touch base with my contact, Lucien, who met with Alpha Varga yesterday. Can you all stay?"

"Of course," was echoed around the room as he dialed the number and placed his cell on speaker at the edge of his desk.

I leaned closer to Reed, asking in a whisper, "Why is he meeting with Varga?"

"We got intel right before you showed up that Varga is the one who tipped off the ODL at the great pack gathering, also before you showed up. But, he's been conveniently unavailable each time Kane's man called, until yesterday, when there was an opening in his schedule."

Conveniently, indeed. He might as well have gotten a skywriter to announce that he was scheming. Besides, working with the ODL—even if you thought it would come to nothing but a headache—was low. Verboten among wolves. *They killed our children,* for Goddess's sake. It was a major red flag.

We fell silent as the phone rang once, twice, before the man picked up.

"Lucien," he stated.

Kane leaned forward, resting his elbows on his desk as he spoke. "Lucien, it's Kane. I've got my top men here as well."

"High Alpha, I hope you're well."

"Thank you. What's the word from Varga?"

There was a pregnant pause. "He refused to see me."

"What?" Reed leaned forward indignantly. "You've got the royal seal. Turning away the high alpha's emissary is the equivalent of spitting on Kane's boots."

"Well, he hocked a big old loogie, then, because I wasn't even allowed on the grounds, despite the fact that he gave me the appointment."

"Holy shit," Gael muttered under his breath, too quietly for the phone to pick up.

"I arrived at the appointed time, pulled up, provided the seal, and was promptly asked to leave the premises. His butler sends his regards from the gate intercom."

"Butler, really?" I resisted the urge to laugh. Some of the European packs had the whole Old World-money, stiff-upper-lip thing on lock, and Varga was definitely one.

"That's a problem," Reed said with an indignant huff.

"You're telling me. Old bastard didn't even like Brigitte."

Brigitte? I mouthed the question to Reed.

"His motorcycle," he answered with an eye roll.

"Motorcycle, girlfriend—regardless, she was insulted," Lucien said, picking up on our sidebar conversation.

"More to the point—" Kane cut us off from the rabbit trail with rage in his eyes. "He refused to see an emissary of the high alpha, appointed with the royal seal."

"Something isn't right, and it may be more than your

parents' murder," Gael said. "You know those old windbags don't like the thought of bowing to a younger alpha. They respected your father, but there have been arguments for years that the high alphaship should have passed to one of them, not you, until you were 'of age,' whatever the hell that means."

"I remember, but they're too damn late. More than forty Alphas have already pledged their packs to me."

"But not all of them," I said. "What about the European packs?"

Kane leveled a questioning gaze on me. "Some were present, and they pledged along with the rest."

I nodded slowly, thinking. "I've got some contacts back in the old country from when I was still an enforcer for Pack Caelestis. I could reach out, ask them to sniff around and see what the rumblings are. Discreetly, of course. But whatever they find, we should probably make time to go over there and get the remaining pledges. Once you control all the pack bonds, they won't be able to pull this sort of shit."

Kane nodded gravely. "I'd appreciate any help you can offer. Reed can get you a phone." I expected anger or more bluster from someone as young as Kane with this much on his plate, but his father had trained him well. He was calm, if visibly troubled by the update.

"Anything else for me, Alpha?" Lucien asked, the sound of an engine revving coming over the line.

"No, Lucien. Keep your head down and your ears open. Call me immediately if anything changes."

"Will do." The sound of tires squealing came through the line before the click of him hanging up, which left us in heavy silence.

Gael was the first to speak. "So, we're heading to Europe. Can't say I'm thrilled about going to the ODL's home turf, frankly."

"Neither am I," Kane admitted. "But an interpack war can't

happen. Our populations aren't so great anymore that our species can handle sustained conflict."

"Brielle might be able to change that, not that I'm condoning war," Reed added hastily. "But if Jada is right, if she's going to affect packs around her, save the mothers like she did Gracelyn... in ten years, we might be looking at a significantly different supernatural landscape."

I froze momentarily as my own terror of fathering a child and having the Fetya snatch it away reared its ugly head. Brielle was certain she'd prevented the possibility, but until we knew the Fetya's stance for sure ... it would remain the stuff of my nightmares.

"We have to survive for that to happen," Gael interjected. "And right now, we're reacting, dodging, just trying to stay on our feet. We need a center of power, with defenses and weapons. Backup beyond the seven of us would be great too."

"What did you have in mind?" Kane asked.

"Your ancestral seat."

Kane blanched. "In Romania? You want to move Pack Blackwater out of Alaska?"

Gael leaned forward, both forearms resting on his thighs. "Not necessarily, but Kane, you're also the Alpha of your father's pack. They can't be left alone, without leadership. Surely you've thought about what would happen if..." He waved his hand uneasily, not wanting to remind Kane of his father's untimely passing.

"I thought I would have more time."

"Well, you don't, unfortunately. You—"

Kane held up a hand, stopping Gael midsentence. "I'm not saying you're wrong. I'm just saying I don't have all the answers yet. For now, I think Dirge is right. We should schedule a visit. We can set up shop at the castle, of course. But... I'm not making any permanent decisions while we're under the gun."

I couldn't agree more. "Smart. Moving too fast is a great way to make mistakes."

Kane nodded his acknowledgment. "Shall we go fill in the women? We could join them for lunch. I need my mate's touch right about now." He rubbed his chest as if he could feel an ache there in her absence, even though she wasn't far.

"Sounds good to me. I'm starved." Reed was on his feet in a flash as I carefully turned to open the door to our clown car of an office.

But before I could step out, Kane stopped me. "Dirge, stay a moment?"

"Of course, Alpha." I stepped to the side, letting Reed and a reluctant Gael exit first. "What can I help you with?" My hands dropped to link behind my back as I assumed the military rest stance out of old habit.

"Have you considered coming back as an enforcer? I know Julius and Gael would welcome the help, and you're experienced."

I rocked back on my heels, considering. It shouldn't have surprised me, but it did. Part of me wanted to say no, that I needed to focus on Shay. But I knew her, and I knew how deep her love for her friends ran. She would want to help and want me to do anything and everything I could to keep them safe.

"I'll need some time to think it over, but I'll get back to you."

"Thank you." He nodded again and rose, clapping me on the back as we strode out the door, the two of us both eager to see our mates.

FORTY-FOUR

Shay

"**B**rielle?" My head snapped up from my spinach salad at the unfamiliar voice. The she-wolf who'd approached our table seemed timid, almost afraid of us. She was a petite redhead, wearing jeans and a light hoodie that said *Run Wild* on the front.

"Yes?" Brielle's tone was kind, not an ounce of worry evident as she addressed the small female.

"Excuse me, I'm so sorry to bother you. But you've been in your rooms since you've been back, and, well—" She picked at her thumbnail with her pointer finger, and I noticed that the digit was red and agitated, as if she'd been picking at the cuticle for a while. *Very* nervous, then. But why? I took as unobtrusive a drag of her scent as I could, and it suddenly made sense.

Anxiety. My own shoulders loosened as soon as I pegged it. She could probably feel the dominance rolling off these four males from a mile off, and as far as I could tell she was *maybe* a nu in the pack hierarchy. Not much stronger than Bri, anyway.

"Do you have a medical concern? I was previously the pack's healer, but I've heard there's a fill-in since I was mated into another pack."

"Er, yes. It's me. I'm the fill-in, Olivia." She pasted on a forced smile, half lifted her hand as if for a shake, then seemed to think better of it. "It's just... I'm primarily an herbalist, and I've heard that you have *actual* medical training, as well as the best maternal-infant survival rates of any healer in the state. I was wondering—and I know it's a big ask—but could I maybe be your apprentice? I've only been an assistant healer for a year in my old pack, and there's a lot that I don't know."

Brielle frowned over at Kane before letting the expression sweep our group. Our insular, private group of people who knew her secret. This girl—no matter how sweet—was a safety risk, and beyond that, letting her into our circle could put a target on her as well.

"I'm not sure that's—"

"Please don't say no. Even if you're only here a few more days, I'd love anything you can share with me. I want to serve my pack well, but it's difficult when I don't know... actually, a lot of things. Your notes have been incredibly helpful, so I know I could learn a lot from you. Please." She stammered to a halt, a rampant blush creeping up her neck.

She might have been a nu or lower, but she had gumption. I instantly liked her.

"We'll probably only be here a few more days, but I don't see why I couldn't swing by the healer's clinic and show you some things." Brielle smiled warmly at Olivia, who nearly fainted in obvious relief.

"Thank you so much. I'll let you get back to your lunch," she said, already backing away.

"That's a bad idea," Gael groused as soon as the little she-wolf was out of earshot.

"Think she's undercover with the ODL?" Bri teased, then a little wrinkle formed between her eyebrows. "They don't even employ wolves, do they?"

"No, they don't," Dirge said, shooting my friend an amused

look. "Even if they tried, there's not a wolf alive who'd take the job of murdering our children. Gael's just an unfriendly ass."

"It was nice of you to offer to help." Leigh said, taking an imperious sniff and a testy bite of her big, greasy cheeseburger.

"Well, she seems sincere. And I always love someone willing to talk medicine." There was an excited gleam in her eyes.

"Just don't get too close," Gael persisted, ignoring everyone's eye rolls. "We don't need any safety risks, and if she figures out" —he dropped his voice so low, even I could barely hear him from right across the table—"the truth of your nature, she could be the weak spot the ODL finds and leverages."

"Considering I've lived my entire life as a psi and we had to travel to see a centuries-old bear shifter to get confirmation, I think my secret's fairly safe." Brielle cocked an eyebrow at Gael, as if testing to see if he'd challenge her directly.

Gael ducked his head, whether in deference or resignation, it was hard to tell. But he didn't take another bite of his steak, and it wasn't lost on me that *his* shoulders were still tight as barbed-wire cattle fence.

Maybe I should go to the clinic with her. *Just to be safe.*

THE CLINIC STANK OF ANTISEPTIC, which was far too sharp for my wolf's nose. Frankly, I was bored out of my skull as I sat on the paper-covered cot and watched Brielle and Olivia with their heads bent over an endless string of random tools, herbs, and notes, but after an entire morning of watching Leigh debate if she should box her shoes by color or by style, it was a welcome reprieve. We just wouldn't tell Leigh until we were back on Blackwater land that I'd stuffed all her leggings into one box instead of sorting them by season. What in the blue blazes did that even mean?

I didn't know, and I didn't intend to find out.

Brielle's phone buzzed in her purse, which she'd dumped next to me on the cot when we'd walked in.

I ignored it, but the sound came again a moment later. The third time annoyed me enough that I spoke up.

"Bri, you want me to check that?"

"Sure," she called over her shoulder, not tearing her eyes away from whatever the two of them were studying.

"Oh, I see. But what about the moon? I mean, human medicine has a longer history of study, but we're not really a one-to-one—"

I tuned them back out as I pulled out her phone. It was easy to spot in its bright teal case, *Smart Bitch* written on the back and studded with black rhinestones. Leigh's gift to her for Christmas last year. To match the one she'd made me, in purple, with *Fierce Bitch*, and her own *Alpha Bitch* in hot pink.

Leigh was special. Even if she did have an abnormally large collection of clothes to sweat in.

Bri had a text, so I swiped in her unlock pattern and checked, expecting something—hopefully not too raunchy— from Kane, but finding instead a message from Aunt Kari.

Aunt Kari: *I'll be in town tomorrow.*

Aunt Kari: *Are you still with the Johnson City pack?*

Aunt Kari: *I'm glad you reached out. I've missed you.*

"Bri? It's from your aunt."

"What?" She straightened, and I watched as it clicked. "Oh. Olivia, can you excuse us for a moment? I was waiting to hear from her. Family matter."

"Of course. I'll keep reading." Olivia smiled, not a hint of malice detectable on her by look or scent. The time spent watching the two of them geek out over their shared love of medicine had only underscored my impression of her as a sweet, nervous wolf. But I now had to add to that list that she idolized Brielle.

If I wasn't mistaken, she had a total girl-crush thing going on.

"What did she say?" Brielle whispered.

I held up the phone, which she took and then quickly tapped out a response.

"Thanks," she murmured, handing it back. She left it open so I could see the exchange.

Brielle: *Yes, we are. I've missed you too.*

Aunt Kari: *Three p.m. tomorrow. My place on the lake?*

Brielle: *Sounds perfect.*

I didn't know where her aunt's place was, but nervous anticipation already filled my belly at the thought. Would she know more about the curse, or were we about to run full speed into a dead end?

Despite her own future being up in the air, Brielle was already smiling when she crossed the small clinic back to Olivia, where they immediately jumped back into their discussion.

A familiar warm, tantalizing scent of cedar and bergamot filled the room, and I was on my feet, spinning toward the door before I consciously realized what I was doing. He was my magnet, always drawing me in, pulling me closer without meaning to do it.

Dirge grinned, wide and predatory, as I closed the distance between us.

"Everything okay?" I murmured, not wanting to disturb Bri and Olivia.

"Everything is fine, but I was wondering if I could steal you for bit? I'm itching for a run, and I'd much rather do it with you."

I cast a regretful look over my shoulder, but Brielle had turned to face me with a stern look, hands on her hips.

"Go."

"But—" I protested, even as excitement thrummed in my

veins. A run with my mate sounded *glorious* after days of packing and waiting. My wolf was itchy too. Loyalty, though, demanded I stay with Bri.

"I mean it, *go*. You two have had barely any time together, so take it where you can." She stepped closer, lowering her voice as she put her hand on my shoulder. "I'm fine, and things aren't slowing down any time soon, that I can tell. Please, spend some time with your mate and stop worrying about me. You deserve it. Both of you." She looked up at Dirge, encompassing him in the demand with a smile.

"Okay, but we're going to send someone else to hang out with you guys," I insisted, even as Dirge pulled me out of the small clinic, not needing to be told twice.

"I can handle that. You two have fun!" she called cheerily after us as Dirge dragged me out the door.

FORTY-FIVE

Shay

The ride to the lake house the next morning was long and bumpy. Dirge and I had stayed out way too late, our wolves not wanting to cut the run short under the waxing moon. It wasn't full yet, but the pull was already getting stronger. Now, as our rented black SUV bump-bumped down the pockmarked clay road, I had a pounding head and regrets about not getting more sleep.

Other parts of me had *also* been pounded, but they weren't complaining. I smiled as I glanced down at Dirge's hand twined around mine, a warm glow in my chest at the memory. We were dynamite together, and I'd never felt so content, let alone so safe. So cherished.

I was happy with my life before, but now I felt complete. It was subtle, but... life-changing.

When we finally pulled to a stop, it was outside a postage stamp of a house, tucked between trees and blending in with its weathered cypress siding. Spanish moss blew in the breeze off the lake, trailing from the trees like ball-gown sleeves.

It was utterly lovely, the sort of place where I'd happily hide away, spend a few weeks enjoying the perfect solitude. But as we all climbed out of the SUV, I was immediately hit by a powerful witch's aura. All thoughts of swimming in the shimmering lake fled as my wolf surged to high alert. My forearms itched as her tawny fur prickled along my arms. It took two deep breaths to will her back down and regain control.

"You okay there?" Dirge whispered at my temple, planting a kiss to cover it.

"Yep. My wolf just doesn't like unknown magical beings, after..." I swallowed down the flood of memories, the flash of the assassin's blade arcing toward me with deadly intent.

"We can wait in the car if it's too much. We don't have to go in." He gripped me by the upper arms, concern etched into his handsome features.

I shook my head, not interested in missing this. Bri's curse had changed her entire life. If Karissma knew about it, I wanted to hear it.

"I'm under control now. Thank you, though." I smiled and did my best to make it look calm. I was on edge, yes, but I was back in the driver's seat.

He held my hand as we walked up the front steps and didn't comment on how I tensed as we walked behind the witch over the threshold into her domain.

She was powerful, even more so up close, though it was evident she had some sort of shield on her aura. Witches had a certain *sparkle* to them, visible only to that sixth sense that could spot auras. Every now and then, they'd twinkle if you watched them long enough.

Watching Karissma was like viewing a mini fireworks show. Her aura popped and fizzed with light almost constantly. Beyond that, she was stunning. She had deep-ebony skin and wore her hair shaved on the sides, with a thick thatch of natural curls on top. The witch also had keen plum-colored eyes, missing nothing as she watched us file in. She stood with her arm tossed over Bri's shoulders, at ease despite the number of powerful wolves standing in the teeny-tiny living space. There was only one bedroom, as far as I could tell, and only enough space for us to all stand if some stayed in the kitchen.

Granted, the men were all heavily muscled, but still.

"You've got more of an entourage these days than the last time we were together," Karissma said with a chuckle. "Care to introduce me?"

"Of course, where are my manners?" Bri's smile was watery, and I could tell she was trying not to cry at the reunion with her long-lost family friend. "This is Kane, my mate."

"And he's the high alpha. No less than you deserve." Karissma hummed her approval as she shook his hand. Her eyebrows slowly lifted as she felt his aura firsthand. "You've got quite a punch. I bet you're good in bed."

"Aunt Kari!" Brielle gasped.

She winked at her niece's scandalized expression. "What? You're grown now. He's a fine-looking boy." There was no levity in her tone when she turned back to Kane, though. "He had better keep you happy, or I'll zap all the fur off his tail."

"Yes, ma'am," he murmured, not the least offended by her protective manner.

"Good," she murmured, but we all heard it.

She had a brass set of balls, a lone magic user threatening the high alpha and six of his pack mates. Although, as her aura continued to crackle with power, I amended that thought. She was confident in her power, and I had a feeling she knew well how to use it.

"These are my two best friends, Leigh and Shay." She pointed to each of us in turn. "This is Shay's mate, Dirge, and these are Kane's second and third, Gael and Reed."

Karissma nodded to each of us. "It's lovely to meet you all. Please call me Kari. So, as fantastic as this meet and greet has been, I have a feeling something more has caused you to seek me out after all these years."

Brielle looked down at the floor, guilt radiating off her. Kane spoke up, keeping a comforting hand on her shoulder. "Yes, Kari. We appreciate you going to the trouble to fly in. Brielle's mother died young, which you know. And within the past few years, Brielle has started having the same symptoms of her disease. But after a visit to a shaman who lives near our pack, he was able to confirm for us that it's not a disease at all."

"Of course not. It's a curse." Kari's statement was decisive, her eye more critical now as she studied Brielle as if she could see the curse hanging off her like so many cobwebs.

She was a witch, so perhaps she could.

"You can tell? Did you know that's what killed my mom?"

Leigh gripped my arm, fingers digging in just shy of painfully as she watched the exchange at my side. We were all tense, and the touch helped take the edge off slightly.

"I did, unfortunately."

"Is there anything you can do to lift it?" Brielle asked. "We were told that it can only be lifted by the witch who laid it."

"Your source was partially correct. A curse of this nature can only be removed by the witch who applied it or by killing her and securing a removal from one of her coven, which is often incredibly difficult to do after you've murdered one of their kind."

I bit my bottom lip. That sucked. I mean, I'd really hoped that her aunt would be able to just remove the thing.

"Oh. So, there's nothing you can do." Brielle glanced worriedly up at Kane.

"Can you identify which witch or coven is responsible for the curse? At least if we know the origin, we can keep working on the removal," Reed said, politely not commenting on the fact that as soon as we left here, we'd be hunting down whatever witch she named, probably to brutally murder them.

Anxiety radiated through me, which had my wolf pushing forward once more. She didn't know why this witch made me so nervous or that it was fear that she might not give up one of her own kind, adopted niece or no. She just knew I was anxious and fearful.

"That won't be necessary... because *I* cursed your mother," Kari said, grim honesty in her eyes.

FORTY-SIX

Dirge

C all it a sixth sense, call it supernatural. Whatever you called it, I knew Kane was about to lunge before he did. His eyes glowed, his fangs descended, and his fingertips were razor-tipped claws as our chests clashed. Somehow, I'd moved fast enough to block the other alpha from tearing the witch's head off her shoulders.

He couldn't do that, because we needed her to lift the curse. He'd realize that, I was sure of it. But however long that took to sink in, I was facing the full wrath of the high alpha, mano a mano.

And holy *shit*, did it not take long for him to pull on his pack bonds, because the wave of dominance he hit me with a half second later almost knocked me on my ass. Thankfully, Reed copped to the same thing I had and joined me in restraining Kane.

"*Move!*" The command thundered with so much alpha dominance that I felt all the women skitter back from his fury, unable to withstand the power lashing us. Reed and I together were nothing close to a match for him, and it was only Gael's quick thinking to jump on his back that gave us a fighting chance. His thick biceps curled under Kane's chin—not choking, yet, just applying enough pressure to get his attention.

"Alpha, please!" Reed tried to reason with him, while I tried not to get gutted by his claws. My wolf was howling for release, but I kept him locked down behind steel bars. We could *not* start shifting in this small space, or one of the females could get hurt.

"That's enough, Alpha. Allow me to explain, and all will become clear," Kari said, taking her own life in her hands as she stepped forward instead of giving Kane space.

He strained again, but her own power crackled in the air, sending an unpleasant buzz over my skin.

Kane was still in our grip as she stood toe to toe with him. "I promise, if you don't like what I have to say, you can rip my head off yourself before the sun sets on this day. But you're not going to want to."

He shook us off, still riled as he ran a hand through his close-cropped hair. Brielle was at his side in an instant, hanging on to him and leaking that lightning-struck stream scent I'd come to associate with her being stressed out.

It made me want to jump to her defense, even though rationally, I knew that wasn't the move here. The witch was too calm, and if she meant her harm, why tell us?

Shay stepped up to my side as well, her fingertips ghosting over my chest as if checking I was in one piece before settling on the back of my arm.

"Please, have a seat. Would any of you like a cup of tea, before I tell you the story? It's a long one, and not pretty."

"No, thanks," Leigh scoffed, arms crossed over her chest.

"Very well." Kari inclined her head slightly, sadness clear on her sharp features. "Your mother was my best friend, a fact you well know," she said to Brielle, like the rest of us weren't here.

The witch was bold, ignoring a room full of edgy alphas.

Brielle nodded hesitantly.

"Our friendship wasn't one many approved of. Neither my coven at the time nor her pack. It wasn't done, friendships across species lines, and at that time in America, racial tensions were high as well. We were doomed to fail, yet somehow, our friendship bloomed. Two women ahead of their time."

She smiled softly then, stroking one of her thumbs idly as she relived the memories. She didn't have the body language of a killer. Not that she wasn't *able* to kill—she was strong enough to fry a person if she was so inclined—but my wolf sensed no malice in her, no whiff of a lie to this tale.

"She met your father about a hundred years after the two of us became friends, and it was instant love, as it so often is with your kind. They were over the moon when they found out you were on the way. She'd lost a son before you—I don't know if they ever told you in the end—and it took all my skill to save her. So when she found out she was pregnant again, well, your mother immediately put herself on bed rest. She was so eager to be a mom, even though pregnancy is fraught for wolves. She didn't care. She just loved you, from the moment she knew you were coming."

I drew in a shallow breath, confused about the direction this was going. If they were so close, why the fuck had Kari cursed her?

Brielle's scent changed again as sorrow plunged into the mix.

"Around halfway through the pregnancy, she began to have complications. Small things at first. Early contractions here and there. And then one day, she was walking back from the bathroom and collapsed. Your father called me after the pack's healer left. He hadn't been able to do anything for her besides a few herbal teas. And that's when I sensed it for the first time. Your magic."

She smiled at Brielle, the saddest expression I could imagine.

"You knew," Brielle said, the words a statement, not a question.

"I knew what you were, yes. And when I told your mother, she nearly died of a broken heart. She couldn't bear to lose another child. She begged me to do anything I could, to change you, to save you. But there was nothing I could do to take away your very nature. An omega is who you are, what you were destined by the Goddess to be. We tried everything: masking spells, glamours, even lesser curses, but still, I could sense you. The only possible option was to dampen your magic, smother it under a curse so vile, it would kill her. But she didn't care. She wanted you to live, to have a chance at a normal life and happiness. She insisted that she'd rather spend however many years she could loving you. Your father agreed, though I think given any other option, he would have chosen his mate's life."

Brielle and Leigh were both crying now, my own mate swiping away silent tears as she leaned into my side. I wrapped my arm around her, wanting to stop the pain, even though we all knew how this story ended.

"I placed the curse in her fifth month. Your power was already so strong, we were concerned the ODL would sense you early, and it was the only way to mask your true identity. The effects were immediate, the taint so strong, your mother's health almost didn't recover after the birth. It once more took everything I had to save her, return some semblance of her health, but she refused to let me lift the curse. You were her everything, and if I lifted it from your line, you'd have been exposed."

She cleared her throat, doggedly continuing the story. "It worked, obviously. Your magic has been slowly draining away for your entire life, and as you age, the symptoms will worsen. I can lift the curse, but... you'll be hunted. The power I felt when you were still in your mother's womb..." She shook her head sadly. "It can't be hidden any other way. As soon as we reveal the truth, the ODL will come for you with the full weight of the organization. You'll be hunted until the day you die."

The silence was so thick, you could have cut it with a knife.

"She died to protect me," Brielle whispered, her voice full of agony. "She could have lived for hundreds of years more if it weren't for me."

"No, sweetheart, no. You don't understand. Bringing you into this world, saving you, that was her purpose. She couldn't have borne another blow. It changed her, losing your brother. She'd had a long, hard life. You were the light that saved her." Karissma stepped forward, ignoring the way Kane tensed as she folded Brielle into her arms.

After they'd both regained their composure, she stepped back. "I can remove the curse, today if you wish. But you need to be prepared. Your kind hasn't walked the earth since the Renaissance. While I know you'd never harm another living being, the Omega Defense League won't care. They will see it as their singular mission to destroy you."

"We should wait," Reed was quick to interject, holding up apologetic hands as he addressed Kane. "Alpha, with all due respect... If Brielle isn't in immediate danger of the curse doing permanent damage"—he cast a questioning glance at Karissma, who nodded her agreement—"we should wait. We need time to plan, to make a strategy. The ODL threat is real. The faintest whisper of her magic at Ushagat Island, and they struck without any hesitation or preliminary investigation. They won't be any less willing to strike when her powers are unleashed in full."

Kane was silent, his expression stony as he held Brielle tightly to his chest, and I couldn't blame him for his stunned silence. I'd held my dying mate in my arms. It was enough pain to end me, but they faced a devil's bargain. It was no choice I ever wanted to have to make.

"So, what? Her only choices are to live her life as a shadow of what she was destined to be in relative safety until she dies young. Or, unleash her full potential, only to be hunted into an early grave?" Leigh said, her words stricken with anger and grief.

"Those aren't the only options." Shay surprised me by speaking up at my side. Her voice shook with emotion, and her grip on me was tight, as if she was scared she'd float away if she let go. "There's another choice."

"What? Because all I hear is shit sandwich after shit sandwich!" Leigh's face crumpled into tears, and in an instant, Gael was there. He pulled her against his chest, running a soothing hand down her back. For the first time since meeting them, she didn't push him away. She accepted the comfort, turning her face into his broad chest and letting her tears soak his shirt.

"We bide our time, and we keep fighting. You don't quit when the chips are down, not when your life is at stake. We figure out how to keep Bri as strong as we can, and then we go to war against the ODL. On *our* terms." Shay straightened, leveling a pleading gaze on Bri. "You deserve better, Bri. Your mom did too."

Brielle bit her bottom lip and looked up at Kane, as if asking him a question. They communicated silently for a few moments until he cleared his throat.

"We agree with Shay. We will change the laws, or we will dismantle the Omega Defense League brick by brick." He pinned Kari with a heavy gaze. "What can we do for Brielle in the meantime, while she's stuck with this curse?"

Karissma smiled then, giving a slow nod of approval as she peered around at the seven of us. "Physical contact with her mate, of course. The stronger your bond is, the more the toll of the curse is spread between you. Your position as high alpha may help, given the greater pool of power you can access. There are some potions I can provide, generally good for the constitution and good health. But beyond that, it's trying not to tap in to your omega powers while they're shuttered. The more power you use, the larger the drain."

Brielle gasped. "Is that why I can't hold my shift?"

Karissma nodded. "Any use of your power is going to cause you pain and exhaustion. The more you can limit it, the better. Though given you've never experienced your powers without the curse, you may not even realize when you're doing it. Omega gifts take time and practice to master, like any other. Surrounding yourself with power, whether at a natural seat of power like a convergence of ley lines or by those gifted with extreme magical energy"—she nodded at Kane, then Shay as she spoke—"can also help replenish your stores more readily and lessen the effects of the drain."

"Ley lines?" Gael asked. "Where are those located?"

Kari sighed. "You young people are supposed to be running this whole damn world, and you don't even know about ley lines?" She muttered a few curses under her breath as she waved her hand, magical glitter trailing in its wake until a four-foot-high world map shimmered in the air before us. Purple lines began to appear, pulsating and glowing especially strong anywhere they intersected. I was surprised to see that one was centered in Alaska, near Pack Blackwater grounds. But the thickest lines were over Europe.

"Holy shit, that's right where your father's pack house is located," Reed murmured, pointing to an inky pool of purple settling right over Romania.

"Imagine that, a world leader who actually knew about the magic he depended on." Karissma said, sarcasm practically dripping from her tone as she let us finish studying the map. After a few more moments, she waved it away as easily as she'd waved it into existence.

"There's an intersection in Alaska too," Reed said a little petulantly.

Kari's mouth pressed into a thin line. She had that same look our mother used to get when Reed was a toddler.

"I have a question. You mentioned beings of great magical power helping Bri," Shay interjected. "But... how? I don't have any more power than any other shifter, as far as I know."

"You do, actually," Kari said with a gentle smile. "Your fae nature hasn't been fully awoken, as it doesn't for fae until they've bonded with their life mates. Once you two have tied the knot... You'll be sitting on a near-nuclear level of power. I can't say for *certain* that you could best the high alpha here in an arm-wrestling match, but I'd say there's a strong chance."

Shay blinked, mouth hanging open briefly as she turned to me, then back to the witch. "But how does that help Bri?"

Karissma bobbed her head back and forth, considering. "Think of it like a battery pack. Brielle's battery only has one bar. She's always low. Her bond to Kane allows her access to a second bar of energy. You could give her a third, at full power. That bar could be the difference between her surviving the lifting of the curse, or not."

So, Brielle was some kind of energy vampire? I glanced with concern between Shay—my loving, selfless mate, who'd already thrown herself on a literal blade to save her friend— and Kane, his gaze hopeful as he hung on the witch's every word. I didn't like it, not one bit.

I cleared my throat. "We've got a lot to discuss and to think about. Perhaps we should head back to the pack lands?"

"Of course. I'll be here when you're ready to discuss next steps." She stared me down as I led Shay past her, and I knew she saw right through me. Centuries-old witches tended to have that ability. It was how they survived all the witch hunts.

FORTY-SEVEN

Shay

We were barely out of our rental on Johnson City pack grounds when a harried beta rushed up to us.

"High Alpha! I'm so glad you're back. Alpha Todd has put together a last-minute fete to celebrate your historic visit to Texas."

"Historic?" Kane asked with a heavy dose of skepticism.

"Apparently, it's been more than two hundred years since your father visited, and that was before Alpha Todd's time. The neighboring pack Alphas, ah, would like the opportunity to *participate* in history. Or so they bellowed over the phone. Repeatedly. Until he agreed to host the event, which begins in less than two hours."

The beta's harried expression suddenly made a lot more sense. Dread built in my chest. A room full of alpha energy was *not* my idea of a good time ever, but especially not now. I was processing everything we just heard from Kari and really struggling. My not bonding Dirge—right away, thank you very much —was one skosh shy of actively hurting my best friend. But were we ready for that? There was still so much we didn't know about each other, and sure, the attraction was through the roof...

But bonding was for life.

Granted, at this point, I couldn't imagine life without him. Even when I thought he'd be doomed to permanent wolfhood, I had still wanted him close. But now... now we spent our nights tangled up and our days getting to know each other. I couldn't imagine it any other way.

Did that mean we should bond, though? Right now? It was so fast.

I was conflicted. And the more I thought about it, the more it felt like I was keeping secrets from him, secrets that might make him want nothing to do with me.

"I see," Kane said with a chuckle. "Well, we'll be staying in town for a bit longer, and we'd be happy to meet the neighbors."

Reed cut in, his politician voice firmly in place as he took the aide by the elbow. "Unfortunately, though, we didn't bring formal attire for an event of this type. We packed light." He bestowed the man with a dazzling smile, and I swear on the Goddess's hem the man nearly swooned.

"That's no trouble at all. I've already called in a tailor, and his team is staged with formal-wear options for each of you, just outside your lodgings."

"Excellent...?"

The man wasn't breathing. He stared into Reed's charming face for a long moment before he realized he was waiting for an introduction. "Marvin," he finally stammered.

"Thank you, Marvin. Please let Alpha Todd know we'll be there with bells on."

"Of course, I'll update Alpha Todd." He wandered off in the direction of the other alpha's office, but not without casting a few looks back over his shoulder at Reed, who'd already jumped into business mode.

"Okay, as usual, I'm approving outfits for you." He leveled a disapproving glare on Gael. "But I suppose your mates might want to handle your outfits now?" He looked at Brielle first, then me.

"Umm, can we just say that we're not exactly formal, and we'd appreciate you handling all menswear decisions?" Brielle asked with a grimace.

I nodded my agreement.

"Excellent." Reed gleefully rubbed his hands together. "Let's go see what Texas tailors can do in... an hour and forty-nine minutes."

A LOT, as it turns out. A Texas tailor with a team of ten—yes, *ten*—assistants could dress us all in ninety minutes flat, in clothing fancier than we'd worn for Bri and Kane's bonding ceremony. I tugged nervously at the neck of the gown where the strapless side swooped down under my arm, only to have my hand smacked by my assigned dresser, Jewel.

She studied me with pursed lips from the floor to the tips of my hair, which had been styled into a sort of braided-sides, swoopy-curled mohawk. That part was pretty cool. The dress, though ...

"It's perfect, and if you touch it again, I'm going to bite your hand off." The she-wolf lifted her lip in a snarl, not a hint of joviality in her stance as she nodded. "You're ready. You can head into the hallway—you're expected in about five minutes. But if you need more tape, I'll be in the back of the room with my kit."

"Uh, thanks," I murmured, eager to get away from her. She was all sharp angles with not a hint of soft edges, and her personality matched. By the time I stepped into the hallway, my stress was through the roof, which was ridiculous given all we'd been through. But between her salty personality and the impending crowds, I was not a happy wolf.

"Shay?" My name on his lips was low and husky. It sent a thrill straight to my pussy, panties going damp with just a single word. I forced myself to turn slowly, even though I was tempted to throw myself at him.

I didn't want to know what Jewel's punishment would be for getting horizontal with my mate after she'd perfected every detail of my appearance. And then I spotted him, in a freaking *tuxedo*, hair slicked back and that devilish grin that made my knees turn to jelly. Fuck, forget horizontal. I'd accept vertical, up against the wall, if it meant I got to muss him up a little.

"Hi," I whispered, slowly looking up to meet his glowing eyes.

"Hot damn, you are a vision." He closed the distance between us, and between one blink and the next, his hands were skimming up the sides of my plum gown, fingering the lace trim at the edge. His erection throbbed hot against my belly, which was swooping in somersaults.

It might be worth it to get smacked around by the tailor.

He reached up and touched a curl, twirling it around one finger with an appreciative hum low in his throat.

Shit. I could take her.

"You can't expect to come out dressed in this hot little number, looking all perfect and untouchable, and just say hi, muzică mea. You'll give a man a heart attack like that."

I rolled my eyes at his over-the-top flirting, but deep down inside, I felt like I was having a vagina attack. She wanted him, stat. He was gorgeous in formal wear; his usually unruly hair was slicked back, and the sleek black tux he wore hugged his broad shoulders before coming in to frame his narrower waist. It was ridiculous to feel this turned on when I'd seen him naked, but somehow, that just made it hotter. I was the only one who knew what was under all that fine window dressing. I knew the real man, and I couldn't wait to peel him out of it all later. Drive him wild, like I knew he could be.

Settle down, hussy. I have to be presentable for at least two hours.

His fingertips grazed the top of my breast, just the swell that crested above the curve of the dress, and my clit tingled with pure, unadulterated lust as I inhaled a deep breath of his scent. The cedar and bergamot was laced with his own answering need as I slid my hands inside his tux jacket.

Fuck, fine, one hour. You just have to make it one hour.

Dirge's chest was warm and solid under my fingertips, and suddenly, the anxiety about tonight's event was gone. He was here. He was my touchstone.

A shudder racked me, the last bit of the nerves working their way out, and he frowned down at me.

"Was that—"

"Bitches, this better be a good night. Because I don't want to waste all this fine ass on a boring, freaking political dinner." Leigh strutted into the hallway with both hands on her hips, doing a little spin to show off a fire-red mermaid gown that hugged every curve she had. She stopped with her hip cocked, displaying said ass with flair.

I laughed and felt Dirge's chest shake with laughter under my fingertips. What else could you do?

"I wouldn't get your hopes up, Leigh. We already know all the Johnson City folks, and I think only a few neighboring alphas are coming," Brielle stood in front of her own door, Kane appearing at her back as she shoved a white-gold earring into place.

Leigh rolled her eyes. "Listen, I need to get laid, okay? They better have some hot seconds, or I'm going to be hitting the Howler solo tonight, and we all know that's not a good look."

I cringed. The Howler was a dive bar about ten minutes off pack grounds where in-the-know humans came to get lucky with a shifter. It was seedy as hell and not at all safe for her to go to alone. The bouncers were good enough, but every now and then, a disgruntled hunter snuck in to take a swipe at a tipsy shifter.

"If you're looking for a second, look no further," Gael said smoothly, eyebrow cocked defiantly.

Leigh's mouth flapped a few times, much like a fish, before she angrily snapped it shut. "You wish you were that lucky. You and your sugarcoated dick are off-limits."

He threw his head back and laughed, a sound I'd never heard before. "Sugarcoated? My, you must have enjoyed yourself more than I thought."

The top of Leigh's head was going to blow off. I was sure of it.

But she just smiled, sickly sweet as poison, and swayed toward him. "Ooh, big bad alpha thinks he's got a hold on the little she-wolf." She ran her hands up his chest, and he froze, a deer in the headlights under her fingertips. "But I've got news for you. It could be *gold fucking plated* and I wouldn't touch it again with a ten-foot pole. The asshole it's attached to isn't my style." She gave him a little shove backward, then stormed down the hallway.

"Those two are going to be endless trouble, aren't they?" Dirge murmured as we watched him watch her walk off.

"Either that, or they're going to kill each other," I agreed, concern about the night growing again as I watched them dance around each other again.

It was starting to look like my inner hussy was going to be disappointed tonight, because we were going to be on babysitting duty.

THE EVENT WAS ACTUALLY LOVELY. They'd chosen an indoor-outdoor party space, though most of the guests were milling around outside chatting under the twinkle lights or gyrating on the dance floor. The music was okay, but not what I'd have chosen. The breeze carried away many of the overwhelming scents, the fresh pine from the woods cleansing as well as soothing.

The food was good too. The waiters had just handed me some sort of seafood things that were too fancy for me to be able to pronounce, but I ate two of them with gusto.

"Do you want to dance?" Dirge asked as we set our empty plates on a passing waiter's tray, his breath tickling my ear as his arms went around me.

"Mm, yes and no?"

"And why is that?"

I sighed, watching as Leigh danced with a tall, brooding alpha male from Pack Timberwood. He was handsome enough, I supposed, but not at all her type. Meanwhile, Gael was knocking back hard liquor like it was water and pretending he couldn't see her.

We really didn't need a multipack altercation added to the pile of shit we were already trying to climb out of.

"Your friend is a grown woman, and while she might bluster in private, I don't imagine she'd ever do anything to hurt Brielle or Pack Blackwater's reputation."

"You're right," I said with a sigh, leaning back into his warmth.

A raindrop splattered right on my nose, but before I could wipe it away, another hit my cheek. Then my hair, and then it was like someone opened up the floodgates. Good-natured screams and squeals rang out as people made a mad dash for the indoor space.

I was laughing as I pulled Dirge along, not really all that

concerned. Although, I didn't want to look like a drowned rat either.

The indoor space felt cramped after our freedom, and within ten minutes, the many clashing scents and alpha pheromones were already getting to me.

I had been slowly edging us toward the back door, preparing myself for an early escape as soon as the party started to wind down, when a quick burst of cold air hit the back of my neck, and a too-familiar scent blasted me.

My pulse pounded, and the whole world seemed to narrow as I spun.

"Shay? Are you okay?" Dirge's voice sounded far away, as if he were yelling down a tunnel.

He was here, and I was not even close to okay.

So I ran.

FORTY-EIGHT

Dirge

One minute, we were holding hands and making small talk, pretending like we weren't working our way through the crowds toward the exit, and the next minute, a lightning bolt of emotion hit me dead center in my chest, so strong it nearly knocked the breath out of my lungs.

Before I could even process what had happened or why, Shay dropped my hand and bolted like someone had just shot a starter's pistol. I tore after her as she deftly wove through the crowd, nearly bowling a few people over in the process. I wondered if Gael had finally snapped and torn some poor schmuck's head off for Leigh grinding on them on the dance floor. But no. We passed Leigh—still grinding and impossible to miss in that fire-engine-red dress—and I followed Shay straight out the small side door and into the torrential downpour outside.

But she hit that wall of water and didn't hesitate. In one stride, she went from my stunning mate in the purple dress that I planned to peel off her with my teeth to the tawny wolf who landed in a full-speed run.

My own wolf rose to the surface just as quickly, determined to stay with her, find out what had set her off.

That tuxedo was probably very expensive, I thought with fleeting regret as I tore after her on four paws. I couldn't say how long she ran or if she even knew where we were going. Fuck, were we even still on Johnson City pack lands? No idea.

But still, she raced on tirelessly through the woods. The waxing moon was past its apex before she finally slowed, her wolf's sides heaving as she staggered to a stop, head hanging low. I gave her space, stopping a dozen feet away before yipping softly to let her know I was there.

Shay was so exhausted, she didn't even look up. She must have known it was me, for there was no visceral pain left in my chest. *Her* pain, I'd realized somewhere along the run through the towering, endless pines. Our bond had progressed again, slowly filling in the cracks. That fractured bond was no joke, for it had taken... quite a lot of physical contact in order to progress even this far. Or perhaps it was her wolf, calling out to mine in her moment of terror that had done it. I couldn't say.

All I knew was that she was feeling a torrent of pain, sadness, and regret. It burned behind my breastbone as if someone had lit a torch and shoved it behind my sternum. I wondered if she realized, but I couldn't ask, not in this form.

Could I? Excitement for the possibility of our mental link forming was hard to suppress, but whatever she was going through right this second had to take precedence.

When she didn't flinch back from my presence, I paced slowly forward to nuzzle her, our noses passing briefly as my wolf sought to comfort hers by exchanging scents. He didn't know or care why, only that our mate needed comfort. Physical comfort, preferably.

She acquiesced, sides still heaving as she leaned her face into my shoulder, so like her favorite pose when we were in human, it made me smile inside.

Eventually, her wolf shuddered and faded, leaving behind my beautiful human mate, naked and shivering in the night air. I shifted back as well, though years of living in wolf form meant my stamina wasn't taxed nearly as much as hers had been. When I opened my arms, she came to me gratefully, wrapping herself around me and tucking her head under my chin.

She was chilled to the bone, lips a little bit blue and goose-flesh covering her as I chafed her lightly with my hands to warm her up.

Slowly, she absorbed my warmth, and the knot of pain in my chest began to ease. I was overflowing with pride that I was able to comfort her, support her, even as the curiosity was eating at me. Why had she run from the room like her tail was on fire?

"There are some things I haven't shared with you yet," Shay said, her voice a whisper I could barely hear, even in the stillness of the forest. The crickets were singing louder than her.

"Whatever it is, I'm here, muzică mea. And I'm not going anywhere." I stroked down her back, urging her to sit with me so she could rest. She was still trembling as she lowered herself into my lap, curling up like a kitten against my chest.

"It's not a happy story."

"Some aren't. They're still worth telling." I continued stroking her back, long and slow, not prying even though I wanted to. I knew so little of her past, but our present had been pretty all-consuming. We had time to learn each other, bask in every nuance. We had forever. So I'd take whatever she was willing to share, and I'd hold space for the rest until she was ready.

"I was found on the side of the highway when I was six years old. I don't remember my life before that, and I have no memories of my parents. I didn't even know what I was, in the beginning."

I stayed silent, letting her work it out.

"They put me into human foster care. There were no parents to terminate their rights, so I bounced from home to home for several years. I was always quiet, a little timid. But it wasn't until my fourth home, when I was eleven, that I stopped speaking altogether. He wasn't really a good man, or I guess he was a terrible one. He fostered for the paycheck more than anything. So I lived in a room with three other girls, and across the hall was a room with four boys. We all had bunk beds."

Dread grew in my stomach as I feared where this story was heading. If that man had touched her, I'd rip his head off. I didn't care if it was cold-blooded murder. Anyone who had hurt a child, *especially* a vulnerable one under their protection? They deserved every scrap of pain coming their way.

"It was crowded and noisy. I didn't speak, so no one spoke to me, which I preferred after a while. I was invisible. But one of the girls was unhappy there. She was thirteen and claimed she'd met an older boy who she was going to run away with. One night, she slipped out our window and made a run for it. I was curious, more than anything. I didn't know much about boys, but I was starting to develop an interest." She chuckled mirthlessly.

"But what my foster sister was too naive to know was that her older boyfriend was just bait. He was part of a sex trafficking ring."

All the breath left my lungs, and it took all I had in me to stay still instead of shifting into my wolf form and howling my rage at the sky. Even though I knew what she was going to say next, the words still cut like knives.

"The men waiting there were not this pretend boyfriend, and they scooped me up with her. We were blindfolded and drugged, and when I woke up, it was on a dirty mattress inside what I later learned was a shipping container."

She shuddered at the memory, and I gripped her tighter. I had to force myself to loosen my hold.

"It's okay. You don't have to tell me if you don't want to." Though I *really* needed to know if that wolf was one of these despicable men. I had full confidence I could tear him limb from limb, but if he was part of this *ring*... I'd need Kane's backing to wipe them off the face of the planet.

"I need to, Dirge. It's time you know who you're mated to."

Her voice was full of misery and guilt, and I wanted to light something on fire. But that wouldn't help her. I cupped her chin, forcing her eyes up to mine.

"Whatever you tell me, wherever this story goes, it doesn't change my opinion of you. I already knew you were a survivor. This only confirms that. You are *mine*, and nothing can ever change that."

FORTY-NINE

Shay

—————

Dirge's eyes burned with unfettered devotion, and the sight of it nearly clogged my throat. But I had to finish this awful tale, get it over with so he could make an informed decision about who I was, the terrible things I'd done.

I was a murderer. A cold-blooded killer in a feminine package. And part of me was screaming not to tell him, not to let him see this darkest sliver of my soul, but how could I not? How could I let him complete a bond with me without full disclosure? I couldn't. It was bad enough it had gone this far. I pushed on with the tale, though everything inside me was screaming that he was going to run, to leave me and never speak to me again.

"They came at night. For the first few nights, I just squinched my eyes closed and prayed they didn't come to my mattress. It was terrible, and we all cried. Endless tears." I closed my eyes as if it wasn't real if I didn't let the outside world in. "But on the fourth night, a man came. I felt the edge of the mattress dip, and I froze. Even the tears wouldn't keep coming."

Dirge tensed underneath me, and I could smell his rage as

his scent turned acrid and bitter. I rested a hand on his bicep to calm him, even as the words poured out of me faster and faster.

"When he grabbed my ankle, something inside me just... snapped. One minute, I was a terrified little girl. The next, my body burned, everything hurt, and people were screaming. Somehow, I had fangs and claws, and I was tearing him to shreds. Another man ran in when he heard him screaming and tried to stop me. But my wolf... She tore him up too. The other girls were screaming, there was blood everywhere... but thankfully, the second man left the door open."

I swallowed hard. The memory of that waiting sliver of moonlight—that ultimate freedom at a time when I was so desperate—was something I would never forget.

"We all ran. More men came and tried to stop us, but I tore every single one of them apart. They shot me four times. She didn't stop, though. We killed every last man."

I ducked my face against his chest, the steady thrum of his heart comforting me now, while he was processing. I knew the jig was up. Even among shifters, such bloodthirsty destruction wasn't okay. Feral wolves who killed humans were put down, no exceptions. He was going to stand up and leave me here any second, but I'd take this last crumb of connection and hold it tightly, even if it was all I had left.

His hands came up to cup the backs of my arms, and I braced myself for him to shove me away. But he didn't. He skimmed my arms, up my throat, to cup my jaw. Gently, he urged me to look at him. I was so afraid of his judgment, I wanted to resist, but a part of me knew I needed the closure.

But when our gazes clashed, mine terrified and his stormy, he still didn't let me go.

"Good."

The word shocked me to my core.

"What?" I spluttered. "I murdered more than twelve men that night. How can you say *good*?"

"Those sons of bitches deserved it. Don't you see? They were kidnapping and sex trafficking *children*. You were eleven, Shay. That was self-defense if ever I heard it. And you saved all those other girls."

I sat in his lap, too stunned to argue.

That night had been my greatest shame, my recurring nightmare, for fifteen years. I'd never shared the truth of my background with another soul, for the horror. But... good?

He must have seen the disagreement written on my face, because he let out a frustrated growl. "Shay, I know it was traumatic. And you've got the right to remember it however you want. But put the Shay of *today* on the outside of that situation. I know it's hard. But let's say there was a trafficking ring nearby, and we went to bust it. Would you feel sorry for the mother-fuckers hurting little girls? Or would you let your wolf loose and tear them limb from limb?"

"I—" My mouth went dry as my wolf snarled, pushing forward against my control, even as exhausted as she was. "I'd rip their throats out, every last one." The answer shocked me.

I'd never stepped back and analyzed my trauma, not from an adult perspective. I'd been holding on to it as a scared little girl, too afraid to let anyone know what she'd been through or what she'd done.

But maybe... maybe it was time to give her a break. Younger me was a survivor, and that wasn't something to be ashamed of. Though, I wasn't sure I was ready to let it all go. Some part of me... some part of me still felt the stain of those nights. The gore splattered in my fur, dry and crusty and stinking for over a week until I found a stream and finally got brave enough to plunge myself in it. Thinking myself some kind of monster, before I'd known my wolf was part of me. That I wasn't crazy.

"There's my girl." He smiled down at me with pride. "Those fuckers don't deserve another *second* of your time. You hear me?

They got off easy. If you hadn't taken them out, I sure as fuck would've, and it wouldn't have been fast."

He meant it too. My pulse was pounding as I looked up at him, held him. He wasn't going to leave me.

"But the shifter here. How does he fit into the story?" he asked softly. He stroked both sides of my neck with his thumbs very distractingly.

"Oh," I murmured, letting my gaze drop back down to his chest. "That's Brand. He's... he's the one who found me after."

Dirge went still again, listening intently.

"I didn't understand what had happened to me, not for a while. I didn't *know* what a shifter was, let alone that I was one. I thought I'd gone crazy or was some sort of mutant. So, I lived alone in the woods for... a while. A full year, in the end. But one day, a man found me. Spoke to me like he knew I could understand him. And then he shifted right in front of me."

Dirge chuckled, giving me a little squeeze as I continued.

"It blew my mind that I wasn't the only one. He told me I was safe, I wasn't a monster like I'd thought, and he was going to take me to a pack, a place with other wolves where I'd be safe forever. It took us a full week to hike back to civilization, and the whole time, he told me stories, cooked for me over campfires at night. He made me feel cared for, for a little while. Normal." I swallowed hard, feeling silly.

"But..." Dirge prompted.

"But when we got there, it wasn't *his* pack. He left me with the Johnson City pack like... a piece of luggage. I felt abandoned all over again, and I haven't seen him since." Goddess, I was pathetic. He was going to see that. It wasn't bad enough that I was a murderer—even when he'd gone feral, he'd never killed anyone—but I was also a sad sack whose only fond childhood memories were of a random alpha who couldn't be bothered to keep her around.

"Until tonight," Dirge murmured, understanding dawning.

"Until tonight," I agreed. "All those memories came rushing back, and I couldn't bear to face him. So, I just... ran."

He smiled, hugging me to his chest. "I can understand that."

We rested for a few moments, and then he said, "Can I ask you something?"

"Hmm?" I hummed, happily ensconced in his arms and not looking to move any time soon. Granted, his legs were probably falling asleep and his back was getting tired from leaning against the hard tree trunk, but if so, he didn't complain.

"There's a full moon in just over a week."

"That's... not a question."

"Will you bond with me?"

I froze, my heart thudding at double speed.

"I saw your face earlier. When Karissma said you could help Brielle. And at first, I was against it. Frankly... the scene where you threw yourself in front of that assassin before I could get to you? It has played on repeat in my mind every single night since. But the truth is, I want you. I want this bond between us sealed up tight. It's selfish, really. We've been through a lot, and if you want to wait, I—"

"I don't." I cut him off, then blushed.

"You don't want to bond with me, or you don't want to wait?" he asked, studying me intently.

"The second thing. I want you to be mine too." I wove my fingers between his, holding him tightly. "I don't want to wait."

A grin started to bloom then, slowly spreading like honey until his whole face was a breathtakingly handsome grin. Goddess, he looked like a fallen angel when he smiled like that. Just a hair to the wrong side of holy.

"Yeah? You sure?"

"Yeah," I said, waggling my eyebrows at him. "I'm sure. If... if you still want me. After hearing everything, about me being a broken mess of a murderer." I hated myself just a little for ruining this moment with my ugly insecurities. Goddess, I kept on shooting myself in the foot. But—

"You are *not* a murderer," he admonished, giving me a stern look. "You're a hero. You saved not just yourself, but every other little girl in those shipping containers from a horrible fate. And if you're broken, well, I guess I am too. But maybe together, we can rebuild something beautiful. The fact that I didn't kill when I was feral doesn't mean I didn't in my time as an enforcer or even since. I have no regrets about taking out the assassin who stabbed you."

I nodded, too emotional for words at his acceptance. After all the things I'd kept hidden, even from my very best friends, he'd just wiped away the stigma, the shame, with an easy smile like it was nothing.

But to me? It was everything.

He kissed me then—both a reprimand and a promise—and I felt the tingles from the top of my hair to the very tips of my toes. And everywhere in between. *Everywhere.*

We stayed like that for a long while, just basking in the comfort of a mate's touch and kissing as we talked, until the moon had traveled far across the sky and even his banked-coal-level warmth wasn't enough to keep the cold at bay any longer.

"Ready to head back?" he asked.

"Yes, I just wish it weren't so far. I'm exhausted." And I was, to my very bones.

"Luckily for you, I'm not. Hop on," he said, then shifted into his wolf form.

He was big, yes. Almost chest height when I was still in human form.

"Are you sure? You ran just as far as I did."

He yipped his assent, and I pursed my lips, considering the long, *long* way back.

"Okay, here goes nothing," I muttered, and climbed on his back.

FIFTY

Shay

By the time we made it back, the sun was already kissing the horizon. The twilight was fading into soft lavender, the deep orange of sunrise hot on its heels.

As beautiful as it was, though, I couldn't look away from the man standing outside our lodgings. He stood tall and proud, but quiet, patient. He looked exactly as I remembered from my childhood, as if time hadn't touched him, the same hint of silver at his temples, the same laugh lines at the corners of his eyes.

Brand.

He'd waited. I'd tried to run from the past, from the shame and hurt of a little girl's memories, but he'd waited.

Suddenly, I was really glad we'd stopped at a cache at the edge of the woods to pull on sweats and weren't walking up buck freaking naked.

"Shailene," Brand said, warm familiarity in his tone. "I'm so glad to see you again."

"Everyone calls me Shay now." It was an asinine thing to say, but it was all I had.

Well, not all that I had. Dirge was holding my hand, his

solid presence at my side an easy reassurance. I wasn't alone and scared anymore. I had a mate, and a pack who had my back.

I had a *family*. The realization nearly knocked me down. All my life, I'd wanted a family. And now I had one. I'd thought back then it would be Brand and his pack, who was my family. But it was time to let that go. He had saved me from a feral life in the woods, and that was enough.

"Shay." He said the name like he was testing it, rolling it around on his tongue. Then he nodded. "I wanted to give you something." He held up a coin, waiting to see if I'd take it.

I closed the distance, accepting the weathered and ancient-looking piece of metal. "What kind of coin is it?" I asked, looking up to meet his eyes.

"An Etruscan coin. Very old, from ancient Italy."

My eyebrows shot up as I turned it over in my hand. There wasn't a date stamped on it, but it seemed weathered enough to be ancient, and it was heavy. Nothing like the newly minted thin coins we had nowadays.

I closed my fist around it as if it was going to vanish from my grip like he had from my life all those years ago. "It's cool, but why did you want to give it to me?"

"It's a token. A way to call for help, if ever you need it again. It can only be used once, but if you kiss the coin and say, 'In time of greatest need, I call for greatest might.' Help will come."

"Umm, okay." I was confused. So very, very confused.

He smiled then, the look oddly wistful. "I wanted you to have it before I left."

"Thank you," I murmured.

He looked down, and I realized his hand seemed to waver in the burgeoning light.

"My time draws to an end, and I must go. Fare thee well, until we meet again," he said with a soft smile, and then faded away, right before our eyes.

"Okay, that was weird as hell," Dirge said. "Is the coin still solid?"

I opened my fist, and there it was. Solid and real, glinting in the sunlight even though the mysterious man who'd given it to me was long gone. Suddenly, I had all new questions about why he hadn't kept me all those years ago.

"Huh. Well, can't hurt to hang onto it, right?" He squeezed my shoulder, and I nodded.

Couldn't hurt, indeed.

WE CRASHED for three hours before the noise from the living room woke us. Dirge was up and out of bed first, using the bathroom and heading to his suitcase to pull on fresh clothes. He froze in front of it, then spun to face me.

"Did you leave this here?" he asked, holding up a piece of folded parchment. His name was scrawled across the front in swirling calligraphy that I didn't recognize. The back was sealed with ruby-red wax.

"No. What is it?" I sat up, clutching the blankets to my chest as curiosity won out over exhaustion.

"A note."

"Who's it from?" I prompted when he didn't say more, scanning the inside.

"I don't know. It's only one line: 'The Fetya have been paid.'"

What the fuck?

"What does that even mean?" I asked, reaching for him to hand me the letter. He was right. One line, and it was unsigned. I didn't recognize the handwriting, but it was sepia ink on heavy paper, a little scratchy, as if someone had written it with a quill rather than a modern pen.

"I think it means they're not going to exact another price.

But… who even knows about that? And why wouldn't they just tell us if it were true?"

"I have no idea." I paused, hesitating before I passed the note back to him. "Dirge, does this impression in the wax look familiar to you?"

He accepted the note and stared at it long and hard before answering. "No? Does it look familiar to you?"

I reached over to the nightstand, picking up the coin Brand had given me. Two faces pointing away from each other were etched into one side. But the other was a circle of numerals in some ancient language that I didn't recognize. And that was what was pressed into the wax.

I held them up to show him, and he looked surprised. "Brand? But… I would ask how, but the man literally disappeared in front of us, so he's clearly not all wolf, or he's mated to someone incredibly powerful." He shook his head, fingering the bit of wax thoughtfully. "How did he even know about the Fetya?"

"I don't know. But he said help would come, and he's saved me before." I clutched the coin a little tighter, as if it could steady the jumble of unruly feelings in my chest. Who was this man, and why had he appointed himself my guardian angel? "If it's true, that's a huge relief."

"If it's true," he echoed, tucking the parchment into his bag. "I guess we can figure it out together," he said with a crooked smile.

I froze, my eyes going wide as a thought struck me. "Do you think he was fae?"

"What?"

"I'm half-fae. Do you think… He disappeared. He knows about the Fetya without us telling him. He's oddly invested in me. What if he was my fae parent?"

Dirge sank onto the bed next to me. "That would explain some things, but I don't know how we'd verify it without calling him back here with the coin to ask. Is that what you want to do?"

Was it?

"No. I have a feeling that we're going to need this." I bit my bottom lip as I stared down at it. A tiny bit of metal, but somehow more. And I knew in my bones that now wasn't the time. My answers would have to wait a little longer.

But there was still a thrill humming in my veins that I might have just met my fae father.

He restlessly ran a hand through his hair and shrugged. "Okay, then. Do you want showers first, or coffee?"

I didn't even hesitate. "Coffee, please." I tucked the coin into my pocket and made a mental note to get it put into a setting so I could wear it on a necklace.

Something buzzed before we could walk out of the room. "Is that your phone?" I asked. Mine was in my pocket.

He crossed to the nightstand and scooped it up. "Yep. It's one of the men I contacted from the old country."

"Good news?"

His face turned grim as he quickly scanned the message. "It's news, but it's not good. We'd better go fill in the others."

"THERE YOU TWO ARE! Did you have a wild night?" Brielle smirked as we walked into the shared living area.

"Something like that," Dirge answered.

"Well, hurry up and get in here. We need to work out our next steps, and we were waiting for you two sleepyheads. There's coffee."

"Thank the Goddess." I was anxious about the next steps, but taking a moment to fix a cup of coffee wouldn't change it.

We poured two oversized cups of black gold, then headed back to the living room, where the rest of our pack was waiting.

They'd saved space for us on the love seat, which I accepted gratefully. I stifled a yawn with my palm as we sank into the cushions.

It really was a long night, and not in a hot way.

"So, Kane and I were up half the night talking," Brielle started, shooting Kane a smile. "And we've both agreed that as much as we want this curse gone, we need to be smart about it. Aunt Kari has said there's no rush, and we need a plan for handling the ODL before we just pull the plug and bring them down on our heads when we're not ready."

Reed nodded, clearly relieved by this decision. "I have an idea on that, actually. Kane, you're high alpha now. Maybe it's time to address the Interspecies Governing Council."

"To what end? The IGC doesn't even have a wolf shifter as a sitting member," Kane said.

"To the end of getting the law overturned. Why should wolves still be suffering centuries later for one pack's bad decisions? Fuck, wolf representation would *also* be a step in the right direction."

Kane nodded, but seemed tense. "I agree, but we all know what the outcome will be."

"I wouldn't jump to that conclusion, Alpha." Dirge surprised me by speaking up and leaning forward to rest his forearms on his knees. "The ODL attacked the Kodiaks and showed up at the great pack gathering without real cause, but off a completely bogus tip. They're reaching, and that's a great reason to push back. Based on the Kodiak attack... other species might stand with us."

"Bears alone won't be enough," Gael commented. "We'd have to reach further, garner some support from other species."

"The goblins were opposed from day one. They had religious beliefs that the loss of omegas—of any one important magical species or subspecies—would impact the balance of power in the magical world." Reed offered, rubbing his chin thoughtfully.

"I don't know about religion, but many species have been in decline in the last century. Everyone's chalking it up to human expansion, hunters." Gael vaguely waved a hand. "The point is, we'd have some major barriers to overcome. People have disbelief, and goodwill is in short supply among other species who're also feeling pinched by modern life."

"It's a place to start, though," Brielle said with a smile. She was far too calm for someone whose life was on the line.

"It's not just other species, unfortunately," Dirge said. "I got a message this morning from one of my contacts from Romania. He says there are rumors starting that the Hungarian pack has called back all their pack mates from around the globe, and that they're in talks with Poland about forming a new alliance."

"A new alliance?" I asked, confused. European pack politics hadn't ranked high on our list of priorities before meeting Pack Blackwater. Our pack was small, out of the way of most of that.

He nodded at me with his lips pressed into a firm line. "Yes. Currently, Kane is high alpha of the majority of wolf packs. Australia does their own thing, and some parts of Asia. But... probably eighty percent of the world's wolf population in some way or another filters up to him. Or they did to his father, at least. The Hungarian Alpha is talking about taking a chunk out of Europe, including those alphas that *haven't* pledged yet. They're shopping for new allies."

Reed kept a cool head, but it was clear the wheels were already spinning. "Any confirmation of that?"

"He got word from a supplier that they're ordering mass amounts of arms. Not just the usual, though. Silver bullets, crossbows, and wolfsbane."

Gael swore. "That's not just a new alliance, Alpha. They're prepping to come after their own kind. They want a full coup."

"We have to go back to Europe," Kane said. "We can't let the world fall apart, not now when we need the might of all the packs to enact change at the IGC level. The council will see us as a joke if we're not united."

"Agreed," Dirge murmured.

I studied the others in the room, dread tossing in my stomach as I took in Brielle's grim expression and Leigh's pale face. Our lives were changing fast. It was disconcerting at times, but there was nowhere else I'd rather be.

I drew in a deep breath, realizing this pause was all the opening we were likely to get to share our news.

"While we're talking about what's next... Dirge and I came to a decision last night." Every eye turned my way, and yes, it still made me pause, even though most of these pack mates were family. "We're going to bond under the next full moon. We know it's soon, but with everything that's going on, we don't want to wait. We love each other, and... whatever's next, we want to do it together."

Dirge reached up and ran his thumb down my cheek, sending a little shiver running through me as our eyes locked. That smile of his made my stomach flip for a much better reason and was one I wanted to wake up to every day for the rest of my life.

Leigh squealed in delight, and she almost knocked me off my seat with the force of her hug. Brielle was there a moment later, wrapping her arms around both of us. The guys all shook Dirge's hand, offering congratulations as well.

"OMG, we have another bonding ceremony to plan!"

"Do you want to do it here or in Romania?"

Romania? Oh, that's where Kane's father's pack mansion was.

"Umm, here? We don't want a big to-do, just us and the moon," I said, wincing at their crestfallen expressions. "Just our *pack* and the moon," I clarified.

"As if you could keep me away!" Leigh pinned me with a

look, then shifted gears so quickly, it made my head spin. "Okay, so, we need to get you a dress, and flowers, and—"

She was talking so fast, I could barely keep up. It was a little too much, and when I looked over at Dirge, the anxiety must have been clear on my face, because he squeezed my hand.

"It's all going to be okay, muzică mea," he whispered against my temple before pressing a kiss there.

Even that simple touch grounded me, as my friends gestured excitedly and tossed rapid-fire ideas back and forth like a Ping-Pong ball.

"Okay, but bluebonnets are classic for a Texas wedding. You have to want bluebonnets, right?" Bri asked, turning to me for input.

"Umm, sure. Bluebonnets are nice." I didn't care what kind of flowers I held or walked over. Only that the man waiting for me in the circle was Dirge.

"See? Classic."

Leigh rolled her eyes but didn't argue. About the flowers, anyway. She'd moved on to dress fabric.

My life might have been changing at full speed, but as I held my mate's hand and listened to my friends argue about the details of our perfect bonding ceremony, I was deeply grateful to be exactly where I was.

FIFTY-ONE

Dirge

O*ne week later, full moon*

THE JOHNSON CITY pack's bonding clearing was in a peaceful spot, a nice little meadow sandwiched between a small lake and the forest. The moon was almost at its peak, and I stood quietly off to the side, watching the circle be prepared. Leigh had just scampered off to be with Shay, but she'd been overseeing the pack volunteers as they piled the circle high with bluebells, delphiniums, and several other types of blue flowers I didn't know the names of. They smelled nice, though.

Her ring weighed heavily in the pocket of my dress slacks, and my thoughts were nebulous as I stood barefoot in the grass. Anticipation for what was to come, gratitude that people I didn't even know had pulled together to make this happen on short notice. Shay was quiet, yes, but in the past week, I'd heard from many, many members of her old pack what a sweet, kind soul she was. They'd stopped and taken time to share little memories with me, and each one made me smile.

My mate had impacted *so many* more people than she ever

knew. I absently patted my other pocket, where her gift lay. It was bittersweet, and I'd gone back and forth a hundred times in the span of a few days, because while I knew the memories were painful, I hoped they'd be healing.

I should have bought a backup gift. Just in case.

Shit.

Who thought it was a good idea to give their mate something *sad* on their bonding night?

A heavy hand fell on my shoulder, and I froze as Gael spoke.

"You look as twitchy as a squirrel in the middle of rush-hour traffic. What's wrong? Not having second thoughts, I hope?"

I shook my head, relieved to have company. "Not about Shay, just about what I chose as a gift."

"Ahh." Gael rocked back on his heels and regarded me thoughtfully. "You don't seem the type to choose something flippantly."

"No, I uh... no. I put a lot of thought into it, but what if she doesn't like it?"

"Doesn't like what?" Reed asked, jogging up a little short of breath.

"His bonding gift."

"Well, shit. What did you buy her? You've been out of society for a while, but I assumed you had this on lock." Reed seemed dismayed as he scanned me, as if the gift was going to be stamped on my forehead.

"I didn't buy her anything. I found her something."

"Which is ...?" Reed gestured for me to spill, but I shook my head.

"It's private. If she wants to share it, that'd be up to her. But here are the rings." I passed him the box from my pocket.

Reed groaned as he accepted them. "Do I need to go into

town? It would be tight, but I could find a decent tennis bracelet and get back in time."

Gael shoved him, giving him a stern look. "A tennis bracelet? You're such a douche."

"I'm fine," I chided my brother. Then quickly added, "But thank you."

He nodded, then surveyed the clearing. "For a small pack, they've got a really nice setup. The cabin is all ready to go, and the ladies who run the bonding ceremonies went above and beyond."

I smiled, excitement and anticipation starting to outweigh my nerves. I was going to be bonded tonight. To Shay, my sweet, beautiful Shay.

It was more than I ever dared dream of, ever allowed myself to hope for. And yet... it was happening.

Kane arrived shortly thereafter, and the three of them shot the shit and joked, trying to keep me entertained and out of my head, but I mostly let the chatter wash over me. I appreciated the company, but I wasn't in a chatty mood.

My wolf was pacing, pressing up against all my boundaries, wanting our mate. Eager to see her, eager to bite her, make her ours forever.

I adjusted myself, the semi I was already sporting not at all appropriate for an official ceremony.

Gael and Reed were arguing over something asinine when Kane leaned in close with a serious expression.

"You ready for all this?" He gestured to the women trailing flowers away from the mound into the woods where Shay would be walking out to meet me any moment.

I nodded, suddenly choked up. I was so ready, it felt like my entire life had been building to this one moment and the rest of my happiness hinged on it. She was everything, and I was prepared to spend the rest of my life loving her, making her happy.

"Good man." He patted me on the shoulder. "I wanted to ask you something now, before things get underway. If you don't mind?"

"Shoot."

"You acted as an enforcer before. And I will happily reinstate you as a working enforcer for the pack as we discussed previously, if that's what you want. But... you seem to have bonded with the women. They're close, but they let you in. And I was wondering if you might accept a less traditional role, but one that I think is doubly important given Brielle's special talents."

My eyebrows rose in surprise. "I'm listening."

"I'd like to make you the personal guard for the three of them. It'll be a paid position, same level as head enforcer. But your duty will be to protect them, specifically, instead of splitting your focus across the entire pack's security."

"You don't have to pay me to guard my mate," I said drily, even though I was already warming up to the idea. His parents had been killed, and while he had Gael watching his back, Brielle—any of the alpha mates, really—didn't have anyone permanently assigned by the pack order. It was an oversight long overdue for correction. "Shay is more than capable of taking care of herself. But I tentatively accept, as long as she agrees."

He nodded, his relief plain to see. "I don't know what's coming in the next few months. But I know it's going to be dangerous, for Brielle most of all. And while I'd normally assign Gael—"

"He and Leigh can't stop fighting? I understand."

He gave me a grim smile in answer, then cast a glance up at the moon. "It's time. Are you ready?"

"I'm more ready for this than anything else in my life."

Kane chuckled. "Let's do this, then."

He called the other two, and we stepped into the circle of

flowers, the sweet scent of them perfuming the air as we took our positions. Kane stood at the top of the circle, ready to officiate. Gael and Reed had my back, ready to serve their ceremonial duties.

It was different, being back in a pack. Sometimes, it felt like a too-tight pair of shoes that I was going to bust out of any second. And other times, like this, it was as easy as breathing.

As soon as we were in place, music began to waft softly through the trees. It was only the four of us, per Shay's request. There were some grumbles from the rest of the Johnson City females, but in the end, they acquiesced to Shay's desire for a private ceremony.

Within minutes, Brielle appeared, wearing a simple green gown and holding her bottle of perfume. Then came Leigh, holding a jar of special herbal water. I didn't know what was in it and I didn't care, because the sight that came behind her took my breath away.

Shay was everything beautiful and good in my life. And when I saw her wearing the frothy white gown, I almost choked at the lump in my throat. She gazed shyly down at the ground as she stepped up to take her place between her two best friends, her dark curls styled into a waterfall over one shoulder, the thin straps of her gown hiding nothing of her mating marks, the beautiful swirls calling me, inviting me in to finish them with my bite.

What had I ever done to deserve such perfection? I was unworthy. But I loved her with every cell of my being, every hair on my head. And I would work every day of forever to keep her content at my side. To show her how much I cherished her.

She was halfway across the clearing when she looked up, and our eyes met. She seemed uncertain, and it was like my own nerves evaporated. I wasn't here for stuffy traditions or for my pack mates. It was her. It had always been her.

And traditions were made to be broken.

I stepped out of the flowers, eating up the ground between us in long strides. And then she was there, close enough to kiss, to see the little blue blossoms woven into her hair. She was my own fairy, come to life from the pages of a book.

"Don't be afraid," I said, meaning every word as I stroked the line of her jaw with my thumb. "It's just me, and you, and the moon."

FIFTY-TWO

Shay

"So, given what we've learned recently about my gifts, Leigh and I were discussing that it might be best if she applies the fertility water during the ceremony." Brielle was biting her bottom lip nervously. "Unless you guys *want* to have a baby right away, but frankly, I don't really know how much control I have over my..." She waved idly at herself, at a loss.

"Her mojo's running wild, Shay, and you do not want her sprinkling hyperpowered preggo juice on your feet instead of the regular rose hips." Leigh shook her head and pointedly took the jar from Brielle. "I'm vetoing that option."

I nodded wordlessly, sudden, intense nerves making it impossible to speak.

I was ready to bond—so ready, I could practically feel the way his fangs were going to sink into my neck tonight. But something about the *official ceremony* vibes was making me incredibly anxious. We'd minimized it as best we could, but there were only so many ways you could change the actual ceremony. I even felt a little nauseous, which was super weird. My wolf was quiet, so clearly, I wasn't picking up any latent danger. Just regular old social anxiety, fueled by childhood trauma and a healthy dose of *people are scary as fuck.*

Walking across the clearing while everyone stared... I swallowed hard, staring down at my dress with major second thoughts. It was gorgeous, the prettiest dress I'd ever seen, frankly. But I was so exposed in it. Thin spaghetti straps were all that held it up, my mate marks on full display. Even the parts between my breasts were framed by the deep V-neck. It dissolved from the bodice down into a skirt of organza ruffles, feeling silky and soft around my legs as I walked.

I'd loved it on sight, knew the peek at my marks and my bare throat would drive Dirge wild. And yet... now I was second-guessing even this.

Brielle laid a hand on my arm, the touch gentle. She didn't say a word, but the room flooded with a soft, soothing scent. A gentle stream in the summer sun.

I looked up to see Brielle frowning in concentration. "Is anything happening? I can't tell."

A wave of calm washed over me, and the lump in my throat finally eased. "Yes, actually. Thank you."

"Oh good." She shot me a happy smile before grabbing her glass bottle of ceremonial perfume. It was full of lovelace, a potent aphrodisiac for shifters. I swallowed hard at the reminder that we were about to head to the clearing.

"One last thing," Leigh said with cheer as she stopped us by the door. She lifted the hem of her own dress and stuck out her foot. "Show me the toes!"

I rolled my eyes, but grinned at the memory of Gracelyn doing the same to Brielle a few short weeks ago. I lifted the hem of my gown, showing off my freshly painted digits and the anklet of bells circling my left ankle.

"Excellent. Let's roll out!"

Brielle groaned at her movie-quote tone. "What are we now, robots?"

304

"Hey, we *transform* into wolves. It counts," Leigh joked as we stepped out into the cool night air.

I LET their quiet chatter roll over me, comforting me as we walked. It didn't take long to get to the walkway that led into the bonding clearing, just long enough for Brielle's soothing omega scent to evaporate. The lump was back in my throat and my nerves were thrumming double time by the time we stopped next to a few of the older pack females who'd volunteered to prep the clearing.

One of the women addressed me with a warm smile. "Good luck tonight, honey. You look beautiful. Ready for us to start the music?"

I was frozen to the spot, but Leigh answered for me.

"Yep, she's ready. Just got a case of the prebonding jitters."

The older woman laughed, resting a hand on my shoulder. "It's going to be just fine, honey. I saw him out there, and he's nervous as a bee with no honey. You two are going to be a lovely couple." She gave me a squeeze, then they walked off as soft notes began to weave into the air.

"Do you need a minute, or are you ready to get this show on the road?" Leigh asked, eyeing me up and down. She reached down to adjust a layer of fabric that wasn't lying perfectly enough to suit her, then nodded.

I bit my bottom lip, still not able to answer her.

"Bri, she needs some more of your mojo if you can work it up."

"I can try," she said with a tired smile, but I knew it took a lot out of her—and hurt, if I'd interpreted Karissma's information correctly.

I shook my head, forcing myself to speak to put them both at ease. "I just need Dirge."

Brielle smiled with a knowing look. "Well, then, let's get a move on."

They each kissed me on the cheek before they started walking down the path.

In a matter of a few heartbeats, I was standing all alone in the forest. My toes dug into the soft grass, and I let out one big exhale before I followed them. I was still nervous, but that wasn't the most important thing now, was it?

I didn't want to be alone and afraid anymore. I wanted him.

As I stepped into the clearing, I kept my eyes on the ground, afraid to trip and ruin the beautiful gown. But despite my fear, my eyes were drawn to Dirge's like magnets. He was breathtakingly handsome in dark gray dress slacks and a creamy button-up. His hair was slicked back, his sleeves rolled up to just below his elbows, showing off bitable forearms.

He must have read my anxiety on my face. I sucked in a surprised breath as he stepped out of the circle, breaking all the protocols that had been drilled into us over the past week as he nearly jogged to stand before me.

"Don't be afraid. It's just me, and you, and the moon."

I leaned into his calloused palm, soaking in his touch like a plant starved of sunlight turned to the sun. He was my grounding place. He was my home. His voice, his touch, his scent—everything that was him soothed me, brought me back down to center. I was okay, and I was more than ready to bond with my mate.

Shifting the bouquet of beautiful flowers to one hand, I held out the other to him. He laced our fingers together with practiced ease, and together, we walked to the moonlit circle of flowers, Leigh and Brielle trailing behind us with their ceremonial gifts.

It was stunningly beautiful in its simplicity. The moonlight reflected on the lake, the heady scent of crushed flowers rose from underfoot, and the sparkle of stars high overhead made the perfect symphony of beauty. As soon as we were all in place, I passed my bouquet to Brielle so I could hold Dirge's hands in both of mine. But now that we were here, now that I'd gotten over the nerves about all the formality of this night... I was ready. Like a thoroughbred chomping at the bit, I was ready to run away with him.

Suddenly, this ceremony couldn't happen fast enough. I shifted on the balls of my bare feet in anticipation.

Gael stepped forward first, holding up his palm. My mouth dropped open at the blueish gem the size of an egg he cupped there. Even in the dim light, it sparkled like a diamond.

"For prosperity," he said with a smile, leaning down to place the stone at our feet.

Leigh was next, waiting until Gael had stepped all the way back behind Dirge before entering the same space. "For fertility," she said with a cheeky grin as she knelt and splashed the rosehip water over our feet and ankles.

Brielle's eyes were misty as she came forward, unstoppered bottle of perfume in her hands. To my surprise, she dipped her fingers straight into the thick oil as she spoke. "For passion," she said, and then dabbed the warm, dripping oil behind both my ears and inside my wrists. She turned to Dirge and repeated the action. My blood heated as his eyes grew dark when they met mine.

Reed was the last one to make an offering, as was custom. He held up two shining golden rings. "For eternity." There was love and pride in his eyes as he handed each of us the other's ring. "And may you have all the joy in your lives together," he added, sneaking a hug for his brother before stepping back into place.

"Dirge and Shay." Kane nodded to each of us in turn as he stepped forward to complete the ceremonial binding. "We gather here under the Goddess's moon to bind you two together as mates. It is an eternal bond, forged by the love of the Moon Goddess, lasting in life and beyond the pall of death. Alpha Dirge, what do you offer this woman to prove that you are worthy of her love?"

Dirge swallowed hard, and I'd swear that the pinch of anxiety I felt behind my breast wasn't mine, but his. Was our bond finally snapping into place? The thought brought me such joy, such peace.

He reached into his pocket, slowly pulling out a piece of paper. "This might be a really bad idea. But, I wanted you to have this. And if you don't like it, I'll buy you anything you want. Hell, I'll let Reed buy you anything you want. But you deserve to know the truth."

I took the paper with curiosity, not sure what could be printed on it to give him such apprehension. But when I unfolded it, the news headline nearly jumped off the page.

Sex Trafficking Ring Dismantled, More Than Two Hundred Young Girls Saved

A messy, masculine scrawl of green ink was on the side, right between the headline and the article. He'd written: *You saved them.*

I hastily folded it back up, clutching it to my chest like the most precious artifact. "Is this what I think it is?"

My voice was hoarse with emotion, but for once, I didn't care. It was an emotional night.

"It is," he murmured.

I had tears in my eyes as I hugged him, practically crushing him to my chest. He hugged me back just as hard. I don't know how long it was before we pulled apart.

But when we did, Kane smiled and asked, "Do you accept his offering?"

"I do," I said, nodding as happy tears trailed down my cheeks.

Dirge's thumbs sneaked up and wiped them away, love and joy practically radiating from him. He mouthed something to me, and it took a moment for me to catch it.

My warrior.

I almost didn't hear Kane as he told us to exchange rings. Almost.

Dirge slipped a stunning ring on my finger, the band made of two golden threads twined endlessly around. I couldn't see where one ended and the other began, just beautiful continuity. Centered on top was an emerald, the giant rectangular stone as heavy as it was gorgeous.

"It was hard to get so quickly, but as soon as I saw the color of your marks, this piece from our family collection came to mind."

Family collection? I was wearing a piece of his history? Tears pricked my eyes again, but I dashed them away with the heel of my free hand. I didn't want to spend this night crying, happy tears or no. I wanted to spend it reveling in the moment, drinking in every second, burning it all into my memory.

"It belonged to my grandmother and was made for her bonding ceremony. But if it doesn't suit you, you can choose—"

I shook my head, stopping him in his tracks. "It's perfect, just like the man who gave it to me."

Dirge smiled, the pleased look he wore sending a bolt of *want* singing through my veins. He held up his hand for his own ring, and I tried to put the lust aside to focus on the ceremony.

I slipped the heavy gold band over his knuckle, and it slid home perfectly. It was carved by the pack's jeweler with images of two running wolves. Little bitty diamonds were worked into the scene, sparkling like stars over the wolves' heads.

It was nowhere near as precious or even as important as his centuries-old family heirloom, but I hoped he liked it.

"It's perfect. It's us," he murmured, pinning me with a

heated look. I didn't know if it was the moon or the lovelace or just the incredible intimacy of the shared moment, but I was burning up with need. This ceremony needed to *end*.

Kane cleared his throat, but he didn't look annoyed that we'd interrupted his ceremonial words to chat. He smiled warmly instead, one eyebrow raised, asking if we were ready to continue.

We both nodded, so he continued, reading the last part from the little black book clutched in his hands.

"The bond between mates is sealed with a bite. It is tradition for this to be done privately, and it must be completed before the moon sets on this night. In the eyes of the Moon Goddess and these witnesses, I bless this joining. Go forth and claim your mate."

As soon as he snapped the little book closed, Dirge's hands were in my hair, pulling me close so he could devour my lips in a ravishing kiss. His wolf was there, eyes aglow as we clashed, both of us too eager to hold back.

Our closest friends cheered and clapped as we kissed, but the noise faded quickly. When we pulled apart, gasping for air, they were gone, the clearing quiet, the two of us alone.

"Are you ready, muzică mea?"

"I am so ready," I murmured, eyes still locked on his lips. I didn't want to stop kissing him.

He grabbed me by the hips and lifted, the motion surprising me at first, but I quickly wrapped my legs around his waist. The heat of his erection was there, burning deliciously through the layers of clothing still separating us. Dirge wasted no time grabbing a handful of the gown's train so he wouldn't step on it, and then fastened his lips back to my neck.

We were moving, but I didn't care. His tongue was laving sinful circles over my neck, my collarbone. By the time he kicked the front door of the little cabin open, my straps were off my shoulders, most of my chest bared to him.

Dirge barreled straight through the door, making a beeline for the bedroom, when something finally clicked.

"Wait! Stop!"

He froze, worry etching a line between his eyebrows. "What's wrong?" He held me gently, even though I could feel the tension in his shoulders. He was a man on a mission to claim his mate, eyes aglow with his wolf, but even still, he stopped for me.

Goddess, I loved him.

"I have a gift for you too."

"Can it wait?" he asked, letting the edges of his fangs scrape along my clavicle, the implication making me shiver. He was ready.

Fuck, I was ready. The friction between us was driving me insane, and I was soaked. But I'd worked so hard this week to get it ready for him.

"It'll only take a second, I promise."

He smiled, the corners of his eyes crinkling as he set me carefully on my feet. Thankfully, he didn't let go, because my knees were already liquid and it took a second to get my bearings.

As soon as I could stand without falling down, I walked over to the sound system tucked into a cabinet right outside the bedroom door. I'd set it up this morning, so all I needed to do was push Play.

One click, and I wrapped my arms around myself as now-familiar notes began to play over the cabin's sound system.

Dirge's arms went around me from behind, his chin resting lightly on my shoulder as he listened. We stood like that for several minutes as the music rose and fell, weaving into the air, becoming part of the memory.

"It's gorgeous. Did you compose this?"

I nodded, too caught up in the thrum of heat in my veins, of want pulsing in my pussy to answer. My wolf was pushing me now. She wanted to claim our mate, the visceral *need* was growing overwhelming, and while I wanted him to enjoy his gift, I wanted him to sink his teeth into my throat a little bit more.

There was no more time to waste. I spun in his grip, my hands going around the back of his neck like a lasso, pulling him tight against my mouth.

Dirge didn't hesitate, a bit of that old, feral need still burning in his eyes as he reached down, looping his hands under my thighs, which he somehow still found through the many layers of skirt fabric. I could feel his heat burning through me. Between the two of us, we had enough fire burning to turn this house to ash, yet somehow, the only thing that ignited was *need*.

He navigated the small cabin with our lips still fastened together, each of us too far gone to separate. I hardly noticed the dip of a mattress beneath his knees because the delicious friction of his hard chest against my needy nipples was too great for me to care about anything else.

When my back hit crisp, cool sheets, I finally let our mouths fall apart on a breathless groan. He took the opening, peeling the thin straps of my dress the rest of the way down, exposing my breasts in one motion. A growl rumbled through his chest, his eyes glowing bright green with his wolf.

He kneaded my breasts with surprising gentleness given the speed with which we were racing toward the finish. I arched up into his touch, wanting more, more, more.

Dirge tweaked a nipple with one hand, sending a spiral of need straight to my clit as the other hand trailed down, slowly pushing the dress the rest of the way down. The thin prick of his wolf's claws at his fingertips showed me just how on edge he was and nearly sent me over the edge to an early orgasm.

He exposed my lacy white thong a moment later as another

rumble of pleasure barreled out of his chest, sending vibrations through me everywhere he touched me. But what really shook me to the core was one little word, projected as clearly as if he had spoken right into my mind.

Mine.

FIFTY-THREE

Dirge

Mine.

I didn't mean to speak to her; not really. I was intent on two things—making her feel good and giving her my bite. But when it happened, it demanded a pause, an acknowledgment of this momentous shift between us.

Dirge? Her mental voice was laced with wonder, even as it shook with need.

Muzică mea, I practically purred through the bond, letting my mouth drop to her navel, sucking and nipping at her flesh as I worked my way across her flat stomach toward the edge of that lace. It was blocking the view I really wanted, of her sweet pussy.

I was torn as she once again arched beneath my ravenous kiss between whether to rip it to shreds or save it for a memento of this night forever.

She moaned low in her throat as my tongue worked the junction of her hip and thigh, and the decision was made. The sides of the skimpy fabric gave under my touch, and I tossed them away. Her pussy was bare and glistening in the soft lamplight, and the urge to throw back my head and howl was embarrassingly strong. My wolf was riding me hard, urging me to take, feast, *claim*.

Yes, she urged me. Her hands were woven into my hair, urging me forward, urging me to feast on her sweetness.

I shifted my position so I was between her legs, letting the fabric of the dress still tangled over her knees trap her beneath me. It kept her tightly in place, so I controlled the motion, the depth. I skated over her slick flesh with my thumb, but my fangs were low and aching for a taste. I used my hands to press back on her thighs, giving myself as much room as the dress would allow, and dove into her folds.

Her cries turned high and keening as my tongue pressed in, and I could feel an echo of her pleasure in my own chest, the feeling so overwhelming, I ground my erection down into the mattress with need.

Goddess, I was riding the knife's edge of pleasure before I'd even taken my pants off. I was going to suffocate the first time I sank into her heat, when I could feel both sides of this tornado of pleasure rising between us.

She must have felt the same, because when I slipped my middle finger between her folds, I was still twirling my tongue lazily around her clit when the spark turned into a flame, and she quaked around me with a scream.

Her orgasm nearly made me lose my head, and my control. I groaned against her skin, dropping my forehead to her mound as I dragged in a hit of her scent, fighting for my composure even as I stroked her higher with my hand. The man wanted to tease her, torture her slowly to make this last all night. But the wolf had his needs too, and when my fangs grazed the crease of her groin, she cried out again, a feral pleasure burning through the bond in my chest.

She didn't want to wait either. Her hands dragged at my shoulders, trying to pull me up, pull me in. But I couldn't give her what she wanted just yet.

I lifted up, burying a second finger inside her as I used my other hand to snatch the dress the rest of the way down, leaving it to puddle on the floor as I yanked my dress pants so hard, a button pinged across the room.

She was lost with need now as I pumped into her faster, adding a third thick digit, stretching her wider for me. As soon as we were both completely naked, I lay back between her knees, laving the groove at the top of her thigh, working my way to the curve of her upper thigh.

Her legs were quaking around me, and I could feel that she was right there, at the precipice of another orgasm.

I pressed my thumb to her clit, following the pleasure as I applied just the right amount of pressure. But when I felt her about to go over that edge, I struck.

My fangs sliced into her thigh like butter, the heady hit of her blood at the back of my throat laced with her pleasure as she screamed my name. My wolf was howling to be buried inside her, her pussy clenching around my fingers so tightly, the bones hurt.

I withdrew my fangs, never stopping the pressure on her clit, keeping her riding the wave of pleasure as I licked and sealed the wound, pressing a reverent kiss next to my mark as I finally withdrew my fingers.

Euphoria nearly overwhelmed me as her tart-sweet pomegranate flavor bloomed on my tongue.

Goddess, she was everything. Perfection.

Before I could sheath myself in her, she was up on her knees, eyes glowing gold with her wolf. The tips of her fangs peeking out over her bottom lip took my breath away. *She* was the goddess, a golden shimmer of power hanging in the air around her like nothing I'd ever seen before. Her fae half, shining through?

I didn't resist as she pushed me down on my back, erection straining against open air in an invitation for her to take, ride, own me. Her hands were hot as a brand on my shoulders as she straddled me, the blunt tip of my dick bumping her slick folds, parting them easily as she paused, meeting my eyes.

The tension in that moment was unreal, and I swear I could feel her pulse as she swallowed me with her heat. The perfect grip of her made me want to close my eyes and arch up against the bed, but she held me frozen in the trance of her need. She was in control now, and I was hers to play, to take. My wolf rumbled his approval as she sank all the way, taking me to the hilt.

Shay groaned, her chin dropping against her chest as the vibrations teased her already overstimulated clit.

She rose up, taking me out to the tip, then slammed down again, harder, establishing a blistering pace that made me work to hold on to my orgasm. She was fire and lightning, fireworks streaking through the night sky. She was magnificent, and she was mine.

When Shay leaned forward, I skated my hands up her sides, urging her to do it, mark me, finish this bond burning up between us.

But still, I wasn't ready for the intense wave of pleasure that burst through me when she sank her fangs into my left pectoral muscle, right above my heart. Euphoria wasn't a strong enough word for it as the bond snapped into place all at once. I grunted as I came, one hand tangled in her hair, keeping her mouth against my skin, the other on her hips, driving her down harder as I thrust up into her, over and over as we both climaxed, and she squeezed every drop of cum out of me.

When she finally pulled back, swiping her tongue over my chest, sealing her mark over my heart, I was a man replete with love, destroyed by the force of nature that was my mate. She slid off me to curl up at my side with a satisfied sigh as I stroked her soft curls.

She was mine, and I was hers. Forever.

Forever, she agreed, stroking a hand lovingly over my jaw as I wrapped myself around her. The music she'd composed for me, for us, had fallen to a soft hush, the twinkling piano notes a perfect accompaniment to this moment.

I held her to me like the most precious woman in the world.

Because she was, and I was never letting her go.

Forever.

It was a promise, and a benediction.

It was ours.

Epilogue - Leigh

Three days later

I stared down at the single word, taunting me, destroying me.

Pregnant.

It was insulting, the way it stared up at me in defiance from the pee stick like some sort of smug proclamation.

You're up the duff, lady, and you were too stupid to see all the signs.

No, not stupid. Somewhere, deep down, I suspected. Denial? She was the queen bitch of this fucked-up scenario.

How in the actual fuck had I, a single, unmated she-wolf, managed to get pregnant? Pregnancy was rare, even among fully bonded, committed shifter couples who rode out week-long heats together, barely coming up for air.

And yet here I was, apparently too fertile for my own good.

I wanted to blame Brielle, her stupid-potent omeganess clearly playing a hand in this. But I couldn't when I knew *exactly* how this had happened. Shit, I could pinpoint it, the moment clear as a bell ringing in my memory.

I could be twelve hundred years old, a decrepit crone of a

wolf, and that memory would still send a shot of lust through me.

The sight of Gael, hovering over me, hands on either side of my head, cords straining in his neck as he worked his hips, grinding into me, and then—

I shook my head, forcing myself to let that memory die a slow, painful death. Let's not talk about the fact that I was slick with arousal just from the memory, okay? That was embarrassing and *so not happening ever again*.

But, damn. I was pregnant. It was too big, too much, too... everything. Overwhelming. But even as my mind spun with the absolute shitshow that was the drama this would cause, a tiny spark of joy burned in my chest.

I was having a baby. A tiny, perfect child to love and raise and spend the rest of my life with. It was nothing that I expected, and yet... I didn't regret it either. I could never regret her.

Her felt right. Granted, I'd probably have to wait a really long time to find out for sure, but something inside me was convinced it was a girl. My little perfect flower. No, she was too tiny to be a flower. *Petal.*

I could already see a little blonde mini-me, but with Gael's whiskey eyes, running and giggling, a crown of flowers on her head as I chased her through the sunshine. A bloom of protective instincts nearly overwhelmed me, and I rubbed the heel of my hand over my sternum, the intense need to *protect* this little miracle almost taking me to my knees. My brain was spinning, trying to process, trying to figure out a plan.

The world was dangerous, but I wasn't without resources, without friends.

But protecting her meant two things.

One, I had to tell Brielle, immediately. She was an omega, with fertility gifts. She could make sure my baby girl came safely into this world, and that was priceless beyond words. I barely knew my little Petal, but I knew I would give my life for hers.

Two, I was absolutely not sharing this news with Gael, at least not yet. He was too volatile, too hotheaded. Everyone thought he was so composed, but from where I was sitting, he might as well have been a stick of dynamite, and I was carrying news that was nothing less than incendiary.

This just didn't happen. Unplanned pregnancies for wolves weren't a thing, so how was he going to take it? We weren't fated, as far as I could tell. We were just... I didn't want to reduce it to a one-night stand, but fuck. He was a scorching-hot lay, but that was all.

Well, not all. He was now the father of my child. It was complicated, and when one of us did eventually find our mates, it was going to hurt like Satan's asshole to watch.

I dropped a hand over my lower belly cupping the space where I thought she was hiding.

We'll tell your daddy, just... not yet. I'll take care of you, Petal.

A knock at the door dragged me out of the internal conversation and into the harsh reality of our pack's situation.

"Leigh? The jet is ready. Do you need help with your bags?" Reed called cheerfully through the door, right as a wave of nausea burned up my esophagus.

Shit, shit, shit. Not now, please, not now!

I tried to swallow it down, but it was impossible. I abandoned the four pregnancy tests on the counter and ran for the toilet.

I dropped to my knees and heaved as quietly as I could but, with Reed waiting right outside the door—

"Leigh?" He rattled the doorknob. "Leigh, are you okay in there?" He pounded the door, concern evident in his voice, even as I was stuck, every muscle locked in the tortured rictus of dry heaving.

I felt the smack of the door hitting the wall as much as heard it, dread filling me, while I was helpless to stop it.

He pounded through the door, crossing the threshold of the bathroom door in what felt like slow-mo, like a car crash you saw coming, but no matter how hard you slammed the brakes, you knew the collision was imminent.

"Leigh? Shit. Have you got the flu or something?" Reed, Goddess bless that man, dropped a comforting hand on my shoulder, not the least put off by a sick pack mate.

I sat back on my heels, finally through.

For the moment. This is officially morning sickness, not just airplane ick. Or the stomach flu. Or any of the nine thousand lies you've told yourself in the last month.

"I'll get you a washcloth." He turned to the sink, and my eyes fell closed.

There was no way he was going to miss—

"Oh, fuck." He froze, his hand on the tap, washcloth dry in his hand as he stared, jaw slack at the evidence, plain to see.

He didn't say another word, though. He turned on the tap, quickly wetting, then wringing the cloth, before bypassing my extended hand and pressing it to my forehead himself.

His eyes were heavy with concern when they met mine.

"Does he know?"

I shook my head weakly, taking the cloth so I could wipe my clammy face and, finally, my mouth.

"Are you... keeping it?" I could tell it pained him to ask, but he didn't say it with judgment. It was verboten among wolves to terminate a pregnancy because pups were so rare. But he was right. I did have that choice.

"Of course I am," I murmured without hesitation.

His shoulders sagged with relief. I could imagine. It was one thing to keep my secret from his best friend; it was another entirely to keep a secret abortion from his best friend.

But if I had gotten to know Reed half as well as I thought I had, he would have kept that secret too if I'd asked it of him. He was a good man.

He extended a hand, helping me up from the cool tile floor —which wasn't half bad, actually, when you were hot and sick —and guided me to the bed.

"You just sit here. I'll run your bags to the plane and come back with one of those sodas. What kind is it?"

"Ginger ale." The memory of Gael pressing the only drink that soothed my tossing stomach hurt, like a dagger to the chest.

He paused at the doorway, his eyes filled with compassion as he held my bags.

"I can't believe it. You're pregnant," he murmured, shaking his head. "It'll work out, okay? Let's just get to Romania and worry about what's next then."

I nodded woodenly, though I wasn't sure I believed it yet.

"What the fuck did you just say?"

Ice water ran in my veins as a second figure stepped into the doorway.

A very pissed-off, towering, snarling male.

Gael.

Oh, fuck.

Thank you so much for reading Fated to the Feral Wolf! Leigh and Gael's story is book three, Fated to the Warrior Wolf!

I. Am. Dying. For you guys to see what happens next, for Bri and Shay as well as Leigh! Gael is all alpha, super protective hero. But Leigh's stubborn, and they've got a lot to work through. It's sparks around the clock!

Scan to order Fated to the Warrior Wolf, Coming November 2024:

I appreciate you spending your time with me and my words, because I *love* creating this world, and YOU make it possible. 🩶 Your kind words in the reviews mean the world to me, I have cried more than once reading them.

If you would like a bonus scene with Leigh and Gael's wild night (the one where they left the dance floor together...) you can get that here: https://dl.bookfunnel.com/m3am609qkb. I'm also in a reader Discord run by my friend Ciara, where I have my own channel, which you can join here: https://discord.com/invite/dWCFbYGZFz.

XOXO,

April

Pack Hierarchy

Alpha - The strongest of all designations. These are the leaders of most packs, but not all alphas lead packs. They possess the ability to command weaker wolves.

Beta - Often the alpha's second or third, they possess a lot of strength, but don't have the dominance of an alpha. If a pack does not possess an alpha, they can lead, but the pack is considered weak.

Gamma
Delta
Epsilon
Zeta
Eta
Theta
Iota
Kappa
Lambda

Mu - Middle of the road. An average wolf without a significant amount of dominance. Wolves below this point are more likely to need protection from the pack and stick close to pack lands.

Nu

Xi

Omikron

Pi

Rho

Sigma

Tau

Upsilon

Phi

Chi

Psi - The weakest member of the pack, often overlooked and looked down upon.

Omega - A designation only for females touched by the Moon Goddess and granted special abilities, now hunted into extinction.

Author's Note on Native Alaskan Cultures in this Book

Hello, April here. I wanted to take a minute to discuss something very important, and that is the basis of some characters in this book on actual native traditions and cultures in Alaska, the Athabascan or Dena'ina people. Now, to start with, I am not a member of this culture, and as such, I've tried to tread both lightly and respectfully on ground that isn't mine.

That being said, I also wanted to accurately represent the people of Alaska as a whole, and to exclude native people will never feel right to me. So, I've done extensive research on the culture and language, but there is no intended representation of *actual* people, tribes, or locations. I hope that my fictitious representation, to the best of my abilities as an outsider, is as respectful and inclusive as it is magical.

I have traveled to Alaska myself, and one of the things I was so intrigued by was how many rich and diverse native cultures there are. I knew as soon as I set this wolf pack in Alaska that there would be some of that diverse beauty woven into the story. If you are interested in researching the United States' history of treating unfairly with native people—and poor treatment as a whole—I have provided some links below that could be educational. I feel that positive representation, even in works of fiction, can only help us all see each other as we are: people and equals. Or perhaps wolves. 😉

For more information on Native Alaskan cultures, I have some handy links below:

https://www.alaskanative.net/learn/cultural-tourism/

https://www.travelalaska.com/Things-To-Do/Alaska-Native-Culture/Cultures/Athabascan

https://geriatrics.stanford.edu/ethnomed/alaskan/introduction/native_cultures.html

Land Acknowledgment: https://www.facebook.com/watch/?v=760392721359358

Language Resources:

https://uafanlc.alaska.edu/Online/TI974WK1979/wassillie-1979-den_dictionary.pdf

https://www.alaskanativelanguages.org/language-planning

https://web.kpc.alaska.edu/denaina/pages/vocabulary_pages/greetings_and_expressions.html

Playlist

"A Symptom of Being Human"—Shinedown
"The Sound of Silence"—Disturbed
"When I Get There"—P!nk
"Hold Me"—Teddy Swims
"Gymnopedie No. 1"—Erik Satie
"Teeth"—5 Seconds of Summer
"Only Girl"—Rihanna
"Lose Control"—Teddy Swims
"Stay With Me"—Sam Smith
"Exile"—Taylor Swift feat. Bon Iver

Also by April L. Moon

The Hunted Omegas Series

Fated to the Wolf Prince

Fated to the Feral Wolf

Fated to the Wolf Warrior

Made in United States
Orlando, FL
26 July 2024

49446043R00203